# MAYDAY

# MAYDAY

*A NOVEL BY*

## Nelson DeMille

*AND*

## Thomas Block

Book-of-the-Month Club
New York

*The authors would like to thank*
*Mel Parker*
*for his careful editing*
*and his unwavering*
*enthusiasm for this novel.*

# About the Authors and the Book

Thomas Block and Nelson DeMille met for the first time at Dutch Broadway Elementary School, in Elmont, Long Island, New York. They were both second graders, but due to some fluke in the system, Nelson was a full eighteen months Tom's senior, an age difference that was advantageous to Nelson in Dutch Broadway School, but which became less important in their later years.

Tom and Nelson successfully completed elementary school together, perfect products of the suburban 1950s. They entered Elmont Memorial Junior and Senior High School and became involved with numerous activities, such as football, track, wrestling, and operating the stage lights for school plays. Nelson was elected to student government, while Tom wrote a column for the school newspaper, *The Elmont Oracle*, which exposed corruption in student government. "That's what friends are for," said Tom recently.

Tom had begun flying lessons when he was fourteen years old and obtained his pilot's license at seventeen, the minimum legal age. Nelson, at Tom's suggestion, started lessons when he was seventeen and got out of the flying business at eighteen, much to the relief of his flight instructor.

After high school graduation in 1962, Tom attended Morehead State College in Kentucky, and Nelson attended Hofstra University in New York.

Tom left college and pursued his aviation career, joining the former Mohawk Airlines at age nineteen, becoming the youngest airline copilot in the United States. Mohawk survived the experience and went on to become Allegheny Airlines, USAir, and subsequently US Airways. Today, Tom is a Senior Captain for US Airways, flying wide-body jets to Europe.

Nelson completed three years at Hofstra and, bored, joined the United States Army in 1966 to see the world, not fully realizing there was a war heating up in Vietnam. Nelson went to Officer Candidate School, was commissioned a Second Lieutenant, and trained in Panama, then was assigned to lead an infantry platoon in Vietnam, where he served from October 1967 to November 1968 with the First Cavalry Division.

Upon discharge, Nelson returned to Long Island, where Tom was living. Nelson went back to college and obtained his degree as Tom moved up the airline seniority ladder. Tom and Nelson discovered they both had developed an interest in writing. Tom had begun writing for aviation magazines, and soon became a columnist for *Flying Magazine*, the world's largest-circulation aviation publication. Nelson began writing the Great American War Novel based on his combat experiences in Vietnam. Unfortunately, no one wanted to publish a Vietnamese *Naked and the Dead*. Tom

# ABOUT THE AUTHORS AND THE BOOK

transferred to Pittsburgh in 1972, while Nelson remained on Long Island.

In about the mid-1970s, Tom and Nelson began collaborating on general magazine pieces, none of which was published, but the experience of working together was a prelude of things to come. The years passed, and Tom became an internationally known aviation writer, while Nelson published a series of paperback novels.

In 1977, Nelson began an ambitious novel, *By the Rivers of Babylon*, in which Arab terrorists hijack two El Al Concordes. Nelson soon discovered that he didn't have the technical expertise to write the aviation scenes that were important to his novel, so he turned to his old friend Tom for help with those portions of the book.

The process worked well, and *By the Rivers of Babylon* became a Book-of-the-Month Club Main Selection, a *Reader's Digest* Condensed Book, and a national and international bestseller.

There is a section in *By the Rivers of Babylon* that reads:

Then there was the thing that bothered Becker from the first day he had taken the Concorde up to 19,000 meters. It was the problem of sudden cabin decompression of the type that can happen if you are hit by a missile, or if there is a small explosion on board, or if someone shatters a window with a bullet . . . at 19,000 meters, you needed a pressure suit to make breathing possible, even with an oxygen mask. Lacking pressure suits, you had only a few seconds of usable consciousness to get down to where you could breathe with a mask. There was no way to do that at 19,000 meters. You put the mask on, but you blacked out anyway. The on-board computer sensed the problem and brought the plane down nicely, but by the time you got down to where you could breathe with the mask, you woke up with brain damage.

One day, Tom said to Nelson, "We should collaborate on a novel about the high-altitude decompression of a plane, and what happens to its passengers and its crew." And thus was born *Mayday*.

Tom and Nelson worked on the novel for over a year. *Mayday* was published in hardcover by G. P. Putnam in 1979 and was a critical and commercial success. The paperback appeared on bestseller lists across the country and around the world.

Tom went on to publish five more aviation adventure novels, and Nelson went on to publish eight bestselling novels. Although they never collaborated again, *Mayday* was a fun and exciting experience for both of them, a convergence of their interests in writing as well as a friendship-strengthening episode for the two kids from Elmont, Long Island.

Nelson has reached the pinnacle of success in his writing career, and Tom has done the same in his flying career and as an aviation magazine writer.

While neither Tom nor Nelson has any immediate plans to collaborate again on a novel, they both felt that *Mayday*, a timeless and edge-of-the-seat tale of high-altitude terror, deserved to be republished.

Working with me at Warner Books, Tom and Nelson updated some of the politics and technology in the story to bring it into the '90s.

For old fans of *Mayday*, the authors hope this up-

# ABOUT THE AUTHORS AND THE BOOK

dated version is as immediate and exciting as the one you read in the late 1970s. For new readers, welcome to Flight 52. Fasten your seat belts and prepare for takeoff. You've never had a ride quite like this.

### *MAYDAY!*

MEL PARKER
Publisher
Warner Paperbacks

SUCCESS/FOUR FLIGHTS THURSDAY
MORNING/ALL AGAINST TWENTY-
ONE-MILE WIND/STARTED FROM
LEVEL WITH ENGINE POWER ALONE/
AVERAGE SPEED THROUGH AIR
THIRTY-ONE MILES/LONGEST
FIFTY-NINE SECONDS/INFORM
PRESS/HOME CHRISTMAS

—Telegram to the Rev. Milton Wright,
from Kitty Hawk, North Carolina,
December 17, 1903

# MAYDAY

# 1

Silhouetted against the deep blue horizon of the stratosphere, Trans-United Flight 52 cruised westbound toward Japan.

Below, Captain Alan Stuart could see pieces of the sunlit Pacific between the breaks in the cloud cover. Above was subspace—an airless void without sun or life. The continuous shock wave generated by the giant craft's supersonic airspeed rose invisibly off its wings and fell unheard into the mid–Pacific Ocean.

Captain Stuart scanned his instruments. It had been two hours and twenty minutes since the flight had departed San Francisco. The Straton 797 maintained a steady Mach-cruise component of 1.8—930 miles per hour. The triple inertial navigation sets with satellite updating all agreed that Flight 52 was progressing precisely according to plan. Stuart picked up a clipboard from the flight pedestal between himself and the copilot, looked at their computer flight plan, then glanced back at the electronic readout of position: 161 degrees,

1

14 minutes west, 43 degrees 27 minutes north—2100 miles west of California, 1500 miles north of Hawaii. "We're on target," he said.

First Officer Daniel McVary, the copilot, glanced at him. "We should be landing at Chicago within the hour."

Stuart managed a smile. "Wrong map, Dan." He didn't care for cockpit humor. He unfolded the chart for today's mid-Pacific high-altitude navigation routes and laid it on his lap, studying it slowly with the motions of a man who had more time than duties. The chart was blank except for lines of longitude and latitude and the current flight routes. Flight 52 had long left behind any features that mapmakers could put on a chart. Even from their aerie of over twelve miles altitude, there was no land to be seen over this route. Captain Stuart turned to First Officer McVary. "Did you get the fourth and fifth sectors in?"

"Yes. Updates, too." He yawned and stretched.

Stuart nodded. His mind drifted back to San Francisco. His hometown. He'd done a television talk show the previous morning. He'd been anxious about it and, like an instant replay, snatches of the conversation kept running through his brain.

As usual, the interviewer had been more interested in the Straton than in him, but he'd become accustomed to that. He ran through the standard spiel in his mind. The Straton 797 was not like the old British/ French Concorde. It climbed to the same altitude the Concorde did, but it flew a little slower. Yet it was measurably more practical. Armed with some aerodynamic breakthroughs of the '90s, the Straton engineers had aimed at less speed and more size. Luxury coupled with economy of operation.

The aircraft held 40 first-class and 285 tourist-class passengers. For the interview, he remembered to mention the upper deck where the cockpit and first-class lounge were located. The lounge had a bar and piano. One day when he was feeling reckless he would tell an interviewer that it had a fireplace and pool.

Stuart had spouted the advertising hype whenever he couldn't think of anything else to say. The Straton 797 flew faster than the sun. Slightly faster than the rotational velocity of the earth.

At a cruise speed of close to 1,000 miles per hour, Flight 52 should arrive in Tokyo at 7:15 A.M. local time, though it had departed San Francisco at 8:00 A.M. At least that was usually the case. Not today. They had departed San Francisco thirty-nine minutes late because of a minor leak in the number-three hydraulic system. While the mechanics changed the bad valve, Captain Stuart and his flight crew spent the delay time reviewing their computer flight profile. An updated winds aloft forecast had been sent to them, and Stuart had used the new wind information to revise his flight plan. They would fly south of the original planned routing to stay away from the worst of the newly predicted headwinds.

Time en route would be only slightly greater than usual, at six hours and twenty-four minutes. It was still impressive; grist for the media's mill. Across seven time zones and the International Date Line in less than a working man's day. The marvel of the decade.

But it was a little frightening. Stuart remembered the time he had been candid during a magazine interview.

He had honestly explained the technical problems of supersonic flight at 62,000 feet, like the subtle effects of ozone poisoning and the periodic increases in radiation from sunspots. The interviewer had latched on to some of his points, exaggerated others, and had written an article that would have scared the hell out of a Shuttle astronaut. Stuart had been called in to speak to the Chief Pilot about his candor. Never again. "I did another one of those damned TV interviews. Yesterday morning."

McVary looked at him. "No kidding? Why didn't you tell us? Not that I would have gotten up that early . . ."

The junior pilot in the cockpit, Carl Fessler, who sat behind them at the relief copilot's position, laughed. "Why do they always pick on you, Skipper?"

Stuart shrugged. "Some idiot in public relations thinks I come across good. I'd rather fly through a line of thunderstorms than face a camera."

McVary nodded. Alan Stuart was every inch the image of the competent captain, from his gray hair to the crease in his pants. "I wouldn't mind being on TV."

Stuart yawned. "I'll suggest it to PR." He looked around the flight deck. Behind McVary, Fessler was typing into a portable computer—an electronic equivalent of a ship's log—with backup data from the instrument panel. McVary had returned to staring blankly ahead, his mind, no doubt, on personal matters.

The usual mid-flight routines had laid their blue veil over the crew. The blue mid-Pacific blues. The doldrums, as they were called by seamen—but this ship was not becalmed as a ship caught in the doldrums. It was ripping along at close to the velocity of a bullet.

Yet there was really nothing, at that moment, for the three pilots to do. At 62,000 feet, all the weather was beneath them. An hour before, they had flown over an area of bad weather. Some of the towering cumulus clouds had reached up high enough to at least give any of the crew and passengers who cared to look at them something to see. But there had not been even the slightest turbulence at those altitudes. Stuart would have welcomed a little bump, the way truck drivers did on a long haul across endless smooth blacktop. He glanced out the front window again. There was one thing to see that never ceased to fascinate him: the rounded horizon line that separated earth from subspace.

The autopilot made small and silent corrections to keep the flight on the preprogrammed course. Stuart listlessly laid two fingers of his right hand on the control wheel. He had not steered the 797 manually since right after takeoff. He would not use the control wheel again until the final moments of their landing approach at Tokyo.

Carl Fessler looked up from his portable computer. He laid it down on the small table next to him. "What a lot of crap this backup data is. Most of the other airlines don't do this crap anymore."

Stuart took his eyes off the horizon and glanced back at his relief copilot. "I bet we could find some eager young new-hire pilot to take your place. He'd probably type faster, too." Stuart smiled, but he had been pointedly serious. He had little patience for the new breed. They had a job that was fifty times better than what had come before, yet they seemed to complain constantly. Did they realize that thirty years ago Alan Stuart had to hand-plot each and every route segment before climbing into the copilot's seat? *Spoiled*, Stuart said to himself. Telling them about it was a waste of time. "If we land in the teeth of a monsoon at Tokyo, you'll earn your day's pay, Carl."

McVary closed his copy of *Playboy* and put it into his flight bag. Reading was not authorized, and Stuart was starting to get into one of his Captain moods. "That's right, Carl. Or if one of these lights starts blinking, we'll find something useful for you to do real quick."

Fessler could see which way the wind was blowing. "You're right. It's a good job." He swiveled his seat slightly toward the front. "In the meantime, are you guys any good at trivia? What's the capital of Rwanda?"

McVary looked back over his shoulder. "Here's a trivia question for you. Which one of the stews has the hots for you?"

Fessler suddenly looked alert. "Which one?"

"I'm asking you." He laughed. "Look, I'll press the stew call button, and if fate brings you your secret lover, I'll nod. If not . . . well, you have ten left to wonder about." He laughed again, then glanced at Captain Stuart to read his mood. The old man seemed to be taking it well enough. "Skipper, anything for you?"

"Might as well. Coffee and a pastry."

"Coffee for me," Fessler said.

McVary picked up the ship's interphone and pushed the call button.

Flight attendants Sharon Crandall and Terri O'Neil were in the first-class galley in the main cabin below when the light blinked. Terri O'Neil picked up the phone. After a brief exchange with McVary, she hung up and turned to Sharon Crandall.

"They want coffee again. It's a wonder they don't turn brown with all they drink."

"They're just bored," said Crandall.

"Too bad. Walking all the way upstairs every time the cockpit crew needs a diversion is no fun." O'Neil took out a dish of pastry and poured three coffees.

Crandall smiled. Terri was always carrying on about something. Today, it was walking to the cockpit. "I'll go, Terri. I need the exercise. I have to go down to the pit pretty soon to help Barbara Yoshiro." She nodded toward the service elevator that led to the lower kitchen. "There's no room to move down there."

"No. Take a break. If anyone needs the exercise, it's me. Check these hips."

"Okay. You go." They both laughed. "I'll do the cleaning up," Crandall said.

Terri O'Neil picked up the tray, left the galley, and walked the short distance to the circular staircase. She waited at the base of the stairs while an elderly, well-dressed woman worked her way down.

"I'm sorry I'm so slow," the woman said.

"Take your time. No rush," O'Neil answered. She wished the woman would move a little faster.

"My name is Mrs. Thorndike." She introduced herself with the automatic manners of the old, not recognizing or caring that modern travel didn't require it. "I like your piano player. He's quite good," the woman said. She stopped on the bottom step to chat.

O'Neil forced a smile and balanced the tray of coffees and pastry against the handrail. "Yes. He's good. Some of them are even better than he is."

"Really? I hope I have one of the better ones on the flight home."

"I hope you do."

The old woman finally stepped aside and the flight attendant trudged up the stairway. Strands of "As Time Goes By" floated down to O'Neil over the normal in-flight noises. With each step the singing of the more gregarious passengers got louder.

When O'Neil reached the top of the staircase, she frowned. Three of the male passengers stood arm-in-arm around the piano. So far, they were content to sing softly. But she knew that whenever men acted openly chummy while they were still sober, they were certain to become especially loud after they began to drink. Alcohol released the Irish tenor in them. O'Neil knew they would soon get their chance, since she was supposed to open the bar in a few minutes. She wished the airline would go back to the old-fashioned lounge instead of the aerial nightclub.

"Hello," O'Neil called to the young piano player. She could not recall if his name was Hogan or Grogan. He was too young for her anyway. She edged her way around half-a-dozen passengers, across the heavily carpeted lounge, and toward the cockpit. With the tray balanced in her hands, she tapped against the fiberglass door with the toe of her shoe. She could see from the shadow that someone in the cockpit had leaned up against the door's tiny section of one-way glass to see who had knocked.

Carl Fessler unlocked the door for her, and O'Neil walked into the cockpit.

"Coffee is served, gentlemen."

"The pastry is mine, Terri," Stuart said.

Everyone took a plastic cup, and she handed Stuart the pastry dish.

Stuart turned to Fessler. "Carl, see if the passengers' flight-connection information has come in yet." Stuart glanced down at the blank electronics screen on the pedestal between the two flight chairs. "Maybe we missed it on the screen."

Fessler looked over his shoulder toward the right rear of the cockpit. He had left the data-link printer's door open. The message tray was still empty. "Nothing, Skipper."

Stuart nodded. "If we don't get that connection information soon," he said to Terri O'Neil, "I'll send another request."

"Very good," said O'Neil. "Some of the first-class passengers are getting nervous. Having a printout of connection updates works even better than giving them Valium." While she spoke with the Captain, O'Neil could see out of the corner of her eye that Fessler and McVary were looking at each other in a peculiar way, evidently conveying some sort of signal. Terri realized that the First Officer and Second Officer were playing a game—and that she had become part of it. Boys. After everyone mumbled his thanks, O'Neil left the flight deck and closed the door behind her.

Captain Stuart had waited for the coffee and pastry as though it were a special event—a milestone along a straight desert highway. He ate the pastry slowly, then sat back to sip at his coffee. Of the three of them on the flight deck, only Stuart remembered when everything they ate was served on real china. The utensils then were silver and the food was a little less plastic as well. Now even the aromas were a weak imitation of what he had remembered as a new copilot. The whole cockpit smelled different then. Real leather, hydraulic fluid, and old cigarettes; not the sterile aroma of acrylic paints and synthetic materials.

Alan Stuart's mind wandered. He had flown for Trans-United for thirty-four years. He'd crossed the Pacific more than a thousand times. He was a multimillion-miler, although supersonic speeds had made that yardstick meaningless. Now he was losing count of his hours, miles, and number of crossings. He sighed, then took another sip from his plastic cup. "I don't know where the company buys this lousy coffee," he said to no one in particular.

Fessler turned around. "If that's a trivia question, the answer is Brazil."

Stuart didn't answer. In a few seconds his thoughts had slid comfortably back to where they had been. Supersonic transports were not actually flown; they were just aimed and watched. What modern pilots did mostly was to type instructions into onboard computers, and that was how actual flight tasks got accomplished. It had become such a passive job—until something went wrong.

In the old days, there was much more work, but much more fun. There were the long layovers in Sydney, Hong Kong, Tokyo. Some days in the Straton he would sit in his twelve-mile-high perch and look down on the routes he had flown as a young man. Old Boeing 707s—the original jets. And the captains that he had flown with had once flown the DC-4s, DC-6s, and DC-7s on those very routes. Even with the old 707, they needed to make refueling stops everywhere. The lighter passenger loads meant that the flights operated only a few times each week, so they had several days' layover in lots of remote and faraway places. Life, he was certain, had been simpler yet more exciting then.

Carl Fessler tapped his pencil on the digital readout of the Total Airframe Temperature gauge. He was beginning another round of required entries into the portable backup computer, entries of their mid-flight aircraft performance numbers. Records of every sort, to be fed into the company mainframe computer and never to be seen again.

The Total Airframe Temperature needle sat on 189 degrees Fahrenheit, closing in on the red-line mark of 198. The operational limits at 62,000 feet were always a matter of temperatures and pressures, reflected Fessler. The Straton transport's skin was not to exceed its designated limit. If necessary, Fessler would tell the Captain and he would slow the ship down. The environment they operated in was hostile enough. Don't press it. "What's the capital of Japan?" he asked without looking up from his paperwork.

McVary glanced over his shoulder. "Mount Fuji?"

"Close," said Fessler. "But not close enough for you to try to land on it." Fessler entered the final figures into the computer and looked up at the windshield. Just beyond the glass and the aluminum-and-titanium alloy skin of the 797 was a slipstream of air moving so fast that anything its friction touched was instantly heated to over 175 degrees Fahrenheit. Yet the actual temperature of the atmosphere outside was 67 degrees below zero. The air itself was thin enough to be nonexistent. Less than one pound per square inch—one-fifteenth the normal sea-level amount. The oxygen composition was less than one percent. The mass was unbreathable anyway, since the pressure was too low to force the few oxygen molecules into the lungs. Subspace, reflected Fessler. Subspace was not what he'd been hired for five years before. But here he was.

McVary suddenly sat erect in his seat and put down his coffee. "Skipper, what's that?" He pointed to his right front. There was a small dot on the horizon—hardly more than a speck against the cockpit glass.

Stuart sat up and put his face closer to the windshield.

Fessler put down his coffee and turned in his seat to look.

They watched the dot on the right side of the windshield. It was moving across their front, apparently at an oblique angle to their flight path. It was growing slightly, but not alarmingly. It did not—at least for the moment—pose any threat of collision.

McVary relaxed a bit. "Must be a fighter. Some military jet jockey horsing around."

Stuart nodded. "Right." He reached into his flight bag and pulled out a pair of binoculars, a good set of Bausch & Lomb that he had bought in Germany many years before. He carried it as an amusement. He used to watch ships, planes, and faraway coastlines when he flew low enough to see something worth looking at. He'd meant to take them out of his bag long ago, but habit and nostalgia—he'd seen a good deal of the world through them—had postponed the retirement of the glasses. He adjusted the focus knob. "Can't make it out."

"Maybe it's a missile," McVary said. "A cruise missile." He had been an Air Force pilot, and his mind still worked in that direction.

Fessler half stood near his console. "Would they shoot it up here?"

"They're not supposed to," said McVary. "Not near commercial routes." He paused. "We did deviate pretty far south today."

Stuart twisted the focus knob again. "Lost it. Wait . . . Got it. . . ."

"Can you make it out, Skipper?" asked McVary, a slight edge to his voice.

"Funny-looking. Never seen anything like it. Some sort of missile, I think. I can't tell. Here." He handed the binoculars to McVary. "You look."

The ex-fighter pilot took the glasses. Even without them he could see that the object had gotten closer. To the naked eye it appeared to be a sliver of dark-colored metal against the blue sky. He raised the glasses and adjusted them. There was something very familiar about that object, but he couldn't place it. It was hard to get a perspective on its size, but instinctively he knew it was small. "Small," he said aloud. "And at that speed and these altitudes it could only be military."

Fessler stepped closer to the front windshield. "Whose military?"

McVary shrugged as he continued to scan. "The Martian Air Force, Carl. How the hell do I know?" He leaned farther forward. For a brief, irrational moment he thought he might be seeing the opening salvo of an atomic war. The end of the world. No. It was too low, too small, and going toward the open Pacific. "It's got to be a jet fighter . . . but . . ."

"If it gets closer, we'll turn," Stuart said. Altering the course of a supersonic transport was no easy matter, however. At cruise speed it would take him nearly four-and-a-half minutes to turn the 797 around, and during that time the ship would have flown sixty-seven miles. At any greater rate of turn, the passengers would be subjected to an unacceptable level of positive Gs. Those who were standing would be thrown to the floor. Those seated would be unable to move. He flipped on the switch for the cabin seat-belt sign, then turned in his seat and wrapped his hands around the control wheel. His left thumb was poised over the autopilot disengage button. He looked at the object on the horizon, then at his crew. The cockpit had changed quickly. It was always that way. Nothing to do, or too much to do. He glanced at his relief copilot, who was still out of his seat and looking out the window. "Fessler. Who played opposite Cary Grant in *North by Northwest*?"

"I don't know."

"Then get back in your seat and do something you do know. Sit down, strap in, get ready."

"Yes, sir."

Small beads of perspiration had begun to form on the Captain's forehead. "I'm going to turn," he said, but still did not press the autopilot release button on his control wheel. Alan Stuart—like most commercial pilots—was reluctant to alter course, speed, or altitude unless absolutely necessary. Jumping headlong into an unneeded evasive action was a student pilot's stunt.

The fourth being in the cockpit—the autopilot— continued to maintain the 797's heading and altitude.

The object was easily visible now. It was becoming apparent to Stuart that the mysterious missile was not on a collision course with the Straton. If neither of the crafts altered course, the object would pass safely across their front. Captain Stuart relaxed his grip on the control wheel but stayed ready to execute a turn toward the north if the object's flight path changed. He glanced at his wristwatch, which was still set to San Francisco time. It was exactly eleven o'clock.

McVary saw the object clearly now in the binoculars. "Oh, Christ!" His voice was a mixture of surprise and fear.

Captain Stuart experienced a long-forgotten but familiar sensation in his stomach. "What, what. . . ?"

"It's not a missile," said McVary. "It's a drone. A military target drone!"

---

At 10:44 A.M. San Francisco time, the helmsman of the nuclear-powered aircraft carrier *Chester W. Nimitz* made a three-degree course correction to starboard. Positioned 2,000 yards astern of the *Nimitz* were the cruiser *Belknap* and the destroyers *Coontz* and *Nicolas*. Their helmsmen also made appropriate corrections. The fleet steered a steady course of 135 degrees, making a headway of 18 knots. They rode serenely over the mid-Pacific, their position 900 miles north of Hawaii. The midmorning skies were clear and the air was warm. The weather forecast for the next thirty-six hours called for little change.

Retired Rear Admiral Randolf Hennings stood on the 0-7 deck of the carrier's superstructure. Hennings's blue civilian suit stood out among the officers and men dressed in tropical tans. The orange ALL-ACCESS pass pinned to his collar made him more, not less, self-conscious.

From the seven-story-high balcony behind the

bridge, Hennings had an unrestricted view of the *Nimitz*'s flight deck. Yet his eyes wandered from the operational activities toward the men who stood their stations a dozen feet away inside the glass-enclosed ship's bridge.

Captain Diehl sat in his leather swivel chair, overseeing the morning's operation. He was, at that moment, in conversation with Lieutenant Thompson, the Officer of the Deck, and with another lieutenant, whom Hennings had not met. The helmsman stood attentively at the *Nimitz*'s steering controls.

The flurry of on-deck activities from the dawn practice maneuvers had subsided. Hennings counted half-a-dozen aircraft on the starboard quarter of the *Nimitz*'s flight deck. One by one, they were being taken to the servicing area on the hangar deck below. The plotting board in the Air-Ops Room had shown only one aircraft yet to be recovered. *Navy 347. F-18. Pilot Lt. P. Matos. Launched 1027 hours, 23 June. Special test. Estimated time of return, 1300 hours.*

Hennings had not liked that "special test" designation. It was too close to the truth—and the truth was not to be openly discussed. He would have preferred something even more routine, like "extra training."

Hennings knew too well why the test was a secret, even though no one had actually spoken with him about it. It was, he knew, because of the new Voluntary Arms Limitation Treaty recently approved by Congress and signed by the President. Hennings had read that the agreement specifically prohibited the development of improved tactical missiles, among other things. Today's secret test would be the first for the updated Phoenix missile. Its range had been doubled to 500 miles, a new self-guiding radar system had been added, and, most importantly, its maneuverability had been vastly increased. All of this was unquestionably outside the limitations of the treaty Congress had decided on. But if the weapon proved workable, it could significantly alter the balance of power in any future air-to-air combat scenario.

Hennings became aware that a young ensign was holding a salute, speaking to him. He glanced at the woman's blue and white name tag. "What is it, Ms. Phillips?"

The ensign dropped her salute. "Excuse me, Admiral. Commander Sloan requests that you join him in E-334."

Hennings nodded. "Very well. Lead on."

Hennings followed the ensign through the hatchway and down the metal stairs. They walked in silence. Hennings had entered the Navy at a time when female personnel did not serve on warships. By the time he left the Navy, it was not uncommon. While in the Navy, Hennings had towed the official line and outwardly approved of women serving with men aboard ship. In reality, Hennings thought the whole social experiment had been and was a disaster. But the Navy and the Pentagon had covered up most of the problems so that the public was never aware of the high pregnancy rate among unmarried female personnel, the sexual harassment, abuse, and even rapes, and the general lowering of morale and discipline. In short, it was a nightmare for the ships' commanders, but it wasn't his problem.

On the 0-2 deck of the conning tower, they stepped into a long gray corridor similar to the thousands that Hennings had walked through in his shipboard career.

There had been an incredible amount of technological innovation aboardship since his day, but the old architectural adage that form should follow function was never more true than on a warship. There was a familiarity about naval architecture that was comforting. Yet, deep down, he knew that nothing was the same. "Did you ever serve on an older ship, Ms. Phillips?"

The ensign glanced back over her shoulder. "No, sir. The *Nimitz* is my first ship."

"Could you imagine what these corridors were like before air-conditioning?"

"I can imagine, sir." The ensign stopped abruptly and opened a door marked "E-334." She was relieved to be rid of her charge, relieved not to have to hear a story about wooden ships and iron men. "Admiral Hennings, Commander."

Hennings stepped into the small gray-painted room packed with electronics gear. The door closed behind him.

An enlisted man sat in front of a console. Standing behind the man and looking over his shoulder was Commander James Sloan. Sloan looked up as Hennings entered the room. "Hello, Admiral. Did you see the launch?"

"Yes. The F-18 was being strapped to the catapult when I arrived on the bridge. Quite impressive."

"That machine really moves. Excuse me for just one minute, Admiral." Sloan leaned over and said something to the electronics specialist, Petty Officer Kyle Loomis, in a voice just a bit too low for Hennings to hear.

Hennings could see that Sloan was unhappy. They were apparently having some technical difficulty. Still,

Hennings had the feeling that he was not being shown all the military courtesy possible, but decided not to make an issue of it. Retired, after all, meant retired. He had one mission aboard the *Nimitz,* and that was to carry back the results of the "special test" to the Joint Chiefs of Staff, to carry on his person untitled and unsigned test results, and to commit to memory everything that could not be written. He was a messenger. The execution of the test was not an area he cared to get involved with.

His old friends in Washington threw him these consulting plums as a favor. He had little else to do. This time, however, he was beginning to wish he hadn't been home when the phone rang. Hennings had the feeling that all those soft jobs to exotic places and those generous "consulting fees" had been a setup for the time when his friends might need a special favor. Could this be that special time? Hennings shrugged. It didn't matter. His friends had earned his loyalty, and he would provide it.

Commander Sloan was pointing to a panel of gauges above the console. Loomis mumbled something. Sloan shook his head. He was clearly not happy.

"Problem, Commander?"

Sloan looked up and forced a smile. "Only the usual . . . Admiral." He paused and considered for a second. "One of our high-frequency channels to San Diego isn't working. Can't figure out why." He glanced at the equipment panel as though it were an enlisted man who had jumped ship.

"Will it delay things?"

Sloan thought it might, but that wasn't the proper answer. "No. It shouldn't. We can go through Pearl.

Just a procedural step." He paused again. He wondered how much of this Hennings was taking in. "We could eliminate the step anyway. The things we need are working."

"Good. I'm to be at a conference tomorrow morning."

Sloan already knew that. The famous breakfast meetings of the Joint Chiefs, where bleary-eyed old men turned the talk from golf scores to nuclear holocaust with the ease of a piano player going through a familiar medley.

"I'm set up on a commercial flight out of Los Angeles late tonight. I need to be off the carrier by 1600 hours."

"The mission should be completed shortly."

"Good. Now, do you mind telling me why you summoned me here, Commander?" His tone was as gentlemanly as always, so the words were more, not less, terse.

Sloan was taken aback for a second. "I didn't summon . . . I mean, I thought you would want to be here."

"This . . ." Hennings waved his hand around the room, ". . . this means very little to me. I would rather have just gotten an oral and written report from you at the completion of the test. But if you want me here, I'll stay." He sat in a small swivel chair.

"Thank you, sir, I would." Sloan didn't trust himself to say any more. He had treated Hennings in an offhand manner since he'd come aboard, but now he was reminded, in case he had forgotten, that Randolf Hennings had friends. More than that, though, the old saying, "Once an admiral, always an S.O.B.", was brought home.

# MAYDAY

As Hennings watched Sloan shuffle through some papers, he realized for the first time how much Sloan wanted him to be here, as an actual accomplice in the missile test. They were, Hennings now realized, doing something *criminal*. But it was too late to turn back. Hennings pushed those disquieting notions out of his mind and forced himself to think of other things.

Sloan turned to the electronics. He peered at the panel intently, but he was trying to recall all that he knew about Randolf Hennings. Action in and around Vietnam. He was considered a likable man by his peers, but you never knew about admirals, retired or otherwise. They could change as quickly as the North Atlantic weather. Hennings was known for having enough perseverance to get his job done but not enough to be a threat to his seniors. Those very seniors who had made it to the top had now picked Hennings to carry out a most sensitive mission. Hennings was known to be the epitome of dependability and discretion. Like a dinghy caught in the suction of a battleship's wake, thought Sloan, retired Rear Admiral Hennings had followed at a speed and course set by others. Yet Sloan had to reckon with him. He glanced back at Hennings. "Coffee, Admiral?"

"No, thank you."

Sloan's mind was still not on the electronics problem but on the politics of the test. He thought about asking Hennings for some information, but decided that would be a mistake. At any rate, Hennings wouldn't know much more than he, Sloan, did.

"Sir, the patch to Pearl isn't carrying."

Sloan looked at the electronics man. "What?"

"The problem might be on their end."

"Right. Probably is." Sloan glanced at Hennings. Hennings was drumming his fingers restlessly on the arm of his chair. His attention seemed to be focused on the video screen that was displaying routine weather data.

Petty Officer Loomis glanced back over his shoulder. "Sir? Should I keep trying?"

Sloan tapped his foot. Time for a command decision. He felt acid in his stomach and knew why officers had more ulcers than enlisted men. He considered. The test elements were nearly all in position. A delay could disrupt things for hours. Hennings had to be at the Pentagon the next morning with the report. If the report said only "Special test delayed," Commander James Sloan would look bad. The men behind the test might lose their nerve and cancel it for good. Worse, they might think he had lost his nerve. He considered asking Hennings for advice, but that would have been a tactical blunder.

"Sir," the electronics man said, his hand poised over a set of switches on the console.

Sloan shook his head. "Get back to the mission profile. We can't spend any more time on routine procedures. Send the approval for the release, then get another update from Lieutenant Matos."

Petty Officer Kyle Loomis returned to his equipment. He had begun to suspect that all was not routine here, but as a former submariner, his knowledge of fighters and missiles was too limited to allow him to piece together what was not routine about this test. Without anyone telling him, he knew that his ignorance had gotten him out of the submarine that he'd come to hate and onto the *Nimitz*, which he found more tolerable. He also knew that his transfer request to the Mediterranean Fleet was secure as long as he kept his mouth shut.

Sloan watched the electronics procedure for a few seconds, then glanced at Hennings, who was still staring at the video screen. "Soon, Admiral."

Hennings looked up. He nodded.

It occurred to Sloan that perhaps Hennings, like himself, wanted to go on record as having said nothing for the record.

Petty Officer Loomis spoke. "Sir, Lieutenant Matos is on-station. Orbiting in sector twenty-three."

"All right. Tell him that we expect target information shortly."

"Yes, sir."

Sloan tried to evaluate his own exposure in this thing. It had begun with the routine delivery of the two Phoenix test missiles to the carrier a month before. He had signed for the missiles. Then came a routine communication from Pearl informing the *Nimitz*'s commander, Captain Diehl, that Hennings was coming to observe an air-to-air missile testing. Not unusual, but not routine. Then came the brief communication that directed a routine practice firing of the missiles. The only exception to the routine was that "procedures and distances" be in accordance with the manufacturer's new specifications for the AIM-63X version of the Phoenix. That was when Sloan had known that there was a top-level conspiracy—no, wrong word; *initiative*—a top-level initiative among the Joint Chiefs. They were going to secretly ignore the new arms limitation agreement that Congress had enacted. And by a stroke of fate, Sloan had been named the technical officer in charge of conducting the test. Within a year, he'd be a captain . . . or he'd be in Portsmouth Naval Prison. He looked at Hennings again. What was in this for him?

Sloan knew that he could have backed out at any time by asking for shore leave. But those old men in the Pentagon had done their homework well when they studied his personnel file. They knew a gambler when they saw one. A small stream of perspiration ran down Sloan's neck, and he hoped Hennings hadn't noticed it. "Approximately ten minutes, Admiral." He punched a button on the console and a digital countdown clock began to run.

Sloan had an inordinate fascination, mixed with phobia, for countdown procedures. He watched the digital display running down. He used the time to examine his motives and strengthen his resolve. To rationalize. The updated Phoenix was a crucial weapon to have in the event of war, even though the idiots in Congress were acting as if there would never be any more wars. One discreet test of this missile would tell the Joint Chiefs if it would work under combat conditions, if the increased maneuverability would mean that the kill ratio of this newest weapon could be nearly one hundred percent.

The Navy brass would then know what they had, and the politicians could go on jawing and pretending. American airpower would have an unpublicized edge, no matter what happened in the future. Russia could go back to being the Soviet Union and the Cold War could refreeze; U.S. combat forces would have something extra. And with modern technology, a slight edge was all you could ever hope for. All you ever needed, really. There was also the matter of the Navy finding its balls again, after countless years of humiliation at the hands of the politicians, the gays, and the feminists. Nine minutes.

Commander Sloan poured a cup of coffee from a metal galley pitcher. He glanced at Hennings. The man was looking uncomfortable. He could see it in his eyes, as he had seen it several times the day before. Did Hennings know something that he didn't?

Sloan walked to the far end of the console and looked at the gauges. But his thoughts were on Hennings now. Hennings seemed to be almost uninterested in the testing. Uninterested in Sloan, too, which was unusual since Sloan was certain that Hennings was to make an oral evaluation report on him. Sloan felt that almost forgotten ensign's paranoia creeping over him and shook it off quickly. A seasoned officer turns everything to his advantage. He would turn Hennings's detachment to his advantage, if necessary.

Hennings stood suddenly and moved nearer to Sloan. He spoke in a low voice. "Commander, will the data be ready as soon as the testing is complete? Will you need to do anything else?"

Sloan nodded. "Just a few qualitative forms." He tapped his fingers on a stack of paperwork on the console desk. "Thirty minutes or so."

Hennings nodded. The room was silent except for the ambient sounds of electronics.

Randolf Hennings let his eyes wander absently over the equipment in the tight room. The functions of this equipment were not entirely a mystery to him. He recognized some of it and guessed at what looked vaguely familiar, as a man might do who had been asleep for a hundred years and had awakened in the twenty-first century.

When he was a younger man he had asked many questions of his shipboard technicians and officers. But as the years passed, the meaning of those young men's answers eluded him more each time. He was, he reminded himself, a product of another civilization. He had been born during the Great Depression. His older brother had died of a simple foot infection. He remembered, firsthand, a great deal about World War II, the Nazis and the Japs, listening to the bulletins as they came across the radio in their living room. He recalled vividly the day that FDR died, Hiroshima, Nagasaki, the day the Japanese surrendered, the day, as a teenager, that he saw a television screen for the first time. He remembered the family car, a big, old, round-bodied Buick, and how his mother had never learned to drive it. They'd come an incredibly long way in a short span of time. Many people had chosen not to go along on that fast ride. Others had become the helmsmen and navigators. Then there were people like himself who found they were in positions of command without understanding what those helmsmen and navigators were doing, where they were going.

He walked over to the single porthole in the room and pushed back the blackout shade. The tranquil sea calmed his troubled conscience. He remembered when he had finally made the decision that he would have to evaluate his men on their personal traits and then trust their technical advice accordingly. Men, he understood. Human beings did not really change from generation to generation. If his sixty-seven years were good for anything, it was that he had arrived at an understanding of the most complex piece of machinery of all. He could read the hearts and souls of his fellow men; he had peered into the psyche of Commander James Sloan, and he did not like what he saw.

Petty Officer Loomis turned around. "Commander Sloan." He pointed to a video display screen.

Sloan walked over to the screen. He looked at the message. "Good news, Admiral."

Hennings closed the blackout shade and turned around.

Sloan spoke as he read the data. "Our elements are in position. The F-18 is on station, and the C-130 is also in position. We need only the release verification." He glanced at the digital countdown clock. Five minutes.

Hennings nodded. "Fine."

Sloan gave a final thought to the one command check he was not able to complete. If the test had not been a secret, and if delay had not meant possible cancellation, and if cancellation had not meant potential disadvantage in a future war, and his career weren't in the balance, and if Hennings weren't evaluating him with those steely gray eyes, and if it wasn't time for the Navy to gets its balls back, and if that damn digital clock weren't running down . . . then, maybe, maybe he would have waited. Four minutes.

The video screen's display updated again, and Sloan looked at the short message. He read it first to himself, smiled, and then read it aloud. "The C-130 has launched its target and it was last tracked as steady and on course. The target drone has accelerated to Mach 2, and is now level at sixty-two thousand feet." He glanced at the digital countdown. "In two minutes and thirty seconds I can instruct Lieutenant Matos to begin tracking the target and engage it at will."

---

"Would you like another drink?"

"No, I think I'll wait." John Berry put down his empty glass and looked up at the flight attendant. Her shoulder-length brunette hair brushed across the top of her white blouse. She had narrow hips, a slender waist, and very little visible makeup. She looked like one of those models from a tennis club brochure. Berry had spoken to her several times since the flight had begun. Now that the job of serving the midmorning snack was nearly finished, she seemed to be lingering near his seat. "Not too crowded," Berry said, motioning around the half-empty forward section of the Straton 797.

"Not here. In the back. I'm glad I pulled first-class duty. The tourist section is full."

"High season in Tokyo?"

"I guess. Maybe there's a special on electronics factory tours." She laughed at her own joke. "Are you going on business or pleasure?"

"Both. It's a pleasure to be away on business." Disclosures can come out at unusual moments. Yet, for John Berry, that particular moment wasn't an unusual one. The young flight attendant was everything that Jennifer Berry was not. Even better, she seemed to be none of the things that Jennifer Berry had become. "Sharon?" He pointed to the flight attendant's name tag.

"Yes, Sharon Crandall. From San Francisco."

# MAYDAY

"John Berry. From New York. I'm going to see Ka-
bushi Steel in Tokyo. Then a metal-fabricating company in Nagasaki. No electronics factories. I go twice
a year. The boss sends me because I'm the tallest. The
Japanese like to emphasize their differences with the
West. Short salespeople make them nervous."

"Really?" She looked at him quizzically. She
grinned. "No one ever told me that before. Are you
kidding?"

"Sure." He hesitated. His throat was dry. Just the
thought of asking this young woman to sit with him
was mildly unnerving. Yet all he wanted was someone
to talk to. To pass the time. To pretend for a few relax-
ing moments that the situation in New York didn't
exist.

Jennifer Berry's tentacles reached even this far. Her
presence stretched across a continent and over an
ocean. The image of his difficult and complaining wife
lay over John Berry's thoughts. Their two teenaged
children—a son and a daughter—were on his mind,
too. They had grown further from him every year. The
family tie had become mainly their shared name.
Shared living space and shared documents. Legalities.

The rest of what was termed these days their lifestyle
was, to Berry, a cruel joke. An outrageously expensive
house in Oyster Bay that he had always disliked. The
pretentious country club. The phony bridge group.
Hollow friendships. Neighborhood gossip. The cock-
tails, without which all of Oyster Bay, along with the
neighboring suburbs, would have committed mass suicide long ago. The futility. The silliness. The boredom.
What had happened to the things he cared about? He
could hardly remember the good times anymore. The

all-night talks with Jennifer, and their lovemaking, before it became just another obligation. Those camping trips with the kids. The long Sunday breakfasts. The backyard baseball games. It seemed like another life. It seemed like a lifetime ago.

John Berry found himself dwelling on the past more and more. Living in the past. A 1960s song on the radio made him yearn for Dayton, Ohio, his hometown. An old movie or serial on television brought on a nostalgia so acute that his heart ached.

He looked up at the young woman standing over him. "How about having a drink with me? Never mind. I know . . . you're on duty. Then how about a Coke?" Berry was speaking quickly. "I'll tell you about Japanese businessmen. Japanese customs. Very educational. Wonderful information. Great stuff to know if you ever want to become an international corporation."

"Sure," she said. "Love to hear it. Just give me a few minutes to finish up. A few more trays. Ten minutes." Sharon Crandall gathered Berry's tray and half a dozen others. She smiled at him as she walked past on her way to the service elevator in the rear of the first-class compartment.

Berry turned and watched as she stepped inside. The narrow elevator was barely big enough for both her and the trays. In a few seconds she had disappeared behind the sliding door, on her way down to the below-decks galley beneath the first-class compartment.

John Berry sat alone for a minute and collected his scattered thoughts. He got out of his seat and stretched his arms. He looked around the spacious first-class section. Then he looked out the window at the two giant engines mounted beneath the Straton's right wing.

*They could swallow the Skymaster. One gulp,* he thought.

His company, Taylor Metals, owned a four-seat Cessna Twin Skymaster for the sales staff, and if Berry had any real interest left, flying was it. He supposed that flying was mixed up somehow with his other problems. If he found the earth more tolerable, he might not grab every opportunity to fly above it.

Berry turned toward the rear of the first-class cabin. He saw that the lavatories were vacant. He looked at his wristwatch. He had time to wash up and comb his hair before Sharon returned.

On his way to the rear of the cabin, Berry glanced out the window again. He marveled at the enormous size and power of the giant airliner's engines. He marveled, too, at the solitude of space. What he failed to notice was that they were not alone. He did not see the tiny dot against the horizon that was rapidly approaching the Straton airliner.

———————

Lieutenant Peter Matos held the F-18's control stick with his right hand. He inched the power levers slightly forward. The two General Electric engines spooled up to a higher setting. Matos continued to fly his Navy fighter in wide, lazy circles at 54,000 feet. He held the craft's airspeed constant at slightly less than Mach 1. He was loitering, flying nondescript patterns inside a chunk of international airspace known to his country's military as Operations Area R-23. He was waiting for a call from Home. It was overdue and he was just beginning to wonder about it when his earphones crackled with the beginning of a message. It was the voice of Petty Officer Kyle Loomis, whom Matos vaguely knew.

"Navy three-four-seven, this is Homeplate, over."

Matos pressed a button on the top of his control stick. "Roger, Homeplate. Three-four-seven. Go ahead, over." He began another turn through the tranquil Pacific sky.

The voice of the electronics mate in Room E-334 carried loud and clear. "The target has been released. We estimate an initial in-range penetration of your operational area within two minutes. Operation status is now changed to Foxtrot-alpha-whiskey. I say again, Foxtrot-alpha-whiskey."

"Roger, Homeplate. I read Foxtrot-alpha-whiskey." Matos released the transmit button and simultaneously pulled back on the control stick. Foxtrot-alpha-whiskey. Fire-at-will. He would never see the target, the hit, or the destruction except on his radar, yet the predator's stimuli were there and his heart beat faster. The F-18 tightened its turn, and Matos felt the increase in G forces as he accelerated around the remainder of the circle he had been flying. He leveled the fighter on a northeasterly heading and spooled up the engines again. He felt like a knight charging into the field to do battle.

Peter Matos, like most military men who were not born in the continental United States, was more loyal, more patriotic, more enthusiastic than the native-born Americans. He had noticed this right from the beginning. Wherever the flags of the American military had flown—Germany, Guam, the Canal Zone, the Philippines—young men had rallied to those flags. There was also the Cuban officer subculture, the Mexicans, the Canadians, and others who saw the American armed forces as more than a military organization, more than a necessary expense, or just an organization you sent your tax money to, but never your sons. To men like Pedro Matos, who came out of the most abject poverty that his homeland, Puerto Rico, had to offer, the military was home, family, friends, life itself.

Matos worked hard at his duties, studied his manuals, watched what he said, never bucked the chain of command, expressed opinions only when asked, and carried out all orders with enthusiasm and without hesitation. Outwardly, he was sure he was getting it all right, but inwardly, he prayed to San Geronimo that he wouldn't be passed over for promotion. One pass-over could mean the end of his military career, especially in a peacetime Navy.

Loomis's voice jarred him out of his reverie. "Navy three-four-seven, do you have target acquisition?"

Matos glanced down at his radar screen. "Negative, Homeplate."

"Roger, Navy. Keep us informed."

"Will do." Matos kept an eye on the radar screen as he let his mind drift back to the larger problems. Matos was certain that the results of this test would determine how the rest of his life would run. The test was secret. That much he was told. It was also illegal. That much he had figured out for himself. What he could not figure out was why they had chosen him to fire this missile.

The new AIM-63X Phoenix missiles rode on the belly mounts of his F-18. For this test, the missiles were fitted with dummy warheads of stainless steel and titanium, and the target was a supersonic military drone launched several hundred miles away by a Navy C-130 Hercules turboprop. Except for those facts, thought Matos, he could have been aiming a pair of live missiles at an attacking Tupolev bomber or a Chinese MiG-21. Of course, both Russia and China were friends of the United States at the moment—but like most military people, Matos knew that friends like these could turn into foes in a heartbeat.

Matos glanced down at his radar screen. No target yet. Today's mission was a maximum-range exercise to test the updated maneuverability of the new weapon. The radar's normal 200-mile range had been modified to accept a 500-mile limit. Once launched, the new Phoenix would require none of his usual follow-through guidance. His orders were to fire the first missile, wait for it to stabilize, fire the second missile, then turn 180 degrees and proceed at top speed away from the combat area. The new self-guidance system would seek out the target and continue to track it with no further assistance from Peter Matos.

Tactically, this missile was much safer for a combat pilot. Before the enemy craft knew they had been attacked, the fighter was gone. Matos wasn't sure he liked this innovation. It called for less personal skill than guiding the missile from the F-18, and it was not as . . . manly . . . as remaining in the area. Too, there was no longer even a remote possibility of seeing the hit. But none of that was his business.

He focused on the radar. An electronic blip began to track across the outer fringes of his screen. He pressed the radio button on his control stick. "Homeplate. Three-four-seven has preliminary target acquisition."

His voice was cool, almost laconic. He smiled at the image of those German and Japanese pilots on the late-night movies screaming into their aircraft's radio, while the American and British pilots always sounded so bored as their craft was falling apart around their ears. Cool. "Do you copy, Homeplate?"

"Roger, three-four-seven. Preliminary target acquisition. Proceed. Out."

Lieutenant Matos punched a console button, then raised his eyes toward the firing control processor. An electronic symbol slewed to the target's blip. Matos watched the screen for a few seconds. Suddenly, another blip appeared. Matos blinked. He looked again. The second blip looked weaker and smaller. It was directly behind the first one. *False image*, Matos thought. *Some screwy transistor or diode a tenth of a degree too warm. Something like that.* He'd experienced these electronic aberrations before. So had most of the fighter pilots in his squadron. Glitches, or angels, they were called. False images. Echoes. Bounceback. Reflections from some other radar set. Reflections from the surface of the sea. Apparitions with no more substance than a vapor cloud. Vaporware, in the parlance of modern-day computer-speak.

Matos pressed a button on his console. He twisted a knob to adjust the screen's resolution setting. The aft target began to fade. Then it disappeared. It appeared to have merged with the original, stronger blip, which he was certain was the target. He pressed his radio talk button. "Homeplate, Navy three-four-seven has the target in good resolution. Distance is four hundred and eighty miles. Over."

Loomis's voice was flat, neutral, like every radio operator's in the military. "Roger, three-four-seven."

Matos hesitated. He thought about mentioning the glitch, but decided against it. If there was one thing they didn't want to hear about, it was nonexistent problems. He looked back at the radar screen. Good target. He flipped a safety switch, then lifted a cover that guarded the firing trigger. He was about to fire the longest air-to-air missile shot ever attempted. He pressed his radio button. "Fire number one." He waited a second, took a deep breath, then pressed the triggering button.

The AIM-63X Phoenix missile dropped away from the F-18's supporting structure. For a brief moment the missile appeared dormant as an electronic delaying device allowed the weapon to clear itself from any potential conflict with Matos's aircraft. When the proper interval had passed, a microvolt was internally induced. Flowing down a maze of printed circuit boards, the current reached its goal—the proper solenoids were activated and the rocket engine was ignited.

A stream of orange flame roared out of the Phoenix's tailpipe. Within seconds the missile accelerated to twice the speed of the F-18.

Matos saw the missile streak off. He was about to begin the launch sequence for the second Phoenix. He glanced down at his radar screen. The target had again split into two images. *Two targets.* Matos pressed the console resolution buttons. No change. He pressed them again. Still the same. *Two distinct targets. If one was the target drone, what was the other one? Jesus Christ.* The self-guided missile that he had already launched was completely out of his control.

# MAYDAY

The Phoenix's self-guiding system was working on the problem. The conflict between the two electronic images presented the missile with a quandary. In keeping with a logic and priority array that had been formulated in a conference room thousands of miles away, a trickle of voltage moved down yet another decisive path. The AIM-63X Phoenix, with its enhanced tracking and maneuverability, made a slight adjustment in its course. It steered toward the larger of the two targets.

# 2

John Berry stared at the reflection of his face in the mirror of the first-class lavatory. He ran a finger through the streaks of gray in his brown hair. There were a few wrinkles around his eyes. Still, at forty-one, he looked good.

Some of the women he knew from the country club or at work used words such as "interesting," "charming," and "solid" to describe him. He knew that he was supposed to make a move toward these women, but he could not work up the enthusiasm for it. Except once. A saleswoman at the office. And that had been a disaster.

John Berry thought about his father, as he did more and more these days. At forty-one his father had had a loving wife, four loyal children, his church, his community, his country, his own small business that he enjoyed. But that was in another time, another country almost. John Berry had none of those things, and at forty-one would never have them. Still, there was a way out. He could leave Jennifer and make a fresh start of it; just another divorced couple, just like so many of his friends. At least then he'd have hope. Whenever he flew the Skymaster he thought about it. But somehow he wondered if he could bring himself to do it.

Berry ran through the conversation he'd just had with the flight attendant. Why had he done that? Who the hell was Sharon Crandall? An hour ago, he didn't know she existed. She wasn't going to solve his problems. Yet he felt less alienated, felt more of a bond with the rest of humanity for having made that contact.

A light flashed on at the end of his peripheral vision. It was several seconds before he realized that it was the return-to-cabin light above the door. Berry knew that the cabin seat-belt lights were on as well. As a seasoned air traveler, he found that unusual since the flight was smooth. *Another flight must have reported some chop ahead*, he thought. It did not occur to him that the Straton was the only commercial aircraft using that route and altitude. His thoughts were on Sharon Crandall. With the seat-belt sign on, she would probably sit with the other flight attendants. Then there would be lunch preparation. *Damn it.* He took his time washing his hands and ignored the return-to-cabin light.

Lieutenant Peter Matos kept staring at his radar screen, hoping that the second target would disappear. He knew he needed to make some sort of report. The seconds were flashing by on his console clock. *They're waiting to hear from you, Matos.* Reluctantly, he slid his thumb back to the microphone button. "Homeplate, this is Navy three-four-seven."

# MAYDAY

"Go ahead, three-four-seven," replied Loomis.

"I . . . I'm having difficulty with target resolution. Will delay second firing. Stand by for updates."

"Roger. Out."

Matos's throat was dry. He had evaded the problem. Lied. But if the worst had happened, then nothing could save that other aircraft—if that's what the second radar blip was. On the other hand, if it was only an electronic aberration, then there was no reason to report anything more than he'd already said. Trouble with target resolution. They were already probably chewing their lips on the *Nimitz*. *Play it cool, Peter.*

He looked back at the screen, hoping again that it was all resolved. But there were still two targets. The weaker of the two crossed in front of the stronger, then disappeared off his screen to the southwest. The stronger blip remained steady on its previous course. Again he reminded himself that even if the stronger target began evasive maneuvers, the outcome would be the same. The Phoenix AIM-63X's guidance system had already chosen the larger object—chosen it to die. Phoenix would stay with its victim like a hunting bird, stalk it, pursue it, and pounce on it. That's all it knew. All it had been created for.

But what was the other target? Who was he? Then it hit him like a fist. It had to be the Hercules C-130. *Jesus Christ*, he thought. *Jesus Christ, I've made a navigation error. My fault. My fault.*

Matos turned to the satellite navigation set on the left side of the F-18's cockpit. He punched in several commands. His hand sweated beneath the leather of his flying glove. He hit a wrong button and had to clear the set and start over. *Damn it. Calmete!*

# MAYDAY

While he fumbled with the navigation set, his memory slid into an unpleasant track. He was seventeen years old and he was driving his first car, a '71 Ford. In the rear of the car were his mother, father, and Grandmother Matos. His sister was seated next to him. He had gotten off the interstate at the wrong exit. While his cousin Dolores was being married, he steered his angry family through the unfamiliar streets of North Miami. His father had hissed at him through clenched teeth, *"Es tu culpa, Pedro."*

He looked down at the navigation display. It verified his position as correct. To be certain, he went through it again. Correct. He was where he was supposed to be. At least that's what the equipment said. Then what was that second target?

He looked down at his radar screen. The Phoenix missile was small and ghostly white as it tracked across the green screen, outbound toward its target. Matos was always reminded of one of those video games. *A game. That's all it is,* he decided. They had introduced another element into the game to see how he would respond. That big white target on the green field was not an aircraft transporting flesh and blood. It was an electronic decoy. A mirage, sent out by the Hercules or the target drone. He should have reported it. They had tested *him,* and he had failed. He had compromised himself. He was through.

He kept staring at the screen. It all made sense. It all fit. Except for one thing. The Phoenix was tracking the large target, and the Phoenix would not track an electronic decoy.

The distance between the hunter and the hunted narrowed to less than 200 miles. The missile was traveling at Mach 3, covering nearly one mile every second.

Matos started to press the radio button but took his hand away. He racked his brain for answers. *Could the Hercules be off course? Could my navigation equipment be wrong?* He knew that if the problem was his equipment, it would still be technically his fault. An error from his craft was equivalent to an error from its captain. It was unfair, but effective. It compelled those in authority to pay close attention to details. The modern Navy was getting away from that concept, but it wasn't totally gone. Not yet. And this accountability did not discriminate between the captain of the 91,000-ton *Nimitz* and the captain of a 64,000-pound naval aircraft. Electronics could betray you, but a navigation set would never stand in the dock with you in front of a board of inquiry. If he had fired at the Hercules, a demonstrable mechanical fault in his navigation set might keep him from being court-martialed, but his naval career would be finished. He reminded himself that the naval careers of the crew of the Hercules would be terminated even more abruptly if that missile were headed for them.

The sound of his own breathing filled his helmet and perspiration collected under his pressure suit. His right hand gripped tightly around the control stick. His left arm tensed against the side console, his fingers touching the throttles. He had stopped trying to make any additional adjustments on the radar. The picture that it painted was accurate.

He felt his nerves becoming steadier as he resigned himself to all the worst possible scenarios. He stared distractedly at the radar screen, then, for the first time since he had fired, he looked out of the Plexiglas bubble at the world he flew in. *Es tu culpa, Pedro. It is your fault, Peter.* He pushed his finger against the thin Plexiglas. Half an inch away was an airless, subzero void.

A glint of hope shook him out of his lassitude. There was one straw he hadn't grasped at yet. He looked back at his console. Working quickly with the radar controls, he slewed a computer readout to the target on his screen. In a few seconds another entry displayed on his information board. The target was cruising at 62,000 feet. It was making a ground speed of 910 miles per hour.

Matos smiled for the first time since he had catapulted off the deck of the *Nimitz*. No Hercules turboprop could match even half that performance. Very few aircraft could. High-altitude supersonic flight was the province of missiles, special target drones, and advanced fighters, bombers, and spy planes. He would know of any such friendly craft in his area unless they had gotten off course. Two possibilities remained: The first was that it was an enemy aircraft, in which case he wouldn't get a medal for shooting it down, but he wouldn't be court-martialed either. It would be covered up and he would be the secret envy of every flight officer aboard. It had happened before.

The second possibility was the more likely. The profile being flown by the target on his screen was very close to the predicted performance of the drone. *The Hercules must have released two drones, either by mistake or by design.* That must be it. Matos felt better. His naval career had a fair chance now. He had to call the *Nimitz* immediately. Explain. He could still relocate the other target, fire the missile, do a turnaround, and get the hell out of there. He looked down again at the radar screen. The distance between the Phoenix and its target lessened rapidly. Thirty miles, twenty miles, ten miles. Then the missile and the target merged, became one. Matos nodded. The missile worked. That much they now knew. But he was left wondering what he had hit.

John Berry pushed the stopper valve halfway and turned on the water until the basin filled, then adjusted the taps until the inflowing water equaled the draining water. He took off his wristwatch and laid it on the aluminum shelf. 11:02. It was still set to California time. Jet lag was not nearly so bad with the Straton as it was on the conventional jets, but it still caused his body clock to become disoriented. Time *was* relative. His body was on New York time, his watch was on California time, but he was actually in an obscure time zone called Samoan-Aleutian, and he would soon land in Tokyo at a different time altogether. Yet at home, time dragged, almost stood still, hourly, daily, weekly. But that hadn't stopped him from getting older—in fact, it speeded up his aging process. *Relative. No doubt about it.* He bent over the basin and began splashing water on his face.

The Phoenix missile, with its updated maneuverability, made one small correction and aimed itself so that it would strike the broad port side of the midfuselage slightly above the leading edge of the wing. Somewhere in the circuitry, the sensors, the microcomputer of the Phoenix—the place that was the seat of its incomplete powers of judgment and reason—there might have been a sense or an awareness that it had succeeded in its purpose. And having no fear, no hesitation, no instinct for survival, it accelerated headlong into its prey, consigning it, and itself, into oblivion.

A middle-aged man sitting in aisle 15, seat A, glanced out the window. He noticed a silvery spot at least a mile away. He blinked. The spot was now as large as a basketball and a few inches outside the window. Before his brain could transmit even the most primitive response of ducking or screaming, the silver orb was through the window, taking a section of the fuselage and his head and torso with it. The Phoenix plowed across the remaining two seats in the section, B and C, disintegrating the passenger's wife and mother. It crossed the aisle to the middle section, pushing some of its grisly harvest with it, and swept away the four center seats, D, E, F, and G, and the passengers in them, then crossed the starboard aisle. It then pushed seats H, J, and K, with three more passengers, through the fuselage and, along with other collected debris, out into the void.

Everything in the Phoenix's path, its wake, and a yard on either side of it, was pulverized by the high-speed disintegration of the fuselage wall. Seats and people were turned into unrecognizable forms and their high-speed disintegration in turn reduced people and objects near them to smashed and torn remnants of what they had been. With no warhead on the missile there was, of course, no explosion—but the impact forces had the same effect on everything in its path.

The deceleration had caused the Phoenix to begin to tumble as it reached the third gang of seats. Its tail rose up and it hit the starboard sidewall broadside, cutting, as it exited, an elongated swath nearly eight feet high and six feet across. It tumbled out into space, dragging more metal and flesh with it. Its energies spent, the Phoenix continued for only a short distance before it faltered and fell, end over end, twelve miles down into the Pacific Ocean.

The first sound that John Berry heard was an indistinct noise, as if a high shelf stacked with rolls of sheet metal had been knocked over. He felt the aircraft bump slightly. Before he could even raise his head from the basin, he heard a rushing noise, a roar, that sounded like someone had opened the window of a speeding subway train. He straightened up quickly and froze for a second until his senses could take in all the stimuli. The flight was steady, the water was still running in the tap, the lights were on, and the rushing sound was lower now. Everything seemed nearly normal, but something—his pilot's instincts—told him he was flying in a dying aircraft.

Outside, in the cabin, the enormous quantity of internal pressurized air began to exit through the gaping holes in the Straton's fuselage. All the small, loose objects onboard—glasses, trays, hats, papers, briefcases—were immediately propelled through the cabin, and were either wedged behind something stationary or sucked out the holes.

The passengers sat quietly for a long second, completely unable to comprehend what had just happened. There was no point of reference in their minds for it. The normal reactions of screaming, quickened heartbeat, adrenaline flow, fight or flight, were absent. They reacted with only silence and stillness amid the noises of rushing air.

Like a growing tidal wave, the escaping air was gathering momentum.

A baby was sucked out of its uncomprehending mother's arms and hurled along over the heads of the passengers and out the starboard hole and into the nothingness of space.

Someone screamed.

Three unaccompanied children, a boy and two girls, in seats H, J, and K, aisle 13, near the starboard hole, had not fastened their seat belts and were picked up by the howling wind and sucked out, screeching with terror.

Everyone was screaming now as the sights and sounds around them began to register on their consciousness.

A teenaged girl in aisle 18, seat D, near the portside aisle, her seat dislocated by the original impact, suddenly found herself gripping her seat track on the floor, her overturned seat still strapped to her body. The seat belt failed and the seat shot down the aisle. She lost her grip and was dragged down the aisle by an invisible and extreme force. Her long blonde hair was pulled taut and her skirt and blouse were stripped from her body. Her eyes were filled with horror as she continued to fight against the unseen thing that wanted to take her. She dug her nails into the carpet as the racing air pulled her toward the yawning hole that led outside.

Her cries were unheard by even those passengers who sat barely inches away from her struggle. The noise of the escaping air was so loud that it was no longer decipherable as sound, but seemed instead a solid thing pounding at the people in their seats. The events in the cabin took on a horrific aura of pantomime.

Some of the bolts that held other damaged seats to their tracks began to fail. Several gangs of seats broke loose in sequence and rammed into rows of seats ahead, some of the seats tumbling over the tops of other seats as they rushed toward the hole. A gang of four seats, the passengers still strapped in, wedged into the smaller entry hole, partly blocking the hole and causing more suction at the larger exit hole on the starboard side. At the starboard hole, a gang of loosened seats seemed to pile up like paratroopers nervously bunching up, waiting for their turn to jump. Another flying seat loosened the logjam and one after the other they all shot out into space, the passengers strapped in them screaming, kicking, and clawing at the air.

---

John Berry, unaware of what was happening outside, turned the handle of the lavatory door and pulled inward on it. It seemed to be stuck. He tried again, pulling with all his strength, but the fiberglass door would not budge, though he could see the latch disengage. He braced both feet against the jamb and with both hands on the latch pulled with every ounce of strength he could summon. Still it would not move even a fraction of an inch. He was frightened and puzzled. He repeatedly pressed the assistance call button and waited for help.

As the internal air escaped from the Straton's tourist cabin, then its first-class cabin and upstairs lounge, the flow of cabin pressure still being pumped into the aircraft was literally piling up in those areas where it could not so readily escape—the five lavatories with inward-opening doors. The pressurized air poured into these lavatories through the normal air vents, and though some of the pressurized air leaked out from around the edges of the lavatory doors, the net trend was positive. Those five inward-opening fiberglass doors were sealed shut with a differential air pressure of two pounds per square inch, which added up to four thousand pounds pressing them shut.

The seven outward-opening lavatory doors blew open into the vacuum, hurling their occupants into the cabin and toward the two gaping holes that awaited them.

In the lounge on the upper deck, drink glasses and liquor bottles were sucked toward the spiral staircase that led down to the first-class cabin. Books, magazines, and newspapers were ripped from passengers' hands and sent into the vortex of rushing air. Every loose object in the lounge spun around the stairwell like a tornado.

The passengers who had chosen to stay in the lounge when the seat belt signs came on watched in horrified fascination as every movable thing in the room was sucked toward the growing vortex of debris around the stairwell.

Eddie Hogan, the piano player, had been playing "Autumn Leaves" when the sudden burst of airflow pulled him backward off the rigidly mounted bench. The bench had been equipped with a special seat belt, but Hogan had declined to use it. He was pulled, head-first, down the staircase, across the main cabin, and then swiftly out through the gaping starboard hole.

A blind man, seated near the piano, screamed repeatedly for someone to tell him what was happening. His body strained against his seat belt and he pulled against the leash of his Seeing Eye dog. The golden retriever seemed to be pulling away from him with an unnatural strength. He yelled at the dog. "Shannon! Shannon! Stop that!" The dog whimpered as she dug her claws into the soft pile. The leash broke and the dog was taken into the vortex and carried down into the first-class cabin, where its limp body wedged under an empty seat.

As the dozen lounge passengers watched from their secured seats, the piano and bench danced in their mounts but continued to hold against the maelstrom. Everyone in the upper deck became hysterical almost simultaneously.

In the first-class cabin below, objects from the lounge ripped through the accelerating air, cutting and smashing against heads and arms held up in protective gestures. The cloud of debris raced through the curtain into the tourist cabin and joined the other, incredibly numerous objects in their headlong rush out into the vacuum as though this void could be filled, satiated, if only enough objects and people were sacrificed to it.

# MAYDAY

In the tourist cabin, a big man strapped to his seat in the aft section was bellowing at the top of his lungs. He was raging against the wind, against the hurtling objects, and against the fates that had conspired to put him on this aircraft for his first flight. He had seen his half-dressed wife pulled out of one of the seven outward-opening lavatories and watched her as she seemed to run, tumble, and fly toward the hole, screaming his name as she went by and looking at him with puzzled eyes. Suddenly, he unfastened his belt and jumped to his feet. He half flew, arms and legs outstretched over seated passengers, skimming their heads as he sailed along. At the starboard-side hole his big body smashed into the jagged aluminum skin, opening his throat and severing his left arm as he was vomited out of the sick and dying aircraft.

In those lavatories that had opened, water gushed out of the taps and commodes into the low-pressure environment. From the bowels of the giant airliner, waste tanks flowed backward and their contents came up through the sink drains and toilets.

In the galleys, water valves ruptured and water overflowed the sinks. Pantries and refrigerators swung open and their contents flew out into the passageways and into the cabins.

In the pressurized baggage compartments below the cabin floor, aerosols and pressurized containers ruptured and disgorged their contents throughout the luggage. The cats and dogs that rode in kennels beneath their masters were banging wildly against their cages in fear.

The outward-opening cockpit door held for a moment. It strained against its lock and aluminum hinges, but the difference in pressure between the cockpit and the cabin was too great and the door finally burst outward into the first-class upper lounge.

Captain Stuart heard the door go. Suddenly, every loose object on the flight deck—maps, pencils, coffee cups, hats, and jackets—lifted into the air and converged on the open door, then disappeared into the lounge and down the stairway. Stuart felt himself pulled back into his seat. His arms flew up over his head and his wristwatch ripped loose. He pulled his arms down into his lap and waited until the initial rush of air subsided. He sat still trying to steady the hard beating in his chest. He calmed his rushing thoughts and tried to reconstruct what had happened in the last few seconds. He remembered that he had felt the jolt of a mild impact on the Straton only seconds before, but he had no idea what had caused it. What he did know was that the autopilot was still functioning and the craft was still under control. He glanced quickly at McVary, then glanced quickly back at Fessler. "What happened?" he yelled.

McVary kept staring silently at his instruments.

Fessler was looking back at the open door and didn't respond.

"Descend!" Stuart commanded, and yanked shut the power levers controlling all four engines, then disengaged the autopilot and pushed forward on the control wheel. The Straton transport abruptly nosed downward. But at their incredibly high cruise speed, the forward momentum slowed their initial descent. Stuart watched the ground altimeter as they moved slowly downward. Fifty-eight thousand feet. Fifty seconds had gone by since the impact.

Stuart quickly scanned his instruments. Cockpit indications were still good, except that he had already lost a major portion of his pressurized cabin air. His first thought was that a fuselage door had somehow opened. He looked at the door warning lights. They showed all the doors closed. Had a faulty window blown out? No. The decompression was much too rapid for that, and what had caused the jolt? A bomb. *It had to be a bomb,* he thought. *What is happening back there?*

Stuart looked at the cabin altimeter—the differential pressure gauge—which told him at what relative altitude the cabin pressure was. The hands of the cabin altimeter were spinning upward like those of a broken clock. The cabin pressure, which had always been kept at 10,000 feet, was now at 19,000 feet. *Losing pressure. Hold the pressure.* They were losing the artificial atmosphere that they had brought with them—this atmosphere from earth that made it possible to live at 62,000 feet—throwing it out into subspace, through some large hole.

Stuart glanced at the two altimeters together. The ground altimeter showed that the Straton had only gotten down to 55,000 feet. The cabin altimeter showed that they now had an artificial altitude pressure of 30,000 feet, then 35,000 feet. Stuart estimated that the artificial atmosphere would bleed off at about the time the Straton hit 50,000 feet. Then the altimeters would read the same. Subspace would be in the cabin.

Stuart started to feel light-headed. Instinctively, he pushed the autopilot button back on. He slammed his hand into the automatic descent selector, pushing it to its maximum rate of descent, letting the computer bring it down as fast as it was safely possible. He sat back in his seat. His head was pounding with pain. Sinus cavities. The air pockets inside his skull could not adjust to the rapid rate of cabin altitude change. His nose began to bleed. A river of blood poured down his white shirt. His lungs had already been emptied of most of their air. He felt hollowed out. His hands and feet were cold, and he didn't know if it was from loss of blood or loss of cabin heat.

The Straton's four engines were sucking up and compressing the thin outside air and pumping all the pressurized air they could into the ruptured cabin. As they descended lower, the air was slightly thicker and the pressurized airflow became stronger. But Alan Stuart suspected, knew really, that it was a losing battle. There was one hell of a big hole back there, and the arithmetic of the problem . . . *If a basin has ten gallons of water and is losing one gallon a second through the drain, and a tap is replacing a half gallon every five seconds, how long before* . . . Too long. His head was bursting, and he couldn't think of anything but the pain now.

Captain Stuart turned his head slowly toward McVary. McVary had strapped on the copilot's oxygen mask and was transmitting an emergency radio message on the international distress frequency. Stuart shook his head. "Useless," he said softly, but he also reached for his oxygen mask and pulled it on, tightening the straps hard against his face. He looked back at Fessler. Fessler was lying slumped across his desk. Blood was pouring from his mouth, ears, and nose.

McVary continued to transmit the distress signal, though his speech and thoughts were fragmented. He sucked hard on the oxygen mask as he spoke, and blood collected in his mouth and he had to swallow it.

McVary knew that the oxygen mask alone was not enough. Without a sustaining pressure to force the oxygen into and through his lungs, it was almost totally useless. The flight deck's emergency oxygen canister, behind Fessler's panel, could just as well be back in San Francisco for all the good it was doing them. Only a military pressure suit—a space suit—of the type he had once worn could exert the necessary pressure on his body so that he could breathe. But he knew that even if he had one, there would not have been enough time to hook it up.

Dan McVary, who as a young man had flown exotic military jets through wild maneuvers, was suddenly more frightened than he had ever been. How had this happened? Commercial transports were not supposed to completely decompress the way military craft did when they were hit in combat. The possibility of sudden decompression was so slight that it had been ignored by the aeronautical engineers who built the Straton. There were no air-lock doors or pressure bulkheads between the sections as there were watertight compartments on a ship or airtight compartments on modern dirigibles. These safety features were too heavy for an airliner. Too costly. A complete decompression was not supposed to happen. But it had. How? He wondered if airtight compartments would have helped anyway. The image of the *Titanic* with its so-called watertight compartments flashed through his mind. Engineering marvels . . . every contingency planned for . . . only a set of the most . . . the most unusual circumstances . . . his head was splitting and he felt a coldness deep down in his body that chilled him in a way he had never felt before. Dan McVary knew he was dying.

Captain Stuart's vision began to blur. He pushed his face forward to read the digital clock. Over a minute had passed since he felt the jolt. The Straton was still on autopilot and was beginning to descend very rapidly. He could see that the vertical descent rate had increased to 12,000 feet per minute. They passed through 53,000 feet. The cabin pressure was up to 45,000 feet. They were definitely not going to get down to a level where the oxygen masks could be used in time to save anyone who was still able to use them. They would not get into the naturally breathable atmosphere for several minutes after that. He shook his head. They were all dead.

For an instant, Stuart considered the passengers. They were his responsibility. But there was nothing he could do, or even say. There were no slow sinkings on an aircraft, no dramatic speeches from the captain, no leisurely good-byes or farewell toasts. There were only a few minutes or seconds of horror, then death.

In the tourist cabin, the noise from the wind and escaping air had lessened considerably as the inside and outside pressure approached equilibrium. People could hear each other now, but there was very little talking. Most people sucked hard on their released overhead oxygen masks, inhaling and exhaling deeply, puzzled by the absence of that familiar feeling of having taken a good deep breath.

A coldness permeated the cabin and deepened the effects of shock and increased the effects of oxygen deprivation. Layers of condensed moisture formed along the ceiling, caused by the natural onboard water vapor that had suddenly been squeezed out by the reduced cabin pressure. The passengers stared up at these forming clouds, unsure of what they were or what they meant.

Someone yelled, "Fire!" and some people screamed, but most remained silent, accepting this new aberration, too numbed and disoriented to react. The cloud moved through the cabin like a sea fog rolling into a coastal city, casting an amorphous gray haze over the silent people. The cabin lights shone with an unearthly luminescence through the cloud. Eerie white ice particles began forming on the walls and windows. Near the starboard hole there was a brief snow flurry.

The moisture dissipated and the cabin atmosphere became dry except for the breath fog still exhaled by the living and the blood pouring from the open wounds of the dying. Blood and breath crystallized and formed frosts of red and white wherever they touched a freezing surface.

The outside sounds of the four Straton engines and the airflow past the gaping holes grew louder as the sound of the outward-rushing air lessened. These new noises filled the tourist cabin and drowned out the weak moans of the injured.

An uncounted number of people were dead or dying, and most of the rest were in shock. But it appeared that the worst of the ordeal was over. The aircraft was still flying and showed no visible signs of crashing. A strange calm, a pleasant languor simulating the effects of alcohol or tranquilizers, took hold of the passengers of Flight 52 as the first effects of oxygen deprivation began to register. There was still the pain behind the eyes, in the ears, but it did not seem so acute now.

Captain Stuart pressed his face against his console. Everything appeared dark in the cockpit, but he could see that the instrument lights were working. They shone like dying suns in a faraway galaxy, yet they seemed to emit no light beyond their surface. He read the two altimeters. Aircraft altitude was 51,000 feet, and descending. Cabin altitude was also 51,000 feet and descending now with the aircraft. The cabin differential pressure was zero. Inside was outside. Outside was inside.

The autopilot was taking the aircraft down, as fast as it could safely go, into the thicker atmosphere at 30,000 feet where they would find enough ambient pressure to make the oxygen masks workable. The rate of descent was racing against the physiological effects of anoxia—suffocation—and suffocation was winning. Stuart could see no way out of it. All the numbers— airspeed, altitude, rate of descent, rate of pressure loss—had been predictable. He knew the numbers before he had ever stepped into the cockpit of his first Straton. *If only the damned hole had been smaller . . .*

In the first-class lounge, an elderly man, John Thorndike, released his seat belt and quickly stood. A familiar sensation gripped his chest and he reached for a pillbox in his jacket. He paled, then turned blue as his heart gave out. He tottered for a moment, then fell forward across the cocktail table, landing on his wife, who tried to scream but couldn't.

In the tourist and first-class cabins, older people began dying. Some slipped away noiselessly, others moaned their protests as hearts and lungs failed.

# MAYDAY

Throughout the aircraft, the old, then those with pre-existing medical conditions began to die. Lungs collapsed, hearts gave up, thin blood vessels burst, and hemorrhaging blood poured from all the body orifices. Internally hemorrhaging blood collected in skulls and body cavities causing a more painful death. Pockets of pressurized air developed in body cavities, and people began clawing at their faces and torsos, irrationally trying to get at the source of the pain.

Everyone, young and old, weak and healthy, experienced hyperventilation, dizziness, blurred vision, and nausea. People choked on their vomit when oxygen-deprived brains and muscles failed to respond to the vomiting reflex. Skin colors went from white to blue. Bowels and bladders released, and if normal breathing and its adjunct, the sense of smell, had been possible, the cabin would have reeked.

More and more people had given up on the masks, but many people still tried desperately to suck from them, silently cursing what they thought was a failure of the system to provide oxygen. But the oxygen was there. The molecules poured out of the masks and swirled around their faces like a cruel joke, then dissipated into the low-pressure atmosphere.

In the freezing tourist cabin, where anyone who cared to look could see the holes, sunlight poured in through the south-facing port-side hold and starkly illuminated the rubble and carnage left in the wake of the missile.

By this time, everyone who was capable of forming thought knew they were suffocating. Yet outside, through the holes, they could see the unlimited sky, a cloudless deep blue, bright with sunlight. It looked balmy, enchanting, but it was as lethal as the bottom of the sea.

Captain Stuart was barely conscious. He moved his head to his right. McVary was still sitting upright, staring straight ahead. He turned his head and looked back at Stuart with an odd expression. Stuart turned his head away and looked over his shoulder. Fessler was still lying across his desk in a pool of blood. The bleeding seemed to have stopped.

Stuart's fingers were numb and his limbs were heavy. His brain seemed detached from his body and he felt as though he were free-floating.

The cells in his brain were dying, but one shining thought, like a faraway landing beacon, was becoming increasingly clear in the darkening cockpit. Ever since he had begun to fly the Straton, the thought of high-altitude decompression had played on his mind and he had formulated a response to this possibility that was so ingrained that it had not yet died or become jumbled like everything else. He knew he must shut off the autopilot and push the aircraft into a sudden dive. It was all coming to him now. He had it. *If they did not all die quickly and someone in the cockpit was still functioning when the aircraft descended into the breathable air, then that person might have enough intellect left to put the aircraft down somewhere.* He looked at McVary again. Young. Good health. Sucking hard on his mask. Half his brain might survive. The idiot would save them from death and condemn them to that shadowy place, that place of perpetual eclipse, that state of being which is called half-life—speechless, blind, paralyzed, dim-witted. He thought of his wife and family. *Oh, God. No.*

Stuart reached his hand out toward the autopilot release button on the control wheel. No good. McVary might turn it on again. He pushed his hand toward his console and found what he wanted—the autopilot master switch, which was not duplicated on the copilot's side. He pushed his hand over the guarded cover of the switch and rolled it back. His fingers found the small toggle.

He hesitated. The instinct for survival—any kind of survival—began overtaking his fading intellect. He had to act quickly. *Quickly! Act what?* He tried to remember what he was supposed to act on, then remembered for a flash of a second and tugged on the switch. It held fast. He recalled clearly that the solenoid was designed to require a good deal of force to shut down the auto *. . . auto what? What?*

Captain Alan Stuart sat back in his seat and stared out the windshield. He frowned. He had a headache. Something was bothering him. *Coffee. Brazil.* He had to go to Brazil for coffee. He smiled. A small trickle of saliva ran down his chin.

The automatic pilot continued to steer the Straton 797 through its programmed emergency descent. Its electronic memory bank and preset responses were in no way affected by the oxygen deprivation. Never once did it consider the effects of anoxia on its human charges. It was true that one young creator of this autopilot had suggested once that a sudden and complete decompression at altitudes of over 50,000 feet should induce a shutdown of the autopilot. But that young man no longer designed autopilots and his "self-destruct response," as the Straton executives had labeled it, was not part of the autopilot's repertoire. The autopilot could and would descend to 11,000 feet where the air was breathable and warmer, and would continue piloting the Straton on its flight path to Tokyo. It could do that and more. The thing it could not do was land the plane, not without additional inputs from the crew.

---

John Berry felt the effects of the rarefied atmosphere. He had begun to hyperventilate. His head ached painfully and he was dizzy. He sat on the small commode until he felt a little better.

He rose again and pulled at the door. It was still firmly stuck. He felt too weak to try it again. He glanced at his watch on the shelf. 11:04. Only two minutes had gone by since he had felt the bump. It seemed longer.

Berry began pounding on the door. "Open up! Open the damn door! I'm stuck in here!" He put his ear to the door. Odd sounds were coming from the cabin. He pounded again, then sank back against the bulkhead. He wanted to try the door again, but decided to wait until he felt stronger.

John Berry knew that if the aircraft made an emergency landing in the ocean, he would not be able to get to the life rafts. He would drown when the aircraft sank. He put his hands to his aching head, bent over, and vomited on the floor, disregarding the commode. He straightened up and inhaled deeply several times, but a light-headedness rolled over him like a giant wave. He wanted to wash his face and mouth, but remembered that the tap had run dry. *Why?*

The lavatory seemed to get darker, and he felt

weaker. He slipped to the floor. His transition to unconsciousness came slowly, and he allowed his body to untense. He felt a strange euphoria and decided that death would not be that bad. He had never thought it would be. He recalled his childhood, which did not surprise him, even thought of his children, which made him feel less guilty about the way he felt about them. He remembered Jennifer, the way she once was. He closed his eyes and lapsed into blackness.

The vent in the lavatory continued to send a steady stream of pressurized and heated air into the enclosed space. The pressure leaked out around the edges of the door, but it leaked slowly, slowly enough to keep a pressure of over two pounds per square inch on the door, sealing it shut. The pressure loss was also slow enough so that the atmosphere in the lavatory never rose above 31,000 feet.

John Berry lay crumpled on the floor, breathing irregularly. Five more minutes at the altitude of 31,000 feet would cause him permanent and irreversible brain damage. But the Straton's autopilot was bringing the airliner down rapidly.

---

In the tourist cabin, the first-class cabin, the first-class lounge, and the cockpit, the passengers and crew of Trans-United's Flight 52 had fallen, one by one, into a deep, merciful sleep; the level of oxygen being supplied to their brain cells had dropped too low for too long.

---

# MAYDAY

At 11:08 A.M., six minutes after the Phoenix missile had passed through the Straton 797, the airliner reached 18,000 feet. The autopilot noted the altitude and began a gradual recovery from the emergency descent. The speed brakes were automatically retracted, followed by a slow and steady autothrottle power advance to the four engines.

In the cockpit three figures sat slumped over, strapped to their seats. The two control wheels moved in unison, the four throttles advanced, the ailerons made slight and continuous adjustments. The aircraft was flying nicely. But this was no ghost ship, no Flying Dutchman; it was a modern aircraft whose autopilot had taken charge as it was told to do. Everything would be fine, at least for a while.

As the autopilot's electronic circuitry sensed the proximity of the desired altitude, it leveled out the giant airliner and established it at an altitude of 11,000 feet and a slow, fuel-saving speed of 340 knots. The air-pressurization system had automatically disengaged as the aircraft sank into the thicker atmosphere. The fresh sea breezes of clean Pacific air filled the cabin of Trans-United's Flight 52.

A few minutes after leveling off, the first passengers began to awaken from their unnatural sleep.

# 3

Lieutenant Peter Matos flew his F-18 fighter on a straight and level course. Reluctantly, he pushed his radio-transmit button. "Homeplate, this is Navy three-four-seven." He continued to hold down on the transmit button so he could not receive a reply from the *Nimitz* until he was ready to deal with it. His mind whirled with conflict. Something was still not quite right. Finally, he slid his finger off the button, which freed the channel so he could receive their reply.

"Roger, Navy three-four-seven. We have also registered the intercept," Petty Officer Kyle Loomis answered. Matos knew that the carrier had been equipped to monitor the missile, and that the men in electronics Room E-334 had watched the needle that registered the sudden end-of-transmission from the AIM-63X as it had impacted against the target, destroying its transmitter.

"Navy three-four-seven, this is Homeplate."

The voice in Matos's earphones was unmistakably

that of Commander Sloan. Even though a special encoding voice scrambler was being used to prevent anyone else from monitoring their channel, the deep and measured qualities of Sloan's voice came through. Matos discovered that he had suddenly braced himself, as if he had run across Sloan in one of the *Nimitz*'s below-decks corridors.

"We are receiving conflicting signals," Sloan said.

Matos sensed a growing anger at the edges of Sloan's voice. He had never personally experienced a run-in with the Commander, but too many of the other pilots had. Sloan's wrath was legendary. *Don't get jumpy,* Matos said to himself. *It's just an electronic echo that makes him sound that way. Keep your mind on the job.*

"Our monitors agree with your report of missile impact. But we're still monitoring the target drone," Sloan continued. "Its condition reads as steady. That conflicts with the Phoenix's readout. Do you have the engagement area in good radar resolution?"

Matos slumped lower in the cockpit seat to the limits that his cinched-up harness would allow. His heart sank with the words, and he could taste the bile from the pit of his stomach. *Christ Almighty, Mother of God.* He moistened his lips and cleared his throat before pressing the transmit button. "Roger, Homeplate. This is three-four-seven. I'm beginning to get the impact zone in good resolution. Stand by."

James Sloan had no intention of being put off, even momentarily, by one of his subordinates. "Three-four-seven, execute a radar lock-on with the Phoenix," he transmitted. "The test missile must have failed before it engaged the target. That would explain why we still read the target drone."

"Roger, Homeplate." But Matos knew that the Phoenix had hit *something*. He had watched the radar tracks converge. He also knew that the *Nimitz*'s shipboard radar could not see the impact area. The carrier was hundreds of miles astern of his F-18, which put it out of radar range of the test site. All that the carrier people would be able to tell from the equipment in the electronics room was that there was no longer any radio signal coming from the test missile, and that the target drone continued, inexplicably, to send a loud-and-clear transmission.

Matos huddled over his radar screen. The target had maintained a steady course for a short while after the intercept. Matos turned on two cockpit switches, then made an adjustment to the radar. He could now plot both the target drone and the Phoenix's altitude losses on his vertical display board. Beyond the target was the faint radar reflection that was the remains of the AIM-63X Phoenix missile. It was visible for half a minute, and Matos tracked it continuously as it fell into the sea. "Homeplate, this is three-four-seven. The test missile has dropped into the ocean. I am now tracking the target drone. I am locked to it in the vertical scan. It is descending. Altitude is approximately fifty-one thousand feet. Descent rate registers as twelve thousand feet per minute."

"Okay," Sloan answered, "that's good. Our readout still shows the target as level at sixty-two thousand. The target's transmitting equipment must have been damaged by the impact. Maybe the Phoenix just grazed the drone." With no warhead, Sloan knew that complete destruction would require a full-face hit. "Continue to track, and we'll consider our shipboard monitors as dysfunctional."

"Roger." But something else bothered Matos. The target was not falling very rapidly. His own jet could dive faster than the target was going down. For what should have been a smashed target drone tumbling through the sky, it was not performing as expected.

*Data is missing*, he thought. The only reason it made no sense was that he was operating without all the information. Garbage in, garbage out, as they said in the computer classes at Pensacola. Don't jump to wild conclusions. Leave the emotional responses to civilians. Military technicians waited for the data. Technology was really the science of hindsight. When they corrected and analyzed all the material, they would easily discover what had made this test seem so bizarre.

Matos was no longer apprehensive. There was something about rote procedures that was calming and comforting. As long as he stuck to the technician's routines, then he could push his fears away. The blips on his radar had again become no more than game pieces, and the entire maneuver had taken on the aura of electronic chess.

*The impact has distorted the drone's shape*, Matos thought. It's been bent into some sort of low-drag lifting body. Flattened out into a metal parachute that has already reached its terminal velocity. Wilder things have happened. Matos felt that Commander Sloan's idea that the test missile had only nicked the target drone was probably right. That would explain how and why the drone's misleading signals were still being routinely sent to the *Nimitz*.

"Vertical scan indicates twenty-five thousand," Matos reported. Events had settled down, and things were beginning to make sense. "Seventeen thousand feet. The target is now tracking thirty-eight degrees to the right of its intercepted course. I am showing . . ."

As Matos's eyes traveled over the array of data readouts, he froze when he saw the new trend. It was too far from normal to pretend otherwise. "Homeplate . . . the target's descent rate has decreased." Matos's voice was pitched higher. "Eight thousand a minute. Now it's six thousand a minute. The altitude is fourteen thousand feet. The descent rate has dropped to three thousand a minute. The target is leveling out at eleven thousand feet!"

After just a few minutes' pause, Sloan's voice filled the void. "Navy three-four-seven, I don't know what the hell has happened out there, but you better find out. Fast." There was no longer any mistake about the timbre of Sloan's voice or its intent.

"Roger, Homeplate. Proceeding toward the target. I'll obtain a visual sighting." Matos pushed the throttles forward. The F-18 accelerated rapidly, pushing him back against his seat. A flood of disjointed emotions swelled in him, but he held them at bay. He directed all his energies at the technical task of intercepting the moving radar target.

---

"That's a good question, Commander. What the hell has happened out there?" Randolf Hennings had begun to allow himself a small measure of an admiral's anger. He had played silent errand boy far too long. Retired or not, Hennings's natural propensity for leadership—in mothballs for the past several years, like his naval uniforms—had begun to emerge. Sloan was losing control of the situation.

Hennings had not liked Commander James Sloan from their first handshake. There was something too shrewd and calculated about the man. He had shown no hint of good nature. It was as if the universe had been created solely for the benefit of Commander Sloan.

Sloan had ignored the Admiral's question. "We'll take over," he said to Petty Officer Loomis. He dismissed the technician, and Loomis left the room quickly and quietly. "Nothing wrong has happened, I'm sure," Sloan finally answered, turning toward Hennings. "But even if something has . . . there's no need to let it get beyond the two of us. I won't call the electronics specialist back until we've resolved whatever the problem is."

"There are three of us," Hennings said. "Don't forget your pilot. He knows more than we do. He's the one who's out there. We don't get a very clear picture . . ." He motioned toward the stack of electronics. ". . . from all of this."

"Matos is no problem," Sloan answered. "I know how to pick men. I know how to assign jobs."

Randolf Hennings looked with marked disdain at the young commander. *He doesn't command men. He uses them*, Hennings thought. Men like him were no good for a crew, a ship, or a navy. "Don't be surprised if your subordinates sometimes take a tack against the prevailing wind."

"*Surprised?* Hell, no. I'd be *amazed*." But as soon

as he said it, Sloan knew he had gone too far. He had let the remark out too quickly, on the heels of all the wrong turns that events had taken. The remark hung in the air between the two men, and Sloan regretted it. An unnecessary indulgence.

Sloan tried to eradicate his error. He smiled at Hennings, then forced a small laugh. "You're right, Admiral. They sometimes try to tack against the wind. We all do, on occasion."

Hennings nodded slightly but said nothing. He resented being linked to Sloan, no matter how minor the inference. If this were the old days back on the *John Hood*, he would have called this officer to his quarters and, in private, reamed him out. *Remember the mission*, Hennings thought, quoting to himself what a lifetime of experience had taught him.

"We're trying to do a job, not win points," Hennings said. The retired Admiral had built his naval career on precisely that premise. Embarrassing your subordinates was, he felt, counterproductive. You would get a man's best only when he cared enough to produce. Threats would get you no more.

Sloan grunted an unintelligible reply, then turned his eyes toward the electronics console. He basically understood how to work the equipment, and he checked it over to refresh his memory. Sloan moved quickly and competently around the gangs of switches and dials, like a skilled surgeon performing a familiar operation.

Hennings watched him for a few moments, then sighed. Perhaps he had been too critical. Perhaps he was getting too old. Times had changed. It was Sloan's show. Undermining the Commander's confidence or taking exception with his methods would do no one any good, least of all the Navy. No one should try to be the captain of every ship.

"Just a few more minutes, Admiral." Sloan was aware of Hennings's displeasure. It was another factor to be considered. The successful completion of the mission was the first concern, but not alienating the retired Admiral was an important second. He had gotten off to a bad start with the old man, and would need to do some work to get things even-keeled. A successful test firing would make it easy to bridge the gap. Nothing made people friendlier than a shared success.

Hennings sat down on the edge of the console. He gazed blankly across the room at the closed hatchway door.

Sloan found himself tapping his fingers against the glass face of the panel-mounted clock. He shifted positions. Then he coughed lightly to clear his throat. If things went well, it could all be wrapped up within the hour. "Not much longer," he said to break the silence. "Matos should be just about in visual range of our target."

———————

Matos's first sight of the target was routine enough: a black dot that hung motionless against the blue sky. Without anything nearby to provide perspective, size was an indeterminate thing.

The target maintained a steady course of 342 degrees. It had gradually slowed during its descent, and it now held a speed of 340 knots. Flying the F-18 over three times the target's velocity, he was quickly closing the remaining distance between them. He would intercept the target shortly.

Matos had been splitting his attention between the radar and the windshield, and now that he had the target in visual contact, he kept his eyes fixed on it. "Navy three-four-seven has visual contact," he transmitted.

"Roger," Sloan answered, his tone impatient.

Matos paid no attention to the implied message. He had stopped worrying about Sloan, and instead concentrated completely on the job at hand. To stay emotionally uninvolved was the proper attitude in any scientific trade.

Matos's left hand eased back the F-18's throttles. He began a reduction that would have his aircraft flying at a similar speed when he pulled alongside the target, thus avoiding an overshoot. Formation flying was still a matter of practice, skill, and gut reactions. In the modern fighter pilot's repertoire, it was one area that had yet to be taken over by electronics. Peter Matos was particularly good at high-speed formations. He would sometimes lay far astern of his squadron, then zoom up and rapidly tuck into his assigned slot. "Nice showboat," his buddies would radio, but everyone was impressed. Matos was good.

Yet today he was having a problem. The target stayed its distance. Matos had misjudged. He had begun a speed reduction from a point too far away. The hundreds of subtle clues that went into compiling a pilot's instinctive reactions were somehow off base. Something was wrong. Matos took his eyes off the black dot on the horizon and glanced at his radar screen.

*Six miles. Christ*, he thought. *How could it still be*

*that far?* Matos looked out the windshield. He sped up again, and the distance shortened. The black dot was apparently not a drone. It was too big. That was what had thrown off his speed adjustment and perception. His mind's eye had expected a ten-foot object, and he had played off his airspeed accordingly.

As the space between them narrowed, the size of the target grew rapidly. It was huge. The first distinguishing mark was a horizontal line across the middle of the structure. A wing line. Then the tail section sprouted from the indistinctness. Matos sat stunned. It was an aircraft. A large jet. "My God!"

A commercial transport! There was no doubt in his mind that this was the target he had hit. The craft appeared ghostly, like a ship abandoned on the high seas. Dead in the water. He closed the remaining distance without any additional thoughts or feelings.

Matos pulled alongside. The Trans-United logo seemed incongruous. Vibrant colors—green, blue, and yellow. Living colors on a dead ship.

The Straton 797 looked eerie, as if the aircraft itself knew what had happened to it and who had done it. It flew with its nose canted slightly upward. Its four jet engines produced a continuous flow of exhaust gases. It was holding steady at 11,000 feet and was making an airspeed of 340 knots. Matos guessed that it was being flown by its computer.

Matos maneuvered his fighter closer. He scanned the port side of the wide-bodied fuselage and saw what he was looking for. The hole. A black spot on the silver body, like an ominous spot on an X-ray. He took his craft around to the starboard side. The exit hole, like an exit wound of a bullet, was much larger. Huge, jagged, ugly. His hands, then his knees, began to shake. He threw his head back and looked up out of his bubble into the sky. "Oh, Jesus. Oh, God."

He did not look at the Straton for a long time. Finally he forced himself to study it again. There were no people visible at any of the windows. No eyes looked back as he flew parallel with the rows of Plexiglas, only thirty feet from where the people should have been. He had flown intercepts on transports before, and he knew he should be seeing the people. Matos nudged the throttles and flew forward to get beside the cockpit. No heads in the cockpit, either. There were no people anywhere. No passengers, no crew. No survivors.

"Three-four-seven!" the radio shouted, and Matos jumped. Sloan's sudden transmission had startled him. "Are you there? What the hell's happening?"

"I . . . Homeplate . . ." Matos's thumb stayed locked to the microphone button. As he allowed his F-18 to drift aft and fly a looser formation, the shadow from the transport's upper fuselage crossed his canopy. From below, the 797 appeared incredibly immense. Matos's F-18 seemed an insignificant speck. He was piloting a toy compared to the mammoth machine he hovered beneath.

Yet the unimaginable had happened. Matos's toy had destroyed a great airliner. Beyond all doubts and all talk lay the reality of what was in front of him. His face was covered with sweat, and his eyes welled up with tears. "Homeplate. We have hit a transport. A Straton 797. Trans-United."

There was no reply from the *Nimitz*.

# 4

John Berry lay unconscious in one of the first-class lavatories of the Straton 797. His breathing, which earlier had been forced, had relaxed to its normal rate again. He was motionless except for the involuntary trembling of his left hand. His mind wrestled through layers of troubled dreams triggered by his unnatural sleep. Slowly, like the imperceptible lifting of an early-morning fog, John Berry awoke.

He opened his weighted eyes. He turned his head slowly and looked around the small room without comprehending where he was. At first he could recall nothing beyond his own identity.

John Berry attempted to raise himself from his slumped and uncomfortable position on the floor, but his muscles would not respond. *No strength*, he said to himself. That had been his first rational thought. Lying on the floor while he gathered the energy to get up, he spotted a shiny object near him. His wristwatch. He picked it up. 11:18. It jarred his memory, and all the missing pieces fell into place. Gradually, he remembered where he was, and then why. He realized that he had been unconscious for fourteen minutes. *Decompression,* he thought. *An opened door. A blown-out window.* He could figure out that much. He had read articles about it in aviation magazines.

*Still flying.* His senses told him that the Straton airliner was being held straight and level, and he could feel the reassuring pulses of engine power through the airframe. The knowledge that the crew still had the ship under control was comforting.

Berry grabbed at the rim of the washbasin and pulled himself up. His legs were still wobbly, and he was light-headed. He vaguely recalled having vomited, and he saw the evidence of it in the corner. But he had already begun to feel better. He looked at his reflection in the mirror. He looked all right. No cuts or bruises, although he had dark circles around his eyes. The eyes themselves were red and watery.

Berry took a few deep breaths and shook his head to clear it. He felt as though he had a giant hangover, except that the symptoms were disappearing rapidly. He would be all right, he assured himself. Decompression was a temporary thing. No permanent damage. It was like passing out from too many martinis. Too many martinis was probably worse. He already felt nearly normal.

Berry reached for the door handle. He pulled on it tentatively, remembering that he could not open it earlier. But the Straton's pressurization system had automatically shut down once Flight 52 had reached a life-supporting altitude, and there was no longer any airflow coming from the vents behind him. To Berry's surprise, the door yielded easily. He opened it and stepped into the passenger compartment.

John Berry had no preconceived notion of what to expect in the cabin. He had not let his mind get that far ahead, yet subconsciously, he certainly expected nothing too far from the ordinary. As his eyes took in the scene, what he witnessed caused him to step backward against the fiberglass wall. The appalling sight filled his brain, and a primeval scream rose from the depths of his soul. Yet he made no outward cry.

Utter devastation. The worst of the damage was in the forward section of the tourist cabin, only twenty feet from where he stood. That was where his eyes were instantly drawn and his attention riveted. The curtain that had separated the first-class from the tourist sections had been torn away, exposing the entire length of the Straton's huge cabin.

Through the ragged hole in the left side of the 797, Berry could see the wing, and below that, the blue waters of the Pacific Ocean. Spread out from the hole for a distance of ten feet lay an unrecognizable heap of debris. As he focused on the mound, he began to separate the component parts: chair rails, seats, and hand luggage.

While his eyes darted around the boundaries of the rubble, he tried to understand what he was seeing. There were two holes in the aircraft's fuselage. The hole in the right sidewall was considerably larger and more irregular than the hole in the left. On both sides there were sheets of metal that vibrated continuously in the slipstream. They added a strange undertone to the noises of the howling wind. There was no evidence of there having been a fire. But John Berry did not connect what he saw to any probable cause. His inexperienced eye could not separate the pieces of the puzzle into suitable clues.

Berry slowly realized that the puddle beneath the mass was actually blood. He was suddenly covered with cold sweat. From the pile of debris he recognized what seemed to be chunks of flesh, sections of arms and legs. A mutilated torso rested against the edge of the hole in the fuselage.

A movement from beneath the debris caught Berry's eye. A woman. She was pinned beneath the wreckage. Berry took a step toward her. As he did, the wind that blew through the gaping hole shifted the wreckage.

Berry froze. The woman's face, which appeared unmarked and unhurt, turned. Beneath the falls of her blonde hair was the bloody stump of her neck.

Berry turned his eyes away. His throat constricted and he began to gag. His heart pounded. For a moment, he thought that he might pass out. He closed his eyes and steadied himself against the bulkhead.

John Berry looked to the front of the airliner. At first glance it seemed normal enough, except that oxygen masks dangled from the overhead compartments above each seat. Briefcases and pieces of clothing were jammed in the corners. But what caught his attention was the thing that was glaringly absent: life. The passengers sat motionless in their seats, like a display of mannequins strapped into the mock-up of an airplane.

Berry walked to where his seat had been. In the row ahead was a man Berry had exchanged friendly words with. Pete Brandt, from Denver, he recalled. Berry reached for the man's wrist and felt for a pulse. Nothing. He put his hand up to Brandt's mouth. He felt no breathing.

Berry looked around and then realized that Brandt, and all those seated within five rows of him, had no oxygen masks. For some reason the masks had failed to drop from the compartment above each seat in that section. Berry looked down at the seat he had been in. No mask. *I'd be dead*, he thought.

He turned around and looked across the cabin. Most of the passengers on that side had their oxygen masks strapped on. Berry went directly toward the row where a balding, elderly man was seated. They had nodded politely to each other when they had boarded the flight.

Even before Berry laid his hand against the man's chest, he knew. The white clamminess of his flesh and his frozen facial expression told Berry he was dead. Fear and agony were etched into his face. Yet he wore an oxygen mask, and Berry could feel the trickle of life-sustaining air still being pumped through its plastic tube. Then why had he died?

Berry looked to the next man. It was Isaac Shelbourne, traveling with his wife. Berry knew the famous pianist by sight and had recognized him while they waited to board. He had hoped to strike up a conversation with him during the flight.

Berry laid his hand on Shelbourne's shoulder. The man stirred. *Alive*, Berry thought, and his heart filled with hope. He could hear Shelbourne mumble incoherently beneath his oxygen mask, and Berry slipped the mask off the man's face.

He grabbed Shelbourne's shoulders with both his hands and shook him. "Wake up," he said in a loud voice. He shook him again, more violently. Shelbourne's eyes were open, but his gaze was blank. The pianist's eyes teared and blinked involuntarily. Saliva ran out from one corner of his mouth. Sounds emanated from the depths of his throat, but they were no more than unintelligible noises.

"Shelbourne!" Berry screamed, his own voice taking on an ominous sound as it cracked. In a sickening moment, Berry understood how totally and irrevocably impaired Isaac Shelbourne was.

Berry looked around the cabin. Others had awakened, and they too exhibited the same signs that Shelbourne had: dysfunctional speech, spastic muscular action, and no apparent capacity for rational thought. *Brain damage!* The hideousness of that notion hit Berry full force. He released his grip on the man he had attempted to revive.

John Berry took a few steps away from where he stood. He was now both afraid and revolted. The people in the cabin were apparently all brain damaged. He understood that a sustained lack of oxygen could do that. Having an oxygen mask on was evidently not enough protection. Vaguely, he recalled an article about pressure versus the percentage of oxygen. Above a certain altitude, even pure oxygen wasn't enough. *No pressure, no flow,* was the line he remembered. He wondered if it applied to the Straton's cruise altitude. Sixty-two thousand feet. Yes, that was it. Of course. They had been traveling in subspace.

He knew for certain that everyone he had seen without an oxygen mask was dead, and those who had worn them had lived—only to become brain damaged. Yet he was alive, and capable of rational thought—and he had not worn an oxygen mask. Why had he not been affected? The idea that the brain damage might be progressive jarred him. His mind might still begin to fade, as the result of oxygen deprivation began to have its effect.

*Nine times seven is sixty-three,* he said to himself. *Newton's first law concerns bodies at rest.* He *was* rational. That was no illusion. He had the impression that brain damage caused by oxygen deprivation was not progressive. He was sure of that. At least he felt that he was sure of it.

Some of the passengers had gotten up from their seats. Berry saw that those who moved around were disabled to varying degrees. Some had difficulty walking, while others seemed to move normally. But up close, he could see that even those who retained normal muscular control had been affected; he could see it in their eyes.

Berry stepped aside to allow a college-age boy to move down the aisle. The boy stumbled a few times. Several feet past Berry he suddenly stood rigidly upright, then fell to the floor. His body writhed in convulsions. An epileptic seizure. Berry remembered that he should do something to prevent the boy from swallowing his tongue. But he could not bring himself to step toward him. He turned away feeling disgusted and helpless.

A young girl, hardly more than eleven or twelve, moved slowly down the aisle. She had come from somewhere in the rear of the airplane. Her face showed that she was afraid, and that she understood the horror. She turned to Berry.

"Mister. Can you hear me? Do you understand me?"

Her voice was tenuous and her face was covered with tears.

"Yes" was all that he could think to reply.

They looked at each other for a brief, intense moment. In a flash of recognition, she suddenly understood that Berry was like her and not like the others. He was no threat. She ran up to him, buried her face in his chest, and began to cry.

"We'll be okay," Berry said. His words were as much for himself as for her. For the first time since he had awakened he allowed himself a small measure of emotion. "Thank God," he said to himself, choking back tears of gratitude for this small miracle. The child continued to cry, but more softly. He held her small, tense body against his.

While his attention was focused on the young girl, he failed to notice that several of the passengers had gotten up and were moving toward them. John Berry and the girl huddled together in the center of the forward cabin as the silent passengers encircled them.

Commander James Sloan was transfixed by the radio message that had come from his pilot. He stared at the towering panel of electronic gear as if he expected to find a way out of the situation in its switches and meters. Yet there was nothing on the console but the neutral data of frequencies and signal strengths. What Sloan wanted to know was available from only one source.

"Matos, are you sure?" Sloan asked. His perspiring hands gripped the microphone. His normally stern voice had a strange, new tone woven through it, and his words sounded out of place.

There was no immediate response from the F-18, and while he stood in the silent electronics room, Commander James Sloan realized that he was suddenly afraid. It was an emotion he was not accustomed to, and one he seldom allowed himself to experience. But too much had happened too quickly. "Matos," he said again, "take your time. Look again. Be absolutely certain."

Retired Rear Admiral Randolf Hennings, who had remained silent since Matos had sent his first startling message, stepped closer to the radio. He could hear the loud rhythm of his own heartbeat, and he was sure that Sloan could hear it too.

But James Sloan was not listening. His entire universe had shrunk. There was nothing he cared about now except the words that were about to come through the radio speaker. There was no other inroad to his thoughts.

"There's no doubt, Commander," Matos's transmission began.

Sloan's face went pale. He listened to the remainder of the pilot's message through a filter of personal static, as his mind raced.

"It's right in front of me. I'm only fifty feet in trail. Trans-United, a Straton 797. There's a three-foot hole on its port side, and another hole in the starboard fuselage. The starboard hole is bigger—three or four times as big. I don't see any movement in the cockpit or the cabin."

Sloan stood with his eyes shut, both his hands laid against the console. He had not been face-to-face with fear since he was a young boy. All his body muscles tensed and he wanted to run, to bolt from the room and get away. He wanted to shake himself awake from the incredible nightmare.

"Now what?" Randolf Hennings finally asked, his mild voice barely breaking the silence. "What can we do? What should we do?"

Sloan slowly opened his eyes, then turned his head to stare at Hennings. As he held eye contact with the Admiral, James Sloan pulled himself out of the deepest emotional pit of his life. He had very nearly lost his self-control. The Commander's frown had returned, as had his iron-willed expression and bearing.

"What do you suggest, Admiral?" Sloan asked in an obviously sarcastic tone; he was goading the old man. Hennings appeared puzzled. Sloan waved his hand nonchalantly. "Perhaps we should take a walk below-decks. We could lock ourselves in the brig. Better yet, let's go to the officers' ward room. They've got a nice pair of ceremonial swords on the wall. We could take them down and fall on them."

Hennings uttered an unintelligible sound that showed his surprise.

"Listen, Admiral," Sloan continued, "we've got to evaluate this situation realistically. Figure out precisely where we stand. The last thing we want is to rush off to do something we'll regret. Something bad for the Navy."

Sloan hoped he had not pushed the old man too far. Or too quickly. Still, it was his only chance. Without Hennings along, there was no way he could pull off some sort of cover-up. Sloan had done it once before, when, because of a foul-up, one of his pilots had shot up a Mexican fishing boat. The responsibility for that one might have wound up in Sloan's lap, so he moved quickly to fix it. It had taken only a quick helicopter ride and a small pile of Yankee greenbacks. This one would require more. Much more. But it could still be done.

"I don't know what you mean. What is it you want to do?" Hennings finally asked.

Sloan sat down in the seat in front of the console. He took out a cigarette. He took his time lighting it, then inhaled deeply. He swiveled the seat around to face Hennings and sat back.

"Let's list the obvious things first," Sloan said. His words were slow, full measured, and carefully picked. "Neither of us wanted this. It was a pure accident. God only knows how it happened. That area was supposed to be clear of air traffic. I checked it myself this morning."

Sloan paused. Procedures had required him to re-check, in case of a last-minute change. He had tried, but he hadn't been able to get through on the normal channels, even on the patch. The chance that a flight would have altered its course during the short time he was without a clear channel was minuscule. Less than minuscule. Yet it *happened,* Sloan thought. He managed to dispel the miscalculation with a simple shrug of his shoulders, then returned his attentions to Hennings. "How that aircraft got there is beyond me. I guess our luck was super-bad."

"Our luck?" Hennings said. "What the hell's the matter with you? What about that airliner? It's got people aboard. Women and children." The old man's face was red and his hands trembled. The volume of his voice filled the room and made it seem smaller than it was. Hennings had the sudden disquieting sensation of being closed in. The smallness of the electronics room had trapped him, and he desperately wanted to go above-decks.

James Sloan sat motionless. He continued to wear the same ambiguous expression. "You're right," he said. "It's a tragedy. But it's not our *fault.*" Sloan stopped speaking for a moment to let his words sink in. He took another deep drag on his cigarette. He knew that it was his fault, at least partially. But that was beside the point.

Hennings looked down at Sloan in disbelief. "Are you somehow suggesting that we pretend this never happened?" He was beginning to wonder if Sloan was insane. For a person to even entertain such wild notions seemed evidence enough of insanity. "We've got to help those people."

Sloan leaned closer to Hennings. "That's the point, Admiral. There are no people."

A dead quiet hung between the two men. Numbers paraded by on the digital clock, but time stood still. Finally, the Admiral shook his head. He did not understand. "But it's an airliner," he said. "Trans-United. It's got to have passengers. It must have a crew."

"No, Admiral. Not anymore." Sloan was choosing his words carefully. "The impact of the missile punctured two holes in their pressurized shell. At sixty-two thousand feet, they couldn't survive. They're dead, Admiral. All dead."

Sloan sat back and watched as the words registered on the old man. Sloan had known, as soon as he had begun to think clearly again, that the hole made by the

Phoenix missile would make the aircraft decompress. A decompression at 62,000 feet would be fatal.

Hennings's expression had changed. Shock had been replaced by pain. "Dead? Are you sure?" he asked.

"Certainly." Sloan waved his hand in a gesture of finality. But he knew that there was still a measure of technical doubt. If he let those doubts surface, they would erode his resolve and eat away at the basics of his plan. He knew that Hennings would need an excuse to go along with a cover-up. He figured that the old man *wanted* an excuse. Sloan would be happy to provide one. More than likely, everyone aboard that airliner was already dead—or soon would be. The harm had already been done. It was now a matter of saving himself. And the mission. And, of course, the reputation of the Navy, which needed all the help it could get these days.

Sloan leaned closer to Hennings. "I know that Matos won't say anything. He's in this with us. We do no good by turning ourselves in. This was an accident. If the truth came out, the entire Navy would suffer."

Sloan cleared his throat. He took a few seconds to gauge how Hennings was reacting. So far, Sloan still had him. Hennings had nodded in agreement. The good of the Navy was his soft spot. It was worth remembering. Sloan might need to play on it again, now that he was coming to the sensitive part.

"Our best bet," he continued, "is to have Matos put his second missile into the . . . target. It's being flown by its autopilot. At close range, he could direct his missile toward the Straton's cockpit. It would wipe out the ship's controls." The coup de grâce to the back of the neck, he wanted to say, but didn't. "It will go down. No evidence. Just a sudden disappearance in mid-Pacific. Terrorists. A bomb. Structural failure. We'd be off the hook. The Navy—"

"No!" Hennings shouted, pounding his fist on the console. "It's insane. Criminal. We've got to help them. They could still be alive. They've probably sent out distress signals. More than just the three of us know. Everyone knows." Hennings pointed to the radio equipment. "They must have sent an SOS."

"That's not true, Admiral." The conversation between them had taken on the atmosphere of a debate, and James Sloan was not unhappy about that. He had hardly expected to reach an agreement with Hennings without some sort of fight. Hennings was still talking and deliberating, and that was a good sign. Now all Sloan had to do was find the right words.

"We monitor both international emergency channels on these two sets," Sloan said, pointing to two radio receivers at the top of the console. "There's been nothing from them. You've heard that for yourself. Our shipboard communications center, down in CIC on the 0-1 level, would instantly get any word of a problem from ships or planes anywhere near here. We even get the routine stuff. Things like ships with minor leaks and aircraft with minor equipment difficulties. There's no way that a distress message was sent from that aircraft without our CIC getting involved in it. The CIC duty officer would immediately call me if he had gotten something."

"But what about the people?" Hennings said. "We just can't assume that they're dead."

"Matos reported that he saw no activity. There was no one in the cockpit. He can get within fifty feet of that aircraft. If there's no one visible, it's because they're dead. Slumped in their seats."

"Well . . . I don't know," Hennings said. What Sloan said seemed to make sense, although he wondered for an instant if the Commander was being completely honest. Hennings wanted to do what was best for the Navy. The accident was a monumental tragedy. But, as Sloan pointed out, nothing could change that. Nothing could erase the errors, oversights, and coincidences to bring those people back. Disgracing the Navy was the last thing he wanted to do. Hennings's friends in the Pentagon would be exposed. He knew that they were vulnerable, since the testing had not been authorized. He realized that he, too, was in an impossible position if the truth became known. The faces of his old friends in the Pentagon flashed through his mind. *Protect the Navy. Protect the living*, Hennings thought.

"Admiral," Sloan said, sensing that Hennings could now be pushed to the conclusion he had steered him toward, "I understand your reservations. Your points are valid. I want to check them out. I'll call down to CIC to be sure that no emergency message was sent by the Straton. Then we'll get Matos to take another look. A close look. If he reports that there's no one alive, then we know what we need to do."

As Sloan reached across the desk for the direct telephone to CIC, he kept his eyes riveted on Hennings. Sloan was playing the percentages. He wanted to cement the retired Admiral into the conspiracy. He needed him. The odds were low that Matos would be able to see any life aboard the Straton transport.

Hennings stood rigidly, every muscle of his body tensed. He watched as Sloan held the telephone. His eyes wandered to the digital clock. Half a minute ran off while his mind stayed as blank as the *Nimitz*'s gray walls. Hennings turned to Sloan. Everything seemed to be in a state of suspended animation, waiting for him. Finally, with a nearly imperceptible motion, retired Rear Admiral Randolf Hennings nodded his head.

The young girl clung to John Berry as he stood in the aisle of the forward cabin of the stricken airliner. The din from the Straton's engines and the noise of air rushing past the two holes in its fuselage filled the cabin, yet Berry could still hear the girl's sobs and feel her wet tears against his arm. He was thankful for her physical presence. Facing the nightmare alone would have been too much. Any companion, even a child, was better than none.

Berry's first notion that something unforeseen would break into their moment of tranquillity came from a muffled noise from behind. Berry, still holding the child, turned.

"Down!" he yelled, and he shoved the girl into an empty center row of seats. A tall and muscular man with wild eyes rushed toward them, a jagged section of a serving tray held high in his right hand. The people who had followed the man up the aisle stopped a few rows before reaching Berry and the girl. They seemed more curious than aggressive. They stood in mute wonder, watching the encounter in front of them.

The man yelled incoherently. His facial muscles were contorted with hatred, and sweat covered his forehead. Somehow, in his damaged brain, the man had formulated the thought that the young girl was crying because Berry had hurt her. The man would protect the young girl. He would kill Berry.

"Stop!" Berry screamed. As the man approached, Berry wheeled himself to one side. The jagged serving tray was flung harmlessly past him. Deranged and acting alone, the crazed man was no match for a normal adult. With a right uppercut against the man's jaw, Berry knocked him backward across a row of seats.

John Berry stood in the center of the aisle. His right hand throbbed with pain, and for a few seconds, he thought he might have broken it. He rubbed his aching hand, and while he did he felt an awakening, a long-forgotten sense of pride. He had successfully defended himself and the girl.

Berry glared at the other passengers and raised his fists. It was an act, a show of force for the half dozen of them who stood around him watching. Inwardly, Berry wanted to run. But if they were to attack en masse, he would have no chance. Deranged or not, there were simply too many of them. Too much muscle. He hoped that his threatening gesture would be enough to keep them away.

In the minds of the passengers, rivulets of rational thoughts ran across arid areas of damaged brain cells. They could still sense personal fear, and it had caused them, one by one, to back off. Berry thanked God that they did not have enough presence of mind to gang up against him. Not yet, anyway.

Berry took the young girl's arm and ushered her toward the circular staircase.

"You okay, mister?" she asked.

"Yes." His heart pounded, and his mouth was dry.

He flexed his fingers and could tell that nothing had been broken. He would need to be careful. If he allowed himself to be hurt, they would be defenseless. He would get himself some sort of weapon as soon as he could, and get one for the girl, too.

Berry inhaled deeply and felt his body begin to calm. "Keep your eyes open. Stay alert."

"Okay," she answered.

They climbed up the staircase and into the upper lounge. The stairway creaked under their feet.

The scene in the lounge was a welcome relief from the madness below. Except for the dangling oxygen masks, everything appeared normal at first glance. But as they walked through the lounge, the abnormalities became obvious.

There were nine people in the upper lounge, and Berry's impression was that they were asleep. Then he noticed that they sat in tensed and contorted positions. On their faces they wore expressions of soul-chilling terror. Two of them, a flight attendant and an old woman, were semiconscious.

The flight attendant leaned against the bar and ranted nonsensically. She had a crazed look in her eyes, and she groped spastically at the edges of the bar to maintain her balance. Berry could see from her name tag that she was Terri O'Neil. He had noticed her during the morning snack service. A little more than a half hour before, she had been serving food and drinks in the first-class cabin, and now she could hardly stand straight. Berry turned away.

On the other side of the lounge was the old woman. She was stroking the head of her husband as he lay face down across the table in front of her. She spoke to his dead body in singsong tunes, the snatches of her pathetic and childlike words filling Berry's ears.

Three men and two women sat on a horseshoe-shaped couch near the piano. They all wore oxygen masks, and they looked unconscious. A man wearing the black glasses of the blind sat near them, his arms outstretched in a futile search for the oxygen mask that dangled only inches to his left. He appeared to be dead.

The opened cockpit door was a dozen feet ahead, and Berry could see that all of the crew were slumped over in their seats. With each step Berry slowed his pace, reluctant to enter the cockpit.

Finally, he stepped across the threshold. All three of the pilots were unconscious. *Pull yourself together*, Berry thought.

The young girl stood directly behind him. She said, "No one's steering."

"It's automatic. Like an elevator." The flight controls moved gently in unison, responding to small electronic commands of the gyrostabilized autopilot to keep the aircraft on its programmed course.

The girl looked around the cockpit and saw Carl Fessler's lifeless body draped across his desk. She could hear the hissing sounds that came from the continuous flow of oxygen pouring out of his dislodged mask. She took a step backward and looked in wonder at him.

Berry was hardly aware of the girl. He had guessed correctly at Fessler's condition as soon as he saw that the engineer's mask was off. The Captain, who was still strapped to his oxygen mask, was Berry's concern. He approached the man and tried to shake him into consciousness. Their survival depended on it.

Captain Alan Stuart was breathing, but comatose.

Slowly, Berry accepted the fact that the Captain was probably beyond help.

Berry looked toward the copilot. He, too, was unconscious. Berry and the girl had survived this far, only to discover that there was no one left to fly the aircraft.

Berry glanced around the cockpit. The walls that surrounded the pilot stations were crammed with instruments. He understood some of what he saw, but entire panels and rows of gauges were a total mystery. The difference between a giant jetliner and his four-seat private propeller airplane was like the difference between an airliner and the Space Shuttle. All they had in common was that, on occasion, they flew through the sky.

John Berry knew that he could not fly this huge supersonic aircraft. He was backed against an insurmountable wall of anguish and despair. All he now cared about was their immediate survival—to stay alive within the confines bounded by the sweep second hand of the cockpit clock.

The copilot stirred in his seat and his arm swung off his lap. It fell, with a thud, onto the center console. Berry held his breath while he waited to see what would happen. If the man moved again, he might inadvertently disengage the autopilot or do some other harm to their stable flight condition. In that maze of switches, Berry knew that he could not hope to find the proper combination to set things straight.

"Quick. Help me get him out of the seat," he said to the girl. She came over and grabbed clumsily at the copilot's legs as Berry lifted McVary's limp body out of the chair.

"Don't let him touch the controls."

"I won't." She raised his feet above the equipment

on the center console as Berry lugged the man backward.

"I'll do the lifting. Don't let his legs touch anything." Once they had cleared the center console, Berry let the copilot's feet drag on the floor as he pulled the man back into the lounge.

"Is he sick?" the girl asked. She could see that he was not dead. He was breathing and his head occasionally swayed from side to side, although his eyes were shut.

"Yes. Lay him there. Pull his legs out straight. Give me that pillow." Berry propped the pillow under the copilot's head. He rolled back the man's eyelids. The pupils seemed dilated, although he wasn't sure. Berry looked at the girl. "He might get better. Make him comfortable. That's all we can do."

"I'll get a blanket." She pointed to one wedged beneath a nearby seat.

Berry nodded. The copilot might come out of it, at least enough to help Berry fly the airplane. With the copilot talking him through it, Berry thought he might be able to steer the 797. Maybe.

The young girl brought the blanket over. The two of them knelt in the center of the upper lounge and busied themselves at making McVary comfortable. Berry glanced back at the cockpit. He knew that, shortly, he would have to get the girl to help him take the unconscious Captain out of his seat, and also drag the lifeless body of the flight engineer out of the cockpit. But he could put those things off for a few more minutes. In the meanwhile, he focused his attention on the copilot. He was, without question, their best hope.

Berry asked the girl, "What's your name?"

"Linda. Linda Farley."

"Are you alone?"

"Yes."

"How old are you?"

"I'll be thirteen in four days. . . ."

Her voice trailed off, and Berry forced a smile. He thought, *Happy birthday, Linda.*

Berry and Linda worked on making First Officer Daniel McVary as comfortable as they could. They remained oblivious to the aircraft outside the cabin windows that had flown within sixty feet of where they knelt.

"Homeplate, I see no life in the cabin." Matos split his attention between the long row of windows and the technical needs of flying a close formation. His hands played constantly with the throttles and control stick as he made the corrections to keep his F-18 as near to the Straton's port side as he dared.

His position in the formation was a little higher than optimum, but to put his aircraft in direct line with the fuselage windows would have been tricky. The airflow across the Straton's giant supersonic wing made that region too turbulent. Matos opted to fly in the smoother area a dozen feet higher.

"It's hard to see clearly. The cabin is dark. Stand by." With the bright Pacific sunlight shining down on them, any attempt to look across the intervening distance through one of the small windows and into the cabin was bound to fail. Matos already knew that it would. His first guess had been that the two holes in the fuselage would give him a clear view. But they did not. Too much debris and too many shadows. Even if someone were alive, they certainly couldn't be expected to get close to the holes. The wind alone would keep them back. Matos knew that all he could hope to see were those people who wanted to be seen. Those on the 797—if anyone was left alive—would need to press themselves against the windows to become visible. Once they moved a foot or two back they would vanish into the relative darkness inside.

Surely they would try to be seen. They would want to get Matos's attention. To get Matos's help.

"Okay, Matos. Nothing in the cabin. Go to the cockpit." Sloan's voice was again impatient. Commanding. Bullying, according to most of the *Nimitz*'s pilots. The man obviously wanted the job done quickly. For what purpose, Matos could not even guess. He wondered for a moment what sort of orders he would receive next.

Matos nudged the throttles and maneuvered his aircraft slowly forward. As he passed the widest section of the Straton's fuselage, he inched his F-18 to the right, placing his wingtip within a dozen feet of the 797's flight deck.

As he finished his maneuvering, something caught his eyes. He had been directing most of his attention toward his wingtip clearance, but suddenly he had an impression of movement. Something on the Straton's flight deck. *Someone in the cockpit. Someone alive,* Matos said to himself.

He stared intently at the Straton. The relative narrowness of the cockpit and its broad expanse of glass made it easier to see into than the cabin. *Far side. Copilot's seat.*

# MAYDAY

Something on the right side of the 797's cockpit had moved. At least he thought that it had. Now he was not sure. On closer scrutiny, he could see nothing. No one. If anyone was still there, they were slumped down below the window line.

*It must have been a reflection. A glint of sunlight. A distortion in the cockpit glass. No one alive,* Matos thought. He sat there for another minute and looked at the Straton, then he maneuvered the F-18 outboard and slightly away.

Lieutenant Peter Matos's emotional wound had re-opened. "Homeplate. There is no one in the cockpit. There is no one alive." As much as he tried to control himself, Matos could not be the uninvolved technician any longer. His heart had risen to his throat. *Es tu culpa, Pedro.*

The F-18 slackened its formation on the Straton. It drifted aft. As it did, it flew alongside the upper lounge and within sixty feet of the rows of windows that lined it. Unable to force himself to look at the devastated Straton airliner any longer, Peter Matos kept his eyes focused straight ahead.

# 5

Jack Miller sat at his long, functionally modern desk in the center of the starkly lit, windowless room. He glanced at the wall clock—11:37—then looked over at his assistant, Dennis Evans, who sat at a smaller desk, flipping desultorily through some papers. "I'm breaking for lunch in five minutes, Dennis."

Evans glanced up from his desk. "Okay."

The Trans-United Airlines dispatching office at San Francisco International Airport was experiencing its usual midday lull. The morning departures were well into their routines, and it was too early to begin the flight plans for the late-afternoon trips. The half-dozen dispatchers read newspapers, their assistants made an attempt to look occupied, and the junior aides tried to appear busy and eager.

Miller yawned and stretched. After twenty-eight years at Trans-United, he had enough seniority to get the two things he'd always wanted: a nine-to-five dispatcher's shift, and assignment to the Pacific desk.

# MAYDAY

Now that he had them both, he was bored. He almost yearned for the night shift and the more hectic South American desk again. Such was life.

Miller flipped absently through the pages of his *Sports Illustrated*, then laid it aside. He looked at his computer console, at the display of assigned trips. He was, at that moment, responsible for monitoring only four flights: 243 from Honolulu, 101 from Melbourne, 377 to Tahiti, and 52 to Tokyo.

The weather across the Pacific routes was good, and all the flights had ample reserve fuel. No problems. Not much to do. On days like this, he found himself watching the clock. Miller's eye caught an empty entry on his display screen. He regarded the blank column for a second. "Dennis." He spoke in a voice that years of practice had trained to penetrate the ambient sounds of the room without actually rising above the noise. "Dennis, did you forget 52's update?"

"Hold on." The young man walked over to a stack of computer messages on a countertop and leafed through them. He went through them a second time, more slowly. He looked up and called across the room. "Didn't get one. It's overdue. Want me to send a request?"

Miller didn't like Dennis Evans's choice of the word "overdue." *Overdue* connoted something quite different from *late* in airline parlance. Miller looked at the wall clock. The fuel and position report was only a few minutes behind schedule. Late. It was purely routine. Minor information. Yet Miller would not, under any circumstances, turn anything over to Evans that wasn't perfect. Twenty years before, he had left an open item on his sheet and gone to dinner. When he returned, he'd found the dispatcher's office full of company executives. One of their new Boeing 707s had gone down somewhere over the Gulf of Mexico. That was the night that the euphemism "overdue" became clear.

Miller glanced back at the wall clock, then at the computer screen again. He didn't like it, but he wasn't overly concerned. "Well . . . we've got time." He punched the computer keys to get a different screen, then looked down at the names of the crew. He was familiar enough with the name Alan Stuart. Like a lot of modern business relationships, this one was totally electronic. Just a voice on the telephone and the radio. Yet he felt he knew the man, and he knew that Flight 52's captain was dependable. Miller wasn't familiar with the other names on the crew list, but he knew that Stuart ran a tight ship. Miller was certain that Stuart would soon discover the oversight and send an update. Bugging a pilot, especially a conscientious one like Stuart, was the quickest way to become a disliked dispatcher, and Jack Miller had no intention of doing anything like that during the remainder of his career. It was the sort of stunt that Evans was noted for. He looked up at Evans, who was going through the messages again. "We'll get the update soon. If we don't, then . . ." Miller paused and considered. He didn't want to request Flight 52's updates by relaying a message through air-traffic control for everyone to hear. His eyes fixed on the door to the small glass-enclosed communications room that housed the data-link machine. "If we don't hear from them by, say, twelve o'clock, type out a request to them on the link."

Evans grunted a reply. The radio was faster and easier than the data-link—sometimes link messages just didn't get through—but Miller was always concerned with discretion and politeness. If a captain was sitting on his thumb up there, he ought to be called on the radio and told about it. Evans pushed the computer messages aside and sat back at his desk.

Miller glanced at the computer screen again, then punched a button to turn off the display. "It's a nice day out there," he called to Evans. "They're drinking coffee and daydreaming."

Evans mumbled something as he worked on another flight's data.

Miller watched the clock. The room became still except for the background noises of the electronics. Miller focused on the sweep second hand. He was accustomed to this kind of waiting, but it always made him uneasy. Like the times his wife was overdue. Late. Or his teenaged son or daughter. The clock moved, not slowly, but quickly, at times like this, running through the minutes, making the awaited party more awaited. Making one wonder all sorts of things.

John Berry sat strapped into the captain's seat of the Straton. The midday sun poured through the cockpit windows, bathing him in bright sunlight. He pressed the talk button on the hand microphone again and spoke loudly. "Do you read me? Does anyone read?" Beads of perspiration dotted his forehead, and his mouth felt dry.

With his right hand, he made careful adjustments on the audio panel. "Mayday. Do you read Mayday? Any station. Do you read Mayday?" He sat back and listened. Listened for the familiar crackle, the squelch-break that was the electronic equivalent of a man clearing his throat before he spoke. But there was only the persistent, unbroken hum of the speakers.

Berry slumped into the seat. He was confused. If there was one thing he knew from his years of flying, it was how to work a radio. It seemed simple enough even in the Straton. The airliner's radios did not seem much different from all the other sets that he had operated. Yet there must be something different about them, some small esoteric task that had to be performed before the radios would transmit. But *what*? And *why*? Why should these radios be different? "Damn it." Berry wondered how in God's name he could ever fly the aircraft if he couldn't even work the radios.

The urge to talk to someone had become overwhelming. It had gone beyond the simple necessity to report the disaster and ask for assistance. It had become an overpowering need to hear a human voice just for the sake of hearing it. But as each minute of silence passed, Berry was losing hope and was becoming alternately frantic and despondent. His hand shook so badly now that he stopped trying to transmit and sat back and tried to calm himself. He glanced at the instruments. Everything looked good, but after his failure with the radios, he was beginning to doubt his ability to read even standard gauges. And the majority of the Straton's instrumentation was standard enough to be familiar. But the markings—the altitudes, speeds, fuel reserves, engine temperatures—were incredibly amplified. He tried to imagine he was in the Skymaster and tried to reduce the problems and the instrument panels to manageable proportions.

# MAYDAY

He looked at the fuel reserves. Less than half full. What this meant in flying time at the present speed and altitude, he didn't know. But he'd figure it out soon enough as the needles drifted leftward and the minutes passed. He stared at the control wheels as they moved slightly—inward, outward, left, right. The rudder pedals made small movements. The flight was steady.

Something odd caught his eye and he looked down near his left knee. He stared at the open protective cover and read the words above it. AUTOPILOT MASTER SWITCH. He stared at the toggle, which was pointing to ON. He understood. The Captain had either lost his nerve or lost consciousness before he could complete his last mission. Berry nodded. It sort of made sense. But for Berry, there was no such easy way out. Not yet. He reached down and snapped back the protective cover.

He found he was building up a healthy anger toward fate and toward death, if for no other reason than to tell his wife what he really thought about her. Unfinished business. He reached down and grabbed the microphone. "Mayday! Mayday, you sons-of-bitches! Answer Mayday!"

He began changing the frequency he was using, alternating between the frequencies left on the radios. When he transmitted, he knew he should keep to the universally understood words. He could save the explanations for when he made contact. "Mayday! Mayday! Mayday! Mayday!" He waited for a reply, but again there was none.

Out of desperation he began to randomly turn the dials and transmit on every channel and on each of the four radios in the cockpit. "Mayday, Mayday, Mayday, Mayday."

He switched back to the original frequency. "This is Trans-United Flight . . ." What was the flight number? What difference did it make? He tried to remember his boarding pass but couldn't. "This is the Tokyo-bound Trans-United Airlines Straton 797. Mayday. Do you read Mayday? Trans-United Operations, this is the Tokyo-bound Straton 797, we have an emergency. Do you read?" He waited. Nothing.

He could see that the radio's transmission lights blinked whenever he pressed the microphone button. He could tell from the sidetone in the cockpit speakers that the radios were operating. But for some reason they were not putting out. He suspected that something—the antenna perhaps—had been damaged. He had hoped that someone in the cockpit had been able to put out a distress signal, but he was fairly certain now that they hadn't. The fault in transmitting was not his—he'd known that, really. The radios were all set by the pilots to transmit. They simply weren't sending. That's all there was to it. No distress call had been sent and none ever would be sent.

No radios equaled no chance of flying the plane home. He almost felt a measure of relief. The responsibility of flying and landing this huge machine was not a prospect he'd looked forward to. But he *did* want to live. He put the microphone down and stared at the clear skies around him. His problems on the ground were in their proper perspective now. He could and would change a lot of things if he ever got back to New York. But everyone facing death must make that observation. One more chance. But more often than not, nothing changed if you were lucky enough to get a second chance. Still, he didn't want to *lie down* and die. That's what he'd been doing for the last ten years. He had to think it all out. Later.

John Berry turned and looked back through the open cockpit door into the lounge. He could see Linda Farley sitting in a club chair, weeping quietly.

Berry slid out of the captain's seat and walked back into the lounge. The Captain and the copilot lay near the piano where he and the girl had dragged them, covered with blankets. The body of the flight engineer lay against the far bulkhead, his face and torso covered with a lap blanket.

Berry watched the flight attendant whose name tag said Terri. She was sitting on a small sofa, speaking incoherently to herself. Her face was smeared with blood and saliva. She seemed calm, but he'd have to watch her carefully for signs of violence. He'd have to keep her away from the cockpit, where she could do real harm.

Berry noticed that the old lady had stopped babbling to her dead husband and was now crouched behind a club chair peering over the top and making odd clucking sounds. Blood and drool covered her face also. Her husband's body was still slumped over the cocktail table, but it seemed to have shifted. Berry wondered if rigor mortis was setting in already.

The five passengers on the horseshoe-shaped couch were still unconscious. One, a pretty young woman, was making odd sounds that came from her throat, and Berry wondered if that was what was called the death rattle.

The lounge smelled of feces, urine, and vomit. Berry

closed his eyes and pressed his fingers against his temples. His head still ached from the oxygen loss, and he was becoming queasy.

He opened his eyes and surveyed the scene again. He'd thought that the confusion of these people might improve, might be reversible. But he was fairly certain now that it wasn't. His world was divided neatly and irrevocably, with no fuzzy lines, between Us and Them. And there were a lot more of Them.

Berry walked over to the girl and put his hand on her shoulder. His daughter had been this girl's age when her remoteness and alienation had begun. But that was on the earth. Here, an adult enjoyed all the old prerogatives. "You're going to have to calm down and start helping me."

Linda Farley wiped her eyes and nodded.

Berry walked to the bar and found a can of Coca-Cola and opened it. He rummaged through the debris under the bar and extracted a miniature bottle of liquor. Johnny Walker Red. He opened it and drained off the ounce and a half, then carried the cola to the girl. "Here."

She took it and drank. "Thank you."

Berry knelt down beside McVary and pushed his eyelids back. Partly dilated. Breathing regular, but shallow. He looked up at the girl. "Did he move at all?"

Linda nodded. "He opened his eyes once. He said something, too, but I couldn't understand it." She pointed to Stuart. "That one never moved."

Berry turned to Stuart. The blood and vomit on his face were dry and crusty. Berry pushed back the eyelids. The pupils were fully dilated. The Captain's skin was clammy and his breathing was irregular. The man was dying.

Berry rose and looked down again at McVary. If the copilot regained consciousness, and if he was at all coherent, they might have a chance. The plane was flyable. All it needed was someone to fly it. Berry thought he could do it if someone talked him through it. Someone on the radio, if he could get it working, or this copilot. Without help, he'd have to wait out the hours in full consciousness of his impending death. He almost envied the others.

"Listen!"

Berry shot a glance at the girl, then steadied his breathing and listened.

"The stairs," she whispered.

Berry nodded. "Be quiet." The circular metal stairway that led down to the first-class cabin had apparently been loosened, and Berry remembered it creaking when he'd used it. It was creaking now.

Berry heard the footsteps on the stairs clearly now. They were coming slowly, hesitantly. He thought there was only one person, but he couldn't be certain.

He walked quickly around the lounge searching for something to defend himself with. The barstools were fastened to the floor, the scattered bar bottles were miniatures, and the mixers were in small cans with pop tops, which meant no openers were needed. A canister of precut lemons and limes was in the galley. No knife. "Damn it." He looked over the floor. Almost everything else that was movable had been sucked down the stairwell. He searched desperately for an attaché case, an umbrella, the blind man's cane, but he knew he would find nothing. The footsteps got louder.

# MAYDAY

Linda Farley screamed.

Berry looked at the stairwell and saw the top of a man's head. He shouted at the girl, "Get in the cockpit and stay there. Go on!" He then moved quickly past the stairwell and knelt beside the body of Carl Fessler. He pulled the man's belt off and wrapped it around his right hand, which still ached from the confrontation in the cabin. He let the buckle end swing free.

Berry stood quickly and moved to the opening in the rail around the stairwell. He looked down and saw a large man looking up at him. "Stop!"

The man stopped.

Berry saw that the man's hands were on the floor a few inches from his ankles. He moved back a step. "Go down!" He raised the belt.

The man hesitated.

Berry knew that as long as he stood there he could keep anyone from coming up the stairs. But he couldn't stand there indefinitely. "Go!"

The man backed down a few steps. He looked at Berry with an uncomprehending expression. He opened his mouth and made a small sound, then spoke clearly. "Who are you?"

Berry leaned over and looked at the man's face. Flecks of vomit covered his chin and white shirt. His eyes looked alive. No blood covered his face, no saliva ran from his mouth. "Who are *you*?" Berry asked.

"Harold Stein."

"Where are you from?"

"What?"

"What is your home address?"

The man took another step down. "Where's the pilot? I was in the lavatory when . . ."

"Answer me, damn it! Tell me your home address!"

"Chatham Drive, Bronxville."

"What day is this?"

"Tuesday. No, Wednesday. Look, who are you? Good God, man, don't you realize what's happened down here? Where is the pilot?"

Berry felt his chest heave and his eyes almost welled with tears. There were now three of them in that small minority. "You're all right?"

"I think so." Things were becoming more clear to Stein. "The people down here . . ."

"I know. Come up. Come up, Mr. Stein."

Harold Stein took a hesitant step.

Berry backed off. He unwound the belt from his hand and stuffed it into his trouser pocket. "Come on. Quickly." He glanced over his shoulder at the three men and two women sitting on the horseshoe-shaped couch behind him. Some of them were starting to stir. "Hurry."

Stein pulled himself up to the lounge deck. "What in the name of God . . ."

"Later. You wouldn't be a pilot by any chance, would you?"

"No. Of course not. I'm an editor."

Berry thought he was beyond disappointment, but his heart sank lower still. He regarded Harold Stein for a moment. Fortyish. Big. Intelligent face. He could be of some help.

Stein's eyes were fixed on the cockpit door. "Hey, what the hell happened to the *pilot*?"

Berry jerked his thumb over his shoulder.

Stein looked more closely at the scene in the lounge. "Oh, no! My God . . ."

"Okay, Mr. Stein. Forget that. Let's talk about survival."

"Survival." Stein nodded. He was taking in about ten percent of what was happening. He'd known they were in very serious trouble, but he thought the pilots were still in control. He looked at the cockpit again and saw the captain's wheel move. "Who's . . . ?"

"Autopilot."

"What happened?"

Berry shrugged. "Bomb, I guess." But the two holes didn't look like bomb damage to him, and he'd heard no explosion before the other noises. "Did you see or hear anything?"

Stein shook his head.

The two men stood awkwardly in the middle of the lounge, unsure of what to do next. The overwhelming scope and speed of the disaster had kept them off balance, and they needed the situation to remain static for a few minutes until they got their bearings. Finally, Stein spoke. "Just us two?"

Berry turned toward the cockpit. "Linda, come on out!"

The girl ran out of the cockpit and placed herself beside Berry, and under his encircling arm, as though she were being displayed at a family reunion.

Berry felt her body trembling. He looked down and spoke to her. "This is Mr. Stein. He's going to help us."

Stein forced a distracted smile. His eyes were still darting around the lounge.

"I'm John Berry." He extended his hand.

Stein took it.

Berry looked down at the girl. "This is Linda Farley."

It was surreal, yet comforting, to go through the amenities. That was all they had left. Behave normally, in a civilized manner, and rational thought and action would follow. Berry said, "Let's sit down." He'd developed a proprietary attitude about the lounge and cockpit. He indicated an empty horseshoe-shaped sofa with a cocktail table opposite the cockpit door. "Do you need a drink, Mr. Stein?"

"Harold. Yes, please."

Berry went to the bar and found two Canadian Clubs and another cola. He carried them to the table and sat. He broke open the seal on his bottle and drank. Around him was a scene that had badly shaken him only ten minutes earlier, but like any survivor of a disaster, his mind was blocking out the destruction, the dead, and the dying, which was now irrelevant, and he was focusing on the problems he had inherited.

Harold Stein drank the liquor and let his eyes wander around the lounge. The two men in uniform lay beside the piano in the far corner to the left of the stairwell. One moved, the other didn't. A third uniformed man lay against the rear wall of the lounge, his face and torso covered with a blanket. The bar in the opposite corner was in a shambles. Directly in front of him was another horseshoe-shaped couch. Three men and two women sat strapped into it. Their bodies moved spasmodically from time to time; every change of position presented Stein with a new tableau, each more grotesque than the last.

Stein turned away and focused on a grouping of the club chairs along the left wall. A man wearing dark glasses sat in a frozen position, his hands apparently reaching for a hanging oxygen mask. An old man opposite him lay across the cocktail table, apparently dead also. An old woman, the most animated of anyone, was hiding behind the old man's chair, occasionally peeking out and whimpering. A young flight attendant, also conscious, was weeping by herself, curled up on the floor near the cocktail table. Clothes and sundry lounge paraphernalia were strewn over the plush blue carpet. "This is monstrous."

"Let's stay calm. This," Berry waved his arm, "doesn't concern us . . . unless they become . . . unmanageable."

"Yes, all right." He seemed to be considering. "Maybe we ought to . . . help these people . . . get below."

Berry nodded. "Yes. They're an unsettling influence, but I'm not sure if that's the right thing to do with them. I . . . Anyway, it wouldn't be an easy job. Let it lie for now."

"All right."

Berry leaned forward. "Where were you when the . . . air let go?" Berry had begun to look for answers. If he could figure out what happened, he might be able to figure out what to do next.

"I told you. I was in the lavatory."

The girl put down her cola. "Me, too, Mr. Berry."

"Okay," said Berry. "That's it. I was in the lavatory, too. The lavatories held more of their pressure. Did either of you black out?"

They both nodded.

"Okay. But we're all right now. The people who

didn't put their masks on are dead. Those who did are either dead or brain damaged."

Stein leaned forward and spoke softly. "Brain damaged?"

"Yes. Of course. That's what it looks like, doesn't it?"

"Well . . . yes. I . . . my wife . . . two kids . . ." Stein put his hands to his face.

Somehow Berry hadn't thought of the possibility that Stein was not traveling alone. Berry had traveled alone for so many years that it had accustomed him to think only of himself. Even at home, he seemed to think mostly in ones. Everything had happened so quickly that his thoughts had never gotten to the obvious, even concerning Linda Farley. She most of all would certainly have been with someone. "I'm sorry, Harold. I didn't realize . . ." He could see that he was losing Stein, and the girl was going with him. "Listen, I'm a pilot and I have experience with these things, and the effects of . . . of oxygen deprivation are temporary. I didn't mean brain damage—that was the wrong word. I think I can land this thing, and when everyone gets the proper medical attention, well, they'll be all right. Now, you've got to help me so I can bring us all home. Okay?" He turned to the girl, who was crying again. "Were you with anyone, Linda? Come on. Take a deep breath and speak to me."

Linda Farley wiped her tears. "Yes, my mother. We were . . . I tried to find her before. Then everything happened so fast . . ."

"Yes, I'm sure she's all right. Where was she sitting?" As soon as he asked the question he regretted it. But something made him want to know.

"In the middle. I think near where the hole is." Her eyes filled with tears again. She understood what that meant.

John Berry turned away from them and focused on a picture hanging on the far wall near the piano. Dalí's celebrated *The Persistence of Memory*. A bizarre grouping of melted watches, lying across a surreal landscape. If ever a painting fit a room, it was that painting in this room. He turned away and stared down at the white plastic table in front of him. *He* had been spared any concern beyond his own survival. He was thankful at least for that. If they ever got back, he would be the only one who would not carry any scars of this. In fact, he thought with some guilt, he could come out of it better than he'd gone in. But there were close to three hundred and fifty souls onboard. Souls, he remembered, was the official term. How odd. And most of those souls were dead or dying. It was a hell of a high price to pay for Berry's personal resurrection. If he survived.

Berry glanced at Stein. The man wore a numbed expression. He was obviously haunted by the presence of his brain-damaged family, who sat no more than a hundred feet from him. Berry wondered how he, himself, would stand up under a similar strain. For an instant he conjured up the image of Jennifer and his two children.

He tried to examine his feelings. The thought had crossed his mind to give up and simply wait for the fuel to run out, but he had also thought about trying to fly the airliner, fly it to a landing. He glanced at Stein and the girl. He thought of the others in the cabin of the 797, and the word *euthanasia* came into his mind.

# MAYDAY

Berry knew that the pulse of the engines was lulling him into a false security, a lethargy that made it difficult for him to act as long as there appeared to be no immediate danger. But every minute that passed was a minute less flying time. He wondered if there was actually enough fuel left, considering the high fuel consumption at low altitudes, to get him to a body of land. He supposed he could ditch the plane in the ocean. Did the Straton have an emergency signal transmitter in the tail like his Skymaster did? If so, was it working? If it was there and if it worked, a ship might eventually come. But he didn't know if the three of them could clear the aircraft before it sank. And how about the others? And if some of them did clear the aircraft, how long would they have to float with their life vests in the ocean? He thought of sunstroke, dehydration, storms, and sharks. Clearly they were all as good as dead unless he did something. For some reason, known only to God, he, Linda Farley, and Harold Stein had been given a second chance, an opportunity to save themselves. He suddenly stood. "Okay. First priority. Find others who did not suffer . . . decompression. Mr. Stein . . . Harold . . . you go below into the cabins and make a search."

Stein looked at the staircase. The thought of going down there with three hundred dysfunctional and probably dangerous passengers was not comforting. He didn't move.

Berry had another idea. "All right. Stay here." He went into the cockpit and looked around for a moment. Finally, he found what he needed: He grabbed the PA microphone and pressed the button. He heard the squelch-break and took a deep breath. "Hello. This is

... the Captain speaking." His own voice boomed out in the lounge, and he could hear the echoes of his words coming up the stairwell. "If there is anyone in the aircraft who . . . who . . ." *Damn it.* "Who is not affected by decompression, who feels all right, and who can think clearly, please come up to the first-class lounge." He repeated his message and went back into the lounge.

Berry and Stein stood at the railing of the staircase and watched and listened. Some of the passengers were shaken out of their lethargy by the voice and were making odd noises—squeals, grunts, groans, and growls. A high piercing laugh came from the far recesses of the cabin and penetrated into the lounge. Stein shuddered and shook his head spasmodically. "Good God."

They waited, but no one came.

Berry turned to Stein and put his hand on his shoulder. "I'm afraid that's not conclusive. Someone may be trapped or frightened out of his wits. You'll have to go down."

"I don't want to go downstairs," Stein said in a small voice.

Berry bit into his lower lip. He realized that if he allowed it, Harold Stein would soak up time and attention like a sponge. It was an understandable need. But John Berry could not spare the time, or allow himself a normal man's compassion. "Stein, I don't give a damn what you want. I don't want to die. Neither does the girl. What we *want* isn't enough anymore. All that matters is what we *need*. I need to know if anyone else on this goddamned airplane can help us. We've got to find a doctor, or someone from the crew. Maybe another pilot."

Berry glanced toward the cockpit. The sight of the empty flight deck sent a chill down his spine. He shrugged it off and turned back to Stein. "Take this belt. Find other weapons. We may need them. Linda, you stay here in the lounge and look after these people. Especially look after the copilot over there. All right?"

"Yes, sir."

"If anyone acts . . . funny, let me know. I'll be in the cockpit. Okay? Linda? Harold?"

Stein nodded reluctantly. He half believed that his family would recover and almost believed that Berry could fly the aircraft. "I'll bring my family up here. I'd rather they be up here. They'll be okay in a little while."

Berry shook his head. "They're fine where they are. Later, when they are more aware, we'll bring them up."

"But—"

"I have to insist. Please go. I have other things to attend to in the cockpit."

Stein glanced back at the empty cockpit. "The radio? Are you going to try to contact . . . ?"

"Yes. Go on down below. Let me worry about the cockpit."

Harold Stein rose slowly and took the belt and wrapped it around his right hand. "Do you think they're very . . . dangerous?"

Berry glanced around the lounge. "No more than these people." He paused. He owed Stein more than that. Some lies were necessary. Other were self-serving. "Be careful. I was attacked down there. Different people react differently to oxygen loss. The brain is a complicated . . . Just be careful. Each flight-attendant station should have a call phone. You may be able to use the phones if you want to speak to me."

"All right."

Berry turned abruptly and walked quickly back into the cockpit.

Stein watched as Berry slid into the pilot's seat. He glanced at the girl, forced a smile, and began descending the staircase.

Berry had an urge to shut down the autopilot and take the wheel. Just for a second to get the feel of the machine. To take his fate into his own hands. He stared at the switch on his control wheel and reached out his hand. Steering the giant aircraft could possibly be within his skills. But if the craft somehow got away from him, he knew that he would never be able to get it back under control. Yet eventually he knew he'd take the wheel when the fuel ran out. At that point, he would have absolutely nothing to lose in trying to belly-land in the ocean. So why not try a practice run now? His hand touched the autopilot disengage switch. No. Later. He took his hand away.

He thought about going down in the ocean. If nothing else, he should probably make a 180-degree turn and head south before they left the mid-Pacific's warmer water. He looked up at the autopilot controls mounted on the glare shield that ran between the pilots. One knob was labeled HEADING. Berry put his hand on it, took a deep breath, and turned it to the right.

The Straton slowly dropped its right wing as its left wing rose and the aircraft went into a bank. The tilting motion made him experience that familiar sensation in the seat of his pants. It would take a very long time to turn 180 degrees at this rate of turn, but he didn't actually want to turn around yet. Not until he had a firm plan of action in mind. It was an old pilot's creed not to make course changes aimlessly. He glanced at the fuel gauges. He had time. The water beneath them was probably still warm enough for ditching, and would be for a while. Berry was satisfied that the autopilot would respond to its turn control knob. That was all he had the nerve for right now. He turned the knob back slightly and the Straton leveled out. He looked at the magnetic compass and saw that he was on a slightly different heading of 330 degrees. He turned the knob again to put the proper reading under the cursor, and the airplane rolled back to its original heading of 325 degrees.

He sat back. His hands were trembling and his heart was beating faster. He took a few seconds to calm himself. He considered trying the radios again but decided that they were definitely malfunctioning. Psychologically, it wasn't good to have another failure with them, and he didn't want to cultivate a dependence on them. *The hell with the radios.* If he was going to fly the Straton, he was going to have to do it himself, unless Stein came back with a licensed airline pilot. Berry wasn't counting too heavily on that.

---

Stein stood at the base of the stairs, peering into the dim, cavernous cabin. He'd felt the aircraft tilt and thought it would crash. Then it leveled off. Berry was

# MAYDAY

flying it. He relaxed a bit and waited for his eyes to adjust to the darker shadows around him.

In the center of the first-class cabin, a few feet from the stairs, was the enclosed area that held the two lavatories. He stepped to the side of the wall and looked back into the tourist section. With the section dividers gone, he could see how huge the Straton was. Row upon row of seats, like a movie theater. Shafts of sunlight cut though the windows, and he could see dust motes in them. A larger shaft of sunlight lay across the wide body from hole to hole, and the air rushing past the holes created an odd noise. He noticed a mild and pleasant breeze in the cabin that helped to dissipate the smell of sick people and sewage. The pressure and airflow had leveled out into a state of near equilibrium.

As if they had also reached an internal equilibrium, most of the passengers sat motionless. Their initial bursts of energy had been spent, and they sat with their eyes shut and their faces slack and pasty white, many of them smeared with blood and vomit. A dozen or so people were still making noises, and from the back of the aircraft somewhere came a terrible laugh. A few men and women continued to move aimlessly up and down the aisles, in a sort of trance. It was a cross between an insane asylum and a slaughterhouse. *How,* thought Stein, who was a religious man, *could God permit this to happen?* Why did God give man the ability to reach this high into the heavens and then desert them all like this? And why was he spared? *Was* he spared?

He searched the faces of the people closest to him. None of them offered even the slightest promise of normality. He took a breath and stepped a few feet up the aisle. He forced himself to look at the four center-row seats where his family sat. The two girls, Debbie and Susan, were smiling at him with blood-covered mouths. His wife seemed not to notice him at all. He called her name. "Miriam. Miriam!" She didn't look up, but a lot of other people did.

Stein realized that the noise had made them active. He remained motionless, then glanced back at his wife and daughters. Tears came to his eyes. He stepped back and leaned against the bulkhead of the lavatory. He thought he was going to pass out, and he took several deep breaths. His mind cleared and he stood up straight. He knew there was no way he would walk the length of the aircraft. He'd just wait five minutes and go back. He'd lead his family up the stairs, too.

A peculiar sensation, a mild vibration, began to inch into his awareness. He turned and laid a hand against the bulkhead. The vibration was coming from inside the enclosure, and it was getting stronger. It was the rhythmic hum of a slow-turning electric motor. He remembered that there was a galley elevator adjacent to the lavatories. He quickly went around to the galley opening on the other side of the enclosure. He looked in at a small metal door. The motor stopped. He took a step back as the handle rotated. The door opened.

Stein stood face-to-face with two women. Flight attendants. One tall brunette, the other Oriental. They were huddled close together in the small elevator. He could see pure terror on their faces. Their eyes were red and watery, and traces of smeared vomit clung to their blue jackets? "Are you all right?" Stein asked. "Can you . . . understand me?"

"Who are you?" asked the brunette flight attendant. "What happened? Is everything okay?"

Stein took a deep breath to get his voice under control and replied, "There's been an accident. Holes in the airplane. We lost pressure. A few of us were trapped in the lavatories. The lavatory doors held the air pressure," Stein said, remembering Berry's words. "I guess where you were held its air pressure, too."

The brunette flight attendant said, "We were in the lower galley."

The Oriental girl asked, "Did a door open?"

"No. A bomb."

"Oh, God!"

Sharon Crandall stepped out of the elevator and brushed by Stein. She turned and looked down the length of the cabins. "Oh my God, oh no! Barbara! Barbara!"

Barbara Yoshiro came quickly out of the elevator and stood behind Crandall. She screamed, a long primal scream that died in her throat as she blacked out and collapsed into Stein's arms.

Sharon Crandall put her hands over her face and took a series of short breaths. She turned quickly toward Stein. "The pilots. *The pilots!*"

"Dead. Well . . . unconscious. But there's a passenger who's a pilot. Come on. We have to get out of here."

"What's happened to these *people*?"

"Brain damage. . . . Oxygen loss. They might get violent. Come on!"

A dozen passengers began walking up the aisles toward them. A few more passengers near them tried to stand, but their seat belts held them down. But through trial and error, or because of some vague recollection, some people were beginning to unfasten their belts and stand up. A few of them moved into the aisles. A tall man stood up right next to Stein.

Stein was becoming frightened. "Go ahead! Go first!"

Sharon Crandall nodded and moved quickly up the stairway. Stein dragged Barbara Yoshiro toward the stairway. A male passenger suddenly stood in his seat and stepped into the open area in front of the staircase. With his free hand, Stein straight-armed him and the man spun away, wobbling like a malfunctioning gyroscope.

Stein, dragging the unconscious flight attendant, took the stairs slowly. Someone was behind him. A hand grabbed his ankle. He kicked loose and moved faster up the spiral stairs, almost knocking Crandall over as he reached the top. He laid Barbara Yoshiro on the carpet and slumped over the rail. A half-dozen grotesque faces stared up at him. He thought he saw the top of his wife's head, but he couldn't be sure. His breathing was heavy and his heart raced wildly in his chest. "Get away. Go away!"

Sharon Crandall looked around the lounge. "Oh my God!"

Stein stood by the staircase and wrapped the belt around his hand. "I'll stay here. Go into the cockpit."

Berry looked over his shoulder into the lounge. "Come in here!"

But Sharon Crandall's attention was focused on the flight attendant sitting on the carpet with her legs spread out. "Terri!" She ran over to the girl and knelt beside her. "Are you okay? Terri?"

# MAYDAY

Terri O'Neil opened her eyes wide and looked toward where the sound had come from. It was an involuntary response to the auditory stimulus. Her rational mind had been erased by the thin air at 62,000 feet. The sight of Sharon Crandall's face meant nothing to her. The memory of the hundreds of hours they had flown together had evaporated from her brain like water from a boiling kettle.

"Terri!" Sharon shook her friend's arm.

"Forget it!" yelled Berry. "Come in here!"

Sharon glanced into the cockpit and saw a man sitting in the captain's seat. His voice was vaguely familiar. But she was too shocked to think clearly. She ignored Berry and moved back past the stairwell over to the sprawled bodies of Stuart and McVary beside the piano. She shook the pilot's shoulders. "Captain Stuart!"

Stein watched as a man in the main cabin mounted the spiral staircase. Another man, then a woman, followed. Soon a line of people were walking clumsily up the circular steps. "Go down! Down!"

"Aaahh!"

Stein braced himself on the rail and brought his foot down on the head of the first man.

The man fell to his knees and toppled back, sending the whole line stumbling and falling backward.

Linda Farley knelt beside Sharon Crandall. "They're very sick. I tried to help them."

Sharon glanced at the girl blankly, then looked at Harold Stein by the rail and the unconscious body of Barbara Yoshiro. She walked to the bar and recovered a first-aid box. She carried a vial of ammonium carbonate to Barbara Yoshiro, broke it, and held it under the girl's nose. "Easy, now."

Barbara Yoshiro made a gasping sound, then opened her eyes. Crandall helped her sit up.

The two flight attendants held onto each other, Sharon Crandall comforting Barbara Yoshiro as she began sobbing. "Easy now, Barbara. We're going to be all right."

Stein looked down at them. "Go into the cockpit and see if you can lend a hand there. Okay?"

Crandall helped Yoshiro to her feet and steadied her as they walked toward the cockpit. "Don't mind these people. Come on. Into the cockpit."

Berry glanced quickly over his shoulder. "Do either of you know anything about the cockpit?"

"I thought you were a pilot," said Crandall.

"Yes, I am," answered Berry. "But I'm not familiar with this craft. I can fly it with a little help. Do you know *anything* about the cockpit?"

"No," said Crandall. She helped Yoshiro into Fessler's seat. They both noticed the blood on the desk but didn't comment on it. "How bad are the pilots?"

"They'll be okay."

"There's no need to lie to us," said Crandall.

"They're brain damaged. Maybe—just maybe—the copilot will come out of it with enough faculties left to help."

Crandall considered this for a long few seconds. She'd liked McVary. Liked all of them, actually. Now they were all gone, including the other flight attendants she'd spent so many hours with. Flight crews rarely spoke about accidents, but she had heard talk about decompression incidents. "What exactly happened?"

"I don't know. It doesn't make a lot of difference, does it?"

"No."

Berry turned and looked at Barbara Yoshiro. "Are you all right?"

"Yes. I'm feeling better."

Berry nodded. He had the feeling, no more than intuition, that she would remain calm from here on. It was a good thing to know, and it didn't especially matter if it was true or not. He asked her, "Do you know the cockpit at all?"

Yoshiro shook her head. "I usually stay downstairs in the kitchen. Below the main cabin."

Crandall spoke. "I come to the cockpit often, but I never really noticed much."

"You probably know more than you think. Sit down."

Sharon Crandall sat in the copilot's seat. "This is not going to help."

At first Berry had no special recollection of her, but as he looked at her profile closely, he knew who she was. He felt a smile form on his lips. He was happy that she had made it. It was a conversation that had taken place a century ago, but it had brought him a few minutes of pleasure and he was happy to pick it up where it had ended. "Do you remember me?"

She looked at him. "Yes. Of course. The salesman. I was going to sit with you." Crandall paused. "You're not a pilot."

"Yes, the salesman. I fly, too."

"Fly what?"

"This and that. My company airplane. I can handle this." He had suddenly become an old hand at keeping everything calm. Perhaps he was being too reassuring. He guessed that no one would stay calm for very long once they watched him attempt to fly the airliner. "Where were you two when the decompression began?"

Yoshiro answered. "We were both in the lower kitchen."

Berry nodded. "There must have been pressure trapped down there. The three of us were in lavatories."

"That's what the other man told us," Yoshiro replied. "I guess there might be others."

"Yes. That's why I sent Stein down." He lowered his voice. "His wife and two children are down there. The girl's name is Linda Farley. Her mother was near the hole. I'm John Berry."

"Barbara Yoshiro. You know Sharon."

"Yes," said Berry.

"Look," Sharon Crandall said, "call Trans-United Ops. They'll give you a course to fly, and then coach you through the landing."

Telling him to use the radio was not the sort of information he had been looking for. "Good idea," said Berry. "But the radios don't work."

There was a long silence in the cockpit. Berry broke it. "I'm going to turn and put us on an approximate heading for California. If the fuel lasts, we'll decide then if we should look for a landing area or put it down near the beach. Maybe I can raise someone on the radio when we get closer. How does that sound?"

The two flight attendants said nothing.

Barbara Yoshiro stood. "I'm going below to see if anyone else is . . . sane."

"I wouldn't do that now," said Berry.

"Believe me, Mr. Berry, I'd rather not go. But there were two of our company pilots aboard—going on vacation with their wives—and I have to see if they're alive and sane. And I'm still on duty and I have an obligation to the other passengers."

Berry refused to get excited about the possibility of finding real pilots who could fly the Straton. "The passengers are dangerous."

"So am I. Black belt, judo and karate. And they're not very coordinated, I assume."

"There are three hundred of them."

Crandall turned in her seat. "Don't go, Barbara."

"If it looks really bad, I'll come back."

Berry glanced at her. "I can't let Stein go with you. He has to stay at the top of the stairs to keep anyone from coming up."

"I didn't ask for company."

Berry nodded. "All right, then. Call at the flight-attendant stations every few minutes. If we don't hear from you . . . well, if we can, we'll come after you."

"Okay." She walked quickly out of the cockpit.

Berry turned to Sharon Crandall. "Lots of guts there."

"More than you know. She doesn't know any more about judo or karate than I do. She's trying to make it up to us for fainting. But there *are* two of the company's pilots back there. We both spoke to them. And I hope to God they're all right."

"Me, too."

He tried to picture Jennifer doing something selfless, noble. He almost laughed. God, if only he could get back and tell her what he thought of her.

Crandall picked up the copilot's microphone and held it awkwardly. "I've used this a few times." She held down the button. "Trans-United Operations, this is Trans-United Flight 52. Do you read me? Over."

They both waited in the silence of the cockpit.

Berry looked at her as she sat with her head tilted, waiting for the speaker to come alive the way it always had. "Forget it," he said.

She put down the microphone.

The minutes ticked by. Suddenly, the interphone buzzed. Sharon Crandall grabbed the phone from the console. "Barbara!" She listened. "All right. Be careful. Call in three minutes. Good luck." She replaced the phone and turned to Berry. "The pilots. They're both dead." She added, "It's your ship, Mr. Berry."

"Thanks."

Crandall thought about the government-approved procedures in her manual. It was technically *her* ship, or, more correctly, Barbara Yoshiro's. Barbara was the senior surviving crew member. What difference did it make? Barbara's ship, or Sharon's? Impossible. Absurd.

Berry tried not to show any emotion. "All right. Let's talk about this cockpit. Is there some sort of emergency signal device, for instance? Here . . . what's this?"

She looked at the red button he was pointing to and shook her head. "I don't know."

Berry decided to let her sit and think. He mentally sectioned off the cockpit into six areas and began examining the first one to his lower left, switch by switch, button by button, gauge by gauge. There were things he knew and a lot more he didn't know. He began memorizing locations of the instruments and control devices.

"What about the data-link?" she said.

"What?"

"The data-link. Did you try that?"

"What are you talking about?"

"The *data-link*. This thing." She pointed to a keyboard mounted between the pilots' seats and slightly below the radios. "I saw the crew use it a lot of times. They type on it. Messages come in, too." She pointed to a small video screen on the lower center of the panel. "It's linked to the Operations Center in San Francisco."

Berry stared at the device. He had looked at it before but dismissed it as just another gang of unknown buttons. He thought the screen was some sort of radar. Now it was making sense. He had read about data-links—a discreet electronic screen for sending individual messages to various aircraft. Most airlines had them to link their aircraft together without having to broadcast over the airwaves. He turned to Sharon.

"Do you know how to work it?"

"No. But I think they just type on it. Let's give it a try." There was an edge of excitement in her voice. "Go on. We have nothing to lose. You need a green light to know it's on. Here. This light has to be green."

Berry scanned the keyboard. His hand reached out tentatively and he pushed a button labeled ENTRY. The green light flashed on. Berry assumed this meant that he had a clear channel. He pressed a button labeled TRANSMIT and typed out three letters on the keyboard: SOS. He looked at the video screen. Nothing. "Aren't you supposed to see your message?"

"Yes."

"I don't see anything. Goddamn it. Goddamned airplane."

"I think you type the message first, *then* you push transmit."

"Okay." Berry hit the CLEAR button. "Okay. Let's see." He typed sos again. He reached over and pushed the TRANSMIT button. They both looked at the video screen. sos appeared in white, angular computer letters.

Sharon gave a small shout. "We did it! We did it!" She reached out and squeezed Berry's hand.

Berry was grinning. "Yes. Damn it. We did it. Okay. Okay." But Berry suspected that the video screen's picture meant very little. The only way to determine if the signal had actually been sent from the Straton and received by someone else was to wait for an answer to appear on the screen.

Berry was fairly certain that the data-link couldn't send and receive at the same time, so he resisted the temptation to transmit again and waited for the reply. Unlike a radio, if this machine worked, there was a displayed entry somewhere waiting to be read. He wondered how often the data-links were checked.

The Straton 797 maintained a steady northwesterly heading across the Pacific as the minutes ticked off.

John Berry knew that this was their last hope of surviving. He looked at Sharon Crandall. She seemed to know it too. "Buy you a drink?" He motioned back toward the bar.

"No. Not now. Maybe later. Get one if you want, I'll watch the screen."

"I don't need one." He glanced at the video monitor, then back at Sharon Crandall. "You want to hear about

Japanese businessmen? Japanese customs? It's very interesting."

She looked at him. "Sure," she said, with little conviction and a forced smile. Her smile faded quickly as she looked down at the data-link screen. Except for their own SOS message printed in the upper corner, the screen remained ominously blank.

# 6

Lieutenant Matos had the distinct impression, though he was not looking directly at the Straton, that the aircraft had banked briefly, then leveled out again. He stared at it closely, but it seemed level now. He looked at his magnetic compass. Still 325 degrees. No, the Straton had not banked. It was only an illusion. He rubbed his eyes. He was becoming fatigued.

The F–18 lay back in trail and followed the huge airliner at a distance of a thousand yards. Matos experienced some turbulence in the Straton's wake and lifted his fighter slightly higher. His last message from the *Nimitz* had been bizarre. A bizarre message even for a bizarre situation. *Navy three-four-seven. Follow in trail. Keep out of sight of portholes and cockpit. Do not, I say again, do not attempt to communicate with Straton. Acknowledge.*

Matos had acknowledged and followed orders without question. Had his position been more tenable, he would have asked for a clarification. But he was now numero uno on Sloan's famous shitlist, and that had the effect of putting him in a complete state of psychological dependence and subservience. Whatever Sloan said, Sloan would get. Certainly there was some method to Sloan's madness.

Matos was beginning to recognize tonal qualities in Sloan's voice despite the fact that the voice was scrambled in transmission, then unscrambled on his audio. And there had been a strange quality in Sloan's latest instructions that had not escaped Matos's attention. The voice was not hostile or curt. It was almost friendly, cajoling. The voice seemed to say, *All right, Peter, you screwed up, but just follow orders and we'll be able to square everything.*

But how in the name of God could anyone, even Commander Sloan, square *this*?

It occurred to Matos, now that he had time to think, that his career wasn't the only one that was finished. He'd been thinking only of himself, which was natural under the circumstances. Now he saw the situation for what it was. A monumental fuckup. It started with him, but it would chain-react and obliterate Sloan and anyone else unlucky enough to be in the electronics room. It would also smash the *Nimitz*'s commander, Captain Diehl, and probably his staff as well. The blast would reach into the Halls of the Pentagon, the Department of the Navy, the Department of Defense, and maybe into the White House itself. At whatever level this decision had been made to test-fire a weapon banned by the new Voluntary Arms Limitation Treaty, everyone involved from that level down would be culpable. *No es tu culpa, Pedro.*

Yet Matos, though he didn't fully understand who

ordered the test or how illegal it was, was very much in favor of it. He pictured himself in front of some sort of investigating committee—Senate, House, maybe Department of Defense. He would defend his involvement as a moral decision based on national security. A personal decision that transcended any treaty. He would *not* say he was only following orders. That was the coward's way. He began to take on the mantle of the patriot and martyr: the Ollie North defense. He would show what he was made of when the senators began firing questions at him. The Navy would be awed by his loyalty. Sloan would be impressed by his defense of his superiors. Peter Matos had the feeling that he had arrived at last.

"Navy three-four-seven."

Sloan's voice brought Matos out of his reverie. "Roger."

"Status report."

"Roger. In trail. No change in Straton."

He glanced at the Straton. What had happened was, at the most, only half his fault. Someone on the carrier had failed to note the flight plan of the Straton. The sky was a big test-firing range. It was someone else's responsibility to make certain the range was clear.

But the feeling that Commander Sloan had something else in mind—something that didn't require martyrdom or investigations—nagged at him. He knew if he put himself in Commander Sloan's head, knowing what he knew about Sloan, he would know what Sloan's next transmission would say. But he wouldn't let his mind come to the obvious and final conclusion regarding the Straton.

He glanced at the crippled airliner again. It would

just fly off into the Arctic Ocean on its present heading, and if no Mayday had been sent from it, and if no one on the *Nimitz* made a report . . . Why had *he* made the report? Damned stupid.

He looked at his fuel gauges. He couldn't follow the plane much longer. Yet he knew Sloan would want him to do just that. He'd have to stay with the Straton until its fate was resolved.

His radio crackled and he felt himself stiffen. He cleared his throat and waited for the message.

---

"Navy three-four-seven, this is Homeplate." Commander Sloan's voice was cool, controlled. Sloan looked at Hennings out of the corner of his eye as he transmitted. "Status of Straton."

"Status unchanged."

"Roger. Stand by for mission order."

"Roger."

"Out." Sloan put down the microphone and turned to Hennings. "All right, Admiral. The time for talk is over. I am going to order Lieutenant Matos to fire his second missile into the cockpit of the Straton. I am fully convinced that there is no one alive on that aircraft. If there was a pilot onboard, he would have changed direction long ago." He paused again and switched to a conversational tone of voice. "You know that the Navy is required to sink derelict ships that are a hazard to navigation. Now, the analogy is not precise, but that dead aircraft is a hazard to navigation too. At its present altitude and heading, it can potentially cross some commercial air lanes and . . ."

"That's absurd."

Sloan went on. "And it could also crash into a ship. True, there is no precedent for this, but it seems like an obvious obligation to order a derelict aircraft brought down. We must bring it down on our terms. Now. Hazard to navigation," he said again, hoping the old terminology would produce the necessary response.

Hennings didn't respond, but a flicker of emotion passed over his craggy features. His memory was drawn back to an incident that they had often talked about at the Naval Academy. It had occurred at the beginning of the Second World War. One ship, the *Davis*, had been pulling the crew of a badly damaged destroyer, the *Mercer*, from the water. The *Mercer* was crippled and aflame but showed no signs of sinking, and the Japanese fleet had sent a cruiser and two destroyers toward it. The last thing the Navy wanted was for the Japanese to take a U.S. warship in tow, complete with maps, charts, codes, new armaments, and encrypting devices. The *Davis* captain, John Billings, knew there were wounded and trapped men aboard the *Mercer*. The survivors also reported that the *Mercer*'s skipper, Captain Bartlett, a classmate of Billings, was still aboard. Captain Billings, without hesitation or one trace of emotion, was said to have turned to his gunnery officer and ordered, "Sink the *Mercer*."

But that was war, Hennings thought. This was quite different. Yet . . . they *were* at war, or at least could be someday—contrary to what the fools in Congress thought with their politically correct solutions and reasoning. The Straton, if it was visually spotted or tracked on radar, or crashed near a ship, might be recovered. And if it was, the nature of its damage would be quickly recognized for what it was. And that would lead back to the *Nimitz* eventually. Hennings knew that was what Sloan was really saying with all his bilge about hazard to navigation.

And if the *Nimitz* were suspected, all hell would break loose. America washed its dirty linen in public. The Navy would be subjected to inquiry, scandal, and ruinous publicity. It would be Tailhook a thousand times over. The incident would further emasculate the United States Navy; it was an emasculation that had already gone far beyond belief.

Hennings knew exactly what the Joint Chiefs would say if all that happened. "Why didn't those sons-of-bitches, Hennings and Sloan, just blow the thing out of the sky?" They would never *order* that done, but they expected it to be done by their subordinates. *Someone* had to do the dirty work and protect the people on top. Protect the nation's defense posture and the viability of its military.

Sloan had let enough time slip by. "Admiral?"

Hennings looked at Sloan. If he didn't dislike the man personally—if the suggestion had come from a more morally courageous officer—then it would be easier to say yes. Hennings cleared his throat. "Let's give it ten minutes more."

"Five."

"Seven."

Sloan reached out and set the countdown clock for seven minutes. He hit the start button.

Hennings nodded. Commander Sloan was a man who wasted neither words nor time. "Can you be sure Matos will . . ."

"We'll know soon enough. But I'd be surprised if he

didn't come to the same conclusions himself. I understand Matos better than he understands himself, though I've hardly spoken to the man. Matos wants to be part of the team." He sat down and began writing. "I'm drafting a message to him, and I want you to help me with it. What we say and how we say it will be very important."

"Well, Commander, if you've convinced me, you can convince that unfortunate pilot. You need no help from me in that direction." Randolf Hennings turned his back to Sloan and opened the blackout shade over the porthole. He stared out at the sea. He wondered what fates had conspired against him to make him do such a thing so late in life. The good years, the honest years, all seemed to count for very little when stacked up against this. He thought of the Straton. How many people onboard? Three hundred? Surely they were dead already. But now their fate would never be known to their families. Randolf Hennings had consigned them to their grave. They would lie there in the ocean where so many of his friends already lay, where he himself wished he could lie.

———

Jerry Brewster stood idly in the small communications room of Trans-United Operations at San Francisco International Airport, his hands in his pockets. He waited for the 500-millibar Pacific weather chart to finish printing. Working in this room was the only part of his job as dispatcher's aide that he really disliked. The lights were too bright, the noises too loud, and the chemical smells from the color-reproduction-enhancement machines hung heavily in the stagnant air.

# MAYDAY

The new chart was finished printing. Brewster waited impatiently for it to dry before he pulled it out of the machine. Jack Miller had requested the update on mid-altitude temperatures, and Brewster wanted to get the data to him before lunch. Brewster made it a point to drop everything else whenever Miller asked for something. Brewster liked the old man; Miller was always available for advice and training.

Brewster reached down and carefully pulled the newly printed chart off the roller and held it up. He walked toward the door with the map suspended from two fingers, just to be sure he didn't smudge the still-damp color ink. A bell rang behind him. The tiny sound carried from the far corner of the room above the other electronic noises. Brewster paused. It was the data-link's alerting bell. He listened. The screen was displaying a new message, and even from this far away, he could see that it was unusually short—a few letters or numbers. Brewster knew what that meant. Another malfunction. More gibberish. A segment of some half-digested intracompany transmissions. He watched from a distance to see if the screen would update.

After spending a small fortune to equip the entire Trans-United fleet with this electronic marvel, the data-link communications network was still subject to "technical difficulties," as they called it. Brewster called it screwed up. Garbled messages. Phrases or letters that repeated for screen after screen. Misaligned or inverted columns of data. It was almost funny, except that they were forever calling the system engineers to troubleshoot the damned thing. Fortunately, it was used only for routine and nonessential communications— meal problems, crew scheduling, passenger connections, routine weather and position updates. When it worked fine, it was fine, and when it didn't, you ignored it. Brewster ignored it.

He stepped toward the door. The chemicals in the room stung his nostrils and made his eyes water. He wanted to get into the cleaner air of the dispatcher's office, away from the irritants. He opened the door, then hesitated. Monitoring the data-link was one of his responsibilities. *All right, damn it.* He slammed the door shut, crossed the room and stood in front of the screen. He read the typed message:

S O S

That was all it said. Nothing else. No identity code, no transmission address. Brewster was puzzled, annoyed. *What in hell's name is this?* A prank? A joke? No airline pilot in the world would seriously send an SOS. It was archaic, dating from the days of steamships. It was the equivalent of someone reporting a rape in progress by saying, "Maiden in distress." Who could take that seriously?

Brewster rolled up the weather chart and tucked it under his arm. He stared at the machine in front of him. No, an airline pilot in trouble would transmit a Mayday message on a specific emergency channel using any one of his four radios. He would not send an ancient message on an electronic toy. And even if the impossible had happened and all four radios were malfunctioning, and a pilot resorted to the data-link, then he would send a full message with identifying code. This, then, was either a malfunction in the machine or some pilot's idea of a joke. A very bad joke. And this pilot knew that his joke would go no further than the Trans-United communications room.

Brewster realized that the joke was aimed at him, and that made him angry. He pressed the print button, then yanked a copy of the message out of the machine and held it in his hand.

S O S

Idiots. It would serve them right if he reported them. He didn't know if they could trace which of their flights had sent the anonymous message. It was a stupid, irresponsible thing to do, and the pilot who sent it would be in trouble if they could trace it. Then again, it might only be a malfunction. Why get involved? If he reported it, he'd get a bad reputation with the flight crews. That, somehow, might affect his promotion. Miller had always told him to cover for the flight crews. It would pay off. He was glad Evans hadn't seen the message. He crumpled the data-link's message and threw it in the trash can and left the room.

Jack Miller saw Brewster walk out of the communications room. "Jerry, can you get that mid-altitude stuff to me soon?"

Brewster looked across the room. "Sure, Mr. Miller. Just a few minutes." He glanced at the wall clock. Three minutes to twelve. They would both be late for lunch. He unrolled the chart on his desk, weighted it down at the corners, then picked up a pencil and began transcribing pertinent temperatures onto a blank sheet of paper.

# MAYDAY

John Berry stared at the rotary code selector on the data-link. The thing to do, he decided, was to change codes and send again. A longer message this time. That impulsive SOS had been too brief, enigmatic, he realized. He looked around the cockpit for code books but realized that, even if there had been any, they had probably been sucked out. He would have to try each channel, transmit a complete message, wait for a reply, and if there was none, go on to the next channel. Somewhere, the counterpart to this machine would print. He'd begin monitoring each channel again after he'd transmitted on all of them. It was a shotgun approach, but it was far better than waiting. The urge to hit the key was getting the better of him. "I think I'm going to try another channel. What do you think?"

Sharon Crandall looked at the blank video screen. "Wait a minute or two. I remember that the pilots sometimes waited ten minutes or more for a reply."

"Why?"

"Well, they don't send anything important on it. They just want it so they can leave a message in the communications room—for the record."

"Have you seen the communications room in San Francisco?"

"Once. I used to date a pilot. He brought me in there and showed me the data-link, weather printouts, and all that."

"Sounds like fun. Where's the communications room? Physically, I mean."

"The room's off the main dispatcher's office."

"Anyone on duty there?"

She thought for a moment. "No. I don't think so . . . just machines. But people go in and out, though."

Berry nodded. "Okay. We'll have to wait for someone to go in there and spot the message. Where's the machine located?"

"It's in the middle of the room. The room's small. They'll see it."

"Okay. I hope so."

Crandall felt defensive, but didn't know why she should. She tried to concentrate on the panel. Maybe she could come up with something else. The markings above the controls and gauges seemed so cryptic. RMI. LOM. Alternate Static. Gyro Transfer. "Here. This is something I remember. The ADF. I think it's some kind of radio."

Berry forced a weak smile. "Yes. The automatic direction finder. It's to home in on an airport's signal. Maybe we can use it later."

"Oh." She sat back. "I'm worried about Barbara. It's been a while since we've heard from her."

Berry had found the cockpit clock, but it seemed to be malfunctioning. "What time is it?"

She looked at her watch. "It's six minutes past twelve, San Francisco time."

Berry glanced at the clock again. 8:06. Eight hours beyond San Francisco time. He realized it was set to Greenwich Mean Time and remembered that airlines always measured time from that internationally recognized starting point. Berry shook his head in disgust. Everything in this cockpit seemed to provide him with useless information. The radios were filled with frequencies that wouldn't transmit. The course indicators sat blindly in the center of their scales. The clock told him that at that moment, halfway around the world, neon lights shined on Piccadilly and the London theater had raised the curtain on their first acts. All that useless information was unnerving. He had, he realized, become increasingly morose. He needed to pull himself out of it. He coughed dryly into his hand to clear his parched throat. "At least the weather's good and we have some daylight left. If this happened at night . . ."

"Right." Crandall answered with little enthusiasm.

They both lapsed into silence. Each knew the other was nervous, yet they couldn't bridge the gap to comfort each other. Berry felt himself wishing that Stein were free to come to the cockpit. Crandall wished Yoshiro would hurry back. Neither of them bothered to wish that the accident had never happened; neither of them was thankful for being alive. Their whole existence was reduced to worrying about the next course of action, the next few minutes.

Berry half rose in his seat and looked back into the lounge. "How is it going, Mr. Stein?" he shouted.

Harold Stein called back. "They seem quiet down there. Up here, too. No change in the copilot."

"Call out for Barbara Yoshiro."

Stein called loudly down the stairwell and listened closely. He turned toward the cockpit. "Nothing."

Sharon picked up the interphone and looked at the console. "I don't know which station to call."

"Try any one."

Crandall selected Station Six in the rear of the aircraft and pressed the call button. She waited. No one answered. "Should I call another station, or wait on this line?"

Berry was impatient. "How would I know?"

"I'm frightened for her."

Berry was becoming angry. "I didn't want her to go back in the first place. She's become part of the problem now and no help with the solution." He took a deep breath.

Sharon Crandall rose in her seat. "I'm going down there."

Berry reached out and grabbed her wrist. "No. You're not going anywhere. I need you here." Berry looked intently at her. An unspoken message passed between them: Berry was now in command.

Crandall sank slowly into her seat. Finally, she nodded. "Okay." She looked at John Berry, and he returned her stare. She felt strangely calm and confident in this man's presence.

"Try the rest of the flight-attendant stations," Berry said in a low, calm voice. "I'm going to start changing channels on the data-link. Maybe if we work on it, we can get our luck to change." Berry let his fingers slip gently off Crandall's wrist, and he reached across the console toward the data-link.

---

Jack Miller was trying to decide if he should give Flight 52 more time. He looked up at Brewster. "How's the data-link today?"

Brewster looked up from the weather chart. "What?"

"The link? Is it behaving?"

"Oh." He hesitated. "No. Just got a garbled message, as a matter of fact."

"Okay." He swiveled his chair and looked at Evans. "Okay, Dennis. In ten minutes, call them on the radio. Be gentle."

# MAYDAY

"Always gentle, Chief."

"Right."

Jerry Brewster abruptly laid his pencil down and walked quickly to the communications room. "Damn waste of time," he mumbled. He opened the door, ignoring the stench of color-enhancement chemicals, walked to the center of the room, and slid into the chair in front of the data-link keyboard. He saw that there were no messages on the screen, then set the machine to automatically choose and transmit on whatever channel the last incoming message had used. The SOS. He knew this procedure would work only if the aircraft had not changed the code settings on its own machine. Brewster placed his hands over the keyboard and typed a message almost as short as the one he had received.

WHO ARE YOU?

A copy of his message displayed on his own screen.

---

Berry thought he felt a barely perceptible pulsation in the machine, and had actually seen one of the unit's lights blink for an instant. He jerked his hand away from the code selector as though it were red hot.

The bell that signaled an incoming message rang twice. Its tone filled the 797's cockpit like the bells of Notre Dame on Christmas Eve.

Sharon Crandall let out a startled cry.

John Berry felt his chest heave and his throat constrict.

Letters began to print on the data–link's video screen.

# MAYDAY

Sharon Crandall reached out and grabbed Berry's arm.

WHO ARE YOU?

Berry almost rose out of his seat. "Who are we?" he shouted. He let out an involuntary laugh. "I'll tell them who the hell we are!" He put his fingers on the keyboard. "What the hell is our flight number?"

"Fifty-two. Flight 52! Hurry! For God's sake don't let them get away!" For the first time since it had all begun, tears came to Sharon Crandall's eyes and she sobbed quietly. She watched John Berry's trembling hand type out a message.

———

"Jesus Christ!" Jerry Brewster bent over the data-link screen as he watched its message display.

FROM FLIGHT 52. EMERGENCY. MAYDAY. AIRCRAFT DAMAGED. RADIOS DEAD. MID-PACIFIC. NEED HELP. DO YOU READ?

Brewster hit the print button, then ripped the copy off the machine and stared at it. His heart pounded and his mind raced in a thousand different directions. He took a hurried step toward the door but stopped abruptly and returned to the data-link. He knew they would want an immediate acknowledgment. Anyone in that situation would. With fingers that seemed reluctant to do what they were told, he banged out a short reply.

TO FLIGHT 52. MAYDAY CALL RECEIVED. STAND BY ON THIS CHANNEL.

# MAYDAY

Brewster pushed the transmit button and prayed that the damned machine wasn't having a bad day. He saw his message displayed before he ran toward the door.

Brewster burst into the large dispatch office and shouted, "Quiet! Listen! Flight 52 is in trouble!" His excited voice cut through the droning noises in the crowded office. The room quickly fell silent except for the ringing of an unanswered telephone.

Jack Miller jumped out of his chair and sent it rolling into the desk behind him. "What happened?" He moved quickly toward Brewster.

Brewster waved the message excitedly. "Here! From the data-link."

Miller grabbed the message and scanned it quickly. He cleared his throat and read from it in loud, halting tones. "Mayday . . . Aircraft damaged . . . radios dead." Miller was not completely surprised. In the back of his mind that empty data on his computer screen had grown more ominous with each passing minute. Yet he had put off making the call that would have resolved the open question. It was natural to want to assume that everything was perfectly all right.

A murmur of excitement arose from the dispatchers in the room and grew into loud, disjointed questions and exclamations of disbelief.

Miller turned to Brewster. "Did you respond?"

"Yes. Yes, I acknowledged. I told them to stand by."

"Okay. Okay. Good, good." Miller's eyes darted around the dispatch office. Everyone was looking at him. He was the senior dispatcher, and 52 was his flight. Either way, it was his responsibility. That's what the handbook said. But things never happened the way they were supposed to. For some reason, this emergency message had come directly to him on the data-link, and not through the normal channels. He was unsure of his next step.

Assistant dispatcher Dennis Evans spoke in a flat monotone that reached him over the noises in the room. "We'd better call someone. Quick."

Miller frowned. Evans was a pain in the ass, but this time he was right. "All right, Dennis," Miller said in a sharp tone. "You make the notifications. Use the emergency handbook. Call everyone on the list. Tell them . . ." Miller looked at the message fluttering in his unsteady hand. He knew that from here on they must be very careful. A thousand people, from their bosses at Trans-United to government officials and media people, would second-guess every move they made, every breath they took. Jack Miller and his dispatch office was suddenly onstage. He looked at Evans. "Tell everyone you call that the nature of 52's emergency is still unknown. Give them only the barest details. Fifty-two sent a blind message on the link. Aircraft damaged. Need help. But they're still transmitting, so it might not be too bad." He paused and looked around the room. "Captain Stuart is the best there is."

Evans reached for his telephone and began speed-dialing.

"Let's move." Miller motioned toward the communications room and led the way through the door.

Miller sat at the data-link console and Brewster stood beside him. A dozen dispatchers squeezed into the small stuffy room and jockeyed for positions around the console.

Miller loosened his tie. "Is the code still set?"

# MAYDAY

Brewster nodded. "Yes, sir." He wondered at what point he would confess his negligence.

Jack Miller began to type.

> TO FLIGHT 52. EXPLAIN NATURE OF
> EMERGENCY. NATURE OF ASSISTANCE
> REQUESTED. AMOUNT OF FUEL REMAINING.
> PRESENT POSITION.

Miller pushed the transmit button and sat back.

The room grew very still. Someone coughed. Some brief remarks were passed in low tones.

The data-link's bell sounded and everyone crowded closer.

Miller motioned to Brewster. "Turn on the overhead monitor. I'll work the console and display. Everyone else step back and read the monitor. I need room to work the keys."

The video screen on the rear wall of the communications room lit up. White letters began to appear on the green repeater screen at the same time they printed on the smaller data-link unit.

> FROM FLIGHT 52. TWO PILOTS
> UNCONSCIOUS. ONE DEAD. I AM A PRIVATE
> PILOT. AIRCRAFT HAS TWO HOLES IN CABIN.
> SUSPECT BOMB. NO FIRE. COMPLETE
> DECOMPRESSION. DEAD AND INJURED. ALL
> INCOHERENT EXCEPT TWO FLIGHT
> ATTENDANTS, TWO PASSENGERS AND
> MYSELF. SEARCHING CABIN FOR OTHERS.
> NEED INSTRUCTIONS TO FLY AIRCRAFT.
> AUTOPILOT ON. ALTITUDE 11,000.
> AIRSPEED 340. MAGNETIC HEADING 325.
> FUEL APPROX. HALF. POSITION UNKNOWN.

# MAYDAY

The dispatchers remained motionless staring up at the screen, reading the message through a second, a third time. Each man had been automatically formulating responses to the emergency, but as the words *Two pilots unconscious, one dead* appeared, all the conventional emergency procedures became invalid. Subconsciously, almost everyone was writing off Flight 52.

Miller stared blankly at the printout. "A bomb. Holes in cabin. Complete decompression. Jesus Christ." Miller knew that had he called earlier for 52's fuel and status report, he would have realized much sooner that something was wrong. He wondered if that would make a difference in the outcome. He looked at the printout again. "Decompression. At that altitude. Good God . . . most of them must be dead or . . ."

Evans came through the door. "Everyone's notified. Johnson is on the way. I only told them what you said. Unknown emergency. Might not be too bad."

"I was wrong," said Miller quietly. He pointed up at the video screen.

Evans stared at the illuminated words. "Oh, shit. How in the name of God could . . . ?"

"All right," said Miller abruptly. "The problem now is to get them down. The floor's open for suggestions. Anyone?"

No one spoke.

Brewster cleared his throat. "Can we figure out their position?"

"That's a good idea," said Miller. "It would help. Do you have their last position?"

Brewster nodded. "Yes, sir. From the last fuel and status report." He walked over to another computer and punched up some data. "It's an hour and a half old, but I can plot a probable course and distance from that based on this new information." He motioned toward the video screen. "It won't be an exact position, but it's better than what we have now."

"Do it," said Miller.

Brewster nodded and jotted down the information from Flight 52's emergency message. "One thing's for certain," he said as he finished. "They're headed the wrong way." He turned and left the room.

"That's a good point," said Evans.

"Yes," Miller agreed coldly. He could see the need for a decision pressing against him.

"Maybe you should tell them to turn around," said Evans.

Miller kept his eyes focused on the screen. There was no textbook solution here. And even with all his years of experience, he had never had to deal with anything like this. All he could think of were the consequences for him as well as for the Straton, her crew and passengers. "He's only a private pilot. He could lose control during the turn." He drummed his fingers on the console. "There's no need for a decision right now. We can let them fly on autopilot until we get their position. Maybe the pilots will regain consciousness. I wonder which one is dead?" he added.

Evans slapped his hand on the console. "Damn it, Jack. We have no real idea how much fuel is left onboard and they're headed the *wrong way.* They're headed for the *Arctic Ocean. Siberia* maybe. No matter what happens we've got to turn them around before they reach the point of no return."

Miller shook his head. "The pilot reported half full.

That's enough fuel to get him to this airport or an airfield in Canada or Alaska. We don't have enough information right now to make a rational decision."

"We may never have enough information for that. Look, Jack—" Evans abruptly stopped speaking. Badgering old Jack Miller had always been pure sport. Evans enjoyed taking easy shots at the man in charge. But suddenly he realized that this was life or death; he'd never made a decision like that, and he didn't want to be responsible for making one now. He realized how awesome the responsibility was and realized, too, that Jack Miller, as senior dispatcher, had had to live with the knowledge that one day he would be called on to help decide the fate of an aircraft in distress. "Do what you want, Jack," he said softly. "You're the boss."

Miller nodded. "Need more input." He knew that his superiors would be there soon. They might say, "Jack, why the hell didn't you *turn them around*?" Christ. He didn't want to look like a procrastinator. That would be the end of him. But he didn't want to look compulsive either. He needed more facts. How good was the pilot? How badly damaged was the aircraft? How much fuel actually remained? What was their position? He looked at the clock. The bosses would start arriving soon.

Brewster rushed into the room. Everyone turned toward him. He began without preamble. "The Straton's estimated position is latitude 47 degrees 10 minutes north, longitude 168 degrees 27 minutes west. They are about 2,500 miles out. A conservative estimate of flying time left is 6 hours and 15 minutes, based on last known fuel report and flying time since then. In about 45 minutes they will pass the point of no return regarding this airport. They may have more or less time, depending on the winds. Luckily, they're already at the best fuel-consumption speed for a low altitude. They'd get better range at a higher altitude, but I guess they can't go up with those holes in the fuselage. I just hope none of the fuel tanks are damaged. If so," Brewster said, waving the paper in his hand, "then all this is out the window."

Miller looked up at the video screen. Flight 52's last message was still written there in white letters etched across the dark green screen. The words appeared to pulsate with a sense of urgency as he stared at them. He turned to the console and typed out a short message.

CAN YOU IDENTIFY AND USE THE
AUTOPILOT HEADING KNOB?

A few seconds later, the message bell sounded.

YES.

There was a murmur of excitement in the room. Miller typed again.

CAN YOU RECOVER IF YOU LOSE CONTROL
OR AUTOPILOT FAILS?

The bell sounded almost immediately.

DOUBTFUL.

Miller swiveled in his chair and faced his fellow dispatchers. "Well?"

Brewster spoke. "I'd trust the autopilot to get through the turns."

A dispatcher near the door spoke. "The Straton's control surfaces may be damaged."

Miller banged out a message.

> ANY INDICATIONS OF DAMAGE TO THE
> FLIGHT CONTROLS?

There was a long minute before the bell rang.

> HOLE IN PORT CABIN NEAR LEADING EDGE
> OF WING. SECOND HOLE OPPOSITE.
> STARBOARD SIDE LARGER. NO VISUAL
> INDICATIONS OF FLIGHT CONTROL DAMAGE.

A dispatcher cleared his throat. "Eventually he has to turn. We can't instruct him further on how to twist the autopilot knob. If it gets away from him, there would be no time to give him flying lessons anyway, even if the chief pilot were sitting here."

A few dispatchers nodded agreement.

Evans spoke in a less strident tone. "I think it would be best if he were heading this way when the bosses get here. Everything else has to develop from there. If he can't execute that autopilot maneuver, well then . . ." His voice trailed off and he made a motion of dismissal with his hand that looked too much like a representation of an aircraft spinning out.

Miller looked into the eyes of each man in the room, then turned back to the data-link. He typed.

> TO FLIGHT 52. SUGGEST YOU TURN
> AIRCRAFT AROUND. UNLESS YOU FEEL IT IS
> TOO DANGEROUS. RECOMMEND MAGNETIC
> HEADING OF 120 DEGREES. WE WILL
> PROVIDE MORE ACCURATE HEADING AFTER
> TURN IS COMPLETE. LEAVE AUTOPILOT ON
> AND ALLOW IT TO EXECUTE TURN BY USING

# MAYDAY

AUTOPILOT TURN CONTROL KNOB. ARE YOU
CAPABLE OF DOING THIS? ADVISE YOUR
INTENTIONS.

As the dispatchers waited for the reply, they debated alternatives and theories about what exactly had happened to the Straton. A chart of the Pacific area was brought in and Flight 52's last reported position was marked. Brewster then marked their estimated present position. A few dispatchers reluctantly left the room to attend to other flights and answer the madly ringing telephones. People from other sections drifted in and were promptly asked to leave. It seemed that Flight 52 was taking a long time to answer, but each man knew what the pilot was going through as he tried to reach a decision. Miller drummed his fingers nervously on the edge of the keyboard.

The bell rang to signal the incoming message, and everyone turned to the video screen.

FROM FLIGHT 52. HAVE PREVIOUSLY
TESTED THE AUTOPILOT TURN CONTROL IN
TEN DEGREE TURN AND RECOVERY.
APPEARS TO FUNCTION. WILL USE IT TO
ACCOMPLISH TURNAROUND TO MAGNETIC
HEADING OF 120 DEGREES. WILL BEGIN
TURN SHORTLY.

There was a short pause in the printout, then it began again.

FOR THE RECORD, MY NAME IS BERRY.
WITH ME ARE FLIGHT ATTENDANTS
CRANDALL AND YOSHIRO. PASSENGERS H.
STEIN AND L. FARLEY.

159

# MAYDAY

Miller looked at the last three lines on his printout. He supposed it was a natural human need to identify oneself, to say, This is my name and if anything happens to me I wanted you to know who you spoke to, who we were. . . . Miller typed out a short message.

GOOD LUCK.

# 7

Commander James Sloan sat on the edge of his swivel chair in the small room known as E-334 buried in the bowels of the supercarrier USS *Nimitz*. His eyes focused on the digital clock as it went through its programmed countdown. "Two minutes."

Retired Rear Admiral Randolf Hennings stood silently on the far side of the room, his attention focused on the view outside the porthole, his back pointedly turned to the Commander. He wanted a few moments of peace before the finale began. He watched the gentle swells of the sea. But today his mind was too troubled to be soothed.

"One minute," Sloan announced. He leaned forward and reread the carefully worded order lying on the console deck. He had, he believed, written a minor masterpiece of persuasive argument. The stimuli, the right buzzwords, would produce the conditioned response. "Do you want to hear this before I transmit?"

Hennings wheeled around. "No. Just do it, Commander. Let's get it over with."

Sloan didn't respond, but stared hard at Hennings. He tried to get a reading on the condition of the man's mind.

Hennings took a few paces toward Sloan. "Your pilot may not go along with it." He couldn't decide how he wanted Matos to respond.

"We'll know soon enough." Sloan looked at the paper again. As the situation stood now, he was guilty of criminal negligence and dereliction of duty. But if he transmitted this order and Matos disregarded it and made a full report, then they had him for attempted homicide.

Hennings moved closer and glanced at the written order. "He may not believe this is a lawful order. He may report . . . us."

"Admiral," Sloan replied, "in the new Navy, we cover up all problems of race and gender, problems of poor morale, discipline problems, problems of hetero- and homosexual behavior, and in fact we've become masters of deceit and paragons of political correctness. We had to lie about the death of that female aircraft carrier pilot so it looked like mechanical failure rather than heart failure, which it was. We are awash in a sea of self-serving bullshit. The people in Washington want us to lie about things *they* want us to lie about. So it's no sweat and no big deal to lie about things *we* want to lie about." Sloan added, "Matos, like everyone else in this unhappy Navy, understands all of this. The only report he'll make is the one I write for him to sign. I guarantee it."

But Sloan wasn't quite that sure about Matos. As he

watched Hennings, however, he was reasonably sure his words had hit their mark. Sloan knew exactly which of the old man's buttons to push.

Hennings remained silent.

Sloan's mind went back to Matos. Matos could be a problem, but Sloan didn't intend to give Matos enough time to think. Matos would hear the order and obey automatically. The command would enter Matos's brain through his headset like the voice of God. James Sloan believed that the measure of a good leader was how much he sounded like God. What most men wanted was to be told what to do. A small bell sounded, and Sloan looked at the countdown clock. It read 00:00. He picked up the microphone.

Hennings wanted to stall. "I wonder if burying this mistake in the ocean will be the end of it. The dead have a way of coming back."

"Don't try to spook me, Admiral. But if blaming me makes you feel better, go ahead. That's fine. I don't care. I only want to get this job done."

Hennings's face flushed with anger. The knowledge that Sloan was on the mark kept him from responding. Sloan was unquestionably an immoral man. But what gnawed at Hennings was the thought that he himself was not much . . . not any better. This was not quite like the sinking of the *Mercer*, and Hennings knew it. Yes, it was easy to blame James Sloan. But Hennings knew better. He was doing nothing to stop Sloan. He looked up. "Get on with it."

"I am, Admiral." Sloan reached across the electronics panel and turned on the transmitter. He checked the power output, then verified that the voice scrambler was operating properly. Without it, he would never send a message like this one. To all the eavesdropping electronic ears in the world, Commander James Sloan's voice would be gibberish, but to Lieutenant Peter Matos, the message would come in loud and clear. "Navy three-four-seven, do you read, Homeplate?" Sloan stared at the console speaker and waited.

Hennings moved closer and also fixed his eyes on the speaker.

"Roger, Homeplate. Navy three-four-seven read. Go ahead."

Sloan took a deep breath and cleared his throat. "Lieutenant Matos, this is Commander Sloan." He paused.

"Roger, Commander."

"We have consulted with our commanders at the highest levels and they have advised us on a course of action which will take extraordinary skill and courage on your part. The situation as it now stands has been complicated by several outside factors beyond our control. I will brief you on the details when you come home. The important thing that we have learned is that the accident is in no way our fault. The Straton was off course and did not report its position. How do you read?"

"Read you fine. Go ahead."

"We have been informed that it is physiologically impossible for anyone to have survived a decompression at the altitude at which the accident took place. The problem we face now has to do with that derelict craft. It is a threat to sea and air navigation that must be eliminated. Only a pilot with your personal skills could accomplish this."

"Christ," Hennings murmured in the background.

# MAYDAY

Sloan spoke quickly into the microphone. "Wait one." He turned in his seat and glared at Hennings, but he was thankful for the break. A few seconds' pause would do Matos good.

Hennings leaned over, very close to Sloan. "You should try being honest with him," Hennings said in a low voice. "Tell him you want him to destroy the damned evidence. Tell him you want him to knock it down and stay over it until he makes sure it has sunk. Tell him also that it's possible that someone onboard is alive and well enough to transmit a message. You owe him that much, Commander."

Sloan fixed Hennings with a cold stare and spoke through clenched teeth. "Don't be a fool. I'm making it easier for him, not harder. The last goddamned thing he wants is the truth. The truth," Sloan snarled, "is that the whole damned thing is Matos's fault." He turned back to the microphone. "All right, Lieutenant, we have just received our final authorization." He lifted the written text and noticed that his hands were trembling, which was unusual for him. "You are to fire your remaining missile in such a way as to make inoperable the Straton's autopilot. Since the test missiles weren't equipped with explosive warheads, this can only be accomplished by a direct hit in the area of the cockpit of the derelict craft. The accuracy of your shot is well beyond the profile that you've been trained for. The assignment is beyond the normal call of duty. We, and everyone here, are depending on you and praying for your success." He paused. "Take your time, but try to accomplish this mission within the next few minutes. Good luck, Peter. Acknowledge, please."

A silence settled over the small room. Sloan made an exaggerated gesture of crossing his fingers.

Hennings thought that he had never seen anything so obscene in his life. He turned away, then retreated to the porthole to wait. Perhaps Lieutenant Peter Matos, whoever he was, had more moral courage than they did.

The radio crackled. Hennings turned his head toward the speaker.

"Roger, Homeplate. Proceeding with new mission profile. Out."

Sloan settled back in his chair. Out of habit, he set the countdown clock for five minutes.

Hennings felt a tear forming in his eye and wiped it before Sloan could see it.

Peter Matos stared blankly out the windshield of his F-18. His reply had been automatic. Now he was beginning to fully understand what he was supposed to do. He looked at his console clock, then reached out to push his radio-transmit button. What was he going to ask Commander Sloan? What was left unclear? Nothing that concerned him. He drew his hand away from the radio button and rested it listlessly at his side.

He glanced out of the cockpit. The Straton 797 maintained its heading and altitude with an unerring precision. Far too precise a flight to have been guided by any human hand. He watched carefully for a full minute. He was satisfied that the Straton was indeed being flown by its computerized autopilot.

He settled back in his flight chair. Commander

# MAYDAY

Sloan's earlier orders had not made a great deal of sense. Matos had been certain that Sloan was leading up to something. And he knew, deep inside, what it was. Even though the actual order had now been sent, it was still hard to believe.

Matos considered his options. There were none, really, that he could exercise without a great deal of unpleasantness. The facts were that the Straton had been off course, everyone aboard was now dead, the craft presented a hazard of some sort, and the top brass wanted it brought down. Simple. Follow orders. They would take care of everything. They would look after Peter Matos once he completed the mission.

He stared at his fuel gauges. Less than half full. He glanced at his compass. With every passing minute he delayed, he was getting farther away from the *Nimitz*. Every minute of delay now would add another minute to his trip home. He looked again at his clock. Three minutes had already gone by. He desperately wanted to be done with this within the next few minutes. More than anything else he wanted to be back in his bunk on the *Nimitz*. That was his home—he wanted to go home.

Without another disturbing thought, he began to maneuver his fighter into a better position for the missile strike.

His mind was now filled with the logistics of the difficult shot. The technical trade-offs were complex. The derelict Straton was a large stable target, but its very size presented a problem. How many dummy warheads would it take to bring it down? The first one had not done it. A half-dozen more might not do it. He had only one left. He was reminded of a bull in the ring being stuck with lances and banderillas.

# MAYDAY

The Phoenix missile would hit the Straton. That was no problem. It could do that automatically. But he had to hit a particular spot. He needed a brain shot.

The solution, now that he had a chance to study the problem, was suddenly obvious. He had to fly close to the cockpit and fire his missile at point-blank range. With no exploding warhead he could do this with a fair degree of safety. Then he had to pull out quickly and turn away. The Phoenix would strike the cockpit before its elaborate guidance system could alter its course and steer it toward the target's midsection. Matos managed a small smile. He had outwitted the designers of the weapon. The pilot was still in control after all.

Matos knew that selecting the best angle for the shot would have to be a compromise. He slid his fighter to the starboard side of the Straton. The small shadow of his craft passed over the gleaming silver airframe of the huge airliner. He looked down. Normally, a full side view of the target would be best, but he saw that a missile shot from that angle would be far too risky. He was liable to miss the aircraft entirely because of the high-closure speeds and his need to do the firing manually.

He slid his craft back over the top of the Straton and a hundred yards behind its tail. The shot would have to be made from the twelve-o'clock-high position, right down into the dome that was the lounge and cockpit. The angle would have to be such that the missile would enter the roof of the lounge, pass through the cockpit, and exit from the lower nose. That would wipe out everything on the flight deck. He reached for the manual gun sight above the glare shield and snapped it into place. He looked through it. The gunnery crosshairs seemed to bob and weave as the relative positions of the two aircraft changed.

Matos set his experienced hands to work on the flight control and soon had the calibrated crosshairs steadied and within range. The bulge of the upper lounge and cockpit filled the scope. The sight's bull's-eye swayed back and forth over the protruding dome.

Matos reached down without taking his eyes off the target and turned off the Phoenix's safety switch. He moved his hand laterally and placed his finger on the firing button. He took a deep breath and began nudging the F-18's control stick forward. The fighter came in closer. The bull's-eye was dead center over the dome and holding steady. The Straton's towering tail loomed up in front of him. He would fire when he passed over the tail. He judged that from tail to dome was almost two hundred feet, and that was a good yardstick to use. Closer than that would expose him to danger from debris. And if the stricken airliner suddenly rolled, the wing could come up and hit his fighter.

He looked through the gun sight. Thirty feet from the tail. He had never flown this close to such a large aircraft. Twenty feet. The huge Straton was spread out below him like the deck of a carrier. Ten feet. He could see the rivets in the tail. His heart started to beat heavily in his chest.

The nose of the F-18 passed over the tail of the Straton. The bull's-eye covered the center of the silver dome. The glare of the silvery skin made Matos squint. He exhaled deeply and pressed his finger against the firing button.

John Berry was anxious to get on with the maneuver, yet he was doing nothing. He ran his eyes over the instruments, trying to appear as though he were doing something important.

"John?"

"What?"

Sharon Crandall looked anxious. "Is anything wrong?"

"No. Just a few checks." He paused. "Try to call Barbara again. I want her to know we're turning. When we start to bank, she's liable to become frightened. And tell her to stay away from the holes."

"Okay." Sharon Crandall set the interphone for the mid-ship station and pressed the button repeatedly. "She doesn't answer," she said in a trembling voice.

"Try another station."

Crandall selected the aft flight-attendant station and pressed the button. Almost immediately a muffled voice came back, nearly drowned out by the sound of rushing wind and odd babbling voices in the background. "Barbara, can you hear me? Is that you?"

"Yes. I'm at the rear station," Yoshiro answered in a clear voice.

"Are you all right?"

"Yes."

Crandall turned to Berry. "I've got her. Thank God. She's at the rear station. She's okay."

Berry nodded.

"Barbara, come back up," Crandall said.

"Give me five more minutes. I have to check one more lavatory. I don't see the steward—Jeff Price. Maybe I'll go below to the galley."

Crandall glanced at Berry.

Berry was ready to begin the turn. "Okay. Tell her we're about to turn. Stay where she is until the turn is completed."

Crandall nodded and spoke into the phone. "Wait in the rear station. John is going to turn the aircraft. We've made contact on the data-link. Everything is all right. We're heading in. Stay there until the turn is completed. Take care. See you soon. Okay?"

There was a lighter note in Barbara Yoshiro's voice. "Yes. Good. Very good."

Berry took the phone. "Barbara, this is John Berry. How are the passengers?"

There was a short pause, then the voice came back. "I . . . I don't know. They seem . . . better."

Berry shook his head. They were not better. They never would be. Better meant worse. More animated. More dangerous. "Be very, very careful. See you later."

"Okay."

The phone clicked dead.

Berry exchanged glances with Crandall, then looked over his shoulder into the lounge. Stein had taken the news about the data-link connection calmly, almost without interest. He had other things on his mind. "Harold. Linda," Berry shouted back to them. "Hold on to something. We're turning. Back to California. Be home in a few hours."

Stein looked up from his post at the head of the stairs and waved distractedly.

Berry turned and positioned himself carefully in his seat. He reached out and put his hand on the autopilot heading control knob. He had a vague awareness of a shadow passing over the starboard side of the cockpit's windshield. He glanced at Sharon Crandall, but she seemed unaware of it. He half stood and leaned over her seat and looked out the side windshield. He craned his neck back toward the tail. Nothing. A cloud probably. But he could see no clouds.

"What's wrong?"

"Nothing." He sat down and again placed his hand over the small heading knob. "Okay. We're heading home." Slowly, a few degrees at a time, he began turning the knob. The big supersonic craft banked to the right.

---

For a brief instant, Matos thought that his aircraft was responsible for the apparent movement between them. The action of a missile release would do that. But he had not, he realized, pressed the button hard enough to make contact. His missile-fire light was not on.

The large Straton transport moved rapidly across Matos's gun sight. He removed his hand from the firing button and raised his eyes from the crosshairs. The Straton was in a shallow bank, moving away from the fighter.

*Turbulence*, was Matos's first thought. *No. Impossible. There is no turbulence.* His own aircraft flew smoothly. Yet the 797 was banking. Instinctively, he banked with it and lined up his gun sights again. The Straton moved at a steady rate. Gracefully. Deliberately. Intentionally.

Matos sat up straight in his seat. His hand came down hard on his radio transmit button. "Homeplate! Homeplate! Navy three-four-seven. The Straton is turning. Banking." He followed the airliner as it began its slow, wide circle. "It's going through a north heading. Still turning. Approaching a northeasterly heading. The turn remains steady. The bank angle is approximately thirty degrees and steady. The airspeed and altitude are unchanged." Matos kept his transmit button locked on so he could not receive, and kept up a continuous report of the airliner's progress.

As gently as it had begun, the Straton's bank angle started to lessen. Matos watched as the airliner began to roll to wings-level position. He placed his fighter twenty-five yards astern of the 797.

Matos could see from the rate of the Straton's turn and the symmetry of its entry and exit that the control inputs were being measured electronically. Only a computer-controlled autopilot could provide that sort of precise motion control. He radioed, "Homeplate, the Straton is still on autopilot." But he also knew, beyond any doubt, that there was a human hand working that autopilot.

Matos looked up at the manual gun sight, then down at the unguarded firing mechanism as though he were seeing them both for the first time. *Oh, Jesus.*

His hand was cramped, and he realized he had been pressing hard on his radio transmit button to keep possession of the radio channel between him and the *Nimitz*. But he knew he could not keep the channel away from Sloan forever. He spoke, to justify his finger on the transmit button, and to give himself time to think. "It was a deliberate turn. Someone is flying the aircraft—someone is working the autopilot. I could fly alongside the cockpit to verify." He released the button.

"No!" shouted Sloan. "This is an order. Stay in trail formation. Do nothing to attract attention until you receive orders to do so. And keep your hand off the transmit button unless you are transmitting. Don't try to cut me off again. Do you understand?"

Matos nodded, almost meekly. "Roger. Sorry, I was just . . . excited and . . . must have been gripping the stick. . . . Over."

"Roger. Are you still monitoring the radio channels?"

Matos glanced down at his side console. His monitoring equipment was still on, still silent. "That's affirmative. No radio activity from the Straton on the normal frequencies."

"Okay, Peter. Stay in trail until further notice. Acknowledge."

"Roger, I read, stay in trail."

"Roger, out."

Matos ran his tongue across his parched lips and looked down at his compass. Reluctantly, he reached for his transmit button. When a commander gave an "out" it was the equivalent of, *Don't call me, I'll call you. End of conversation.* But Matos had things he wanted to say. "Homeplate."

There was a short pause. "What is it, Navy?"

"Homeplate, whoever is flying that airliner knows what they're doing. The Straton is flying steadily. Its new heading is 120 degrees. They are heading toward California."

The silence in Matos's headset seemed to last a long time.

"Roger. Anything further?"

Matos could not read the flat tone in Sloan's voice.

He wondered what was going through the Commander's mind now. Why had they thought everyone on-board the Straton was dead? Matos could not hold himself back from asking the obvious question. "Homeplate, I don't understand. Why am I staying out of sight of the cockpit?" He settled back and waited through the long, expected silence.

After a full minute his headset crackled. "Because, Lieutenant, I ordered you to." The voice was no longer neutral. Sloan's words continued, "We are all ass-deep in bad trouble. If you don't want to spend the rest of your fucking life in Portsmouth Naval Prison, you will stay out of sight of that cockpit. Suppose, Lieutenant, you think about why you should keep out of sight and you radio me back with the answer when you figure it out. Okay?"

Matos nodded again and stared at his hands wrapped around the control stick. "Roger."

"Homeplate, *out*."

Matos pushed aside the manual gun sight and snapped back the safety cover of the firing switch. He sat back, deep in his upholstered flight chair, and stared down at the Straton until his eyes went out of focus. He closed his eyes, then made his mind go blank. He erased all the extraneous information he had accumulated and started at the beginning, at the moment he had first seen two targets on his radar screen. Slowly, he realized what Sloan was getting to. Now he knew precisely what he might yet be called on to do. *Say it, Peter*, he thought. *Murder*.

# 8

The Straton leveled, and in the cockpit the sensation of the slight increase in G force lessened, then disappeared. The cockpit returned to a straight and level altitude.

John Berry smiled, and Sharon Crandall smiled back. "We did it! John, that was great. Very, very good."

Berry couldn't suppress a small laugh. "Okay. Okay, we're heading in. Great. The control surfaces respond. We can turn." He felt the wide grin still plastered across his face and knew he looked foolish. He thought ahead to the landing he would have to attempt, and the grin faded without much effort. Flying, he reflected, was like walking a high wire. One slip and it's finished. No do-overs. "All right, let's bang out a message." He reached out and typed.

FROM FLIGHT 52: TURN COMPLETE.
HEADING 120 DEGREES. ADVISE.

He pushed the transmit button.

The incoming message bell sounded almost immediately.

> TO FLIGHT 52: VERY NICE WORK. STAND BY.
> RELAX. EVERYONE HERE IS WORKING ON
> BRINGING YOU HOME.

Berry nodded. *Home.* An evocative word. Its meaning was changing every minute. "Relax," he read. "Okay. I'm relaxed. How are you?"

Sharon Crandall nodded. She looked at Berry out of the corner of her eye. *Very nice work.* Very cool. Competent. Most people would be in a complete state of panic by now. She'd seen men—macho types—whimpering in their seats during an electrical storm. She'd seen a whole football team on the verge of hysteria as their aircraft hit heavy turbulence. She glanced at John Berry. Here was a man who was a sort of low-key salesman who occasionally flew his company aircraft—and he'd acted admirably. More so than she or Barbara had, in fact. She thought she liked John Berry very much. "Do you want something to drink? A glass of water? Something stronger?"

"No, thanks."

She nodded. There were undoubtedly all types of powerful forces at work up here that would draw her to him, but even on the ground, she thought, he would be a person she would want to know. "I'll call Barbara."

"Yes. She should be on her way. Try one of the closer stations."

"Okay." She switched to the mid-ship station and pressed the call button.

There was no answer.

She tried every station, including the below-decks galley.

Berry looked back into the lounge and shouted, "Harold. Call down to Barbara."

Stein called down. He looked up at Berry and shook his head.

Berry reached for the PA microphone, then hesitated. "No. That makes them excited." He tapped his fingers impatiently on the steering column. "She's probably between stations. Or in the galley elevator. We'll wait." He glanced at Sharon Crandall before he turned his head back to the windshield. If she were a bit older . . . But why was he thinking about that now? It was odd how people made long-range plans in terminal situations. His father had planned his spring garden the winter he was dying of cancer. "Sharon, what are you going to do after this? I mean, would you fly again?"

She looked at him and gave him a very big smile. "After this, John, I'll take one week off. Maybe even two weeks." She laughed, but then her expression turned serious. "After that, I'll report for duty as usual. If you have a bad experience in flight, you *have* to go back. Otherwise, the rest of your life becomes a series of avoidances. Besides, what else would I do at my age? Who's going to pay me this kind of money?" She looked out at the horizon line. "And what about you? Will you stop flying that little whatever-it-is for your company?"

"Skymaster. No. Of course not."

"Good." She hesitated, then leaned over toward him and placed her hand on his arm. "How do you feel about landing this plane?"

Berry looked directly at her. Her countenance and

the language of her body were unmistakably clear and had little to do with the question. Yet there was nothing brazen about her. Just an honest offering. Within hours they might be alive on the ground. More likely, they would be dead. Still, her offer did not seem out of place. "You'll help me. We can land this plane." He felt slightly awkward, a little flustered at her touch and her sudden intimacy.

Sharon Crandall settled back in her seat and stared out her side window. She thought briefly about her last live-in lover, Nick, from crew scheduling. Emptiness, boredom. Sex and television. In the final analysis, they'd shared nothing, really, and his leaving left no emptiness, no loneliness beyond what she'd felt when he was there. He had left the same way he had arrived, like a gray afternoon sliding into a dark night. But she was still lonely. "Why don't you send a message from each one of us to someone on the ground?" she said. She instantly wondered whom she would send her message to. Her mother, probably.

Berry considered the idea. "No," he finally said. "That would be a little . . . melodramatic. Don't you think so? A little too terminal. We have some time yet. I'll send one for everyone later. Who do you want to . . . ?"

She ignored his question. "Your wife must be frantic."

Berry considered several answers. *My insurance is paid up. That should take the edge off any franticness. Or, Jennifer hasn't been frantic since she lost her Bloomingdale's charge card.* He said, "I'm sure the airline is keeping everyone informed."

"That's true." She changed the subject abruptly.

"You've got good control of the airplane," she said with some authority. "The flight controls are working okay. And we've still got nearly half our fuel." She nodded toward the fuel gauges.

"Yes," Berry answered, recalling that he had pointed that out to her only ten minutes before. "That's true. It should be enough fuel." But he knew that headwinds or bad weather could change that. As far as the flight controls were concerned, all he knew for certain was that he could make a right-hand turn and level out. He had no information about turning left or going up or down.

"I remember," Crandall added, "how Captain Stuart once told me that as long as the flight controls worked and the engines had a steady supply of fuel, then the situation wasn't hopeless."

"That's true," said Berry. The mention of Stuart's name made him look back over his shoulder. At the far end of the lounge, the two pilots still lay motionless on the thick blue rug, near the piano. Berry turned and scanned the Straton's flight instruments and autopilot. Everything was steady. He stood. "I'm going back to the lounge to see what's going on."

"Okay."

"Scan the instruments. If anything seems wrong, yell."

"You bet."

"If the data-link bell—"

"I'll call you."

"Okay. And watch the autopilot closely." He leaned over her seat and put his right hand casually on her shoulder. He pointed with his left hand. "See this light?"

# MAYDAY

"Yes."

"It's the autopilot disconnect light. If it shows amber, call me—fast."

"Roger." She turned her head toward him and smiled.

Berry straightened up. "Okay. Be right back." He turned and walked into the lounge.

The flight attendant in the upper lounge, Terri O'Neil, was walking around now. Berry didn't like that. The attractive woman on the horseshoe-shaped couch had unfastened her seat belt and was staring out the porthole. The remaining three men and one woman continued to sit on the couch, making spastic, senseless movements with their arms. One of the men had unfastened his seat belt and tried repeatedly to stand, but couldn't seem to manage it.

Berry could see that, as Barbara Yoshiro said, they were all getting better—physically. Mentally, they were more inquisitive. They were beginning to think, but to think things that were not good. Dark things. Dangerous things.

The Straton, reflected Berry, was a protected environment, like an egg. Puncture the shell of a fertilized egg with a pin and the embryo would not survive. And if it did, it would be changed in some terrible way. He formed a mental picture of the Straton sitting serenely on the airport ramp, two small holes on the sides the only outward indication of anything being amiss. The stairs were wheeled up. The crowd cheered. The doors opened. The first passengers appeared. . . . He shook his head and looked up.

Terri O'Neil wandered toward the cockpit door. Berry stepped up to her. He took her shoulder and turned her around. Terri pushed his hand away roughly and spoke to him as though she were berating him for touching her, but the words were gibberish. Berry was reminded of his daughter at fourteen months old. He waited until the flight attendant ambled off, away from the cockpit door, then began walking to the far side of the lounge toward Stein, who was leaning against the rail of the staircase. Stein seemed unaware of Berry's presence and continued to stare down the open stairway. "How is it going?" Berry asked.

Stein pointed down the stairs.

Berry leaned over. A group of men and women were staring up at him, mouths drooling and faces covered with the now familiar, repugnant pattern of blood and vomit. A few of the people pointed up to him. Someone called out; a woman laughed. Berry could hear what he thought were children crying. One man pushed his way to the base of the stairs and spoke directly to Berry, trying hard to be understood. The man became frustrated, and shouted. The woman laughed again.

Berry stepped back from the stairwell, turned, and looked at Linda Farley. She slid off the piano bench and took a few steps toward him. Berry said, "Stay there, Linda."

Stein said to Berry, "I told her to stay away from the stairs. Although this," he motioned around the big lounge, "this is not much better."

Berry asked the girl, "What is it, Linda?"

She hesitated. "I'm hungry, Mr. Berry. Can I get something to eat soon?"

Berry smiled at her. "Well . . . how about a Coke?"

"I looked." She motioned toward the bar. "There's nothing left."

"Well, I don't think there's any food up here. Can you wait awhile?"

She looked disappointed. "I guess."

"How are the two pilots?"

"The same."

"Take good care of them."

Linda Farley was getting all of life's adversities in one big dose. Hunger, thirst, fatigue, fear, death. "Just a little while longer, sweetheart. We'll be home soon." He turned. It occurred to him that he was hungry and thirsty, too. And if he and Linda Farley were hungry and thirsty, then so were many of the people below. He wondered if that would stimulate them to acts of aggression.

"Down!" Stein yelled. "Go down!" Berry moved quickly to the stairs. A man was halfway up.

Stein took a coin from his pocket and threw it, striking the man in the face. "Down! Go down!"

The man retreated a step.

Stein turned to Berry. "Do you have anything I can throw?"

Berry reached into his pocket and handed Stein some change. "I don't like the looks of this, Harold."

Stein nodded. "Neither do I."

Berry looked around the lounge. "How are these people behaving?"

"Erratic. They make me nervous. Too close."

Berry watched Terri O'Neil walking awkwardly toward the cockpit again. He wished he could close and lock the damaged door. The flight attendant stood a few feet from the door and stared into the cockpit, her eyes fixed on Sharon Crandall, who didn't seem aware of the other flight attendant's presence. Berry glanced back at Stein. "I think, as a precaution, we might want to help these people get downstairs."

Stein nodded. "Yes. But I'd like to bring my family up."

Berry turned and faced him. "That's not possible, Harold. I don't think it's really fair." Berry wished that Stein would just accept things as they were, but he doubted that Stein would.

"Fair? Who the hell cares about *fair*? That's my *family* I'm talking about. Who put you in charge here?"

"Mr. Stein, it's entirely too risky to bring your family up here."

"Why?"

"Well . . . anything could happen. It might start a procession up the stairs. We really can't have people in the lounge any longer. They may go into the cockpit. Bump against something . . . they'd be disturbing—"

"I'll watch my family," Stein interrupted. His voice was firm. "My wife and two little girls . . . Debbie and Susan . . . they wouldn't be in anyone's way. . . ." He lowered his head and covered his face with his hands.

Berry waited, then put his hand on Stein's shoulder. "I'm sorry. But there's nothing you can do for them now."

Stein looked up. "Or ever?"

Berry avoided his eyes. "I'm not a doctor. I don't know anything about this condition."

"Don't you?" Stein suddenly took a step down the staircase. "There *is* something I can do for them now. I can get them away from the others. Away from . . ." He looked down the spiral stairs. "I don't want them down there. Can't you see what's happening down there? *Can't you?*"

Berry gripped Stein's arm firmly. He nodded reluctantly. "All right, Harold. All right. After Barbara gets back, we can help these people down into the cabin. Then you can bring your family up. Okay?"

Stein let Berry draw him back up the step. Finally, he nodded. "Okay. I'll wait."

Linda Farley called out. "Mr. Berry!"

Berry walked quickly toward the piano where the girl was kneeling beside Stuart and McVary. "What is it?"

"This man opened his eyes." She pointed to Stuart.

Berry kneeled down and looked into the Captain's wide, staring eyes. After several seconds, Berry reached out and closed Stuart's eyelids, then pulled the blanket over the Captain's face.

"Is he dead?"

Berry looked at the girl. "Yes. He is."

She nodded. "Is everyone going to die?"

"No."

"Will my mother die, too?"

"No. She's going to be all right."

"Can she come up here like Mr. Stein's family?"

Berry was fairly certain that Linda Farley's mother was lying dead in the rubble or had been sucked out of the aircraft. But even if she were alive . . . Berry's mind whirled with the possible answers—lies, really—but none of them was even close to being adequate. "No. She can't come up here."

"Why not?"

He stood quickly and turned away from the dead

pilot. He said to Linda, "Trust me. Okay? Just trust me and do what I say."

Linda Farley sat back against the leg of the piano and pulled her knees up to her chin. She buried her face in her hands and began to sob. "I want my mother."

Berry leaned over her and stroked her hair. "Yes, I know. I know." He straightened up. He was not very good at this. He remembered other occasions of bereavement in his own family. He'd never had the right words, was never able to bring comfort. He turned and walked back toward the cockpit. He took Terri O'Neil firmly by the shoulders and pushed her away from the door.

The glow of his technical triumphs was dying quickly against the cold realities of the personal tragedies around him.

Berry entered the cockpit.

Sharon Crandall was on the interphone. "Hold on, Barbara. John's back in the cockpit." She looked up at Berry. "Barbara's all right. How's everything back there?"

Berry sat heavily in his seat. "Okay." He paused. "Not really. The passengers are getting a little . . . troublesome." He cleared his throat and said, "The Captain is dead."

Sharon Crandall closed her eyes and lowered her head. She said softly, "Oh, damn it." She felt a deep sadness, a sense of loss over Captain Stuart's death. The signs were becoming ominous again.

"Sharon?"

She looked up. "I'm all right. Here. Barbara wants to talk to you about some wires."

# MAYDAY

Berry took the phone. "Barbara? What's up? Where are you?"

"In the midsection." Her voice sounded distant, and the whistling of the rushing air and the jet engines was louder. "There's a bundle of wires hanging down from the ceiling near the bigger hole. Some of the passengers brushed against them and nothing happened. There doesn't seem to be any electricity in them."

Berry thought for a moment. Everything in the Straton seemed to be working except the voice radios. Severed cables might account for that. He hoped the wires had nothing to do with the flight controls. "They might be antenna wires." It was logical that on a supersonic jet, the antennas would be mounted in some low-drag area like the tail. He suspected that the data-link utilized a different signal and a flat-plate antenna, which would be near the noise. That was why the link worked while the radios didn't.

"Do you want me to try to reconnect them?"

Berry smiled. In a technical age, everyone was a technician. Still, it was a heads-up suggestion and a gutsy one, too. "No. You'd need splicing tools and it would take too long, anyway." If those wires were involved somehow with the controls, he'd have to go down eventually and try to connect them himself. "They're not important." Something else was bothering him, and Barbara Yoshiro was in a position to clear it up. "Listen, Barbara, did you see any signs of the explosion? Anything like burnt seats? Charred metal? You know?"

There was a pause. "No. Not really. No." There was another silence. "It's odd. There is absolutely nothing that looks like an explosion—except for the mess and the holes."

Berry nodded. That had been his impression. If the holes had been in the top and bottom of the fuselage, he would have suspected that they'd passed through a meteor shower. He knew that it was an infinitely rare phenomenon, even at 62,000 feet. Could a meteor travel horizontally? Berry had no idea, although it seemed unlikely. Should he put something out about this on the data-link? Did it matter? "Barbara, how are the passengers?"

"About half of them are still pretty quiet. But some of the others are wandering around now. The turn stirred them up, I think. There's been some fighting."

Berry thought that her voice sounded cool and uninvolved, like a good reporter's. "Watch yourself. Work your way slowly. No abrupt movements."

"I know."

"There are people congregating at the bottom of the stairs," he informed her.

"I can't see the stairs from here, but I can see part of the crowd on both sides of the forward galley and lavatories."

"When you get to the interphone in that galley, call me. Or shout to Stein. One of us will help you back up."

"Okay."

"Take care of yourself. Here's Sharon."

---

Barbara Yoshiro didn't feel like talking much longer. As she looked out of the flight-attendant station in the

midsection galley, she saw that the passengers were beginning to pay too much attention to her. The station
was a cul-de-sac, and her only advantage with these
people lay in her mobility.

"Barbara?"

"Yes, I'm coming back now."

"Is it very bad? Should I come down?" Sharon
Crandall asked.

"No." Yoshiro put a light tone in her voice. "I've
been a flight attendant long enough to know how to
avoid groping hands." The joke came out badly and
she added quickly, "They're not paying any particular
attention to me. See you in a few minutes." She replaced the interphone and stepped into the aisle. She
kept her back against the bulkhead of the lavatory and
stared into the cavern that lay between the front of the
airliner and herself, then looked back toward the tail.

The flimsy partitions of the Straton's interior had
been swept away by the decompression. Its entire
length, which she remembered being told was two
hundred feet, lay exposed, except for the three galley-
lavatory compartments. They rose, blue plastic cubicles
in a row, from floor to ceiling—one near the tail, the
midship one she was standing at, and the one in the first-
class cabin that blocked her view of the spiral staircase.

Dangling oxygen masks, uprooted seats, and dislodged wall and ceiling panels hung everywhere. Sixty
feet from her, midway between the galley she was
standing at and the first-class section, were two bomb
holes—if that's what they were.

Barbara Yoshiro studied the possible routes she
might take through the aircraft. She could see that she
had two return routes to choose from. The aisle on the

left—the one she had come down earlier—was now nearly packed with milling passengers. The aisle on the right had only a few people in it, but it contained more debris. Worse, it passed very near to the larger of the two holes in the fuselage. Even from where she stood, she could see the Pacific and the leading edge of the wing through the gaping hole. Perhaps, she thought, she'd travel up the right aisle, then cross over before she got to the open area of debris between the holes. While her eyes fixed on the scene in front of her, she failed to notice that a young man in the aisle next to her was watching her closely.

She drew a deep breath and took a few tentative steps up the aisle. The stench was overpowering despite the fresh, cold breeze, and she felt queasy. She looked up as she walked, her eyes darting quickly in all directions. About a hundred men and women still sat in their seats, blocking the spaces between the rows. Another hundred or so stood in groups or by themselves blocking the main aisles. Some were walking aimlessly, bumping into people, falling into the aisles or into the seats, then getting up again and continuing. Everyone was babbling or moaning. If they would only remain quiet she might be able to ignore them.

It was their clothes, too, she realized, almost as much as their faces or their noises, that gave them away. Their smart suits and dresses were tattered; some of them were half naked. Most people had one shoe or were shoeless. Almost everyone's clothes were stained with blood and splattered with vomit.

Yoshiro noticed that some of the passengers had been wounded in the explosion. She hadn't looked at them, she realized, as individual people who were injured, but as a great amorphous thing whose color was gray and whose many eyes were black. Now she could see a woman whose ear was grotesquely hanging, a man who had lost two fingers. A small girl was touching a terrible-looking wound on her thigh. She was crying. Pain, Yoshiro realized, was one thing that they could still feel. But why could they still feel that and not feel anything else? Why couldn't the sense of pain have died in them, too, and spared them that last agony?

She saw a body lying in the aisle in front of her. It was Jeff Price, the steward. Where were the rest of the flight attendants? She looked around carefully and slowly for the familiar white-and-blue uniforms.

Kneeling almost motionless in the shaft of bright sunlight in front of her, she spotted another flight attendant. The girl had her back toward her, but Barbara Yoshiro could see by the long black hair that it was Mary Gomez. The flight attendant appeared oblivious to everything around her, oblivious to the people stumbling into her, oblivious to the wind blowing her long hair in swirls around her head and neck. Barbara Yoshiro remembered that Mary Gomez had rung up the below-decks galley and asked if she could help. She remembered Sharon's words very clearly. *No, thanks, Mary. Barbara and I are nearly finished. We'll be up in a minute.* It had actually been almost five minutes before they were ready to come up. Had they come up sooner . . . Her religion did not stress fate, but this kind of thing made one wonder about God's sense of timing. She turned away from Mary Gomez.

Someone came up behind her and grabbed her shoulder. She froze, then slowly moved aside. A boy of about eighteen stumbled past her. Someone in the seat she was leaning against grabbed her right wrist. Gently, she pulled it loose and continued up the aisle, her heart beginning to beat rapidly, her mouth dry and pasty.

Yoshiro got a grip on herself and began edging into a corner row of seats. She sidestepped past two seats, then stopped when she saw she couldn't squeeze by the two men who were sitting in the last two seats. Carefully, she climbed over onto the empty seat in front of her and made her way into the left aisle.

She approached the wide area of rubble where stark sunlight illuminated the grotesque dead shapes mingled with the debris. Passengers crawled and stumbled through the twisted wreckage. She watched in horrified fascination as a woman made her way toward the large gaping hole, brushed through the hanging wires and debris, and then stepped out into space. She saw the woman breeze past the cabin windows.

Yoshiro was too stunned to make a sound. Had the woman committed suicide? She doubted it. None of the passengers seemed to have enough intellect left to do even that. As if to confirm this, an old man began crawling toward the same hole in the fuselage. As he neared it, still oblivious to his surroundings, the slipstream took hold of him. He was whisked outside. Yoshiro saw his body bump against the top of the wing before it fell beneath the aircraft. She turned abruptly away and looked down the aisle that would lead her to the safety of the stairs.

Some of the people on the port side had fallen down in the aisle. Others were bunched up, trying to move around and past each other, like wind-up dolls, their feet marking time, their bodies recoiling from the continuous encounters with each other. It was obscene, and

# MAYDAY

Barbara Yoshiro felt as if a string inside of her was tightening, stretching, about to snap.

Barbara moved the last few feet down the aisle to where it opened up into the wreckage. She stepped carefully over the contorted forms on the floor. Less than fifty feet in front of her rose the blue plastic galley-lavatory cubicle, behind which was the spiral staircase.

People kept brushing and bumping her. The noise that came out of their mouths was not human. For some reason, it suddenly swelled into a crescendo of squeaking, wailing, moaning, and howling, then subsided like the noises in the forest. Then something touched it off again and the cycle began all over. An involuntary shudder passed through her body.

She forced herself to look into the faces of the men and women around her to try to determine if they were communicating with each other, telegraphing any movements, so she could act accordingly. But most of their faces showed nothing. No emotion, no interest, no humanity, and in the final analysis, no soul. The divine spark had gone out as surely as if they'd all sold themselves to the Devil. She could more easily read the facial expressions of an ape than the blood-smeared faces of these hollow-eyed, slack-jawed former humans.

There were a few, however, who showed signs of residual intelligence. One young man, in a blue blazer, seemed to have followed her in a parallel course down the right aisle. He was standing on the other side of the rubble area now, near the large hole, and staring at her. She saw him glance at the hole, then move away from it, toward her, pushing his way through the people near him. He stopped abruptly, then looked down at his feet.

Barbara Yoshiro followed his gaze. She noticed a dog in the twisted wreckage. The dog of the blind man, a golden retriever. It sat on the floor, poking its head between the two upturned seats. It was eating something. . . . She put her hand to her mouth. "Oh, no! Oh, God!"

The young man moved deliberately around the dog. A wave of panic began to wash over her. Her knees began trembling, and she felt light-headed. She grasped a section of twisted aluminum brace to steady her balance. The dog pulled something up from the debris. A bone. A rib. "Oh! Oh!" She felt a scream rising in her throat and tried to force it down, but it came out, long and piercing, then tapered off into a pathetic wail. "Oh, dear God."

The people around her turned toward the sound. The young man moved quickly toward her.

Barbara Yoshiro ran. She stumbled over the smashed bodies and seats, then fell. The floor between the holes was damaged and sagged slightly. Her arm plunged through it, into the baggage compartment below. She yanked it out and tore her wrist. Blood ran from the jagged wound. The dog picked up its head and growled at her, a strange growl that sounded more like a man choking or gagging. She rose quickly to her feet. The young man in the blue blazer reached out for her.

George Yates was normally a mild-mannered young man. He was in superb physical condition, a jogger, a scuba diver, and a practitioner of yoga and meditation. For a variety of physiological reasons, the results of decompression had left a large portion of his motor function unimpaired. The thin air had, however, wiped away his twenty-four years of acculturation and civilization, that part of the psyche that George Yates would have referred to as the superego. The ego itself was impaired, but partially functional. The id, the pleasure center of George Yates's brain, the impulsive drives, the instinctive energy, that part of the psyche closest to the lower forms of life, was left dominant.

It had been her movements that had first attracted his attention. When he had focused on those movements, they had begun to separate into perceptible components. A female.

In small flashes that were hardly more than thin sections of memory, George Yates recognized something in her form that he wanted. His last vivid recollection in his seat before things had come apart had been a long sexual daydream. The fantasy had included the women in blue and white who walked through the aisles. Vaguely, he remembered the woman with the long black hair, remembered that she had aroused him. He was aroused now. He reached out for her.

Barbara Yoshiro eluded his grasp. She ran across the remaining area of debris toward the first-class cabin. The forward galley and lavatories loomed in front of her. She slammed into the blue wall, then turned her back to it and began edging her way toward the corner where the wall turned toward the staircase.

People began coming at her, hands outstretched. She hit a woman in the face with her fist and sent her staggering back into the group behind her. Immediately, she realized she should not have done that.

People from all over the aircraft began migrating toward the focal point of the commotion. Some came out of curiosity, some were caught in the tide of bodies, some came to meet the perceived danger—Barbara Yoshiro.

She worked her way to the edge of the lavatory and peered around the corner. Less than twenty feet away she could see the spiral staircase winding upward. But the lower half was filled with people, and the intervening space between her and the base of the stairs was a solid mass of bodies. The open area around her was getting smaller. Hands reached out to her, and she slapped them away. A young boy caught hold of her blouse and pulled at it. The thin cotton tore and exposed her shoulder. Another hand caught hold of her blouse and tore it half off. Someone pulled at her hair. The young man who seemed to be normal was wedged inside the crowd that surrounded her, deliberately pushing his way through. She took a deep breath and screamed. "Help! Someone help me!"

Her voice sounded small against the wind, the roar of the four jet engines, and the excited howls around her. A hundred or more men and women competed with one another to make their sounds supreme in the jungle that was the Straton. She screamed again, but knew that her screams had become indistinguishable from those around her.

She slid around the corner of the bulkhead and groped with her right hand for the lavatory door. Her hand found the knob, and she turned it. The door gave way behind her. She turned her head and peered into the small enclosure, not knowing that it was the same one that had saved John Berry's life a few short hours before. Two men and a woman stood shoulder to shoulder, wall to wall, staring at her. She slammed the door. "Oh God. Jesus Christ." For a second she was reminded of the terror and disgust she had felt when she had opened her kitchen cabinet late one night and found it swarming with cockroaches.

Keeping her back to the wall, she edged farther down toward the staircase. The pressing crowd was only peripherally interested in her, and she found that if she altered between aggressive and passive behavior, she could slide by them. The young man in the blue blazer, however, was still purposefully making his way toward her.

Barbara reached the forward corner of the cubicle, close to the staircase. The press of bodies here was so thick she could barely push through. She called up again, but the din was so loud now that she could not even hear her own voice. She saw that the passengers had gone a few steps higher. One man staggered up the last few steps and disappeared into the lounge. A second later, he came crashing down and caused an avalanche of bodies to tumble over the winding staircase. Mr. Stein, she saw, was putting up a good fight. But he could not hear her, and even if he could, he would not be able to help her.

Yoshiro considered several alternatives. Playing dead was one, but there were so many people pressing around her that this was not possible, and she hadn't the nerve for it anyway. She could see now that she was not being singled out by the crowd any longer, but acts of random violence made it too dangerous to try to mingle with them. Besides, that young man had singled her out. She saw that her only chance was to get into the galley area and ride the elevator to the below-decks galley. She would be safe there and she could call the cockpit on the interphone. With this goal set, she calmed herself and began pushing harder through the crowd. She noticed as she moved that she was becoming light-headed and was tiring quickly. She looked down. The blood was still running from her right wrist. She grasped it with her left hand as she moved. She kept her back to the bulkhead and edged along the forward-facing wall opposite the staircase to the next corner. She made the turn and inched sideways, back in the direction of the tail. She lost sight of the man with the blazer.

Her back slid easily along the plastic wall, and her hand felt the open space of the galley entrance.

*The elevator. Get to the elevator.* Blood continued to seep between her clenched fingers, and her legs were trembling with fatigue. Faces and bodies squeezed against her, foul breath filled her nostrils. Her stomach heaved, and she began to gag on the taste of bile.

Her shoulder slid into the galley opening, and she moved with more force until only her left arm was still pinned against the bulkhead.

The crowd around her seemed to part, and in the opening she saw the man with the blazer. He smiled directly at her. He looked so nearly normal that for a moment she considered calling for him to help her. But, she realized, he could not be normal. She was becoming irrational in her desperation. He stepped up to her.

She fell back into the galley and braced her hands against the door frame. She kicked out with her feet and caught the young man in the groin. He yelled out, and that guttural yell told her beyond any doubt that he was not among the saved.

She reached out and grabbed the accordion door and

slid it shut. It bulged and began to give way almost immediately, but it gave her time to turn toward the elevator.

There were two men in the short narrow galley, both licking spilled food from the counters. She moved quickly, but calmly, past them into the open elevator.

Barbara Yoshiro steadied her trembling hand and slid the manual outer door closed. She frantically pushed against the elevator's control buttons. Finally, the electric inner doors began to slowly slide shut.

The outer doors suddenly parted. Barbara stood eye-to-eye with George Yates. Before the inner door could finish shutting, Yates slipped into the elevator. The electric doors shut behind him. The elevator started down.

Barbara bit her hand to keep from screaming. Tears ran down her face and a pathetic whimpering sound gurgled in her throat. The man in front of her was staring intently down at her. She could feel him pressing against her, feel his body making contact with hers, smell his breath. His hands probed her body, ran over her hips and up to her breasts.

She took a step backward into the corner of the descending elevator. The man pressed against her harder.

The elevator stopped and the doors slipped open, revealing a small, dimly lit galley.

George Yates pressed down on her shoulders until her knees buckled. He stood over her, his hands grabbing her long black hair, and pulled her head to his thighs.

She tried to pull loose and rise to her feet. "No. Please. No." She was bleeding badly now, and she felt very weak. "Leave me alone. Please." She was crying harder now. "Please don't hurt me."

Everything was spinning now, and the dark enclosure became darker. She felt herself being pulled forward by her hair. She lay prone on the floor, trying to feign death or unconsciousness, or anything that would make him lose interest.

But George Yates was still very much interested. From the moment he had singled her out of the crowd, from the second his instincts told him she was different, from that moment, his only thought was to capture her and make her yield. None of these words or abstractions were his to use, but the instincts remained. He turned her over on her back and knelt down with his knees straddling her.

Barbara brought her knee up and caught him in the groin.

George Yates yelled out and stood up. This was the second time she had caused him pain, the second time she had rejected him, and he was partly bewildered, but partly he now understood. She was no longer simply an object of his attraction—she had become a threat, become an enemy.

Barbara raised herself on one hand and lunged for the interphone on the wall. Her hand knocked it off the cradle and it fell to the limit of its cord. She grabbed at it as it swung by her face. She then felt a sharp pain in her eye, then another on her cheekbone. She fell backward. The plastic headset dangled above her. Through the haze of semiconsciousness, Yoshiro realized that the young man had hit her; he had hit her hard with his closed fist. He had hit her hard enough to cause a great deal of pain.

# MAYDAY

The ceiling lights of the galley were blotted out by the huge black shape hovering above her. There was no noise around her, no light entering her consciousness, and this produced a sense of unreality. She simply could not believe this was happening to her; it seemed too remote, so divorced from the world she had been part of just hours before. It was as if she'd stepped into a fog and emerged from it into a netherworld, a world almost like her own but not quite.

For the next few seconds, all Barbara could feel was the cool floor against her bare back and legs, and the steady throb of the engines as they pulsated through the airframe. Then she opened her eyes wider and focused on what was about to happen next.

After striking out at his enemy twice with his fists, George Yates had just enough of his mind and his learned reactions intact to know that a weapon was what he needed to ultimately protect himself from this perceived danger. On the floor to his left was a metal bar that had been used as a locking brace across the liquor supply cabinet. Yates grabbed the metal bar and, in one continuous motion, slammed it down hard against the upper body of his enemy.

The steel bar swept across Barbara Yoshiro's left shoulder and into her skull with a sharp crack. She blacked out immediately from the blow to her head. As it moved across her body, the steel bar had ripped open another and even larger bleeding wound—this one across the top of her left shoulder and neck.

George Yates looked down at the growing pool of blood that surrounded the now motionless body of the person lying on the floor. As soon as he saw the new spurts of blood and her injury, he knew what it meant.

# MAYDAY

The knowledge of her condition was too basic to be misunderstood: she was no longer a threat—this enemy of his had been totally defeated.

Now satisfied, Yates's interest faded and he turned his attention elsewhere. He looked around the galley area. Like a wary animal awakened from sleep, he cautiously stalked around the small area, but he could see no avenue of escape. Yates gave no more notice to the growing mass of blood on the floor, or to the body from which it had poured. As the last of her lifeblood drained onto the metal flooring of the galley, Barbara Yoshiro died.

# 9

Edward Johnson strode briskly down the long corridor toward the blue door marked DISPATCH OFFICE. He stopped abruptly, stuffed an unlit cigar in his mouth, and tried on several expressions in the reflection on a glass door. He picked one that he called disdain mixed with impatience. He stared at himself for a second. Good jawline, hair graying at the temples, cold gray eyes. An executive. Vice President in Charge of Operations, to be exact. He had enough of the ex-baggage handler left in him to be considered salty and intimidating, yet he had cultivated a veneer to make him accepted by the people who were born into the white-collar world. Satisfied with the effect he would produce with the dispatchers, he strode on.

The windowless steel door at the end of the corridor loomed up before him. How many times had he made this walk? And for what purpose? After twenty-seven years with the airline, experience had shown him that nearly every one of these calls had been a false alarm.

# MAYDAY

A real emergency had taken place more than three years before, and even that had been a waste of time. Everyone aboard that flight was already fish food long before he got the message.

So what the hell was it this time, he wondered. Someone in the Straton program probably lost his lunchbox, or some dispatcher couldn't find his pencils. He stepped up to the door and grabbed the knob.

He paused and ran through what he already knew. It wasn't much. Just a brief phone call that had interrupted an important management lunch in the executive dining room. A junior dispatcher named Evans or Evers. *An emergency, Mr. Johnson. Flight 52. But it's probably not too bad.* Then why the hell had he been called. That's what he wanted to say. *Junior* executives were supposed to take care of all the "probably not too bad" things.

Edward Johnson knew that Flight 52 was the Straton 797. The flagship of the Trans-United fleet. The Supersonic Queen of the Skies. But as far as he was concerned it was a 412-ton piece of shit. At one hundred and twenty-seven million dollars per aircraft, any problem with one of their eight 797s was a pain in the ass. The aircraft itself was reliable enough and it produced a small fortune in profits. But as Operations Chief, the fiscal considerations didn't concern him. The goddamned airplane was too precious and too visible to the Board of Directors, and to the media. It made *him* too visible, too vulnerable. To make matters worse, he was one of the people who voted to buy the 797s, and he was the one who had recently pushed through the huge cost-reduction program to cut back on lots of unnecessary maintenance and checks.

Johnson pushed open the door and strode into the dispatch office. "Who's the senior man?" he demanded. He looked around the half-empty office. An awkward silence hung over the room, broken only by the sound of a loud telephone ringing. He took the cigar out of the corner of his mouth. Before the Corporate no-smoking policy, he was able to puff on it to good effect instead of keeping the damned thing unlit. *Wimpy bastards.* "Where the hell is everybody?" His intimidation techniques were working well today, he noticed, but he was not so insensitive that he couldn't read the signs of trouble, smell the stench of fear in this place. "Where is everybody?" he repeated, a few decibels more softly.

Jerry Brewster, standing a few feet from Johnson, surprised himself by speaking. "In the communications room, sir. Mr. Miller is the senior man."

Johnson moved quickly toward the glass-enclosed room. He stuck his cigar back into his mouth, pushed the door aside, and entered the crowded communications room. "Miller? You in here?"

"Over here," answered Jack Miller, his voice the only sound in the suddenly silent room.

Several of the dispatchers backed away to allow Johnson to pass. A few of them quickly left. Dennis Evans moved unobtrusively away from Miller and stood near the door, prepared to go either way. Jerry Brewster reluctantly walked into the small room.

Johnson went up to the data-link machine. He looked down at Miller. "What's the problem?"

Miller had carefully rehearsed what he would say. But now that Johnson stood before him, all he could do was point to the video screen.

Johnson looked up at the screen on the far wall.

TO FLIGHT 52: VERY NICE WORK. STAND BY.
RELAX. EVERYONE HERE IS WORKING ON
BRINGING YOU HOME.

Johnson looked down at Miller. "What's very nice
work, Miller? *Relax?* What the hell kind of message is
that to send to one of our pilots?"

Miller looked up at the screen. He'd been so im-
mersed in this problem for what seemed like so long a
time, he couldn't imagine that someone didn't know
what was happening. "The Straton is not being flown
by one of our pilots."

"*What?* What the hell are you talking about?"

Jack Miller quickly reached down and picked up the
stack of printouts from the machine. "Here. This is the
whole story. Everything we know. Everything . . ." He
paused. "Everything that we've done. I'm afraid it's
worse than we originally thought."

Johnson took the folded printouts and began reading.
He took his unlit cigar out of his mouth and laid it on
the table. He finished reading but kept his eyes on the
printouts in his hand.

Edward Johnson's lunch of poached salmon churned
in his stomach. Less than half an hour before, they had
been discussing his possible presidency of Trans-
United Airlines. Now this. Disasters made and broke
men very quickly. A man had to immediately sense the
pitfalls and opportunities presented by these things and
act on them. If this accident had been caused by any of
the cutbacks he had personally authorized . . . Johnson
looked up from the printout with no discernible expression on his face. He stared at Jack Miller for several

seconds. "You told them to turn around." It was a flat statement, with no inflections that might convey approval or disapproval.

Miller looked him squarely in the eye. "Yes, sir. They're turned."

It took Johnson a second to figure out that cryptic response, and another second to decide if Miller was being insubordinate. Johnson smiled a rare smile. "Yes. They're turned. Nice work."

Miller nodded. He found it odd that the Operations Chief had no further comment on what had happened to Flight 52. But on second thought, he expected no extraneous words from Edward Johnson.

Johnson looked around the room. Everyone was, in a perverse but predictable way, almost enjoying the drama they found themselves in. These were the situations on which were built the legends of the airlines. Every terse statement he made, every expression on his face, would be the subject of countless stories, told and retold. Only Jack Miller and his young assistant, Jerry Brewster, seemed not to be enjoying themselves.

"Sir?" It was Jerry Brewster. He took a hesitant step toward Johnson.

"What?" Johnson could see that the young assistant was nervous.

"I'm afraid I might have . . . contributed to the problem." Brewster was speaking rapidly, getting his confession out as quickly as he could. "When I first saw the original SOS, I'm afraid I didn't respond immediately. I thought it was a hoax."

"A hoax?" Johnson raised an eyebrow. "What the hell kind of hoax could an SOS message be?"

"No, I mean a practical joke. I thought it was someone's idea of a joke." Brewster fidgeted with the clipboard in his hands. This was going to be more difficult than he thought it might be. "But I didn't wait very long. I went back as soon—"

"Any delay is too long," Johnson said, cutting Brewster short. "I'll talk to you later about this," he said angrily, dismissing the young man with a wave of his hand. Johnson turned to the other men in the room. "As for the rest of you, I'd like to remind everyone that there's no room in this business for jokes. Nothing should be treated as a joke. Ever."

Brewster turned away, embarrassed, and left the room.

Johnson stood quietly for a moment. He was glad that he now had at least one ass to hang, if things came to that. He could use a few more. He turned to Miller. "Jack, who have you called? Who knows about this?"

"I had Evans handle that."

Evans spoke quickly. "I did what was in the book, sir. The emergency handbook."

"No outside press, then?"

"No, sir." Evans licked his lips. He had an opportunity to make points, and he didn't intend to blow it by saying or doing something stupid. He had, however, done something daring. He took a deep breath and put a confident tone into his voice. "I followed procedures—up to a point."

Johnson took a step toward him. "What the hell does that mean?"

"I mean I didn't call anyone on the list except you and Mr. Metz from our liability carrier—Beneficial." He shot a quick glance at Miller.

Miller gave him an annoyed look.

Evans continued. "I didn't call the hull carrier either, because we have no real idea of the damage. I also did not call the Straton company's representative." He looked at Johnson.

Johnson's face was expressionless. "Did you also not call the president of the airline or our press office?"

Evans nodded. "I only called you and Mr. Metz."

"Why?"

"There seemed to be no pressing need. I thought I'd wait until you arrived, sir. I knew you were in the executive dining room. I thought I'd let you make the decision about who to call. This is not like a crash. This is an ongoing thing, wouldn't you say, sir? Also, at first it didn't seem too bad. That was my reasoning, sir."

"Was it?" Johnson reached down and picked up his unlit cigar. He put it back in his mouth. He let a few seconds go by. "Good. Good thinking, Evans."

Evans beamed.

Johnson looked up and addressed everyone. "Now, listen to me, all of you. No one does a thing unless they check with me. Nothing. Clear?"

Everyone in the room nodded.

Johnson continued. "Except for Miller, I want everyone to go back to his usual routine. Evans, you take complete charge of the Pacific desk. It's all yours except Flight 52. I am taking personal charge of 52. If anyone asks you about 52, refer them to me."

Miller suddenly felt that he had been relegated to a sort of limbo. He had become a junior assistant. He wished he could get back to his desk, or anywhere that was away from Johnson.

Johnson pointed with his cigar. "No one—I repeat, *no one*—is to say anything to anyone. No calls home to your wives or to anyone else. Also, the normal duty shift is extended indefinitely. In other words, no one goes home. Night-differential and double time will be in effect. The incoming shift is to report to the employees' lounge and stay there until further notice. I want as few new people as possible to know what's happening. We've got a four-hundred-and-ten-ton aircraft streaking back toward the California coast with some weekend pilot in the left-hand seat and three hundred dead or injured passengers onboard. I don't have to tell you why I want the lid on this. Understand?"

Everyone murmured his assent.

"All right, make sure everyone out there understands too. Get back to work."

The dispatchers filed quickly out of the hot, airless room.

Evans hung back a second. "Mr. Johnson, if there's anything further I can do . . ."

"You've done enough, Evans. Good initiative."

Evans smiled. "Thank you, sir."

"And the next time you fail to follow procedures, it had fucking well better make me happy, Evans, or your ass is out. Got it?"

Evans's smile faded. "Yes, sir." He left quickly.

Johnson turned to Miller. "Well. Here we are, Jack."

Miller nodded. He and Johnson went back a lot of years. Now, with the audience gone, Johnson would start thinking and stop playacting. As if to confirm this, Johnson threw his cigar into the garbage can in the corner. Miller was certain that the man hated cigars, but trademarks, like the Trans-United logo and Edward Johnson's cigar—mostly unlit these past years—took a long time to cultivate and develop, and one didn't drop them so easily.

Johnson glanced down at the printout in his hand. "This is one hell of a thing."

"Yes, it is."

"A bomb. Why the hell do people want to blow up an airliner? Shit." He paced a few feet. "Tell me, Jack, do you think they've got a chance?"

Miller glanced at the video screen, then at Johnson. "At first I didn't give them any chance. Now . . . maybe. That pilot—Berry—handled the turn all right. Just to get as far as he did—taking the controls, figuring out the link, turning—that took a lot of guts. Skill, too. He's got what it takes. Read the messages again. He's a cool character. It comes through in the messages."

Johnson stepped up to the Pacific chart that had been hung in the room earlier. He examined the markings on it. "Is this their estimated position?"

"That's our guess. We didn't have much to go on." Miller rose from his seat at the data-link console and walked to the wall chart. He pointed to another spot on the chart. "This is the Straton's last verified position. This one is an extrapolation that Jerry Brewster worked up. Now we're working up another one based on their turnaround and present heading. Brewster will have—"

The thin sound of the data-link's alerting bell cut him off. Both men glanced up at the video monitor.

FROM FLIGHT 52. ALL FIVE SURVIVORS
WERE TRAPPED IN POSITIVE PRESSURE
SPOTS DURING DECOMPRESSION. MOST

PASSENGERS STILL ALIVE, BUT SUSPECT
SUSTAINED LACK OF AIR PRESSURE CAUSED
BRAIN DAMAGE.

Miller stared at each letter as it appeared, knowing what the last two words were going to say after he saw the *B*. The message went on.

SOME PASSENGERS BECOMING
UNMANAGEABLE. ATTEMPTING TO CLIMB
STAIRS INTO LOUNGE/COCKPIT. STEIN
HOLDING THEM BACK. BERRY.

Miller looked up. "Jesus Christ Almighty."

Johnson slammed his hand down violently against a countertop. "Son-of-a-bitch! Goddamned rotten luck!" He turned to Miller. "Is this possible? Could this happen?" Johnson's technical knowledge was sketchy, and he never saw a need to pretend otherwise.

Jack Miller suddenly understood exactly what had happened. A bomb had torn two holes—two big holes—in the Straton's fuselage. Had they been smaller holes, the pressure might have held long enough. Had it been one of their other jets, its lower operating altitude would have made it possible for everyone to breathe with oxygen masks. But at 62,000 feet, where the only commercial traffic was the Straton 797 and the Concorde, a decompression, if it was sudden and complete, could theoretically cause brain damage. Miller would have guessed that it would be fatal, but Berry said that most passengers survived. Survived. *Good Lord. How did this happen?* He stood up and felt his legs wobble a bit. "Yes," he said weakly. "It's possible."

Johnson looked through the glass enclosure into the dispatch office. Dispatchers and assistants in the main room were trying to read the new message on the video screen. Johnson motioned to Miller. "Erase the video screen. Shut it off. We'll use only the small display screen from now on."

Miller pushed the buttons to do away with the video screen's repeater display.

Johnson walked over to the door and locked it. He stood next to the data-link, put his foot on a chair, and leaned forward. "Type a message, Jack."

Miller typed as Johnson dictated.

TO FLIGHT 52: LOCATE SATELLITE
NAVIGATION SYSTEM. IT IS ON RADIO PANEL
AND IS LABELED AS SUCH. READ OUT YOUR
POSITION. ACKNOWLEDGE.

A few seconds passed before the message bell rang.

FROM FLIGHT 52: HAVE PREVIOUSLY
LOCATED SATELLITE NAV SET. IT MUST
NEED REPROGRAMMING FOR READOUT. IT
READS NOTHING NOW. ADVISE ON
PROGRAMMING.

Johnson walked over to the Pacific chart again and stared up at it. He had a vague idea of how to plot positions and no idea of how to program a satellite set. Still looking at the chart, he spoke to Miller. "Tell him that we'll advise later."

Miller typed the message.

Johnson turned. "He really can't land that thing, can he?"

"I don't know." Miller was already in over his head.

Despite years in the dispatch office, he couldn't tell a man how to program a satellite navigation set. In fact, he had a vague memory of having read that they couldn't be altered or reprogrammed en route. Miller had only a textbook image and knowledge of the cockpit of a 797, no conception of what actually flying the craft was about, and he knew that Johnson had even less. "Why don't we get Fitzgerald in here?"

Johnson thought for a moment about the chief pilot. Kevin Fitzgerald was another candidate to fill the president's chair. It would be good to have a pilot in the room with them, but not Fitzgerald. But to ask another pilot in would be an unforgivable insult whose intentions would be obvious to the Board of Directors. Though why give Fitzgerald an opportunity to play hero? The answer was to exclude him from the game for as long as possible. It was generally known that if either of them became president, then the other one would spend the rest of his career in oblivion. Johnson knew that he could easily wind up supervising lost baggage claims instead of in the president's office. He looked at Miller. "Not yet. If that Straton gets within, let's say, two hundred miles of the coast, we'll get Fitzgerald." He thought for a second. "If we can't find him, we'll get the head flight instructor. He'd do a better job of it, I think."

Miller knew that it would be a good thing to start Berry's flight instructions immediately. Either man would do. But Miller also knew that Johnson did not make any decisions based purely on rationality. Edward Johnson's decisions were always based on ulterior motives. "Do you think it's time to put out a brief statement to the press?"

"No."

"Should we have the PR people privately contact relatives of the passengers? We can start booking them on flights to San Francisco and—"

"Later."

"Why?"

Johnson looked at him closely. "Because we are not going to encourage a media circus here. This is not some cheap TV drama. This bullshit about right-to-know is just that—bullshit. There is not one damn reporter or hysterical relative who is going to make a useful contribution to this problem. It's about time somebody started exercising their rights to privacy and secrecy again in this country. This is Trans-United's business and no one else's except, unfortunately, the Federal Aviation Agency. We'll notify them in just a few minutes. As far as a public statement, it may be necessary to release only one. The final one."

"Ed, my only concern right now is to bring that aircraft home," Miller said. "I don't care about any shit that is going to be flying around here later."

Johnson frowned. "You ought to." But then he suddenly patted Miller on the back. Johnson had forced himself to change gears. "You're right. We have to bring 52 home before we can think of anything else."

Miller turned away and walked to the Pacific chart. A little red spot of grease pencil on a field of light blue represented more than three hundred seriously sick and injured people heading home. And the thought that their fate was in the hands of Edward Johnson was not comforting. Miller hoped that John Berry was an exceptionally competent and discerning man.

# MAYDAY

Wayne Metz sat comfortably in his silver BMW 750 as he cruised in the right lane of Interstate 280. He adjusted the knobs on his Surround-Sound CD player until the resonance of Benny Goodman's "One O'clock Jump"—one of his favorites from his old jazz collection—was just right. He glanced at himself in the rearview mirror. Yesterday's tennis had deepened his tan.

He passed Balboa Park and looked at his dash clock. He'd be at the San Francisco Gold Club early enough to review his notes before tee-off with Quentin Lyle. He glanced up at the sky. Beautiful June day. Perfect for business. Before they reached the ninth hole, the Lyle factories would be the latest client of Beneficial Insurance Company. By the last hole he might have the trucking company as well. He hummed along with the music. His reverie was broken by the insistent buzzing of the cellular phone that lay on the passenger seat. He shut off the CD player and picked up the phone. "Yes?"

The voice came through with a slight hollow sound to it. "Mr. Metz, this is Judy. Trans-United Airlines has just called."

He frowned. "Go on."

"A Mr. Evans. The message was as follows: Flight 52, Straton aircraft, sent Trans-United a message saying aircraft damaged. But Mr. Evans said they were still transmitting so it might not be too bad."

"That was the whole message?"

"Yes, sir."

"Not too serious?"

"That's what he said."

"Hold on." He put the phone down in his lap and turned over several alternatives in his mind. But none of them was viable, really. Trans-United was far too important a client for him to pretend that he was out of touch with his office. Still, Beneficial didn't insure what they called the hull—the aircraft itself. They were only the liability carrier. If no one was hurt, he was safe. He picked up the phone. "All right, I'll call them from here. I may have to go down there. Call Mr. Lyle at the club. Tell him I may be late. Emergency. Hope to be there for the back nine. Maybe sooner. Make it sound really catastrophic, but don't mention Trans-United. Got all of that? I'll call you later."

"Yes, sir."

Metz hung up and drove by the San Jose Avenue exit. With any luck at all, his presence at the airport wouldn't be necessary. He slowed his car, picked up the telephone, and punched a pre-stored number. The cellular phone immediately dialed the private New York number for Beneficial's president, Wilford Parke. A few seconds later, Parke's secretary put him through.

"Wayne? You there?"

Metz held the phone away from his ear. Like many older men, Parke was speaking too loudly into the mouthpiece. "Yes, sir." He glanced at his clock. It was almost quitting time in New York. "Sorry to bother you so late in the day, but—"

"That's all right, Wayne. Some sort of problem out there?"

Metz smiled. *Out there.* To most New Yorkers, anything west of the Hudson was *out there*. To Wilford

Parke, anything west of Fifth Avenue was in another solar system. "Possibly, sir. I thought I'd keep you posted." Metz's thoughts were already two sentences ahead. "A call from Trans-United Airlines. Some sort of problem with an aircraft. No details yet, but they said it didn't seem too bad and may only involve the hull. Still, there may be a liability claim. I thought I should call you before you left the office." *And before you heard it from another source,* he thought.

"Good thinking, Wayne."

"Yes, sir. And I thought I might go out there and see to it personally."

"Fine, Wayne. Fine. Keep me posted. Glad to see you're taking care of it personally. Where are you calling from?"

"Car. I'm already on the highway to the airport."

"Very good. Let me know when you have some details."

"Yes, sir."

"Good-bye, Wayne."

Metz spoke quickly. "Sir, where can I reach you later?"

"Later? Oh, yes. Atrium Club. Having dinner. Over on East Fifty-seventh."

Metz did not care where the club was located. "Can I page you there? Is the number listed?"

"Yes. Of course. You know the place. We were there last February. We had a bottle of Chateau Haut-Brion '59. You can reach me there until about ten o'clock. Speak to you later."

Metz tossed the phone onto the passenger seat. Wilford Parke was somewhere between senile and brilliant. In either case, he liked the old man. Talking with him was always a pleasure. He was a real gentleman of the old school. He was a man who believed in his company and who shared management's privileges with those whom he trusted—like Wayne Metz. Metz had always been sure to stress his own Long Island boyhood and his college days at Princeton, which was also Parke's alma mater. But the main reason he liked Parke was that Parke thought Wayne Metz could do no wrong. And he had thought so even before those embarrassing lapses of memory had set in. Wayne Metz hoped that Wilford Parke could hold on to his job long enough to secure Metz's next promotion.

Metz wheeled his BMW through a pack of cars, then accelerated again through an open stretch of highway. He knew he'd been lucky to get the call when he did, on the highway, not far from the airport. From his downtown office it would have taken him over an hour to get there. That was typical of the luck that had propelled him to the head of the West Coast office. Yet he might have to miss the first few holes with Quentin Lyle. That might be ominous. He half believed in omens, and though he found astrology silly, many of his friends read their horoscopes each morning. *Money can be worrisome. Set example for loved ones by cutting down. Do what you believe to be correct. Don't be afraid to trust your heart.*

But certainly his success had not all been luck, thought Metz. It was talent. Wilford Parke had years before seen something in Metz that as a young man he had not been aware of himself. In the corporate hierarchy, where a significant battle could be announced by a gesture as innocuous as the polite declining of a drink, Wayne Metz flourished. He was the master of the oblique and muted signal. He had an uncanny talent for projecting, in the most subtle ways imaginable, his likes and dislikes. He was, to quote his own analyst, perhaps too young a man to be so blessed.

Metz's cellular phone buzzed again. He picked it up. "Metz."

"Ed Johnson, Wayne."

Metz stiffened in his seat. If the Operation VP was calling, it had to be a real problem. "I was just about to call you, Ed. What's the latest?"

"It's bad," said Johnson, evenly. "It's the Straton 797."

"Oh, shit." He and Johnson had once, over drinks, kidded each other about their mutual jeopardy in the Straton program. It had been Metz's idea that Beneficial be the sole liability carrier for Trans-United's fleet of the giant supersonic transports. He'd offered lower premiums with the elimination of the usual, but cumbersome, insurance pool. Johnson, for his part, had been one of the people to vote for the idea. Also, he had once admitted candidly to Metz, after a third martini, that his career was closely tied to the Straton's success for a variety of other reasons. "Where did it crash?" Metz asked. "How many were killed?"

"It was en route to Japan. The good news is that the airliner's still flying, and there weren't many killed . . . yet. But the bad news is worse than you'd ever dream," he said. "A bomb blew two holes in the hull and the air pressure escaped. The passengers suffered the effects of decompression. Up there, as you may know, it's like outer space."

Metz didn't know. No one at Trans-United had told him about this possibility, and he had never had the foresight to have the dangers of high-altitude super-sonic flight researched. It was all supposed to be government approved, so he had assumed that there was no extraordinary risk. "What did you say was the condition of the passengers?" Metz asked.

There was a pause, then Johnson said, "We're not absolutely certain, you understand, but the consensus here—and up there—seems to be that they're brain damaged."

"God Almighty." The BMW nearly went off the road. "Are you sure?"

"I *said* we weren't sure, Wayne. But I'd put money on it."

Metz realized that he had not assimilated all of it. "The survivors . . . how did they . . . ?"

"We're communicating with them on the data-link. That's like a computer screen. Radios are gone. There are only five unimpaired survivors. They were all in the whiffies or someplace like that."

"Whiffies?"

"Bathrooms, Wayne. You'd better get here fast and bring your company's checkbook."

Metz pulled himself out of his daze. "Look, Ed, we're both very exposed with this thing. How many people on board?"

"Nearly a full house. About three hundred."

"When will it land?"

"It may never land."

"What?"

"The aircraft is being flown by one of the passengers. Our—"

"What the hell are you *talking* about?" Metz knew that he shouldn't be speaking so candidly about such a sensitive issue on a cellular phone, but he needed to know more to understand what was happening.

"Our three pilots are dead or unconscious. All that's left of our flight crew are two flight attendants. The passenger who's flying it—some guy named Berry—is an amateur pilot. He still has the Straton under control. In fact, he's turned it around and headed back, but his exact position is unknown. Anyway, I have my doubts that he can land it without smearing it all over the runway."

Wayne Metz was literally speechless. He kept the telephone pressed to his ear and his eyes on the road, but his mind was thousands of miles away—in the mid-Pacific. He tried to imagine the scene. The giant Straton 797 lost somewhere over the enormous ocean, two holes blown through its hull and everyone aboard dead or brain damaged except for a few people, one of whom, a passenger, was flying it. *No, no, no, no.*

"Metz? Wayne? You still there?"

"What? Yes. Yes, I'm here. Let me think. Hold on." As he tried to sort out the incredible facts he had just heard, he inadvertently let the BMW slow. He was traveling at less than forty miles an hour in the left lane of the highway.

A driver in a battered blue Ford behind him hit his horn, then pulled out and passed on the right, glaring at the big sedan. Wayne glanced up distractedly at the other driver, but his mind was on other things. A thought had formed. It was not yet fully shaped, but he could start to see its outline, like a mountain emerging from a fog. The battered blue Ford stuck in his mind, too, for some reason. He cleared his throat. "Listen,

Ed, I'm almost there. Who knows about this? Is it on the radio?"

"No. Not many people know. One of our dispatchers handed me a break by not calling anyone yet. So I still have some space to maneuver."

"Good. Don't call anyone else. If we can't control the situation, at least we can control the flow of information . . . and that may be just as important."

"That's my thinking too. But you'd better hurry."

"Yes. On the way." Metz hung up. He stared out the windshield and began accelerating. He cut in the cruise control at seventy miles an hour, picked up the phone again, and called New York. Parke was still in his office. "Mr. Parke," he began without preamble, "I've got bad news. There's been a terrible accident with Trans-United's Straton 797."

"Aren't we the sole underwriters?" Parke asked quickly.

Metz winced. "Yes, sir. For the liability coverage. We are not involved in their hull insurance." Going it alone was a risky, unconventional way to write that sort of policy, but Metz had never liked insurance pools. He had spent months convincing Beneficial that the airline, and especially the Straton program, was extremely safe. Beneficial did not have to share the huge premiums with anyone. But now they had no one to share the loss.

"Well, Wayne, that's unfortunate. I personally felt that perhaps we were taking on too large a risk, but I don't intend to second-guess you on that issue. The Board members approved it. The proposal—your proposal—had merit and was well-received. Naturally, we'll review our corporate guidelines after a loss of this magnitude. You'll have to make a presentation to the Board. I'll get back to you later on that."

Metz felt the sweat begin to collect around his collar, and he turned up the air-conditioning. "Yes, sir."

"In the meantime, were all those aboard that airliner killed? Do you have a casualty total? Any estimate on our total liability?"

Metz hesitated, then spoke in a firm, controlled tone. "A Trans-United executive told me that it was nearly a full ship. That would mean approximately three hundred passengers and a crew."

There was a long pause as the impact of the tragedy sunk in. "I see. All dead, did you say?"

Metz didn't say. He temporized. "Actually, the accident occurred only a short while ago, over the Pacific. Many of the details are still very sketchy, and nothing has been released to the press yet. It's being kept confidential," he added. "Trans-United didn't want to speak over the phone."

"I understand. We'll keep it quiet on this end also."

"Yes, sir. That would be very good."

"Well, bad day at Black Rock for a lot of people, including us. Listen, Wayne, don't bother to work up a maximum-liability figure. Things are going to be pretty frantic at Trans-United. I'll take care of it at this end. I suppose there won't be any secondary property damages since the aircraft was over the Pacific at the time."

"That's right," Metz lied. "There should be no other claims." He could not bring himself to tell Wilford Parke that the Straton was, at this moment, streaking toward San Francisco, carrying onboard the largest contingent of ongoing insurance liabilities in history.

"Call me when you get more," Parker said. "I'll be

at my club. I'm having dinner with some of the Board. We'll have a telephone at the table. If you'd like some help, I can get people to you quickly out of the Chicago office."

"We should be all right, sir. I've got a good staff here."

"Fine. One more thing, Wayne . . ."

"Yes, sir?"

"I know this is your first loss of magnitude. Paying three hundred death benefits is no small thing. I'm just glad it didn't happen over a populated area."

"Yes, sir." *It may yet.*

"And I'm also relieved that we're not carrying the aircraft's hull insurance. What do those things cost—a hundred million?"

"Something like that." On his desk was the first draft of a memo proposing that very coverage for Trans-United. When he got back to his office, that memo would go into the shredder before he hung up his jacket.

"What I'm trying to say, Wayne, is that there is no insurance executive in the business who at one time or another didn't have his name personally identified with a large loss. I know it's an embarrassment, but the amount we can expect as the total death benefit is manageable. You've had a spot of bad luck. Don't let it get you down. You don't cry over spilled milk in this business. You insure for spilled milk and pay for the spillage out of premiums. The Board might grumble a bit, but you'll come through. We're just fortunate," said Parke in a friendly tone, "that the claim isn't more."

Metz shook his head. *There are three hundred brain-*

*damaged people on that aircraft, and they are coming home. Coming home to Beneficial Insurance. We will be totally liable for the care of each of them for the rest of their lives.*

# 10

Harold Stein stood, coiled, ready to strike again, but the assault seemed to have lost its momentum. The attackers had drifted off; like children, thought Stein, after a game of King of the Mountain, or like wild animals or primitive people whose ferocity subsides as quickly as it begins.

He breathed deeply and wiped the sweat from his face. His arms and legs ached. He peered down into the cabin. The passengers were apparently occupied with something else now. They were not congregating around the stairway any longer, and their noises had subsided. But they might mass again for an attack if something stirred them.

He found it hard to believe that he had actually been attacked. But he found it harder to believe that *he* had been so aggressive, had punched and kicked these men, women, children—people he had spoken with a few hours before.

Stein wondered why Barbara Yoshiro had not come

back. Perhaps she'd been hurt, or maybe she was still searching for something. He looked into the cockpit. John Berry was talking to Sharon Crandall, but he couldn't hear them. They sat, silhouetted against the bright Pacific sunlight, working, he supposed, on bringing them home. "They're quieting down," Stein called out.

Berry turned and called back, "Nice work, Harold. If you need any help, holler."

"Right." Stein looked around the lounge. Berry had his hands full just keeping these people out of the cockpit and trying to fly the aircraft. Stein forced himself not to look at his own trembling hands. He took a deep, measured breath to calm himself, but it was becoming an increasingly difficult task. The more he thought about their situation, the more frightened he had become. Stein knew that he had hardly any emotional or physical resources left inside of him.

His mind drifted back across an ocean and a continent to his home in Bronxville. In his mind's eye he could see its red bricks, white shutters, and rich green lawns. He could see the red azalea bushes in bloom the way he'd last seen them. Every spring people would go out of their way to pass his house and admire Miriam's flowers. Who would tend them now?

He longed for the comfort of the high-backed couch in front of the fireplace where he sat with Miriam most evenings. He pictured the wide stairway that led to the second floor and the bedrooms. His and Miriam's on the left. On the right, Susan's, wallpapered in pink gingham, the aquarium crammed with tropical fish. Beyond that room was Debbie's, all navy and white, filled with miniature toys and the dollhouse he had made for her last birthday.

He began to cry.

He had to act, he decided. He had to do something for them. If he couldn't bring back their minds, he could, at least, comfort their bodies, keep them from being savaged by the others.

Without realizing it, he was standing on the circular staircase. He thought briefly of Berry's admonitions to wait. He thought of his duty to stand there and guard the gates of hell. Hell. To hell with Berry. To hell with them all. He could not wait. Not for Berry, not for Barbara Yoshiro, not for anyone.

He glanced back into the cockpit. Berry and Crandall were busy. He looked toward the piano. Linda Farley was sitting on the floor, half asleep. He glanced down. The stairs were clear. They might not be clear again. He descended quickly into the lower region of the Straton.

At the base of the stairs, he looked around cautiously. People were lying everywhere. Some were slouched against the walls of the lavatories and galley. They seemed to be in a resting state, like wild things after a period of frenzy. It wouldn't last long, he suspected.

The people around him were whimpering softly or chattering to themselves. Now and then he thought he heard a clear word or phrase, but he knew he had not. He wanted so desperately to have someone to help him that he was beginning to create human dialogue out of the animal noises that came from those blood-smeared mouths.

Stein moved cautiously around the lavatories and back toward the area of debris.

Among the sunlit rubble, a golden-colored dog lay sleeping with a meaty bone under its paws. It seemed so incongruous even beyond the incongruity of the sunlight on the twisted deck. Then he remembered the Seeing-Eye dog. *But who would let a dog have a fresh bone onboard an* . . . Then it struck him. "Oh, dear God."

He turned quickly away from the dog and saw, a few feet from him, Barbara Yoshiro. She was sitting on the floor with her head buried between her knees, her long black hair obscuring her face. He moved quickly toward her. She could help him bring his family up to the lounge. He reached down and shook her shoulder. He spoke softly. "Barbara. Barbara, are you all right?"

The flight attendant picked her head up.

Stein recoiled. The face that stared at him was horribly contorted and smeared with blood. "Barbara . . ." But it was not Barbara Yoshiro. It was another flight attendant, whom he vaguely recognized. In the sunlight he could see purple blotches on her cheeks and forehead where blood vessels had burst. The eyes stared at him, red and burning. He stepped back and collided with someone behind him. "Oh! Oh, no, please no!" He stumbled out of the rubble, knocking into people as he moved.

He looked around wildly for Barbara Yoshiro. He called back in to the dimly lit tourist cabin. "Barbara! Flight attendant!"

Someone yelled back at him. "Burbura! Fitatenant!"

Stein put his hands over his face and slumped back against a seat. *God in Heaven.*

Slowly, he took his hands from his face and looked up. His eyes moved reluctantly toward the center row, thirty feet from where he stood. Only Debbie and Susan were still sitting in their seats. Miriam was gone.

Debbie was trying to stand, but each time she rose, the seat belt pulled her back.

Susan was lying slumped over the seat that had been his, her hands clasped together, thrust out in front of her.

Harold Stein moved toward his daughter, slowly, hesitantly. He stood over their seats and looked down. "Debbie. Debbie, it's Papa. Debbie!"

The girl looked up uninterestedly, then resumed her up-and-down movements, patiently, persistently trying to stand. Odd liquid vowel sounds came from her lips.

Susan was breathing, but was otherwise motionless.

Harold Stein knew in that instant that there was neither hope nor salvation for his family or for anyone on this ship. And now he knew what he had to do.

He turned and ran down the aisle, pushing aside the staggering people in his way.

He found Miriam wandering aimlessly near the rear galley. "Miriam! Miriam!"

She did not respond.

He was done with calling their names, done with pretending that anyone was who they had been a few hours before. This wandering wraith standing before him was not his wife.

He took her arm and led her back to the four adjoining seats that had held him and his family.

Stein unbuckled the two girls' belts. He put Susan over his shoulder and pulled Debbie to her feet and led her into the aisle. Alternating with his free hand between his wife and daughter, he maneuvered them both into the area of the rubble.

The two holes that had caused this immense grief were hardly more than a dozen feet away. The wind howled through those open wounds and the noise filled his ears and made it difficult to think clearly. He hesitated, then headed for the larger hole.

Sweating and out of breath, he laid down the burden that was his daughter, then forced Debbie and Miriam to sit. Several cables whipped over their heads, and occasionally one would lash Miriam or the girls, causing them to cry out. A cable whipped across Stein's face and opened a gash on his forehead.

He bent over Susan, and despite his resolve not to speak to any of them, he whispered in her ear. "Sue, honey, Papa's here with you. It's going to be all right now." He turned and looked down at Debbie. She looked at him, and for a moment he thought he saw a spark of life in those dead eyes, but then it was gone. Debbie was their firstborn, and her birth after so many childless years had been the single most joyous event in their lives. He bent forward and kissed her on the forehead.

There was no doubt in his mind that he had been spared the fate of the others for the specific purpose of allowing him to do his duty toward his family. He felt sorry for those who had to go on suffering. He felt sorry for Berry and Sharon Crandall and Linda Farley and Barbara Yoshiro. They had to suffer more than the others and would go on suffering until the aircraft crashed, or worse, landed. He honestly pitied them all, but felt no more responsibility toward any of them. The gates of hell were unguarded, and it was just as well. It might hasten the end for everyone. He, Harold Stein, had been given an unheard-of opportunity to escape from hell and escort his family to a place of eternal rest, and he was not going to shrink from that responsibility.

He wrapped his arms around his daughters' waists, and with no further thought lifted them toward the hole. He watched as they left his hands, one at a time, and sailed away in the slipstream, end over end, through the sunlit blue sky. Each of his daughters disappeared from his view for a moment behind the tail of the craft, then he saw them again, briefly carried by the Pacific wind down toward the sea before he could see them no more.

Without a moment's pause, Stein turned and lifted his wife to a standing position. He walked her toward the hole. She seemed to come along willingly. Perhaps she understood. He doubted it, but perhaps their love— that silent communication that had developed between them—was stronger. . . . Stein forced himself to stop thinking. He looked at the hole, but he could barely see it through the tears in his eyes. He looked back at Miriam's face. Two lines of dried blood ran from her tear ducts down her cheeks. He pulled her face to his chest. "Miriam, Miriam. I know you don't understand, but . . ." His voice trailed off into a series of spasmodic sobs.

He stepped closer to the hole. He could feel the force of the slipstream as it pressed against his body. "Miriam, I love you. I've loved you all." He was going to say, "God, forgive me," but he was certain that this was what God had intended for him to do.

With his arms wrapped tightly around his wife, Harold Stein stepped out of the aircraft and away from the nightmare of Flight 52.

---

Lieutenant Peter Matos fidgeted in the seat of his F-18 fighter. A hundred yards ahead, the Trans-United Straton flew a steady course. Matos forced himself to glance at his panel clock. Its luminescent numbers seemed to jump out at him. He was amazed to see that it had been more than an hour since the Straton had turned toward California. To Matos, it seemed no more than a few minutes. He shook his head in disbelief. During all that time, all he remembered was receiving a few transmissions from Commander Sloan and doing some calculations with his navigation equipment. But other than those brief duties, he could not account for the missing minutes.

*Peter, snap out of it. Do something. Right now.* Matos felt as if he were in a trance, hypnotized by the enormous and unchanging Pacific. He sucked hard on his oxygen mask to clear his head. *Check the flight instruments,* he said to himself. Matos knew that he should get himself back into his normal pilot's routine. It was the best way to get his thoughts back on the right track. The gauge readings were familiar and friendly. Starting on the panel's left side, he saw that the oil pressure was normal, the engine temperatures were normal, the fuel . . .

Matos stopped. His brief moment of reverie ended abruptly. *Jesus Christ.* The F-18's fuel situation was not yet critical, but Matos could see that it soon would be. Even though he had taken off on this mission with the maximum fuel the aircraft could carry, he would, without any question, have to do something very soon.

Matos bit into his lower lip while his mind wrestled with the alternatives. But he knew what he had to do first. He read the hurriedly punched coordinates into his computer. He read the results. "Shit." He had very little extra fuel left. The luxury of waiting out the Straton was coming to an end.

What would happen next? Matos agonized over his choices. Should he defy Commander Sloan? He had never defied an order before, and the idea was unnerving. Bucking James Sloan—and the United States Navy, for that matter—was too drastic a course to consider. It was outside the range of his thoughts, just as the *Nimitz* would soon be outside the range of his fuel.

Matos glanced at the Straton. It was flying evenly and steadily. Too steadily. He knew damn well that he had exaggerated those last damage reports he had sent to Sloan. *Fatigue cracks have developed along the cabin wall. The wing spar may be damaged. It can't fly much longer. It will overstress soon.* None of that was exactly false, but it wasn't true either. There were some cracks and signs of stress, but . . .

"Navy, three-four-seven, do you read?"

Sloan's sudden transmission startled Matos. "Roger," he answered, gripping tightly to the F-18's control stick, "go ahead." He could tell from the Commander's voice that he had grown impatient with their unspoken plan. A sense of dread flooded Matos. He had, he now realized, put off the inevitable as long as he could.

"What's the situation?" Sloan asked tersely.

"No change so far."

"Nothing?" Sloan sounded honestly astonished. "What about the fatigue cracks? What about the wing spar?"

"A little more deterioration. Maybe. Not much." Matos wished he hadn't begun this lie. It had only made things worse. He allowed his eyes to wander over to the missile-firing controls on his side console. He was sorry he had waited. He should have shot the Straton down immediately, before he had time to think about it.

"Matos, your damage reports have been pure bull-shit. You've only made this goddamn job longer and harder for everyone. Don't think I'll forget that."

"No. The Straton was getting worse," Matos lied. "Its airspeed is still steady at 340, but its altitude has drifted slightly . . ." Something caught Matos's eye. It was a small, dark object below the Straton. It was falling rapidly toward the sea. Was it part of the fuselage? Was the airliner finally coming apart? Matos peered over the side of his canopy, and as he did his finger slipped off the transmit button.

"Matos," shouted Sloan as he latched on to the radio's clear channel, "I don't give a shit about airspeeds and altitudes. Will that goddamn airplane go down? That's what I want to know. Answer the fucking question."

"Homeplate—people are falling out of the Straton!" Matos had not heard one word of Sloan's last message.

"What? Say again."

"Yes. They're falling. Jumping." Matos edged his fighter downward, closer to the airliner. He could see clearly now, as he watched another body tumble out of the port-side hold. *Oh, my God.* "There's another one!

There must be a fire inside." It was the only reason Matos could think of for a person to jump to a certain death. He watched the second body turn end over end until it was too far away to see its flailing arms and legs. It receded farther and farther away, until it was no more than a black pinpoint silhouetted against the sea. Then he saw it hit the waves and disappear instantly beneath them.

"Do you see any smoke?"

*Smoke?* Matos jerked his head up and stared at the Straton. But everything appeared as it had before. Too calm. Too steady. Matos ran his tongue across his parched lips, then pushed the transmit button. "No visible smoke. Not yet." His new bubble of hope hadn't yet burst, but it was quickly losing air. No smoke, no fire, nothing. What could be happening in there? For a brief instant he realized the kind of person he had turned into. He pushed that thought aside. He could live with the memory of this accident—even if it was his fault—as long as he didn't do anything else to the Straton. *Please, God, let it go down. By itself.*

"Matos, don't give me more bullshit," Sloan said angrily, but then quickly changed his tone. "Is there any turbulence? Do you see any reason for them to jump?"

"No, but . . . wait . . . wait . . ." Matos kept his finger pressed firmly to the microphone button. "More people are jumping. Two of them. Together. Yes. There must be something going on. Definitely. A fire, or fumes. Something. No doubt. We should wait. Wait. It will go down. I know it will."

Sloan did not answer for a long time. When he finally did, his voice had again assumed a flat and official tone. "Roger, three-four-seven. Understand. We will wait."

---

As he fell with his wife in his arms, Harold Stein raised his head up and stared at the Straton above him. In that split second he saw and identified a jet fighter hovering above and behind the huge aircraft. The silver image of a long rocket hanging from its belly stuck in his mind. In a clear flash of understanding, he knew what had happened to Flight 52.

---

Wayne Metz disengaged the BMW cruise control and took the airport entrance at sixty miles an hour. He drove directly to the Trans-United hangar and slipped the BMW into a VIP space. He sat staring up at the blue and yellow hangar for a full minute.

He had come up with a plan that could greatly reduce Beneficial's enormous liability. A plan that would lessen his own liability as well.

The plan had not been difficult to formulate. It was an obvious one. The problem now was to convince Edward Johnson that their interests coincided, and that these mutual interests could best be served by Wayne Metz's plan. He thought he knew Johnson well enough to risk approaching him.

Metz rummaged around his glove compartment and found his Trans-United ID card. He got out of his car and crossed the hot tarmac toward the hangar. He spotted the personnel entrance and quickened his pace. A group of airline employees stood near the door talking, and Metz brushed by them. He flashed his Trans-United "Official Visitor/Contractor" identification card at the guard, then pushed open the small inner door and mounted a flight of steps two at a time. He moved quickly down a long corridor and opened a blue door marked DISPATCH OFFICE.

Metz approached a clerk. "I'm here to see Edward Johnson."

The clerk pointed to the glass-enclosed communications room. "Over there. But I don't think he's seeing anyone."

"He's seeing *me*." Metz crossed the office and stood in front of one of the thick glass panels. In the small room he could see Edward Johnson looking down at a big machine. Another man stood next to him. In an instant, Metz could see that they were both highly tense, and guessed that the tension was not completely a result of the situation but was partly generated by a friction between the two men. Metz knew that his plan could work only if he were alone with Johnson. He watched for another few seconds. The other man appeared to be a subordinate. Johnson could get rid of him. Metz rapped sharply on the glass.

Johnson looked up, then walked to the door and unlocked it.

Wayne Metz entered the communications room. "Hello, Ed."

The two men shook hands perfunctorily.

Johnson noticed that several of the employees were looking up from their work. He glared back at them, and heads lowered all over the office. He slammed the door and bolted it. "Goddamned center stage." Everything in this damned Straton program was too visible. He motioned to Miller. "This is Jack Miller. He's the senior dispatcher. Fifty-two was his flight."

Metz nodded absently to Miller, then turned to Johnson. "*Was?* Did it . . . ?"

"No. Wrong tense. It's still up there. But it's my flight now. Jack is helping out." Yet Johnson knew that deep down he had already written the Straton off. The past tense fit the Straton, but he'd have to be more careful when he spoke of the aircraft. You had to *sound* optimistic. "Actually, we haven't communicated with them since I spoke to you. But the flight is steady and there's no reason to keep calling. If he wants us, he'll call."

Metz nodded. "It looks like he might make it, then?"

Johnson shook his head. "I didn't say that. We've got to talk him through an approach and landing." He decided to be blunt with Metz. "As far as I'm concerned, that's almost certain death." He motioned toward Miller. "Jack's a bit more optimistic. He thinks this guy Berry can make a perfect three-point landing and taxi to the assigned gate."

Miller cleared his throat. "I do think he has a chance, Mr. Metz. He seems competent. The messages reflect that." He glanced between Johnson and the printout of the data-link messages lying on the console.

Johnson nodded.

Miller picked up the messages. "All the data-link messages are here if you'd like to see them."

Johnson pulled them from Miller's hand and thrust them toward Metz. "Go ahead, Wayne. Read them. They're good for your ulcer. That goddamned Straton. I knew that goddamned airplane would get us."

# MAYDAY

Metz took the sheets and began reading. He subconsciously shook his head. The impersonal words, spelled out in that odd computer type, somehow made the news much worse. Made it infinitely more believable in any case. *Lack of air pressure caused brain damage.*

Miller glanced at Metz, then at Johnson. He barely knew Metz, but felt an instinctive dislike for the man. Too meticulously dressed. His hair was styled like a movie star's. Miller didn't trust men like that, although he knew it wasn't a fair way to judge. The fact that Johnson had asked Metz to come in was indicative of the way this airline was run these days. Ten or twenty years before, this room would have been filled with men in shirtsleeves, smoking, and drinking coffee—pilots, flight instructors, executives, dispatchers, the Straton Aircraft people, anyone who cared about Trans-United and who could lend a hand. Today, when an aircraft got into trouble, they called the insurance man and the corporation lawyers before anyone else. No one dared to smoke a cigarette, or say anything that wasn't politically correct. It was time, thought Miller, to get out of the business.

Metz handed the messages back to Miller and turned to Johnson. "Are you certain these messages are an accurate appraisal?"

Johnson tapped his finger on the stack of printouts. "If he says people are dead, they're dead. I imagine that he also knows what two holes look like."

"I'm talking about the brain damage business. And why do you think it's irrevocable?"

"My expert," he nodded toward Miller, "tells me that, more than likely, what Berry is observing is in fact brain damage. Is it irrevocable? Probably. It's caused by cells dying. That's irrevocable. But who's to say for sure what state those poor bastards are in? Berry is an amateur pilot, not a neurosurgeon. For all we know, Berry could be the son-of-a-bitch who planted the bomb in the first place, although that doesn't seem too likely."

Metz nodded. "Well, it certainly looks bad."

"Very perceptive," said Johnson. "Thank you for sharing. I'm glad I asked you here."

Metz decided to play it cool. "Why *did* you ask me here?"

Johnson stared at him a long time. He answered, finally, "Evans called you because you're in the emergency handbook."

Metz looked pointedly around the empty room.

Johnson smiled to himself. Metz was a sharp customer. He was playing hard to get. "All right, I wanted some assurances from you, Mr. Insurance Man. First of all, are we completely covered for this type of thing?"

"You would seem to be. Your hull carrier will cover the damage to the aircraft, of course. But everything else is our potential responsibility."

Johnson didn't like "seem" or "potential." He said, "Including any claims that arise if the Straton smacks into San Francisco? Everything it hits? Everybody on the ground?"

"That's basically correct."

Johnson paced for a few seconds. He hadn't gotten the bad news that Metz wanted to give him, because he hadn't yet asked the right questions. He looked up at Metz. "Can your company afford this?"

Metz gave a barely perceptible shrug.

Johnson stopped pacing. A chill ran up his spine. "What the hell is that supposed to mean?"

"It means that no one can answer that until the damage is done. It also means that it is the responsibility of the insured to take every reasonable step to minimize the loss. It also means that Trans-United Airlines had better be able to prove that the accident was not a direct result of negligence on its part. It—"

"Wait a goddamned minute. First of all, you'd *better* have the money. Secondly, we *are* trying to minimize the loss. That's what we're here to do. Thirdly, there was *no* negligence on . . ." But even as he said it, Johnson wondered again if any of his recent cutbacks in maintenance could have contributed to the accident—or could be made to look that way by some lawyer.

"Someone with a bomb slipped through your security. Maybe Berry. You almost said so yourself."

Johnson took a step toward Metz, then turned to Miller. "Call the legal department, Jack. Then escort Mr. Metz out of here."

Metz realized he had pushed too far. "Wait. There are a few things I'd like to speak to you about first." He nodded toward Miller. "Privately."

Before Johnson could respond, there was a knock at the door. All three men turned.

Dennis Evans stood on the other side of the glass, nervously clutching a piece of paper.

Edward Johnson walked to the door and unlocked it. "What is it, Evans?"

"I've got a call about the Straton," said Evans waving the paper in his hand. "From Air Traffic Control. They can't contact Flight 52. They want to know if we can contact them on a company frequency. The guy who called, Malone, thought the flight might be having radio trouble."

"What did you tell him?"

"Nothing, sir. I put him off." He handed Johnson the piece of paper. "This is his name and phone number. I told him we'd call him back."

Johnson took the note and stuck it into his pocket. "Okay, Evans. Good work." He closed the door before Evans could reply. Johnson turned and approached the telephone.

Metz placed himself between Johnson and the phone. "Hold on, Ed. Can't we have that talk first?"

Johnson was not accustomed to having someone try to intimidate *him*. He decided that Wayne Metz was either very brash or very desperate. In either case, he had something on his mind. "I have to call them. It should have been done first thing, only this accident is happening all ass-backwards. Normally, there'd be a search-and-rescue operation heading toward them already. We're probably going to be in a shit pot of trouble over these delays as it is."

Jack Miller moved around the men and picked up the phone. "I'll take the rap for that. Give me the number, Ed. I'll call."

Johnson shook his head impatiently. "Don't be an idiot. I'll hang Evans with it. He's the stupid son-of-a-bitch who was supposed to make all the calls."

"I'm the man in charge."

"Jack, let me handle it." Johnson turned and spoke to Metz. "First of all, there was always the possibility that the data-link messages were a hoax. That's why we delayed in calling. Second, like I said, this accident happened ass-backwards. Air Traffic Control is always the first to find out, and they, in turn, notify the airline involved. Having a distress message come in on the company data-link is highly unusual. Actually, it's never happened to any airline. It isn't even covered in the company's emergency handbook. And don't forget that *you* asked me not to call any—"

Metz shook his head impatiently. "This FAA business is no concern of mine. I only want to plan our announcement before you make any calls. We should keep the operations and the liability conversations separate. Otherwise, it might compromise our posture in court. I need a minute with you. One minute."

Johnson looked at Miller. "Jack . . ."

Miller shook his head. "Now, wait a minute. Flight 52 is my flight, Ed. I have to know what's going on."

Johnson put his hand on Miller's shoulder. "This is just insurance crap, Jack. You don't want to hear it, because if you do, you'll be asked about it someday. Give us just one minute."

Miller looked at the two men. Trans-United was still like a big family—but it had become a family that had something to hide. Miller realized that there was no point in trying to buck Edward Johnson—not on this point. "All right . . ." He walked to the door and left the room.

Johnson rebolted the door, then turned back to Metz. "Okay. You have your minute."

Metz took a deep breath and sat himself in a chair. "Okay. We've got to be very careful from a liability standpoint. We can't contribute to the problems of the Straton. Legally, we're better off doing nothing than doing the wrong things."

"In other words, don't give them landing instructions?"

"I'm sorry, but that's the way it is. The courts and juries have set the precedent. Everyone's a Monday-morning quarterback. Whatever you do now will be judged later in court and it will be judged by the results of your actions, not your good intentions. In other words, if you talk him down and he crashes, you're worse off than if you hadn't tried. Your only obligation as I see it is to mount a rescue operation."

Johnson looked at Metz. He was saying one thing but meaning something else. "That sounds like bullshit to me. But if that's true, then we've done the right thing so far by sitting on our thumbs and not giving Berry correspondence courses in flying a supersonic jet. And I'll tell you something else—talking a pilot down by radio is a bitch; talking him into a final approach and landing by data-link is a joke. When I get the chief pilot here and tell him what he has to do, he'll shit." He paused. "Of course, with the way my luck has been going, Fitzgerald will pull it off and become an overnight national hero. He and Berry will do the talk-show circuit. Terrific."

Metz sat up in his chair. "Then there is a chance that the Straton can be landed?"

Johnson shrugged. "There's always a chance. Stranger things have happened in the air. All kinds of bullshit about God in the copilot's seat, bombers landing with dead crews, mysterious lights showing the way to the airport in a storm. And don't forget that Berry may well be an excellent pilot. Who knows?"

Metz nodded. The phone call from Air Traffic Control was something he hadn't planned on, and he wondered what other surprises were still in store. He had to have more facts. "Why doesn't Air Traffic Control know where the Straton is? Aren't they supposed to be watching on radar?"

"There's no radar that far out over the ocean. Each aircraft determines its own position, then radios it in to ATC. They, in turn, work like a central clearinghouse. They coordinate the flights so that none of them try to fly the same route at the same time. With the Straton 797 it's very simple. It flies so high that there's no one else up there except for an occasional Concorde or a military jet. That's probably why ATC isn't too excited by the loss of radio contact with 52. There's nobody up there to conflict with."

Metz leaned forward in his chair. "Then Air Traffic Control still thinks the Straton is on its normal course and headed for . . . Where did you say . . . Japan?"

"Right." Johnson heard an unmistakable tone of eagerness in Metz's voice. Clearly, the man was leading up to something, and his first statement about not giving landing instructions was a clue. That bullshit about courts and juries was just a trial balloon. Maybe Metz had something that would lessen their personal liability in this thing.

Metz stared down at the floor. There was an exact psychological moment to go in for the kill, and it had not yet arrived—but it was close. He looked up. "So it's not unusual to lose radio contact?"

Johnson nodded. "Not too. Radios have problems. I'm told that all sorts of things affect radios at sixty-two thousand feet. Sunspots. The variables of the stratosphere. But all those things are temporary. If contact isn't established soon, everyone will know there's been trouble."

Metz nodded again. "So if ATC can later pinpoint the time of the accident, Trans-United is in trouble?"

Johnson didn't answer.

Metz let the statement take hold for a few seconds, then changed the subject. "How far out will the Air Traffic Control radar pick up the Straton?"

"Depends on altitude. They're flying low now. They won't be seen by radar until they get within fifty miles of the coast."

"That close?"

"Right. But what the hell does this have to do with my liability coverage, Wayne? You're like my goddamned automobile insurance broker. Wants to know all about the accident while I want to know when you're going to pay."

Metz forced a smile. "It's all related."

"Is it?" Johnson could sense that Metz was about to make a proposition, and he tried to look less intimidating and more receptive. He sat down on a high stool and smiled. "What are you getting at, Wayne? Time's wasting."

"I can speak freely?"

"Sure. Just cut through all the bullshit and give it to me straight. If it sounds good for Ed Johnson and Trans-United, you probably have a deal. But if it sounds good for Wayne Metz and company, I'm going to toss your ass out of this office. Hurry. I have to call ATC."

Metz stood. He looked at Ed Johnson for a long time, then spoke softly. "Ed . . . the Straton has to go down. And it has to go down over the water, not over land.

248

No survivors on the aircraft. No further casualties on the ground."

Johnson stood also. Metz's proposition was not a complete surprise. "You're out of your goddamn mind."

Metz exhaled softly. Johnson had not immediately thrown him out of the office, and that in itself was encouraging. He knew enough to say nothing further.

Johnson turned and faced the Pacific chart. He stared up at it, then looked down at the floor and began pacing. He stopped and stared at Metz. "Okay. I'll bite. What do we gain if it goes down in the drink?"

Metz knew he was in a position to score. He let the silence drag on, then he spoke. "We gain everything. We save our companies, our jobs, and we insure our future prosperity in this rat race of life."

"All that? Sounds great. And all we have to do is commit mass murder."

"This is no joke, Ed."

"No, it's not. Murder is no joke." He paused. "And how would you propose we deep-six that Straton? There are no guided missiles or fighters in our fleet at the moment."

"We'll come to that later—if you're interested." Metz glanced at the door as though he were offering to leave.

Johnson pretended not to see the offer. "I'm interested. I'm interested in listening."

Metz nodded. "All right. Listen to this. Beneficial's liability potential is manageable if those people die. The death benefit wouldn't be pleasant to pay, but it's within our calculable exposure. We'll pay it all, and we won't involve Trans-United." He paused. "But . . . if they come back and that pilot is correct about their condition, our liability is enormous. Beyond enormous. It would bankrupt Beneficial Insurance and—"

"Before they paid all the bills?"

"That's right. We will be totally liable for each of those three hundred poor bastards *for the remainder of their lives.* And we'd be totally liable to every relative and organization that is dependent on them. Potentially, that liability might span another seventy-five years."

"And Trans-United might get stuck for the amount you couldn't pay?"

"That's right. The amount we couldn't pay, plus the amount we don't have to pay because of the limits of liability on your policy. Your limits of liability are very high, but I know you'll exceed it if that aircraft lands."

"Maybe it won't exceed it."

"I'm talking billions, Ed. *Billions.* And let me just mention again, without you getting too excited, that Beneficial will undoubtedly subrogate against Trans-United. In other words, we'll try to stick you with half the bills from the first dollar on by going to court and claiming negligence on your part. And that won't be too hard to do. The bomb was on the Straton because *your* people allowed it to be there. There have been cases like this before, you know; Trans-United will be guilty of contributory negligence. Poor security. Poor supervision. Inadequate safeguards. Look at what Lockerbie did to the old Pan Am—it was what finally drove them out of business. Besides, maybe you've done something in your maintenance or engineering programs that'll look bad in hindsight. You know, the

Valujet scenario. Then Beneficial will gang up with the FAA and make you look real bad."

"I'm not buying that," Johnson said, but in his heart he knew that it was all true. Even if the basic cause of the accident was an onboard bomb and nothing more, the lawyers and government bureaucrats could still make his maintenance economy program look responsible. Pan Am had some Arabs blow a 747 out of the sky, and eventually it put them out of business. Valujet put the wrong shipment into the cargo compartment of that doomed DC-9 out of Miami, and the FAA shut the airline down a few weeks later for *bad maintenance*. Metz was absolutely right.

Metz shrugged. "You're not the jury. And there's no sense arguing with me. This is the age of liability and automatic fault. Cause and effect. Modern logic says that whenever something goes wrong, then it *must* be someone's fault. Risk avoidance is today's buzzword. Try to convince a judge and jury that the Straton just ran into a shitload of bad luck and see how sympathetic they'll be to Trans-United. Picture, if you will, three hundred drooling plaintiffs in the courtroom. We'll take you right down the tube with us. The FAA would probably ground you—at least for a month or two. It'll make them look more efficient to the press."

"Unfortunately, you're right about that."

"It's a tough business. Tougher when you don't have an insurance pool."

"We fucked up there, didn't we?" Johnson said.

"Sure did," Metz agreed.

Johnson sat heavily into a chair. "You bastard. Okay. You just try to prove negligence, then."

Metz moved to the door. He put his hand on the

knob, then turned to Johnson. "Ed, I'm sorry I suggested such a thing. The best we can hope for now is that the Straton lands with a minimum loss of life on the ground. Just do us all a favor and suggest to ATC that they try to land him at sea, near a rescue ship. San Francisco is a nice town. I wouldn't want to see a Straton 797 plow through it."

Johnson waved his hand in a gesture of dismissal. "Spare me that bullshit."

Metz nodded. "All right. But I won't spare you from the truth." He paused and seemed to be lost in thought. "When I think of the liability of a few thousand people on the ground . . . over four hundred tons of steel and aviation fuel . . . Jesus Christ. It would be a holocaust. Think of it. *Think* of it. Property damage in the hundreds of millions . . . Well, at least we don't insure the hull. Save a hundred million bucks there."

"A hundred and twenty-five million," Johnson said.

"Right. Well, there's the chance the Straton *will* land at the airport. But it might crash into a crowded passenger terminal or plow into a couple of taxiing airliners. Which reminds me, aren't you supposed to notify the airport of a possible crash landing or something? How about the city of San Francisco . . . Civil Defense or something?" He paused. "And remember, even if we don't stick you with negligence, you still have to cover everything that exceeds your limits of liability and everything we can't cover because of bankruptcy." He let a second pass, then continued, "Beneficial might be able to restructure the company. Trans-United, on the other hand, will go under for good. This is potentially the biggest bad-news media event of the decade. No one even cares to know the name of the insurance company involved. But the Trans-United logo will become as notorious as the swastika. Front page of *Time,* for Christ's sake. And not just for a week or two, as with most accidents. No, sir, if that plane smacks into Frisco, or especially if it lands, the attorneys will parade those poor bastards through the courts . . . through the media. *Three hundred* human beings whose brains have been turned to mashed potatoes. You will personally spend the next ten years in courtrooms. And there won't be a lot of people lined up at your ticket counters in the interim. If we don't take you down, the FAA will and the press will. It's happened in the past, for less nightmarish accidents."

Johnson scowled but didn't speak. Metz was making sense—too much sense.

"How many people earn their livelihood here?" Metz asked. He took a deep breath. "God, I almost wish that thing would go down by itself. I mean, dead is dead. Final. A few weeks of splashy media happenings. Then no one will even remember the name of the airline. Hell, I don't remember the name of the airline involved in the last big crash. All airline names sound the same to the average guy. Like insurance company names. You see, if the thing goes into the drink, then all the facts go down with it. Nothing to photograph. No one to interview. The media gets bored with that. The National Transportation Safety Board can't poke through the debris and sift it all and reconstruct the events. At those depths in the mid-Pacific, and with the Straton's position unknown, the flight recorder with all that information is gone. John Berry and crew are gone. No one knows anything for sure. It would take years of legal hassling to determine who was liable, and to what extent. The airline itself could even be a sympathetic victim, what with the likelihood of a bomb."

"Right," said Johnson. Bombs were out of his jurisdiction, even if the airline's security department could be faulted. And with no physical evidence in hand, there was no way any lawyer could prove that the maintenance cutbacks somehow lessened the aircraft's survivability.

Metz was speaking faster now. "We can implicate the Straton Aircraft people, too. We could drag our feet in court for ages and retire with our distinguished careers intact before it gets untangled. But if John Berry sails into San Francisco International Airport . . . well, there's no room for legal maneuvering when conclusive evidence of the airliner's negligence is parked on the ramp, and the local mental institutions are packed to the rafters with living, breathing, drooling proof of the outcome of Trans-United Flight 52."

Metz had not yet mentioned the idea that those people would be better off dead. It was a touchy argument, so he left it in reserve. "Okay, Ed. That's all the cards, all face up on the table. Think about it. Good luck to you. Good luck to us." He unbolted the door and opened it.

"Shut the goddamned door. Get in here."

Metz shut and bolted the door. He looked at Edward Johnson and asked him, "The question is, can you give Berry flying instructions that will put that aircraft in the ocean?"

Johnson nodded. He'd already given it some thought. "I think so. The poor bastard will never know what happened."

# 11

John Berry turned his head and looked over his shoulder into the lounge. He was about to call to Stein, but Stein wasn't there. Terri O'Neil stood at the door, looking in like a departed spirit who had returned home and who could not cross the threshold without an invitation. Berry looked past her. His eyes darted around the lounge. "What the hell . . . ?"

Sharon Crandall looked over at Berry. "What's the matter?" She turned her head and followed his gaze. "Oh, for God's sake."

Berry jumped down from the pilot's chair and stood in the doorway. Harold Stein was gone. But worse than that, six passengers from the lower cabin had found their way up to the lounge. As he watched, Berry saw another appear out of the stairwell. He looked back at Sharon Crandall. "Stay here and keep them out of the cockpit."

Crandall stood and placed herself in the doorway. Terri reached out toward her. Crandall took her friend's hands in hers and held them, but would not let her pass.

Berry stepped quickly into the lounge, taking Terri by the arm and pulling her along.

He saw Linda Farley sprawled out near the piano. He walked to the middle of the lounge, ignoring the people milling around him. "Linda!"

She didn't answer.

Berry felt an unexpected fear seize him. He released the flight attendant's arm and ran across the carpeted lounge. John knelt beside the girl, took her shoulder, and shook her. "Linda!"

Linda Farley opened her eyes slowly.

First Officer Daniel McVary, lying a few feet away, opened his eyes also. But his eyes opened quickly, in a flash, wide and staring, like a night creature's when the sun goes down. He lifted his head.

Berry helped the girl to a sitting position. He could see that her lips were dry and cracked, and dried tears streaked her face. "Almost home, honey."

Linda Farley's head turned, out of habit, toward the man she had been told to look after. She screamed. "He's awake!"

Berry looked down into the bloodshot eyes of the copilot.

Daniel McVary sat up, his head hitting the leg of the piano. He let out a grunt and rolled over, then crawled toward Berry, his tongue hanging out like a dog's.

Berry pulled the girl toward him and lifted her to her feet.

McVary continued to crawl toward them.

Berry pushed the girl behind him, then slowly, cautiously, bent over and helped the copilot stand. He looked into the man's eyes. This was the man on whom Berry, a few hours before, had placed all his hopes.

But that was before he had fully understood the scope of what had happened to the men, women, and children of Flight 52. Before he had made contact with San Francisco, before he had gained some confidence in himself. He saw now that this man standing in front of him, red eyes blinking and face twitching, could be of no more help to him than the others. Reluctantly, with some sense of guilt, he turned the man around and gently pushed him away. McVary stumbled a few feet, collided with the piano, and lay sprawled across it.

Berry looked up at the cockpit door. Terri O'Neil was again trying to enter the cockpit. Sharon was standing in the doorway with her arms thrust in front of her, pushing her friend away, too gently, Berry thought. A man who had come up from the cabin was also heading toward the cockpit. Berry looked quickly around the lounge. The other passengers were aimlessly stumbling into the lounge furniture and into each other. Berry wondered what force, what residual human intelligence it was that possessed and propelled them in so persistent a fashion. What were they seeking? What were they *thinking*?

Berry took Linda's arm and pulled her to the staircase. He knelt and yelled down. "Stein! Harold! Can you hear me!"

There was no answer from Stein, only the howling wind and the coarse, vulgar sounds of the others. "Stein! Barbara! Barbara Yoshiro! Can you hear me?"

A group of passengers were on the stairs, climbing toward him. Berry waited a second until the first one, a young woman with long blonde hair, came within reach. He put his hand on her face and pushed. She stumbled back, lost her footing, and fell into the man behind her.

Berry rose quickly and wiped his wet hand over his trouser leg. "Oh, Jesus!" he mumbled.

Linda Farley cried out.

Berry turned in time to see the copilot lunge at him. McVary's outstretched hands hit him in the face and Berry stumbled back, almost falling into the stairwell. He recovered quickly and grabbed McVary's arm and pushed him toward the stairwell. He took the girl's arm and walked quickly toward the cockpit door, pushing people aside. At the door, he pulled away Terri O'Neil and two men near her. He pushed Linda into the cockpit past Sharon. "Get back."

He pulled the door by its broken latch and drew it shut as far as its sprung hinges allowed. "Damn it! We can't lock this." He turned and faced Crandall.

Sharon Crandall had her arms around Linda. The girl was sobbing quietly, pressed against her body. Crandall was stroking the girl's hair.

It was several seconds before anyone spoke, then Crandall said, "What could have happened to Stein . . . to Barbara?"

Berry ignored the question. He glanced back at the door. It was open about three inches. Someone pressed on it and it closed a bit more. He was satisfied that the closed door presented enough of an obstacle for the moment. He sat in the pilot's seat and turned back to the girl. "Linda, keep watching the door. Sharon, sit in the copilot's seat."

Crandall sat and turned to him. "John, what about Barbara . . . and Harold Stein? Can't we . . . ?"

Berry shook his head impatiently. "Forget them."

His hands were still shaking. "Stein . . . Stein went below to be with his family, and I don't think he's coming back . . . ever. Barbara . . . well, she must have run into something too big to handle."

Crandall nodded.

---

Daniel McVary focused on the door to the cockpit. Several half-thoughts ran through his mind. The predominant one concerned water. He wanted water, and he remembered that he had drunk water in the place behind the door. He'd sat in a chair surrounded by big windows and drunk from cups. He was beginning to remember a lot more. He remembered that he belonged in the chair. His mind's eye flashed pictures, clear and vivid, but their exact meaning wasn't fully understood.

Daniel McVary's brain still functioned on many levels, but there were huge dead areas, black places, where nothing lived, no synapses connected, no memory was stored. Yet the brain was finding open circuits around these dead areas and thoughts were forming, wants and needs were recognized, action was contemplated.

First Officer McVary's mind focused on the image behind the door that he had seen before it closed. Someone stood near his chair. A woman. He wanted to go back to his chair. The man who had pushed him was in there also. His arm still hurt. He stepped toward the door.

---

Linda Farley shouted. "Mr. Berry!"

Berry spun around and jumped out of his seat, but it

was too late. The copilot crossed the threshold and walked into the cockpit. Berry lunged at him, but McVary lurched out of the way and stumbled against the side wall of the cockpit.

Berry stood still, holding his breath. He watched as the copilot brushed across a board jammed with circuit breakers and several switches, afraid to move toward him again, knowing that if those switches were inadvertently moved, he might never be able to set them right again.

Very slowly, Berry began moving toward McVary and reached out his hand toward the copilot as the man kept groping at the console and electronics board to regain his footing.

McVary got his balance and turned. He came to meet John Berry. Berry proceeded more cautiously, aware that the man had a fair amount of agility and even some cunning. They moved toward, then around, each other, circling cautiously in the confined area of the cockpit.

A group of passengers stood at the door, craning their heads, watching.

Linda Farley moved back and climbed into the pilot's chair. Sharon Crandall edged out of the copilot's chair and tried to get in a position to help.

It occurred to Berry that anyone with as much mental ability as McVary seemed to have might be capable of understanding reason. He spoke softly. "McVary. McVary. Do you understand me? Can you speak?"

McVary seemed to listen to the words, but he kept circling. He opened his mouth. "I . . . I . . . I . . ."

Berry nodded. "Yes. Please go. Go. Out to the lounge. Lounge. Lounge . . ."

# MAYDAY

McVary picked his head up and looked into the lounge, then suddenly bolted toward his flight chair.

Sharon Crandall screamed and tried to get out of his way. McVary grabbed her and threw her to the side.

Berry caught McVary from behind, and both men fell to the floor. Berry struck his head on the seat track and a black, searing pain shot through his skull.

He was aware that he was on the floor and that McVary wasn't. He knew that the copilot could not be restrained by Linda or Sharon, but he couldn't get to his feet. He felt blood running over his forehead and face. He saw McVary's legs near his face. He looked up. McVary was struggling with Sharon. Everything became blurry, then he heard a noise, a noise that filled the cockpit and sounded like the rushing of steam through a burst pipe. McVary screamed.

Berry was aware that Sharon was helping him sit up. He looked around. McVary was gone. The door was closed again. "What happened?"

Sharon Crandall dabbed at his bleeding wound with a handkerchief. She motioned toward Linda Farley.

Berry looked at the girl. She stood, trembling, with a bright red fire extinguisher in her hand, Halon still visible around its nozzle.

Crandall touched Berry's cheek. "Can you stand?"

"Yes. Of course." He stood slowly and looked at Linda Farley. "Good thinking. Very good."

Linda dropped the fire extinguisher and ran to Berry. She buried her face in his chest.

Berry patted her head. "It's all right. You didn't hurt him. Just scared him a little." He cradled her head in his hand and with the other hand reached out for

Sharon. The three of them stood quietly for a few seconds, calming themselves.

Berry heard scratching on the door and stepped over to it. He could see faces through the small piece of one-way glass in the door. He took a deep breath, then hit the door with his shoulder, sending two men and a woman sprawling. He looked back into the lounge. A procession of people were coming, one at a time, out of the stairwell, filling the lounge from wall to wall, pressing closer to the cockpit bulkhead. Berry looked at their blood-red eyes set in those gray, ashen faces. His head swam. His hold on reality was beginning to weaken. An irrational thought flashed through his mind, the thought that he was already dead and this place was not the Straton but some sort of perpetual flight that would never end, never land. . . .

He pulled the door shut tightly and turned, facing back into the cockpit. He felt sweat on his face and his breathing had become difficult.

Sharon Crandall looked from the door to his face, then back at the door. There was fear, thought Berry—no, terror—in her eyes. Berry controlled his voice and spoke to her. "We . . . we've lost a major advantage . . . with them in the lounge . . . but . . . as long as we keep them out of here . . . out of the cockpit . . ."

His world was shrinking, reduced to these square yards—this small room that contained their only link with the world they had left . . . that contained the instruments of their survival and the only mechanical and human intelligence left onboard.

Sharon Crandall held Linda Farley and nodded, but she did not see how they were going to keep the passengers of Flight 52 out of the cockpit.

# MAYDAY

Edward Johnson walked to a long shelf and took down a heavy spiral-bound book. Wayne Metz watched him carefully. The man was still walking a mental tightrope, and the slightest thing could upset his balance.

Johnson sat on a stool and placed the book on the counter. He picked up the telephone.

Metz spoke softly, choosing his words carefully. "Is there anything I can help you with?"

Johnson didn't answer. He placed the slip of paper that Evans had given him on the counter and began dialing. At the same time, he opened the big book in front of him.

Metz was becoming anxious. "Who are you calling? What's in that book?"

Johnson looked at him as the phone began ringing on the other end. "I'm calling ATC."

"Why?"

"Because, Wayne, from now on I have to handle it just like it's supposed to be handled."

"What's in the book?"

Johnson spoke into the telephone. "Mr. Malone, please." He looked up at Metz. "There's a coffeepot in that cabinet. Make coffee." He turned to the phone. "Mr. Malone, this is Ed Johnson. Vice-President of Operations at Trans-United."

"Yes, sir. What's the story with 52?"

"I'm afraid it doesn't look very good. They are no longer transmitting."

"Do you have any idea what's going on?"

"Before I fill you in, take down these coordinates of

their last estimated position. Please take the necessary steps to begin a search-and-rescue operation."

"Yes. Go ahead."

Johnson read the coordinates. "They turned before we lost contact, so they are now on a heading of 120 degrees at a speed of approximately 340 knots. You can extrapolate from there."

"Yes, sir. Hold the line while I get the ball rolling on this."

Johnson flipped through the book in front of him.

Malone came back on the line. "The search-and-rescue operation will be rolling shortly. Is there any chance they could still be flying?"

"Always a chance. Incidentally, when was the last time you heard from them, Mr. Malone?"

There was a short pause. "At eleven o'clock they radioed their position."

Johnson nodded. "Why didn't you call us?"

"Well . . . we were trying to contact them. Actually, we didn't try until they'd missed their next mandatory report. It should have occurred at 12:18, so it's not that long. And all the airlines' 797s have a little radio trouble because of the altitude and—"

"I understand. We've been a little lax here too, I'm afraid. My dispatcher didn't have his regular one-o'clock update from them and he let it go for a while." He would have to fill in the missed 12:00 update. "Then, when he tried to radio, he experienced the same trouble that you apparently did. But, of course, he wasn't concerned."

"That's understandable, Mr. Johnson. But what exactly happened to the aircraft? How did you finally make contact with them?"

"Well, we're not certain exactly what happened. A short while before I called you, we received a message on our company data-link. It was a distress message. It said only SOS."

"SOS?"

"Yes. No identification of any sort. We thought, of course, that it was a hoax of some sort."

"Yes, of course."

"Then, some time later, a dispatcher discovered another message sitting in the data-link. There is no way to determine how long either message sat in the data-link."

"What did the message say?"

Johnson pulled the message toward him and read, "'Emergency. Mayday. Aircraft damaged. Radios dead. Mid-Pacific. Need help. Do you read?'"

"That was it?"

"My dispatcher acknowledged immediately, then called me. Are you writing this all down?"

"Yes, sir."

"Good. They did not immediately call you, I'm afraid, because there was some confusion over the way the message was received and because of the wording in our company emergency handbook."

"Wording?"

"Yes. It says—let me read it." Johnson placed the handbook over the big book in front of him. "It says, 'When Air Traffic Control notifies you of a midair emergency, contact the following.' So my dispatcher called the numbers on the list but never thought to call Air Traffic Control, since your number wasn't listed in the FAA-approved handbook. He may also have believed that someone else was calling you already. You

know how it is, when you see a fire, you think everyone's called. . . . Anyway, it was a damned stupid oversight and he will be properly reprimanded. In any case,
there is nothing lost except some time in getting a
search-and-rescue underway."

"Yes, I see." Malone's voice sounded apologetic.
"Do you know what the nature of the emergency
was?"

"I suspect that the damage to the aircraft was too
great to continue flying."

"What damage is that?"

Johnson put a tone of sadness and anger in his voice.
"A bomb—or structural failure . . . two holes in the
hull. Decompression killed or incapacitated the crew
and passengers."

"Good God. . . . Then . . . who . . . ?"

"A private pilot was in a positive pressure area. The
lavatory, probably. He made the transmissions and
turned the aircraft at our suggestion. I suspect, too, that
he may have touched something in the cockpit that led
to the final . . . led to the possible . . . crash. I hope to
God it's only because of a malfunction of the data-link
machine . . ." Johnson found something in the book
that he needed.

"Yes. Let's hope so. Do you have copies . . . ?"

"Yes. I'll send copies of the printouts to you right
now. It shows everything we know and everything
we've done."

"As soon as possible, please."

"There won't be any further delay on our part. I'm
taking personal charge of the operation at this end."

"Yes. Very good. I'm still a bit concerned—"

"There has, of course, been an unconscionable delay

in getting the ball rolling here, and we will take full responsibility."

"Well, of course, Mr. Johnson, it was an unusual set of circumstances, to say the least." There was a pause. "What time did you say you received the first data-link transmission?"

Johnson took a deep breath. He had figured that it must have been at about 12:15. He looked at his watch. It was now 1:30. "About one o'clock."

"That's a long time."

"Not when you're trying to deal with an unusual set of circumstances. But, of course, you're correct. And please keep in mind that the Straton was still flying up until a few minutes ago, and may still be flying this way, I should add."

"Yes. Well, we've all been a bit . . . slow."

"Please keep me up-to-date on the search operation."

"Of course."

"Meanwhile, the printouts are on the way. I'll have them faxed to this number we show for you."

"Good."

"And we'll keep transmitting on our data-link at three-minute intervals in the event . . ."

"Yes, very good. I'm sorry."

"So are we."

"Thank you." He hung up and turned to Metz. "Well, that went all right. A little trouble with the Federal Aviation Agency is better, I guess, than losing my job and bankrupting the company."

"I'd say so. Will the ATC people come here?"

"Not them. FAA air carrier inspectors. But as long

as they think we're out of contact with the Straton, they won't be in any rush to get here."

"How about the rescue operation you just set up?"

"They'll probably call the Navy and Air Force, and commercial shipping in the area. That'll take hours. By that time we'll have . . ." Johnson stopped, then looked directly at Metz. "By then, we'll be finished with this."

Metz nodded. "How about your Trans-United people? Will they want to come here?"

"I'll take care of that in a minute."

"Good. What's that book you've been looking at?"

"Get me a cup of coffee."

Wayne Metz had not gotten anyone a cup of coffee in ten years. But he turned toward the coffeepot.

Johnson slid off his stool and walked to the data-link. He took the printouts from the receiving basket and quickly read through them again. No times. No indication of spaces between the messages. Nothing that could be considered poor judgment on the part of Trans-United. The last messages since Miller's ". . . working on bringing you home" looked a bit compromising, and he tore them off. With his pen he marked the SOS message: *Discovered by dispatcher in link machine at approximately 1 P.M.* He walked to the door and opened it.

At Johnson's appearance the room became quiet. Johnson's eyes swept the room and fixed each man in turn. He said tonelessly, "Gentlemen, I'm afraid we've lost contact with Flight 52."

There was a rush of moans and exclamations.

"I have called the Air Traffic Control and they have initiated a search-and-rescue operation. Of course, the problem may simply be the link, but . . ." He stepped a few feet into the room. "I will remain in the communications room and continue transmitting." Johnson was aware of Metz behind him. He looked over his shoulder and saw the man holding a cup of coffee. That was good for the dispatchers to see. There was no doubt that Edward Johnson ran things and ran people. He turned and took the coffee from Metz. He spoke in a low voice. "Get back in the communications room and close the damned door. If that alerting bell goes off and they hear it, we're finished." He turned and addressed the dispatchers. "Gather round, please."

The more than two dozen dispatchers moved around him.

Johnson began in an official, but friendly tone. "Gentlemen, there is no doubt in my mind that Jack Miller," he nodded to Miller, "Dennis Evans, and Jerry Brewster," he looked at the two men, "did everything they could do as quickly as possible. However, there was a time lapse between the first link message and now of about half an hour." He paused and studied the faces of the men around him. Some glanced at the wall clock, some at their watches. A few looked surprised, others nodded eagerly. "The first message came in at about one o'clock, I believe someone told me. There will be some problems with ATC and even with our own people over that lag, but I'm solidly behind you, so don't worry too much about it." He looked around the room.

There were more people nodding now.

Johnson looked at Evans. "You call everyone on the list, including our press office. Have the press office call me for a statement. To the president of the airlines and to everyone else, you say the following: Flight 52 has suffered a midair decompression. Radios dead. Amateur pilot flying and communicating on data-link. Communications lost at . . ." he looked at his watch, "one twenty-five P.M. ATC is initiating a search-and-rescue. I suggest an emergency meeting in the executive conference room. Got it?"

Evans nodded quickly. "Yes, sir." He moved rapidly to his desk.

Johnson looked at the men around him. "Each one of you call your flights and tell them to keep off the data-link." He scanned the faces of the men. "Brewster?"

"Here, sir."

"Okay. Brewster, you will take these printouts and make only one copy. Then fax one copy to ATC at the number they show in the Emergency Handbook."

"Yes, sir."

"Then send our copy to the executive conference room in the company office building. The original comes back to me. Quickly."

Brewster took the messages and double-timed out of the dispatch office.

"That's all, gentlemen. Thank you all for your help." He paused. "If any of you are of a religious nature, please ask the man upstairs to look after that Straton and everyone aboard her. Thank you. Miller, come here."

The dispatchers moved back to their desks silently. Jack Miller approached Johnson.

Johnson put his hand on his shoulder. "Jack, fill in the empty updates for 52 and note that they were posted at noon. Leave the one P.M. updates blank, of course."

Miller looked at the big man standing next to him. "Ed . . . we're not going to get away with this."

"Of course we are. I'm doing it for you and the company as much as for myself. There have been a series of errors and blunders here, and we have nothing to lose to try to cover it. If we don't, you, I, Evans, Brewster, and about ten random scapegoats will be fired, then we'll be investigated by the FAA and maybe be charged with something. Your lovely wife can bake cookies for all of us and bring them out to San Quentin on Sundays. Bring the kids along, too."

Miller nodded. He started to move away, but Johnson held onto his shoulder.

"Are the men with us?" Johnson asked.

Miller nodded again. "It's not the first time we've had to cover ourselves."

Johnson smiled. "I always knew you bastards lied for each other. Now you have to lie for *me*. For yourselves, too, of course. Go fill in those updates."

Miller moved off.

Johnson walked quickly back into the communications room. He looked at Metz, who was staring down at the big spiral-bound book. "You know, Wayne, the more I think about it, the more I'm convinced that Straton *should* go down."

Metz looked up at him quizzically. "I thought we agreed on that."

"In principle. Everything I did just now is standard operating procedure. I've done nothing wrong yet, except delay."

"You told everyone the plane went down."

"Did I? I said we lost contact with them. You don't see any new link messages, do you?" He turned and looked out into the dispatch office. "Actually, my responsibility in this screw-up is pretty light. Those idiots out there blew it. ATC was not too swift either."

"They've all given us a chance to save it."

Johnson nodded. "Yes. The man who can really testify to our mishandling of this whole thing is Berry."

"And he's heading home."

"I know. God, I wish he'd just crash," Johnson said.

"He probably will. Right into San Francisco. You've got to put him in the ocean."

"I know."

Metz sat down behind the data-link. "Look, Ed, I know this is difficult for you—it goes against all your instincts. But believe me, there is no other way. Do what you've got to do. If it will make it any easier, I'll type the message to Berry."

Johnson laughed. "You stupid bastard. What difference does it make *who* types the message? There's no difference in guilt, only a difference in nerve. Get out of that chair."

Metz quickly vacated the chair behind the data-link.

Johnson sat down. He glanced up at the dispatch office outside the glass. A few heads dropped or turned away. "As far as they know, I'm still trying to contact Flight 52."

"What are you going to tell him to do?"

"There's only a few things about a cockpit I know for sure. I've ridden in the observer's seat enough times and had to listen to enough pilots give me unwanted flying lessons to know what's dangerous and what can bring an aircraft down. That book I was looking at is the Straton's pilot manual."

Metz nodded appreciatively. "Any ideas?"

"A few. I'm trying to work them out. But they're tricky." He looked at his watch. "That meeting in the executive conference room will be rolling in a while. They'll chew over those link printouts and wail and whine for a good fifteen, maybe thirty, minutes. Then they'll ring me here."

"Then you'd better hurry. Jesus, this is cutting it close, Ed. You didn't leave yourself any room."

Neither man was aware of the insistent rapping on the glass door.

Johnson finally looked up.

Jack Miller stood outside the door.

"Oh, Christ," said Johnson. "If we let Miller in and Flight 52 begins transmitting, that would be the end of the game." Johnson knew that if he turned off the machine, Miller would notice and ask why they weren't trying to reestablish contact. He quickly went to the door and opened it.

Miller took a step in.

Johnson moved forward and edged him out a few steps, but couldn't close the door without being too obvious. "What is it, Jack?"

Miller's eyes moved past Johnson into the small room. He stared at Metz, and without looking at Johnson, handed him a sheaf of papers. "Here's the data-link printouts. Faxed to ATC and copied for the executive conference room." He looked at Johnson. "The chief pilot, Captain Fitzgerald, is on his way here in case we make contact. Mr. Abbot, the Straton Aircraft representative, is also on his way. Is there anyone else you want here?"

"I don't want *anyone* here, Jack. Have a dispatcher intercept them in the parking lot and tell them to drive over to the executive conference room in the company office building. Okay?"

Miller ignored the order as if he hadn't heard it. He said, "I just don't understand what could have happened up there. That aircraft was steady and that pilot—"

"It had two great big fucking holes in it. You wouldn't fly too well with two great big damn holes in *you*." He pushed Miller's chest with his forefinger and backed him up a step. "Go home and get some rest."

"I'm staying here."

Johnson hesitated, then said, "All right. Take over the Pacific desk from Evans."

"I mean here—in the communications room."

Johnson knew what he meant. "It's not necessary."

"Does that mean I'm relieved of my duties?"

Johnson, for some reason he couldn't explain, felt that the data-link bell was going to ring momentarily. He began to perspire. "Jack . . ." He had to be tactful, careful. "Jack, don't start getting sullen. You may have made a few mistakes, but you did a few heads-up things too. It's like in the military. You're somewhere between a medal and a court-martial. Now, don't forget our conversations. Play it my way and we can all save our asses. Okay?"

Miller nodded. "Are you still trying to contact . . . ?"

"Yes. Every three minutes. And you're holding me up now." Johnson was becoming anxious. He kept glancing up at the door across the room. Soon, someone whom he couldn't keep out of the communications room might walk into the dispatch office. In a way, he would almost have welcomed it.

Metz called out. "I have to finish this business with you and report to my people."

Johnson turned his head. "Right." He turned back to Miller. "Do me a favor. Go to the employees' lounge—no, to the executives' lounge—and while things are still fresh in your mind write a full report of everything that happened before I arrived. Make sure the times and actions tally with our estimates, of course. When you finish, report back here and give the report to me and me only."

Miller nodded.

"Did you fill in the Straton's updates?"

Miller nodded again.

"Good. When you come back you can resume your duties here in the communications room. See you later." He stepped back, then closed and bolted the door just as the data-link bell sounded. "Oh, Christ!"

The data-link began to print.

Metz wiped his face with a handkerchief. "That was too close."

Johnson was visibly shaken. "Wayne, just keep out of this. I understand what's got to be done, and I don't need any help from you. In fact, you can leave."

"I'm going nowhere until that aircraft is down."

Johnson walked over to the data-link and sat down. He glanced out into the dispatch office, then quickly pulled the message off and put it in his lap.

Metz looked down and they read it at the same time.

FROM FLIGHT 52: IMPERATIVE YOU HAVE QUALIFIED PILOT BEGIN TO GIVE ME INSTRUCTIONS ON FLIGHT CONTROLS— NAVIGATION—APPROACH—LANDING. BERRY.

Johnson nodded. "He's very sharp." He turned to Metz. "Wayne, do you feel anything for this poor bastard? Can't you admire his guts?"

Metz looked offended. "Of course I can admire him. I'm not completely inhuman. But . . . didn't you once say that you were in Vietnam? Didn't you ever see a commander sacrifice a few good men to save the whole unit?"

"Enough times to wonder if the good men weren't worth the rest of the unit. Enough times, too, to wonder if it wasn't the commander's own ass he was trying to save." Johnson looked up through the glass panels, then down at the keyboard. "I'm going to give Berry a course change that will put them on a heading for Hawaii."

"Why?"

"Because he'll never find Hawaii. He'll run out of fuel in about six hours. He'll go down at sea looking for Hawaii."

"Can't you do something more positive?"

"Too tricky. We'll try this."

Metz suspected that Johnson saw a fine—but to him meaningless—line between actually giving information that would cause the Straton to crash and information that would result in its crash several hours from now. "But he'll keep transmitting. We can't stay in this goddamned room and guard this machine for six hours."

"No, we can't. After he takes up the new heading and stays on it for a while, I'll short out the data-link with a screwdriver through a rear access panel. Then we'll call in a technician and leave. The link won't be fixed for hours."

# MAYDAY

"Are you sure?"

"It'll take over an hour just to get a technician here. Hours, sometimes days, to get parts. These machines are special technology. Never used for vital communications—so it takes a while to get them fixed."

"What if Berry, when he loses contact, turns from the Hawaii heading and heads back toward the coast?"

Johnson shook his head. "He won't. We'll tell him that the air-and-sea rescue units will be intercepting him on his new heading, and that the military and civilian airports in Hawaii are expecting him. He won't want to throw that chance away."

Metz nodded. "Can't he change channels on his data-link?"

"They tell me the different channels are for the relay stations only. There's a computer somewhere that automatically sends all the Trans-United messages to this unit." Johnson pointed at the data-link machine in front of him.

"I see," said Metz, although he didn't see, not exactly. It was, as they said in business school, all PFM— pure fucking magic—and the details of how and why didn't interest him in the slightest. Metz looked up at the Pacific chart. In a vast expanse of blue, a few green dots represented the islands of Hawaii. He spoke to Johnson as he stared at the map. "What if he *finds* Hawaii?"

"With the heading I give him, he won't come close. He'll be lost, alone, with no radio, a damaged aircraft, no idea of how to fly the aircraft, no fuel reserve, and no one looking for him. If he survives all that, Mr. Metz, he sure deserves to live."

Johnson began to type the new heading.

# MAYDAY

John Berry watched the small piece of one-way glass in the cockpit door.

The passengers of Flight 52 moved up the staircase of the Straton like fish or birds on some perverse and incomprehensible migration. Or, thought Berry, like air and water that moves according to the laws of physics to fill a sudden vacuum. They filled the lounge and wandered aimlessly over the thick blue carpet, around the brightly upholstered furniture—men, women, and children—ready to seep into the next empty place that they could fill. Berry felt comforted by this analogy. It denied the possibility that they were acting according to a plan, that they were *looking* for the cockpit.

Berry made a quick count of the passengers in the lounge. About fifty now. If they all suddenly moved toward the door of the cockpit, and if one of them pulled it open rather than pressed against it, then he, Sharon, and Linda could not stop them from flooding the cockpit.

He thought again of the autopilot master switch. Anything was preferable to the nightmare of sharing the cockpit with dozens of *them.*

He noted McVary, sitting in a lounge chair facing the cockpit door, staring hard at it. Berry placed his fingers around the nub of the broken latch. He had very little to grab. He pulled the door shut a few more inches, but it sprang open again.

Berry turned and scanned the cockpit for something that would secure the door, but could find nothing. There was a way to do it, he was sure, but his thoughts, which had stayed so calm for so long, were beginning to ramble; fatigue was dulling his reason. "Damn it! Sharon, we've got to keep this door closed."

She turned in her chair and looked at the door. Forms and shadows passed by the opening between the edge of the door and the jamb. "Why don't I go into the lounge and put my back to the door? I'll take the fire extinguisher. They won't be able—"

"No! Forget it. We've had enough heroes and martyrs already. If we go . . ." he looked at Linda Farley, sitting quietly in one of the extra cockpit chairs ". . . we all go together. No more sacrifices. No splitting up. We're not losing any more of us."

Crandall nodded, then turned back and stared out the windshield.

For a long time there was a silence in the cockpit, broken only by the dull murmur of electronics and the soft, susurrant sound of someone brushing by the door.

The alerting bell sounded.

Berry moved beside Crandall's chair, and they both looked down at the video display.

TO FLIGHT 52: WE HAVE ACCURATELY
DETERMINED YOUR POSITION. CLOSEST
AIRPORT HAWAII. TURN AIRCRAFT TO
HEADING OF 240 DEGREES FOR VECTOR TO
HAWAII. AIR AND SEA RESCUE WILL
INTERCEPT YOU ON NEW HEADING.
AIRPORTS IN HAWAII WAITING FOR YOU
WITH EMERGENCY EQUIPMENT.
ACKNOWLEDGE. SAN FRANCISCO HQ.

Sharon Crandall clutched Berry's arm. "They know where we are." She turned her head to him and smiled.

"We'll be in Hawaii . . ." She looked up at him. Something was wrong. "John . . . ?"

Berry shook his head. "I don't know," he said quietly. "I don't know."

"What's wrong?"

"I'm not sure." He reread the data-link's display screen. "I'm not comfortable with this."

"Comfortable?" She looked at him for a few seconds. She tried to keep the edge of annoyance out of her voice as she spoke. "How in God's name can we be *comfortable* with anything out here? What are you saying?"

Berry suddenly felt angry. "Comfortable," he said coolly, "is a pilot's term. It means that I have no faith in that course of action."

"Why not?"

"Because," he said, slowly but emphatically, "the Hawaiian Islands are a pretty damned small target, as you might know, while the North American continent is pretty big." He leaned back against the side of the pilot's chair. "Look, we are headed somewhere now. North America. California, probably. We can't miss that coastline. If we do what they ask, we'd be putting everything on a long shot. All we stand to gain is a shorter flight time of maybe an hour or two. But if we miss Hawaii—and it wouldn't take much of a navigation error to do that . . . then . . ." he smiled grimly ". . . we'll wind up with Amelia Earhart."

Sharon Crandall looked down at the display screen again, then back at Berry. Her life, she realized, was totally in the hands of this man. If John Berry didn't want to make a course change, she couldn't make him do it. Yet she wasn't going to let him make the decision without some good reasons. She turned away from him and looked out at the far horizon. "How do regular airline flights find Hawaii?"

"With this." Berry pointed to the radio console and the blackened readouts of the satellite navigation sets. "They're either not functioning or I don't know how to work them. And San Francisco hasn't responded to my request for instructions."

"Ask them again."

Berry slid into the pilot's chair and typed.

NEED INSTRUCTIONS ON OPERATING NAV
SETS BEFORE COURSE CHANGE. SETS MAY
BE DAMAGED. FOR THE RECORD, NOW ONLY
3 IN COCKPIT—YOUNG GIRL LINDA
FARLEY—FLIGHT ATTENDANT SHARON
CRANDALL—MYSELF—OTHERS PRESUMED
LOST. BERRY.

Berry knew that sending a list of who was still in the cockpit—who was still alive and rational—was an unnecessary addition to the message. But after his comment to Sharon about them needing to not split up anymore, sending that shortened list of names seemed like a necessary comment to the world. Berry pushed the transmit button, and they waited in the silent cockpit.

Suddenly, the door swung open. Linda Farley screamed.

Berry vaulted out of his chair and stared up at the door. Faces, some grinning, some frowning, peered in at him. Daniel McVary stepped into the cockpit, looking, thought Berry, very irate.

Berry grabbed the fire extinguisher from the floor

and sprayed it into the faces closest to him. The people screamed and tried to move back, but the press from behind was too great and the crowd moved forward, squeezing through the door, one and two at a time, into the cockpit.

Berry was vaguely aware of the sounds of feminine screams behind him and the hands and faces pressing in on him. Without being conscious of it, he had raised the heavy metal extinguisher above his head and brought it down into the face of the man closest to him. The man's face erupted into a distorted mass of red pulp.

Berry swung the extinguisher again and again, striking at the heads and faces of the men and women around him. He was half aware of hitting a young boy in the face. Screams filled the cockpit and the lounge, and drowned out the sounds of even the Straton's engines. Blood and teeth splattered in the air, and he could hear the distinct crack of skulls and jaws. The loudest sound of all was a voice that he identified as his own. The voice bellowed out like an animal in agony.

Berry swung the extinguisher, but nothing stood around him any longer. He dropped to one knee, picked up a body and pushed it out the door, then pushed and pulled the rest of the limp or writhing forms into the lounge. He laid them in an open space made by the crowd, which stood in a semicircle watching curiously, fearfully, but without any hate or anger that he could detect. McVary, he noticed, was among them.

Berry grabbed the edge of the door and drew it toward him as he stepped back into the cockpit. He turned and looked around, trying to focus his eyes.

Sharon Crandall was standing in front of him. She

had kicked off her shoes and was peeling off her panty hose. She pushed by him without a word and tied the feet of the hose around the small broken latch, then pulled on them.

Berry grabbed the top of the panty hose and stretched them out. He looked around quickly for something to fasten it to.

Fingers and hands curled around the edge of the door, trying to pull it open. Berry pulled harder on the hose, drawing the door tight against the probing fingers. He found a cross brace on the left sidewall. He looped the panty hose around the brace and pulled them so tightly that they thinned out, resembling a long rope running between the door and the cross brace. He knotted it quickly, then leaned back heavily against the pilot's chair, his whole body shaking. An involuntary laugh rose in his throat.

Sharon fell into his arms and they held on to each other, her body trembling against his, both of them trying to keep from crying and laughing.

Linda Farley moved toward them tentatively, then rushed to them, circling their waists with her arms.

Berry looked up at the door. There was less than an inch of opening around the jamb, and no fingers probing at the edges. He saw blood splattered on the door's blue-green paint. He pressed Sharon closer to him. "Oh, God, Sharon, good thinking. . . . God, we . . ."

Crandall shook her head quickly and wiped her tears. "How stupid of me not to think of it sooner."

"Me too," Berry said. It was an indication of his state of mind, he thought, that his initial resourcefulness was failing him. He wondered if he hadn't misjudged San Francisco's intentions.

He stepped away from Sharon and Linda, then looked down at his hands. He was covered with blood, and he could see pieces of teeth, gums, and flesh on his arms and hands. The gray carpet near the door was soaked with blood. As the shock wore off, he felt his stomach heave, and his body began to tremble again. He stumbled up to the pilot's chair and sat there trying to get control of himself.

Linda sat in the extra pilot's chair, slumped over the small desk on the sidewall, her face buried in her arms. Sharon stood behind the girl and stroked her hair.

After a full minute, Berry looked up at the data-link screen and stared at the new message that was waiting there to be read.

> TO FLIGHT 52: EXECUTE TURN AS
> INSTRUCTED. SATELLITE SETS NOT
> CRITICAL FOR FINDING HAWAII—BUT WILL
> BEGIN NAV OPERATING INSTRUCTIONS EN
> ROUTE TO HAWAII. UNDERSTAND 3
> REMAINING IN COCKPIT. ACKNOWLEDGE.
> SAN FRANCISCO HQ.

It seemed to Berry that the tone of the last few data-link messages had changed, as though someone new was sending them. But, of course, he knew that it was he, the receiver, who was reading them in a different state of mind.

Sharon stepped over the panty hose at her feet and leaned over Berry's chair. She looked down at the message. She had decided that if she was going to trust him, she would trust him completely, with no reservations, no hesitation. "What are you going to do?"

Berry kept staring at the new message. It seemed to

be patently wrong. If only he could speak to them on the radio, hear their voices instead of reading words displayed on a cathode-ray tube. He remembered his near panic when he had no communication, and knew he ought to be thankful for even this.

Berry thought a minute, then shook his head. "They say they know where we are, but what if they're wrong? Then the new heading is wrong. A few degrees at this distance from Hawaii would put us hundreds of miles off course. And what if this damned data-link malfunctions before we reach Hawaii? They won't be able to send us any course corrections. What if the satellite navigation system doesn't work, or if I can't work it?" He thought of something he'd read once. *The least reliable component of a modern airplane is its pilot.* In this case that was he, John Berry. He looked at the control panels in front of him. "We'd run out of fuel somewhere in the Pacific. I'd have to try to land in the ocean. It would be a race between the rescue craft and . . . the sharks."

Sharon put her hands on his shoulders, then leaned forward and whispered in his ear. "John, Linda is . . ."

"Sorry."

She turned her face and kissed him on the cheek, then straightened up quickly. She looked down at the panty hose and followed it with her eyes to the door handle. It was taut and secure. No hands poked around the small crack in the door. Suddenly, she felt optimistic again. She looked over at Linda. "All right," she said, trying to put a light tone in her voice. "Linda, Hawaii or California?"

The girl picked up her head from the desk. "I want to go home."

Sharon smiled. "California it is, then. John, tell them we're coming home."

Berry felt the tears collect in his eyes and wiped them quickly. He reached out to the console and typed a short, succinct message.

# 12

Edward Johnson stared down at the message that had just come from Flight 52.

> TO SAN FRANCISCO: WE DO NOT WANT TO
> TURN. HAWAII IS TOO SMALL A TARGET.
> WILL MAINTAIN CURRENT HEADING OF 120
> DEGREES. ADVISE US OF EXACT COURSE
> AND DISTANCE/TIME TO SAN FRANCISCO AS
> SOON AS YOUR COMPUTATIONS ARE
> AVAILABLE. BERRY.

"Shit." Johnson took out a cigar and bit the end off. "Smart-ass son-of-a-bitch." He looked at the cigar for a moment, then threw it on the floor.

Metz looked at Johnson. He hadn't liked this idea of heading the Straton toward Hawaii, and he was half relieved that it hadn't worked. "You have to *do* something, Ed. You have to give him instructions that will put him down so we can get the hell out of here before—"

"Shut up, Metz. I know what I have to do." There was some question in his mind about whether or not Berry was onto his game. "I can't push him. He's too savvy."

"What are you going to answer?"

"What choice do I have? I'm going to give him the information he asked for."

"Christ, now we're helping him."

"I have to get him off our backs for a while." Johnson walked to the Pacific chart. He picked up a ruler from the counter and took some crude measurements. "They won't be any better off with this new heading. Maybe a little worse off. But I can't make it too absurd. Berry is . . ."

"I know. Sharp."

"I was going to say he may be suspicious."

Metz walked to the data-link machine and slapped his hand on it. "Don't let this guy spook you. He's some weekend pilot sitting in the biggest, most complicated aircraft ever built—which, incidentally, has two rather large holes in it, and is crammed full of the living dead. Christ. John Wayne couldn't buck those odds." He paused, then said softly, "All Berry needs is a little nudge in the wrong direction and he'll fall."

Johnson ignored him and sat down at the data-link. He typed.

TO FLIGHT 52: WE ARE HERE TO HELP YOU
BUT WILL DEFER TO YOUR JUDGMENT IN
THIS MATTER. PLEASE FOLLOW OUR
TECHNICAL INSTRUCTIONS TO THE LETTER.
IN COMPLIANCE WITH YOUR REQUEST,
ACCURATE HEADING TO SAN FRANCISCO IS

131 DEGREES. DISTANCE IS 1950 MILES.
ESTIMATED TIME EN ROUTE IS FIVE HOURS
AND TEN MINUTES AT CURRENT SPEED. AM
ARRANGING FOR MILITARY INTERCEPT.
PROBABLY INTERCEPT YOU WITHIN TWO
HOURS. SAN FRANCISCO HQ.

Metz glanced up at the wall clock. It read 2:02.

Johnson followed his gaze. "That's right. They won't be in ATC radar range much before six P.M. We have time before anyone sees them on a radar screen."

"What about the military?"

Johnson allowed himself a smile. "If you don't call them, I promise, I won't either."

"I mean, hasn't Air Traffic Control called them already?"

"Sure. Half the Air Force and Navy are headed their way. But they don't have their true heading, and it's a mighty big sky out there." Johnson walked over to the weather map printer and glanced down at it. "To add to the search problems, some bad weather is moving in out there."

Metz looked impatient. "The way our luck is running, they'll probably find them in the next ten minutes."

"*Our* luck? Mr. Berry's luck hasn't been too good today, either. I'll bet this is one flight he wished he'd missed. I'll take our luck over his. Anyway, even if a boat or plane does spot them, they can't do much for them. Only we can do that, because only we are in contact with them, and no one knows that but us."

"Well, what are we going to do for them? What are we going to do to nudge that pilot down?"

# MAYDAY

The telephone rang. Johnson rose, walked to the counter, and picked it up. "Johnson." He paused. "Yes, sir. We're still trying to make contact. No, sir, I think I can be more effective here." He spoke for a minute, then said, "If any questions arise, I'll be here. Thank you." He replaced the receiver and looked at Metz. "That was our illustrious airline president. Everyone is in the executive conference room. And with any luck they will stay there, close to the bar and the air-conditioning. They don't like this room."

"I'm not crazy about it myself." Metz looked at the telephone. "I have a boss, too, and he's probably wondering what the hell is going on. If I knew what was going on, I'd call him."

"You'd better call him before he starts hearing things on the news, or before our president calls him. Presidents are like that. They call people and ask what's going on. Anyway, if insurance company presidents are like airline presidents, he'll really want to know everything."

Metz stared at the phone. "I'll wait." He turned to Johnson. "Well, what instructions are you going to give to Berry?"

Johnson opened the pilot's manual. He glanced at Metz. "There's an expression: the first time you give bad advice it's excusable, the second time it's suspicious, the third time it's enemy action. I suppose I have one more shot at it." He looked down at the book.

"Don't overestimate him. If we're going to sink him, we have to take some chances."

Johnson flipped through the book as he spoke. "When I offered him that vector, I held my breath. You know why? Because there is absolutely no way we could have determined his true position, and I didn't know if he knew that. Also, vector is shorthand for radar vector, and there is no radar out there. That's the equivalent of me telling you that the fastest way to Sausalito is to drive over the bay without using the Golden Gate Bridge. I gambled that Berry knew nothing about over-ocean flying. I also gambled that Ms. Crandall never spent a lot of time hanging around the cockpit listening to our pilots bore her with flying lessons. So don't tell me about taking chances."

Metz wiped the perspiration from his face with a handkerchief. "God, I didn't know it was going to be this complicated."

"Ignorance, Mr. Metz, is bliss. And if you are so ignorant that you think we can yell 'Game's over' and go home and forget what we tried to do, then I have news for you. As soon as I sent that bullshit message, we were committed. Because if he gets back, we may be able to lie about the phony break in communications, but we can't lie about that phony vector."

Metz lowered himself into a chair. "If they get back . . . if they do land . . . we can say they misunderstood. They were suffering from lack of oxygen . . ."

Johnson stopped at a page and began reading, then looked up. "Right. If they do get back and survive the landing, we can say that. Maybe we can make everyone believe that an amateur pilot who was smart enough to land a supersonic jetliner is too stupid to accurately recall the messages we sent a short while before. Besides, there are still three normal people in that cockpit with functioning brains. But the biggest factor of all might well become the printouts. Wayne, do you see the printouts that are coming from our data-link?" Johnson asked.

"Yes." Metz had forgotten about them, and what their existence implied. "We've got to get rid of those."

"Good thought, Sherlock. But before we do, take a guess where the corresponding printouts are. Go ahead. One guess."

"Oh, shit."

"Right. Data-links sure act funny sometimes, but they don't get brain damaged, and don't babble on with conveniently murderous messages. What we've sent to that cockpit is more than enough to have us indicted for attempted murder. If the printer in the cockpit is turned on—and it usually is, as a backup—then they'll have all the physical evidence they'll need."

Metz slumped forward in his chair. "Good God! Why didn't you tell me all this?"

"Why? Because you have no real balls. You were all for this as long as you thought I could come up with a simple technical solution to the problem of putting the Straton in the ocean. If you knew all the problems involved, you would have run off to your group therapy or wherever it is that screw-up insurance whiz kids go."

Metz stood slowly. "It's more than our careers now. If . . ."

"Right. It's our lives against theirs. If they land, we go up for twenty to life. That might affect our promotions." Johnson looked back at the book, then glanced up at the data-link. He turned to Metz. "Instead of standing there with your finger up your ass, go over to the link and very coolly remove the printouts of the last messages."

Metz walked over to the machine. His hands were shaking and perspiration ran from his face. He looked up into the dispatch office. Occasionally a man would glance up at him.

Johnson stood and walked toward the door. "Go on, Wayne. One quick motion, from the printer to your pocket." Johnson put his hand on the doorknob to attract the attention of anyone outside who was watching them. "Go."

Metz ripped the messages off and stuffed them in his trouser pocket.

Johnson pretended to change his mind and walked away from the door. He sat back down at the counter. "Very good. In case of imminent capture, eat them."

Metz walked up to Johnson. "I don't like your sense of humor."

Johnson shrugged. "I'm not sure I like your lack of one. First sign of mental disease—lack of humor. Inability to see the funny side of things. Humor keeps you alert and opened to all possibilities."

Metz felt he was losing control of the situation. He felt he had unleashed forces that were now beyond his control. Everything in this room, including Johnson, seemed so alien. He could manipulate people and he could also manipulate, through them, their technology, their factories, their machines. But he couldn't manipulate the machines themselves. The human factor was really not so unpredictable as the technical factors— the computers and the engines that ran when they should have stopped, stopped when they should have run. "I have a feeling that the Straton will land unless we bring it down."

Johnson smiled. "I think you've finally arrived at the truth. There is nothing radically wrong with that aircraft or its pilot. If his nerve holds, he'll bring it down on some runway, somewhere, and in some sort of condition that will allow him or some of the others in the cockpit, or the flight recorder, to survive."

"We can't let that happen."

"No, we can't." Johnson tapped his finger on the pilot's manual. "In this book is something that will finish him—quickly. And I think I'm onto what it is."

---

The early afternoon sun reflected brilliantly off the tranquil sea that surrounded the USS *Chester W. Nimitz*. The aircraft carrier plodded steadily along its course. A moderate breeze, generated by the ship's eighteen knots of forward speed, swept across its empty flight deck from bow to stern. Belowdecks, the afternoon's activities were routine.

Commander James Sloan and retired Rear Admiral Randolf Hennings sat quietly in Room E-334 on the 0-2 level of the conning tower. Neither of them had spoken for several minutes; each was lost in his own thoughts. For Sloan, the problem was clear and the solution was obvious. For Hennings, the situation was far more complex. Sloan's face was set in a rigid, uncompromising expression. Hennings's face betrayed his inner struggle.

Sloan finally spoke. "The situation has not changed. Our only mistake was waiting for the Straton to go down by itself. But there's no sense continuing this argument. Try to think of it as a tactical war problem."

Hennings was fatigued and his head ached. "Stop giving me those war analogies, Commander. That doesn't work anymore." After Matos's report that the Straton had made a turn, Hennings thought that Sloan would see that they couldn't proceed with the destruction of the aircraft. Hennings was almost relieved at the prospect of confessing to Captain Diehl what they had done. But Sloan, as Hennings should have known, had not given up so easily. To Sloan there was little difference between shooting down an aircraft that they first believed to be filled with corpses, and shooting down an aircraft that showed signs of life. "And stop telling me nothing has changed. Everything is changed now."

"Yes, and for the worse. Let me point out again, Admiral, that I don't want to go to jail. I have my whole life in front of me. *You* may get VIP treatment in Portsmouth—a cottage of your own, or whatever they do with admirals, but I . . . Which reminds me, you'll be the first American admiral to be court-martialed in this century, won't you? Or maybe with your retired status, you'll suffer the indignity of a civilian trial."

Hennings tried to remember—to understand the sequence of small compromises that had brought him so far down that he had to listen to this from a man like Sloan. He was either getting senile or there was a flaw in his moral fiber that he had not been made aware of. Certainly James Sloan wasn't that sharp. "You think a lot of yourself, don't you?" he said. "But if you were as shrewd as you think you are, we wouldn't be in this mess."

"I don't mind sticking my neck out if I can gain by

it. What I do mind is your getting in my way. This would have all been resolved long ago if you hadn't procrastinated, and if we hadn't listened to Matos's bullshit about fatigue cracks and damage."

Hennings nodded. That was certainly true. For the last hour, Sloan had explained to him why Peter Matos should destroy the Straton. For the last hour, Hennings had advised waiting for some word from Matos that the Straton had gone down by itself. Matos's reports had confirmed that the Straton was damaged but still flying, straight and steady, except for one deliberate but unexplainable course change from a 120-degree heading to a 131-degree heading. Also, Matos reported people falling or jumping from the airliner. None of this was comprehensible. "Why did they change course? Why are people falling from a steady aircraft? There was obviously no fire. They can't be jumping. That makes no sense. What the hell is going on up there?"

Sloan wasn't sure he knew what was going on up there either. The first heading seemed to put the Straton closer to its home base of San Francisco. The new heading might put them on a parallel course to the coast. He looked at Hennings. "The pilot must be lost. His navigation sets are probably malfunctioning. As for the people . . ." He thought for a moment about that bizarre happening. "I told you they've probably suffered brain damage." He was beginning to imagine for the first time what it must be like for the people onboard the Straton. "The pilots may be brain damaged, too. That's why they're changing their headings." He looked Hennings in the eye. "They may crash into a populated area. Think about that."

Hennings was through thinking and through arguing.

His only argument had been based on his own understanding of the moral and ethical issues involved.
Against that thin, apparently weightless argument,
Sloan had thrown a dozen expedient reasons for destroying the Straton and the people onboard.

"We're running out of time." Sloan said it casually,
as if he were late for a tennis match at the officers'
club. "Matos is low on fuel."

Hennings stepped closer to Sloan. "If I say no?"

Sloan shrugged. "Then I go to Captain Diehl and tell
him my side of the story."

"You don't bluff well."

Sloan smiled. "Well, I guess it's not important for
you to concur any longer. You've already committed a
half-dozen court-martial offenses. Just stay out of my
way, and I'll call Matos and finish it off. The Straton's
obviously not going down on its own." Sloan picked
up the microphone and glanced at Hennings out of the
corner of his eye. He started to push the transmit button, then hesitated. It would be much better if the Admiral was in on it. As he pondered his next move, the
telephone rang. He put down the microphone and
snatched up the receiver. "Commander Sloan," he said
impatiently, then listened for a few seconds. "Yes. Go
ahead with the message. Exactly as received."

"Who is it?" Hennings asked, apprehension in his
voice.

Sloan ignored him. "Okay. I understand. Then their
request is specifically for a broad-area search, and only
within the boundaries you've described?"

Hennings was certain that it concerned the Straton,
but couldn't guess in what way.

Sloan was shaking his head. "I'm tied up here—with

this special test. Yes, it's still not finished, but that's not your business. Have Lieutenant Rowles lay out the initial patterns and assignments. At least eight aircraft each shift. To be launched at one-hour intervals. Begin the search in the northern quadrant, and expand the search southward." Sloan glanced at the console clock. "Tell Rowles to get the first group off within fifteen minutes." He hung up and turned to Hennings. "A message came from Air Traffic Control to initiate a search and possible rescue mission."

"The Straton?"

"Trans-United Flight 52. A supersonic Straton 797 from San Francisco to Tokyo. Unless the Trans-United Stratons are having a bad day, that must be ours."

"But I thought we would hear any transmissions from them." He gestured toward the radio-monitoring equipment.

Sloan hesitated. He had to pick and choose what to tell Hennings. "They transmitted on a data-link, a typed-out message that displays on a computer screen. I presume only the Trans-United operations office can receive from them. Anyway, the pilot was apparently dying. Brain damage. He made that turn, then made the course change, then they lost contact. They suspect that he died or blacked out, and that the Straton went down and . . ."

"Then they don't know it's still—"

"No. They don't. The good news is that one of the data-link messages from the Straton mentioned a bomb. Everyone thinks there was a bomb onboard. Do you see it all now, Admiral? A pilotless aircraft filled with dead and dying, and with enough fuel left to reach

California. Even if it weren't our fault, I'd say we had a duty to bring it down."

"How soon will your search party be in the area?"

"Soon." Sloan had been asked to search an area that was hundreds of miles from where he knew the Straton actually was. By the time his aircraft worked their search pattern, the Straton would have flown hundreds of miles farther. "Very soon," he lied. He looked at Hennings. "You can't avoid any of the responsibility if I order this aircraft shot down. Silence is acquiescence. You're no better than I am. But if you want to remain silent and let me do the dirty work . . ."

Suddenly, Hennings understood Sloan's insistence on getting his approval for an act that he had the power to accomplish by himself. Sloan was looking for a personal victory over Hennings, and all that Hennings represented. All the old notions of honor, virtue, and integrity. Somehow it would make Sloan feel better to rub Hennings's face in the muck.

Sloan said, "You had no qualms about serving a commander in chief who was a draft dodger, a notorious liar, and who had nothing but contempt for the military. Or, if you had any such qualms, you sure kept them to yourself, Admiral. We all did. Don't talk to me about doing the right thing, about standing up for principle. None of us resigned over Vietnam, and none of us spoke out against the draft dodger in the White House. We're all whores and we're all compromised. The only thing I believe in is the career of James Sloan."

Hennings made no reply, no protest.

Neither man spoke for a long time.

Hennings looked around the room known as E-334.

Sterile, gray metal, covered with mazes of electrical conduit, the smell of electronics hanging in the air-conditioned atmosphere. The world was full of Room E-334s now, on the sea, in the air, underground. Small tight compartments with no human touch. The destiny and the fate of mankind would someday be decided from a room like this one. Hennings was glad he would not be around to see it. He looked at Sloan. This man was the future. He knows how to live in this world. "Yes. Of course. Order Matos to shoot the Straton down."

Sloan hesitated for a second, then sat down quickly at the radio console.

"Make sure he understands what he is to do and why he is to do it, Commander."

Sloan glanced back at Hennings. "Yes. All right. I know what to do. We had him at this point once before." But he knew Matos could go either way. "Navy three-four-seven, this is Homeplate. Do you read?" Sloan looked again at Hennings. "You wanted me to be honest with him, and I will."

The radio crackled, and Matos's voice, strained and perhaps even frightened, came through the scrambler and filled the room. "Roger, Homeplate. Go ahead."

Sloan heard the edginess in the young man's voice. That was a good beginning. "Peter, this is Commander Sloan. I asked you a question before, and now I want the answer. Why have you been ordered to keep out of sight of the cockpit?"

There was a long silence in the room, then the radio came alive with Matos's voice. "I was to keep out of sight of the cockpit because there might be a pilot in there. If he was able to get his radios working, and if he saw me, he might understand what happened to his aircraft and radio the message. Or he might tell someone when he landed."

"Yes. And we have new information from ATC. They think it was a bomb onboard. Go on. What else, Peter?"

"The accident was our . . . my fault. I have a chance to cover it up by shooting the Straton down."

"For the good of the Navy, for the good of national security, for our own good."

"Yes."

"The test we were conducting is in violation of an international treaty. It is illegal. Do you understand?"

"Yes."

"The people onboard are dead or brain damaged. They are heading toward California—like a cruise missile, with enough destructive force to level a small town or wipe out twenty city blocks."

"I understand."

"Every boat and aircraft in the area is heading your way now, including a flight from this carrier. If anyone sees you, we are all finished. Within the next ten minutes, you are to fire the Phoenix missile into the Straton, just as you were going to do before."

"Roger." There was a pause. "My fuel is low."

"All the more reason to get it done quickly. When you complete your mission, keep heading for the coast and I will have a refuel mission meet you. Do you understand?"

"Yes."

Sloan decided it was time to pull out all the stops. He said to Matos, "I have here with me Rear Admiral Randolf Hennings, who concurs with my decision. He will personally debrief you when you land. Understand?"

"Yes."

Sloan glanced at Hennings, whose face had gone white. Sloan said to Matos, "Enough talk, Peter. Fire your missile into the cockpit of the Straton. Do you understand?"

"Yes."

"Get into position, steady aim, and fire. No miss. Ten minutes, max. Call me when you've accomplished the mission."

"Roger."

"Roger. Out." Sloan set his countdown clock for ten minutes, then swiveled his chair and faced Hennings. The Admiral looked pale and was leaning against the bulkhead. "Are you all right?"

"Yes. I think so."

Sloan nodded. "I hope you don't think this is any easier for me than for you."

Hennings wiped the clammy sweat from his neck. "I suspect it is."

Sloan stared at him. The old man looked as if he might be having a heart attack.

Hennings stood up straight. "I think I'll go on deck and get some air."

Sloan didn't want Hennings out of his sight. There was an aura in this room, a spell that could be broken by sunlight and other voices, other faces. "I'd like you to stay around. For ten minutes at least."

Hennings nodded. "Yes. Of course. I'll see it through." He pushed aside the blackout curtain, opened the porthole, and took a deep breath. Then, for the first time in more than forty years, he became sick at sea.

Sloan watched the man out of the corner of his eye. Hennings was a very weak link in a three-link chain. Matos was stronger, but he might break too. Now that the problem of the Straton was as good as out of the way, Sloan thought more about Matos and Hennings. He had pretty much decided how to deal with Lieutenant Peter Matos.

Sloan walked over to the end of the console where a half-dozen interphones, color coded to indicate their function, sat in a row. He picked up the green one and, before anyone answered, reached down and switched it off. "Operations? This is Commander Sloan. We have a problem. Navy three-four-seven, F-18, Matos, is in a critical fuel situation. I want a tanker from the closest coastal base to rendezvous with him." Sloan gave Matos's present coordinates into the dead phone. "Thank you." He hung up and picked up the blue phone and switched it off. "Rowles? Sloan. Alert the Straton search party that they may have to split the mission and look for three-four-seven. Yes. He had a fuel emergency, but I have a tanker on the way and it should reach him in plenty of time. Just keeping you alerted. Right." He hung up and slid a clipboard over the on-off switches, then turned toward the Admiral.

Randolf Hennings was a more difficult problem. As long as Hennings lived and breathed and spoke, with all his pent-up guilt and remorse, James Sloan would never have another good night's sleep, never know when a summons to the captain's office would be arrest. James Sloan couldn't allow that. Not at all.

# MAYDAY

The view from the captain's flight chair of the Straton 797 was spectacular. Berry sat, mesmerized by the churning mass of black boiling clouds in the distance. He had seen them first as a vague haziness on the far horizon, shafts of sunlight streaking from them into the ocean at a sharp angle. The closer he got, the more awesome they looked—and the more he knew he was in trouble.

He leaned forward and scanned the horizon. The line of storms stretched as far as he could see in either direction, like a great solid wall between heaven and earth. They'd dropped down into the sea like a curtain, hiding the horizon line, and towered up above them so high that he knew he could not climb above them.

Sharon touched his arm and spoke softly, worry in her voice. "I haven't seen them this bad in a long time."

Berry had never seen them quite this bad, ever. The only thing they had going for them had been the weather and the daylight, and he had begun to take that for granted, not believing that anything else could go wrong for Flight 52. "You've been through these before?"

"A few times. You?"

"No. Not on a commercial flight."

"In your Skymaster?"

"No." In his Skymaster he would simply have turned and found an airport. Out here there was no airport to turn to.

Crandall looked down at the weather radar screen on

the center instrument panel. "Do you see a break in the clouds?"

Berry stared at the screen. A thin green trace line swept across the radarscope every six seconds, leaving patterns of colored patches in its wake. "I don't really know how to work it or how to read it." He glanced at the line of thunderstorms, then back at the radarscope. What he saw on the scope was supposed to represent what he saw from his windshield, but he could see no correlation. "I've read articles on weather radar, but I've never worked it."

Crandall heard a noise behind her and looked back. Linda was curled up near the cockpit's rear bulkhead, asleep. Crandall looked up at the door. An entire arm, right up to the shoulder, had slid through the opening and the hand was feeling around the inside of the door. The hand found the nylon hose and pulled at it, loosening the tension on the door and allowing his shoulder to slide through. She saw the blue shoulder boards of First Officer Daniel McVary, then saw his face peeking in at the opening. "John. . . ."

Berry looked back. "For God's sake." He hesitated, then stood. He walked to the door and examined the knot around the latch. He took the disembodied arm and tried to force it out, but the hand grabbed his shirt. Berry stepped back. There was something grotesque about this arm reaching out to him. He was reminded of the stories told around a campfire at night. But this was real. He reached into his pocket and found the gold lighter that he carried. He lit it, hesitated, then reluctantly touched the flame to McVary's hand. There was a long scream and the arm disappeared from the cockpit. Berry looked up at Sharon and met her eyes, but there was no censure in them, only understanding.

Berry knelt down beside Linda, who had awakened. "Go back to sleep."

She closed her eyes. "I'm very thirsty."

Berry patted her cheek. "Soon. Don't think about it." He stood and walked back to his chair.

Sharon fixed her eyes on the radar set. "Are these all the radar controls?"

Berry looked at her. There had developed a tacit understanding among the three of them that they were not to talk about the others. Berry looked down at the console. "Yes. Antenna tilt. Gain. Brilliance. Mode selector. . . . Here's one called erase rate. I've never even heard of that."

Crandall looked up again at the black wall outside the windshield. It was closer now, and she could see its inner violence, the black-gray smoke churning. "Can we go around it without the radar?"

Berry shook his head. "These lines sometimes stretch for hundreds of miles. I don't think we have the fuel to try an end run."

"Hawaii?" She didn't want to throw that up to him, but it seemed too important to be left unsaid.

"No. In addition to the other reasons I gave you, we don't have the fuel for that any longer. We have only enough to fly straight to California."

Crandall looked at the fuel gauges. They read less than one-third full.

Berry played with the radar controls. If he could understand the picture on the screen, he might be able to pick out a weak spot in the wall of clouds in front of him.

Crandall remembered other storms she'd gone through in other aircraft. The Straton 797 flew above the weather, and that, at least, was one advantage to traveling in subspace. "We can't climb above it?"

Berry looked up at the sheer wall of clouds. "Not with this aircraft. It won't hold its air pressure." He looked at the oxygen mask hanging beside his seat. An oxygen mask should be enough, as long as they didn't climb much above 30,000 feet. Was that high enough to clear these storms? He couldn't tell for sure, but he didn't think so. Besides, the oxygen tanks would probably be empty, and he didn't know if there was a reserve tank.

Crandall was following his thoughts. "There may be an unused oxygen tank that we could switch to."

"There might be. But do you think we should put those people through another period of oxygen deprivation? Don't we have to draw the line somewhere?"

"Not if it's our lives."

"They are not dead, and we don't know that they won't get better, and even if they won't . . . Besides, in order to gain enough altitude to get over this weather, I'd have to circle—spiral upward. I'd rather not try my flying skills at this point. Anyway, the maneuver would burn off a tremendous amount of fuel."

"What you're saying is that we're committed to bucking into the storm."

"I'm not sure. The other options look better in the short run, but I'm thinking of the California coast."

"Me too." She hesitated, then said, "Will the holes in the cabin . . . could the plane. . . ?"

"I don't think it will come apart." But he didn't know if the structure was weakened, how many longerons were severed. Completely airworthy craft had broken up in storms. He said, "It's the wings that take the most punishment. They don't appear to be damaged."

Crandall nodded. There was something reassuring about John Berry's voice, his manner. Most pilots had that ability to make even bad news sound routine. Yet she felt there was something else troubling him. "If you think the Straton can handle it, then I can handle it."

Berry decided that he had to tell it to her truthfully. It was her life too, and she had a right to know what could happen. "Look, Sharon, the major problem is not the aircraft. If the turbulence gets too rough—and there's no reason to think it won't, by the looks of those clouds—then the autopilot could disengage itself. Then I'd have to hand-fly this thing. Christ, three experienced pilots in an undamaged craft have their hands full during a storm. I have to think about the throttles, the pitch trim . . . I haven't flown this aircraft in *good* weather. The plane could get away from me . . . spin out . . ." Berry suddenly wanted to turn, to run and get away from the black wall closing in on him, even if he had to put the plane down at sea. Anything would be preferable to the nightmare of a bouncing, heaving aircraft caught in the center of a storm of unknown width and breadth. He turned to Sharon. "Do you want to turn? We can outrun it, but we'd probably have to ditch before we reached any land."

Crandall considered the options: Running from the storm knowing that each minute of flight time was another minute from the coast. Then putting it down at sea. And if they survived the landing, there would be the agony of the sea, maybe other passengers floating in the water. . . . She weighed that against the storm. They would live or die in the storm—nothing in between. She looked up at the clouds. Somewhere on the other side of that black veil the sun shone, and over the next horizon was the coastline of America. That's where they said they wanted to go, and that's where they would go. A sense of calm came over her, and she knew that one way or the other the end of their long trial was near. "We should maintain our present heading."

Berry nodded. He also had a need to meet the storm head-on. He thought about his wife and children for the first time in over an hour. Then he thought about his employer and his job. The worst thing that could happen to him, he realized, was that he would survive, only to pick up his life where he'd left it. He believed that somehow the crucible of that storm would cleanse him, even rebaptize him.

Crandall said, "We should call San Francisco and tell them what's happening. They may be able to give us some advice."

Berry nodded. He realized that, subconsciously, he had been avoiding the data-link. Instead of it being a lifeline, the link had become an intrusion into his small world. He typed.

> TO SAN FRANCISCO: WE ARE APPROACHING
> AN AREA OF THUNDERSTORMS. I AM
> UNABLE TO WORK OR READ WEATHER
> RADAR. WE HAVE DETERMINED THAT THE
> BEST COURSE OF ACTION IS TO MAINTAIN
> PRESENT HEADING. IS THERE ANYTHING
> WE SHOULD DO TO PREPARE THE
> AIRCRAFT?

He reached for the transmit button, then decided to type an additional line.

> IS THERE ANY INDICATION AT YOUR END
> THAT WE CAN GET AROUND THE WEATHER
> WITHOUT EXPENDING TOO MUCH FUEL?
> BERRY.

He pushed the transmit button, then looked up at the windshield. Thin wisps of smoky gray clouds sailed past the Straton; the cockpit became a little darker. "I'd say we've got about fifty miles to go before we're into the heavy weather. Nine or ten minutes' flying time."

Crandall noticed that her calm had turned to edginess, as it always did when she entered a storm. It seemed like the waiting was the worst part of it—until you were in it. Then, when you thought the worst was happening, it got even worse than that. But breaking out of a storm into the sun or the moonlight was one of those rare and exhilarating moments in flying. She turned to Berry. "Is there anything you'd be doing in your private plane that we haven't done yet?"

"Yes." He forced a smile. "Turn around and get the hell out of here." The aircraft bumped slightly, and he turned and looked back at Linda. She was awake now, sitting in one of the empty flight chairs with her knees up to her chin. He turned to Sharon. "Buckle her into the observer's seat."

Crandall rose from her chair and walked over to the girl. "Let's get up and sit over here where you'll be more comfortable." She took her by the arm and led her to the observer's seat that was directly behind the captain's chair. "That's right. Here. I'll buckle you in just like when you first came onboard."

"Thank you. Are we going into a storm?"

"It'll be all right. But remember, it's going to get very dark in here. You'll hear the rain against the windshield. It might be louder than you expect. And it will be a very bumpy ride. But Mr. Berry will fly us right through it. You're not afraid of lightning, are you?"

"No. Only when I was little."

"Good. Lightning is nothing to be afraid of." Crandall patted the girl on the cheek, then climbed into her chair and buckled herself in.

The three of them sat quietly in the darkening cockpit as the Straton sailed toward some thin, layered clouds that preceded the wall of thunderstorms. Wisps of light gray flew past the windshield. The Straton bounced suddenly, and from the lounge came a wailing and moaning that Berry recognized instinctively as something very primeval, an ancient inborn terror that came from the very soul of the species. "Poor bastards." They were going to be hurt if it got very bad. There was nothing he could do for them.

The alerting bell sounded.

TO FLIGHT 52: NO INDICATION AT THIS END
THAT WEATHER IS AVOIDABLE
CONSIDERING YOUR ESTIMATED FUEL
RESERVE AND CONSIDERING THE
UNPRESSURIZED CONDITION OF THE
AIRCRAFT. MAINTAIN PRESENT HEADING
AND ALTITUDE AS YOU INDICATED. IT IS
VERY IMPORTANT THAT YOU ALTER
CENTER OF GRAVITY FOR TURBULENCE BY
TRANSFERRING FUEL BETWEEN TANKS.
STAND BY FOR DETAILED INSTRUCTION.

ACKNOWLEDGE A READY CONDITION. SAN
FRANCISCO HQ.

Berry typed.

EXPERIENCING SOME TURBULENCE.
SHOULD I CIRCLE TO AVOID TURBULENCE
BEFORE PROCEDURE IS COMPLETE?

The reply came quickly.

NEGATIVE. MAINTAIN HEADING.
PROCEDURE WILL TAKE ONLY TWO OR
THREE MINUTES. ALL CONTROLS ARE
LOCATED ON OVERHEAD PANEL.

"Okay." Berry looked up at the large panel above
his head. "Sharon, read me the instructions as they
print."

"Here it comes, John. Ready?"

"Ready."

"In the center of . . . the overhead panel . . . four
switches . . . labeled . . . low pressure fuel valve position . . . acknowledge. . . ."

"I see them."

"Good." Crandall typed a quick acknowledgment.
"Okay . . . here comes more. . . . Turn the switches . . .
to off. . . ."

Berry looked over at her. "All of them?" He glanced
down at the display screen himself, but at the angle he
was at it was difficult to read.

"That's what it says."

Berry looked back at the switches. There was something wrong. Some instinct told him to be careful. To
proceed cautiously. He remembered a line from an avi-

ation magazine. *Operate important switches one at a time*. He put his hand on switch number one. Tentatively, he pulled it toward him so it would clear its guard, then pushed down on it and moved it to the off position. He counted off a few seconds.

"Done?"

Berry looked around the cockpit, then scanned the panel in front of him. Nothing unusual was happening.

"Did you do it?"

"Wait a minute. That's just the first one."

Crandall looked back at him. "Is anything wrong?"

"No. I'm just proceeding cautiously."

Crandall turned to the console. "They want an acknowledgment."

"Tell them to hold their fucking horses." Berry hit the second switch, then the third, and finally the last. He sat very still but could feel nothing in the seat of his pants to indicate any transfer of fuel, any shift in center of gravity. Maybe the autopilot was compensating. It probably was. "Finished. Is that all?"

Crandall typed the acknowledgment, then read the next message as it came through. "Last step . . . a covered switch . . . labeled . . . fuel valve emergency power . . . engage the switch . . . then fuel transfer . . . will be done . . . automatically . . . it will take . . . two or three more minutes."

Berry found the switch. Not only was it covered by a special guard, but the guard was fixed in place by a thin strand of safety wire. Clearly, this switch was not used very often. "Are you sure?"

"I'll read it again . . . a covered switch labeled fuel valve emergency power. Engage the switch. . . ." She paused. "John, please hurry. We're almost into the storm."

Somewhere in the deepest recesses of Berry's mind a warning flashed for a thousandth of a second, like a subliminal message on a video screen. He could not see it, though he sensed it for a passing moment, but did not believe what he thought it said. For to believe it was to admit to something he could not possibly handle. Without another thought, John Berry snapped the safety wire with his thumb and lifted the guard.

He pushed the emergency power switch into an engaged position.

Within the span of a microsecond, an electrical signal went to each fuel valve on the Straton's four jet engines. Before John Berry had even taken his hand off the switch, the valves had already begun to choke off the flow of fuel to all four of the engines.

# 13

Lieutenant Peter Matos had never fired a shot in anger, but now he was to fire one in sorrow. His first kill would be an unarmed American civilian transport.

Matos edged his F-18 twenty-five yards astern of the transport's towering tail and one hundred fifty feet above it. He snapped his manual gun sight into place and looked through it.

Shredded clouds flew by his canopy and over the wide expanse of the silvery Straton, causing alternating overcast and bright glare in the gun sight. Matos rubbed his eyes. These were not optimum conditions for a close-in shot.

He looked out toward the horizon. The dark, ugly storm clouds rolled toward him like a high surf sweeping up the beach. In front of the storm were several thin layers of clouds, and he would pass under them within a minute. Then and there, under the heavy veil of gray, he would strike. "Okay, okay, let's go," he said to himself, and pushed forward on the control stick, then hit the transmit button. "Navy three-four-seven beginning the attack."

"Roger."

Matos snapped back the safety cover and put his finger over the missile's firing button.

The target proved more difficult to align this time. The increasing turbulence caused the two aircraft to sway and bounce, and the bull's-eye danced in circles around the center of the airliner's high dome.

They were under the cloud cover now, and the light was subdued but consistent. He stared through his gun sight. Several times he almost pushed the button, but the Straton would sway out of his bull's-eye. He glanced up. He was only a few minutes from the front of the storm. If the Straton got into the black clouds, his chances of holding a trail formation were zero. "Homeplate! I have turbulence. Can't hold it steady!"

Sloan's voice cracked in his ears like a whip. "Shoot the goddamned missile!"

For an irrational moment Matos thought of ramming the Straton's high dome. He went as far as to give a slight forward impulse to his control stick, and the motion carried his fighter closer to its target. Suddenly, he pulled back on the stick and backed off. What held him back was not a fear of death but something he had seen, with a fighter pilot's highly developed sense of peripheral vision, from the corner of his left eye.

As he slid back and above the Straton, he looked down at the airliner's left wing. The flow of hot exhaust gases from the Straton's number-one engine had stopped. Then the number-two engine cut out. Matos looked quickly to the right and saw that the two starboard engines had also stopped producing power. He jammed his thumb on the transmit button. "Home-plate! Homeplate! The Straton is flaming out! I say again, the Straton is flaming out!"

Sloan's response was quick, and his voice was as excited as Matos's. "Are you positive? Where are you? Can you see it clearly?"

Matos composed himself. "Yes. Yes. I'm right on its tail. No vapor trails. Flame out." He watched as the Straton began its slow, powerless descent toward the sea. "It appears that the autopilot is still flying it. Its speed remains at three-forty. The rate of descent is increasing. It's dropping. Going down."

"Stay with it, Matos. Stay with it. I want you to see it hit the water."

Even the scrambler, thought Matos, could not mask the vengeance in Sloan's voice. "Roger, Homeplate." Matos had already begun his descent to follow the dying airliner. He could see that it was still steady on its 131-degree heading, and its glide would take them both directly into the thunderstorms. Matos slammed his hand on the dash panel. "Shit!"

"Situation report," said Sloan tersely.

"Roger. Rate of descent is twenty-one hundred feet per minute. The airspeed has slowed to two-ninety. The wings are level and steady. It still appears that the autopilot is engaged." He broke the transmission, then hit the button again. "Homeplate, there are thunderstorms just ahead. I may lose them shortly."

"Matos, you son-of-a-bitch, your mission is to keep that fucking aircraft in sight until it crashes. I don't give a shit if you have to follow it to hell."

"Roger." Matos put James Sloan from his mind and concentrated on following the plunging Straton. The first scattering of oversized raindrops splattered against his canopy. Within seconds, his visibility had dropped to less than a half mile, then a quarter mile, then five hundred feet. Matos edged as close to the Straton as he dared, but the increasing turbulence made any tighter formation suicidal. There was no reason to throw his life away—not anymore.

"Situation report."

"The Straton is down to forty-eight hundred. Airspeed and descent rates are constant. No power in any engines. They'll hit within two minutes." As he looked up, the huge silver outline of the Straton blended in with the heavy rain and gray clouds, then the airliner faded from sight.

"Roger. Understand two more minutes. Do you still have visual contact with target?"

"Stand by." Matos peered into the grayness in front of him. Now that the Straton was no longer visible, he was afraid of colliding with it. Almost involuntarily, his hand pulled back on the control stick. He considered trying to track it with his radar, but the calibration would take too long and it would not work well at this close range. *Damn it.* He was becoming frightened. At this distance he knew he wouldn't see the airliner until it was too late to take evasive action. He pulled back further on the control stick.

"Matos! Do you have visual contact?"

"Visibility near zero. Heavy rain. Turbulence." Matos's eyes darted around to all the places where the Straton might be, but he saw nothing. Sheets of water ran from his canopy and a bolt of lightning cracked behind him, suffusing his cockpit with an eerie luminescence. *Fuck this.* The only way he'd find the Straton again was if he rammed into it. His hands were shaking as he pushed on the fighter's throttles and pulled back hard on the control stick.

As the fighter began to climb out of the storm, he hit the transmit button. "I have the Straton in sight again," he lied. "Straight ahead. Twenty yards. All conditions remain the same."

"Roger. What is your altitude?"

"Descending through twenty-six hundred feet. Approximately one minute to impact." As he spoke, Matos glanced at his altimeter. Seven thousand feet and climbing. He turned his fighter northwest so he would clear the storm as quickly as possible. Even in a high-performance aircraft like the F-18, the turbulence was jarring. He felt his stomach heave. For a brief instant, Matos pitied whoever might still be alive on that Straton.

"Report."

"Down to twelve hundred feet. Turbulence heavy. Clouds less dense here. I can see the ocean now. No chance of a successful ditching in this kind of heavy sea." The F-18 broke out into the sunshine at 19,000 feet. Matos continued to climb at full throttle, as if the altitude would get him far away from the whole situation. Below him nothing was visible except solid, heavy rain clouds.

"Too heavy a sea for survivors?"

"Roger." Matos glanced down but could see only the thunderstorms he had just risen out of. He turned to the blue sky ahead. When the F-18 continued climbing, he thought about James Sloan. Matos had heard a tone of triumph in Sloan's voice. Not for the first time, he wondered if the Commander was sane. It occurred to him that even the first navigation error that had started this nightmare might not have been his own fault. He thanked God that he had not fired his second missile into the Straton. At the worst, he was guilty of criminal negligence. He could live with that. But he was not guilty of murder.

"I say again—too heavy for survivors?"

"That's correct, Homeplate. The seas are too heavy for survivors," Matos transmitted, reinforcing his lie. But he, too, was relieved. So relieved that tears came to his eyes and he took a deep breath to control his voice. "The Straton is nosing down," he added as he kept his eyes fixed to the distant horizon.

"Roger."

Matos leveled the fighter at 36,000 feet. The storms were far astern and below him, and the warm afternoon sun bathed his face. He looked down at the weather below him. Rising from the top of the large mass were the distinctive anvil-shaped clouds that made the cloud layer easily recognizable as thunderstorms. It was, thought Matos, almost as though God made them that way, in the beginning, so that one day man would recognize that he was approaching the forge and the blast furnace of the heavens.

"We're down to four hundred feet," Matos lied.

The thought that he should go to Captain Diehl crossed his mind. He had to confess, not so much for his own soul but more importantly so that Commander Sloan would be put away where he could do no more harm. "We are down to two hundred feet. The rain is lighter. Visibility improved. The seas are very high. The Straton is nearly in. Nearly in. Stand by." Matos closed his eyes tightly. It was madness. He tried to forget that his playacting was a duplication of what was happening to that airliner. He could see it in his mind's eye very clearly now, hitting the towering water—

"Matos! Matos! Is it in? Is it in?"

Matos took a deep breath. "Yes." He put a heavy tone in his voice and noticed that it was not all an act. "Yes. It's in. Much of it . . . broke apart in the ditching . . . The seas are too rough . . . Most of it has already sunk . . . Only the tail . . . part of one wing remains above the surface. No possible survivors."

"Roger. Circle for a while to be sure."

"Roger."

"What is your fuel status?"

Sloan's question jolted him. He had forgotten to monitor his fuel status for more than an hour. He'd heard stories of pilots in combat doing that under stress. He didn't have to look at his gauges to reply, "Critical." He glanced at the gauges. His climb to 35,000 feet had been a foolish indulgence. "I'm down to forty-five minutes."

"Are you sure?"

"Maybe less. Where is that tanker?"

"Close. Heading westbound from Whidbey Island. Their last position was four hundred miles from your current position. He'll be closer now. Are you looking for survivors?"

"Yes. But my fuel is *critical*. No survivors."

"Roger. Okay, okay, begin your climb and steer a heading of zero-seven-five to expedite the intercept."

"Roger." Without hesitation, Matos turned his F-18 to the easterly heading. He was now pointed into the worst part of the thunderstorms, the part that towered high above his present altitude. "Homeplate, there's a lot of severe weather out here. The new heading is taking me further into it." As much as he wanted to find the tanker, he wanted nothing to do with that line of storms.

"Navy three-four-seven, this is Rear Admiral Hennings. Commander Sloan is on the phone with the tanker. These are your instructions—the tanker is cruising at thirty-one thousand feet, so you might as well get to that altitude to meet it. The weather should be better at that altitude than down lower."

"Yes, sir." Although Sloan had mentioned the Admiral earlier, Matos had no idea who Admiral Hennings was. But the voice was reassuring. Any vague misgiving that Matos had concerning Commander Sloan's intentions was put to rest. He pictured the electronics room crowded with officers and men, all trying to get him home. He looked out of his windshield. He was already above most of the weather at 35,000 feet. Now he had to descend slightly to meet the tanker. "The climb has taken—is taking—a great deal of fuel. I'm really low, sir."

The Admiral's voice came back, gentle, fatherly. "Take it easy, Peter. The tanker is cruising at five hundred knots. He'll be on station within twenty-five minutes. A few minutes for the fuel hook-up and you'll be heading back. Here's Commander Sloan."

Sloan's voice filled Matos's earphones. "It's important to stay calm, Peter. Practice fuel-conservation techniques. Keep us filled in."

Matos pictured himself flaming out just before he reached the tanker. He was glad that Sloan was so calm. It wasn't Sloan's ass. "Roger. Can you arrange air-sea rescue just in case?"

"Roger that," said Sloan. "Way ahead of you. Some of the air-and-sea rescue for the Straton is closing in on your area, including F-18s from the *Nimitz*. Plenty of help out there, but don't think about that now. Hightail it to thirty-one thousand and call me when you're leveled out."

"Roger. What's the frequency of the rendezvous?"

There was a long silence in his earphones. Matos was about to call again when Sloan's voice came on. "I'm speaking to the tanker on a frequency that is not available on your set. I just requested that they put one of their radios on your channel. They have a voice scrambler set to yours, so leave yours on. Give them a call now. Their call sign is Cherokee 22."

"Roger. Break. Cherokee 22, this is Navy three-four-seven. How do you read me? Over."

Matos waited in the silent cockpit, then transmitted again. "Cherokee 22, Cherokee 22, Navy three-four-seven, how do you read?" He waited, but there was no answer. "Homeplate, Cherokee 22 does not respond."

"I can't read them on your channel either. Stand by." After a few seconds, Sloan's voice came back. "They are having radio problems on most of their command channels. But I hear them fine on their administrative channel, which is patched into my interphone. We can work around their problem. I'll relay messages between you. But they're homing in on your channel with a radio navigation homing device and, of course, they'll have you solidly on radar soon. In the meantime, you have to leave your radio set to this channel. Their homing equipment and radar will lead them in."

"Roger."

"And leave your voice scrambler on, too. Try to call

them every five minutes. They'll be on voice scramble. If they hear you, they will tell me. Then you can go back to regular communications directly with them."

"Roger." Matos slid his transmitter override button to the continuous position. As long as he was transmitting a signal he knew he could not receive any messages, and hearing any voice, even Sloan's, would have been reassuring. But the first priority was the tanker.

Matos turned on his radar. He watched the tube as it glowed luminescent green. He adjusted the knobs and looked for the tanker, which should have been on the outer edge of his range by now. Not only did he not see the tanker within the 500-mile limit of his scope, but he saw no other aircraft either. He spoke into his open radio. "Homeplate. Where the hell are all the aircraft that are supposed to be out here? I don't see the tanker on a bearing of zero-seven-five, and I don't see anyone else." He released his transmit override and waited for the reply.

Sloan's voice came back quickly. "Matos, the tanker sees *you*. The rescue aircraft in your area see you. Your radar has been the problem from the beginning when . . . I can't say anything of a confidential nature any longer. Other aircraft are on this frequency now, and we have to maintain the security of this test. Be careful of what you say from now on. Resume your continuous radio signal and keep working your radar. You'll rendezvous with the tanker shortly."

"Roger. I have to release the missile to cut down on weight and drag."

"Negative. That's no longer possible. Too much air-and-sea traffic in your area now. We don't want another . . . Do you understand?"

# MAYDAY

"Roger." Matos thought that the possibility of hitting an aircraft or ship was very remote—absurdly remote—but without functioning radar he could not be sure, and with the way his luck was running he'd probably hit the tanker. But the damned missile was adding to his fuel problems. "Roger, I'll hold the missile." Matos locked his radio on and sat back. There were too many glitches today, too many goblins in the electronics. This was all possible, but not probable. Yet it had happened. This was the stuff that accidents were made of. Fifty percent human error, fifty percent equipment failure. How would they classify this monumental screwup? A little of both, and a lot of bad luck.

Matos worked his radar for a few minutes, but the results were negative. He alternated his attention between scanning the tops of the churning black clouds for aircraft and glancing down at his sinking fuel gauges. It was ironic, he thought, that he should wind up with the same problem that finally killed the Straton. Running out of gas. That was pure stupidity. He never should have let it go that far.

Thirty-one thousand feet. Peter Matos had used every trick he knew to keep the fuel flow as low as possible. Someday he'd learn to think about fuel first and everything else afterward. He remembered his flight instructor at Pensacola: *Gentlemen, even the best fighter-bomber in the world can only go in one direction when the fuel runs out.*

But even if the worst happened, he would be picked up at sea. He tried to settle down into a calm state of mind and anticipate the coming problem instead of reacting to them as they came.

He thought of Sloan briefly. There was no percentage in going to Captain Diehl and confessing. Sloan might be difficult to deal with, but he was all Navy. He anticipated problems and put the wheels in motion to take care of them before they became insoluble. He was cunning and even somewhat dishonest in his methods, but whatever he did, he did for his country, for the Phoenix program, for national security. And in the final analysis, no matter what else he did, James Sloan took care of his men.

---

John Berry sat motionless in the captain's chair. An instant before the failure of the Straton's four jet engines registered on the instrument gauges, it registered on John Berry's senses, and he knew exactly what was happening to them. He felt the aircraft yaw slightly to the left, then felt the deceleration forces against his body.

Sharon Crandall shouted, "John! What's happening? What's happening?" The panel in front of her was a sudden mass of blinking lights and bouncing needles. The engine gauges in the center of the panel unwound rapidly.

A loud warning horn blared from somewhere in the panel and the cockpit was filled with its ominous, deep-pitched sound.

Linda Farley opened her mouth, and her long, piercing scream drowned out the sound of the horn.

In the lounge, the passengers began losing their precarious balance and fell to the floor or crashed against the bulkhead of the cockpit. Deep bellowing cries, punctuated by shrill screeching, penetrated the cabin.

# MAYDAY

Berry's ears were filled with noise, and his eyes blurred from the blinking colored lights in front of him. For a few seconds, he was stunned. His stomach churned from the sinking sensation of the sudden descent. He felt his heart speed up and his mouth went dry. It was only the full realization of what they had done to him, and the anger it produced, that brought him back to his senses. He slammed his fist on the glare shield in front of him. "Bastards! Goddamned sons-of-bitches!"

His eyes ran wildly over the center instrument panel. Nearly every needle and light on the electronic display was active, but the messages they sent him were too complex to comprehend. He could see that the aircraft had lost all engine power. "Flame out in all four" was the expression, he remembered. He was also able to see that their electrical energy was falling off as each of the engine's generators dropped out of the circuit. Berry took a few long, deep breaths and steadied his hands. He reached up and pushed the fuel valve emergency power switch back to its previous position, then reset the four fuel valves.

Crandall turned in her seat and shouted above the noise of the screaming girl and the blaring horn. "John! We're going down! Put the switches back! Put them back! Please hurry!"

Berry looked up and yelled, "They're back. Calm down. Just sit there. Linda! Be quiet." Berry looked down at the panel and waited for some sign from it, or for some physical sensation that would indicate that the engines were producing power again. But nothing happened. Whatever he had done by moving the switches could not be undone by putting them back.

Crandall's voice was choked with sobs. "John . . . John . . . do something. . . . We're going to crash. . . ."

Berry was alternating between periods of trying to disassociate himself from his impending death and trying to find a way to avoid it. He made an effort to sort out the messages that the lights and instruments were telling him, but couldn't keep his thoughts straight. *Valve power. Fuel. Generator.* He knew what was wrong, but he had no idea of what to do about it. It was only the image of a man in San Francisco typing out his death warrant that kept him from giving up.

Most of the cockpit lights had gone out when the generators shut down, but a few remained on, dimly powered by the aircraft's batteries. Suddenly, the cockpit became darker and Berry heard a new noise that completely obliterated all the others. He turned and looked at the windshield. The Straton had entered the edge of the first thunderstorm, and the roar of rain and hail hammered against the windows and the roofline. The hail was so violent he thought the windshield might shatter. "Hold on! Hold on!" he shouted, but he knew no one could hear him.

The Straton began to bounce wildly, then slid dangerously to the right. The nose of the aircraft pitched up and down at the same time that its wings rolled on its axis and its tail yawed left and right.

Berry thought the aircraft might break apart if the violent, unstable flight condition kept up much longer. He saw Sharon Crandall hunched forward in her chair, holding on to the armrests. Linda Farley couldn't get a grip on her chair and was lifted up and dropped, held down only by her lap belt.

The autopilot made the corrections in the flight and

the Straton began to steady out, except for the bouncing caused by the air turbulence as it continued its powerless descent.

Berry tried to catch his breath and steady his shaking body. He turned back to the panel and scanned the small display of emergency instruments, which were all that remained after the generators failed. He was searching for anything that might spark his memory and set in motion a sequence of thoughts that would tell him what he must do. *Circuit breakers.* Berry thought that maybe the panel of circuit breakers on the right would be a clue—maybe one of the breakers was out. He flipped off his seat belt, stood up, and moved aft. He knew he had not much more time before the Straton hit the ocean.

Cutting through the sounds of the weather, the blare of the warning horn and the screaming from the lounge, he heard a voice shouting a single word over and over. He looked over at Sharon, who was turned in her seat, gesturing wildly at him. Her mouth kept forming a single word. *Autopilot.*

Berry looked back at the center instrument panel between the two seats. The amber disengage light now glowed brightly in the darkened cockpit. "Oh, God." With the generators dropped off the circuits, he knew the autopilot was not getting the proper power to stay engaged. The last chance that they had for staying in control until the ditching was now gone. He shouted to Crandall, "Hold the wheel! Hold the wheel!"

The Straton's forward momentum had kept the downward glide steady for a few seconds, but the winds began to break up the controlled descent. The Straton pitched nose upward, and the first step Berry took to get himself back into the captain's chair sent him careening in the opposite direction, backward, into the cockpit door. The door gave slightly under his weight. The aircraft rolled to the right, and he collided with the circuit breaker panel. He lunged at the back of Crandall's chair, but the aircraft rolled left and he headed straight for Linda Farley. He tried to avoid her, but his foot caught the tautly stretched nylons and he tumbled over and fell onto her, then rolled off and came to rest against the left wall.

Sharon Crandall watched for a second, then turned and faced the flight controls. The copilot's control wheel moved by itself, as if it were still safely under the command of the autopilot. But the blinking amber light told her it was not. She reached out and took hold of the wheel.

Berry managed to stand and grabbed the back of the captain's chair. The aircraft remained in a sharp nose-up attitude and he hung on, trying to climb into the chair. He knew that the aircraft's normal stability would keep it upright for a few seconds longer, but unless he could get to the wheel, the Straton could point itself straight up or straight down, go into a spin, or roll, wing over wing, into the sea. "Hold the wheel, Sharon! Hold the wheel!"

Crandall was trying to hold on to it, but it had begun to vibrate with such force that it broke her grip each time she grabbed it.

Berry climbed head first over the back of the pilot's chair. The first violent updraft smacked into the Straton like a giant fist aimed at the solar plexus. The huge aircraft lifted like a toy, then dropped sickeningly, straight down. Berry saw himself rise off the chair, almost hit the ceiling, then fall abruptly to the floor between the captain's chair and the observer's chair. He lay there, dazed and disoriented, not able to tell up from down, or to determine what he had to do to stand upright. He saw Linda Farley's face above him, and heard her screaming his name.

Sharon Crandall seized the wheel and held it, letting it move her arms at first, then slowly exerting more and more pressure to steady it. She focused on the largest and most prominent gauge on the panel in front of her, one of the few of them that was still lit. It was marked ARTIFICIAL HORIZON. This was one instrument that was familiar to anyone who had ever spent any time inside a cockpit. It showed the relative position of the aircraft against a horizon line, and she could see that the Straton was far from level. But inside the clouds she was too disoriented to tell if they were pitched forward or backward, or if the wings were rolled right or left. She tried to get a physical sensation of how the aircraft was moving, but the increased Gs kept her pressed to her seat and she had no sensation of backward or forward, left or right. All she knew for certain was that they were going to crash. It occurred to her that if it weren't for the fact that John Berry was on the floor, they could even be upside down.

She had a firm grip on the vibrating wheel, but her arms and shoulders ached. She knew she had to do something before the aircraft tumbled. She glanced at the artificial horizon, then tried to get a gut feeling based on her thousands of hours in flight. She decided that the aircraft was traveling nose up and the left wing was dropped, though the reverse might be true if she were reading the instrument backwards. She pushed forward with all the strength she had and rotated the wheel to the right.

For an instant, she thought she had guessed wrong as the artificial horizon line traveled even farther the wrong way. Then slowly the line straightened, then moved to align itself. The vibrations subsided and the aircraft flew steady except for the constant buffeting of the winds. She gripped the wheel tightly and held it with every ounce of strength she had left.

Berry pulled himself up and noticed that the aircraft was much steadier. He looked quickly at Linda. She was very pale and her body was doubled over with dry heaves. He climbed quickly into the pilot's chair. He strapped himself in and grabbed the captain's control wheel. He held it very tight, his knuckles turning white. It wasn't the wheel that was shaking, he realized, but his hands. He took several long breaths before he found his voice. "Sharon . . . Sharon . . ." He looked at her but couldn't think of what to say.

Sharon released the wheel and sat back, trying to prepare herself for the coming impact. Several thoughts and memories flashed through her mind, but none of them seemed important. She reached out and touched Berry's arm, then looked back at Linda.

The girl was staring at her. "Are we going to crash?"

"Yes. Hold on tight."

# 14

Commander James Sloan kept up a constant stream of talk into the dead interphones, speaking alternatively to the phantom air-sea rescue and the phantom tanker. He was becoming bored with the charade, but saw no alternative to it. He had to keep Hennings in Room E-334 until Matos was down, and until he could decide what had to be done with the Admiral.

Outside the door of the room, voices and footsteps approached.

Hennings looked up from his chair, an uneasiness in his eyes.

Sloan replaced the green interphone. "Just a changing of the watch, Admiral. Room E-334 is inviolate, off-limits to everyone except the few of us with an official need-to-know. I don't think even the Fleet Admiral would walk in here without calling first."

Hennings slumped back into his chair. That had been the problem from the start. An illegal test, shrouded

333

by secrecy, had concentrated an inordinate amount of power into the hands of James Sloan.

Sloan looked at the old man hunched over in his chair. The long years of sea duty had permanently darkened his face, but the last few hours had cast an unhealthy pallor over his features.

Hennings seemed to rouse himself out of his lethargy and looked up. "Why are we taking the transmissions from the tanker and the rescue operation through the interphones? Let's put a few radios on those frequencies."

Sloan shook his head; he had already thought of an answer for that. "These are not my operations. They are being handled from separate electronics rooms, separate commands. And I don't want two more squawk boxes turned on. I have enough to think about without listening to a lot of jet jockeys talking to each other."

Hennings nodded and slumped back into his chair.

The gold-colored bridge phone rang, and Sloan snatched it up. This was a *real* call. His heart began to pound. "Yes, sir."

Captain Diehl's voice sounded unsure, almost apologetic. "Commander, I'd like a status report on Navy three-four-seven."

Sloan had known this call would have to come eventually. The Captain wanted to know as little as possible about the Phoenix test, and that was the reason Sloan had kept control so long. But now Diehl wanted to know why one of his aircraft was overdue. "Status unchanged, sir." He glanced at Hennings.

There was a pause, then the Captain said, "I can assume, then, that everything is going well with three-four-seven?"

"Right, sir. He's employing fuel-saving techniques at this time."

"I see. That was part of the test profile?"

Sloan paused purposely, as though he were reluctant to commit a security breach. "Yes, sir."

"All right. The Admiral is still with you?"

"Yes, sir."

"Fine. I won't take any more of your time, Commander."

"Thank you, sir." Sloan hung up, took a deep breath, and turned to Hennings. "The Captain is concerned about three-four-seven."

"So am I."

Sloan stared at the radio speaker. Matos's open transmitter filled the room with rushing noises, noises of the cockpit, noises that came from nine miles above the earth. Occasionally, he could hear Matos, forgetful or uncaring that his transmitter was on, talking softly to himself, humming once, cursing many times. Then his voice came through the speaker loud and clear. "Homeplate, no tanker in sight. No air-sea rescue in sight. Fuel estimated at fifteen minutes. Maintaining heading of zero-seven-five, at thirty one thousand feet." He read his coordinates from his satellite navigation set. "Storm still below me. Shutting off transmitter so I can receive you."

The rushing sound stopped, and Sloan quickly picked up the microphone. "Roger. Civilian and military air-sea rescue closing on you. Tanker should be in sight."

"I don't see it."

"Stand by." Sloan picked up the green phone and spoke for a few seconds, then took up the microphones. "Matos, he thinks he has visual contact with you as well as radar contact. As a backup, keep your transmitter sending a signal so he can home in. Hang in there, Peter."

"Roger." The rushing sound of the open transmitter filled Room E-334 again.

Sloan looked at his countdown clock, which had been set at Matos's estimated forty-five minutes of flying time. It read fourteen minutes. Fourteen minutes to keep this incredible juggling act with the dead, colored interphones, with Hennings, with the live, gold interphone to the bridge, and most of all with Lieutenant Peter Matos. A lesser man than himself would have fallen apart long ago, but James Sloan had a strong will, and he knew that one man, with a strong sense of mission and a keen sense of self-preservation, could control any situation. People wanted to believe, and if you gave them no cause for suspicion, if you acted with confidence and assurance, they *would* believe.

Suddenly, the room was filled with a voice that was at once familiar and unfamiliar. "Mayday! Mayday! Navy three-four-seven is flaming out!"

Hennings jumped to his feet.

Sloan grabbed the microphone and glanced at the countdown clock. Eleven minutes left. Matos had made some kind of calculation error, or the fuel gauges were slightly off at the low end. Maybe the missile produced more drag than he thought. "Roger, Peter. I understand. Air-sea rescue has a good fix on you."

Matos's voice was shaking, but he fought for control and replied, "Roger. I'm going through thirty thousand

now. I'll be into the top of the storm in a few seconds."
He read his coordinates, then said, "Violent updrafts,
buffeting the aircraft. Unstable."

Partly out of instinct, and partly because Hennings
was in the room, Sloan gave Matos the best advice possible under the circumstances. "Peter, hold off on
ejecting for as long as possible. When you eject, hold
off on the chute as long as you can."

"Roger." Sloan pictured Matos falling, still in his
flight chair, waiting as long as possible before opening
the parachute, then opening it at the last possible moment, being caught in the wild currents—being taken
up instead of down, then dropping again, then rising
with the currents—a process that could go on for a
long, long time. If that didn't kill him, the sea would.

Hennings stood next to Sloan and watched the radio
speaker, then looked toward the interphones. "How far
is the closest air-rescue craft?"

Sloan grabbed the blue interphone and poised a pencil over the clipboard that covered the switches. "Operator. Patch me into the rescue command craft. Quickly.
Rescue? This is the *Nimitz*. How far is your closest air
or sea craft from the target aircraft? Right. He has
flamed out. Copy these coordinates." Sloan read them
off. "He will eject shortly. Do you still have a good fix
on his transmission signal? Right." Sloan nodded his
head. "Yes, all right. . . ." This absurd monologue into
a dead phone was becoming tiresome. He hoped he was
still doing it well. "All right, we—"

Matos's voice cut into the room. "Homeplate—I am
down to twenty thousand. The ride is very rough. Rain
and hail. No visibility."

Hennings grabbed the microphone. "Navy three-four-seven, we are talking to air-sea rescue now. You will be picked up soon. Stand by." He looked at Sloan.

Sloan spoke into the interphone. "Hold on, rescue." He turned to Hennings. "Tell Matos he will be in the water in less than ten minutes. Tell him to keep the fighter's transmitter signal on. After ejecting, the air-sea rescue craft will home in on his raft transmitter."

Hennings spoke into the microphone and relayed the message. He added, "Don't worry, Lieutenant. We're with you, and we're praying for you. Out." Hennings released the microphone button so that Matos could continue to transmit. Tears came to his eyes, and he turned away and stared out toward the porthole.

Matos's voice broke the silence in the room. "I am down to ten thousand feet. Preparing to eject." His voice had become matter-of-fact, as though he were reporting on someone else's problem. "Eight thousand feet."

Hennings took note of the calmness in his voice. He knew it was important for a pilot, as for a seaman, to do this well, to go down with dignity.

"Still extremely turbulent . . ." The sound of Matos's breathing came through loudly on the speaker and filled the electronics room. "This is my last transmission. I am leaving the aircraft now." The speaker gave a loud pop as the canopy blew off, followed by an ear-piercing rushing sound as the transmitter picked up the three hundred-mile-an-hour wind that filled the cockpit. Then, a split second later, they heard the loud explosion of the ejecting charge as Peter Matos's flight chair was blown clear of the F-18.

The continuous, unnerving roar of the abandoned fighter was broadcast into Room E-334. Hennings thought for a moment that he could hear the crashing sea, then an odd sound, like a muffled slap vibrated through the speaker, followed by silence.

Sloan reached out and shut off the radio. He spoke softly into the interphone. "The aircraft is down. The pilot has ejected. Home in on his raft transmitter when he lands. Yes. Thank you." He hung up. Sloan put his hand on the digital clock and erased the remaining minutes of fuel time that Matos never had. The digits 00:00 seemed appropriate. He sat down. "We can console ourselves, Admiral, with the fact that one F-18 is a small price to pay for the continuation of the Phoenix program. The program, like its namesake, will rise from its own ashes and fly again."

"Your attempt at metaphor is grotesque, ill-timed, and inappropriate, Commander. What I'm concerned about now is Flight Lieutenant Matos."

"Yes, of course. We all are. Lieutenant Matos is trained in sea survival. His life raft will keep him afloat and his flight suit will keep him dry. And at these latitudes, the water is not that cold." Sloan rocked back in his swivel chair and closed his eyes. He pictured Peter Matos dropping quickly into the sea, his parachute ripped apart by the winds. Then another picture flashed through his mind: Peter Matos landing softly, inflating his raft, clinging to it. How long could he live in the sea? No one was looking for him. It might take days for him to die. Then again, he might not die. There had always been that possibility. He suddenly saw Matos being transferred from a rescue craft to the *Nimitz*— stepping aboard, his flight suit covered for some reason with seaweed, walking across the wide flight deck before him. *No.* Even without the storm, he had no chance if no one was looking for him in the right place.

The sound of Hennings's voice penetrated Sloan's thoughts. He opened his eyes and looked up at the Admiral. Hennings was speaking into the blue interphone.

"Hello? Hello?" He pushed repeatedly on the headset buttons. "Hello? Air-sea rescue?" Hennings looked down at Sloan, then down at the series of colored phones in their cradles. He reached over and slid the clipboard away from the switches, saw that they were off, then looked back at Sloan.

Sloan sat silently and met the old man's eyes. Finally, he said, "Sorry, Admiral. It was the only way out for us."

Hennings let the phone fall from his hand and heard it hit the floor. His voice was barely above a whisper. "You . . . you son-of-a-bitch. You murdering son-of-a-bitch . . . How in the name of God . . . ?" Hennings's senses reeled, and he had to make an effort to stand steady. His eyes tried to focus on Sloan, but he saw sitting in front of him not Sloan himself, but Sloan's true essence. "Who *are* you? *What* are you?"

*"We,* Admiral. *We."*

The illusion passed, and Hennings regained control of himself. "Matos was . . . he trusted you . . . he was one of your men. . . ."

"I see you're not giving as much thought to the hundreds of people we sent down on the Straton. Don't civilians count?"

Hennings put his hands on the console and leaned over, close to Sloan. "You know the expression: three may keep a secret if two of them are dead." He looked Sloan in the eye. "Me next?"

"Don't be absurd."

Hennings straightened up. "Call air-sea rescue right now." He reached for the phone switches.

Sloan grabbed his arm and held it tight. "Don't be a fool. We've already consigned a planeload of civilians to their deaths. If we start a search for one man who can hang us, we may as well do it for all of them." He tightened his grip on the Admiral's arm. "And it would be a useless exercise. No one can survive that sea." He released Hennings's arm and spoke in a calmer tone. "Admiral, it's not even jail I mind very much. It's the indignity of the proceedings. We'll be treated as the most vile things that ever lived. Our names will be spit out in the officers' clubs and ward rooms for generations. That's no way to end a career. If you remain silent, no one will ever know. Nothing is gained by confessing. Nothing. The dead are dead. The Navy and the nation are intact." He changed the tone of his voice and spoke as though he were giving an official report. "Flight Lieutenant Peter Matos was killed when the rocket engine of his Phoenix missile exploded while strapped to his aircraft. He will receive full military honors and his family will cherish his memory, and they will receive his insurance and all standard benefits due an officer's family. His name will not be besmirched in any way." Sloan paused for a long time. "Admiral?"

Hennings nodded.

Sloan looked up at the wall clock. Three-ten. "Isn't your flight off the carrier scheduled for 1600 hours?"

"Yes," Hennings answered absently.

"Then I suggest you gather your gear, Admiral.

You've only got fifty minutes, and I expect you'll first want to pay your respects to Captain Diehl."

Hennings glared at Sloan.

"Also," Sloan added, waving his hand at the report sheets that still lay on the radio console, "I expect your report to the Joint Chiefs will stress that this mishap was in no way my fault."

Without answering, Randolf Hennings turned and walked out of Room E-334.

---

John Berry felt the familiar pilot's control pressures in his hands and realized that this was the first time he had attempted to hand-fly the giant Straton. The warning horn sounded weak and the lights became dimmer as the electrical energy was being drained away from the dying airliner. The cockpit became quieter as they dropped beneath the worst part of the storm. From the lounge, Berry could hear the moans of the injured. He released one hand from the wheel and turned on the windshield wipers. Through the rain and clouds, he thought he could see glimpses of the ocean. His heart pounded quickly. He forced himself to look down at the altimeter. "Four thousand feet," he said aloud. They were dropping at the rate of about forty feet a second. "Less than two minutes to impact. Hold on. Sharon . . . the life vests . . ."

"Yes. In the orange pouch against the rear wall."

Berry turned and looked at the orange pouch hanging on the wall, then saw the small emergency exit near the right rear of the cockpit. "When we hit, you get the vests. I'll open the door. Linda, stay in your seat until we come for you."

Crandall grabbed his arm. "John . . . John, I'm scared."

"Stay calm. For God's sake, stay calm." Berry held the controls tightly. He knew he should be thinking about how to bring the aircraft in, and what to do if they survived the crash. But he couldn't get his mind off the problem of the dead engines. *The fuel was shut off. But the fuel is now on again. What else . . . ?*

A bolt of lightning flashed close outside his left window and the cockpit was illuminated with an orange glow, followed by the crackling sound of unharnessed electricity. Berry sat up quickly. Suddenly, all the complexities of the overhead instrument panel were swept away. "Oh, for God's sake!" He saw in a moment of unbridled clarity his old Buick, rolling down a hill in Dayton, Ohio, engine off, and he saw his hand turn the ignition switch, and heard again the sound of the Buick's engine firing into life. "Sharon! The ignitors! The ignitors! Listen. Listen to me. Get up. Get up!" He looked down at the altimeter. Two thousand feet.

As she unbuckled her belt and slid from her chair, the Straton broke through the bottom of the thunderstorm, and Berry could see the surface of the ocean clearly now. The sky was relatively calm, and the aircraft flew without much turbulence. But even from this altitude he could see the towering white foam of the swelling waves. He knew that even if they could get out of the aircraft, they wouldn't survive that sea.

Sharon Crandall was holding his arm and looking at him. Berry realized in an instant that she had perfect trust and confidence in him; as a flight attendant, she must have known that to ditch without a restraining belt meant almost certain death.

Berry spoke clearly and firmly. "I can't look away from the flight instruments. . . . On the overhead panel there are four switches marked 'engine ignitors.' Hurry."

She knelt down behind the pedestal between the pilot's chairs and looked up. Her eyes swept the instruments and switches above her. "Where? Where? John . . ."

Berry tried to reconstruct the panel in his mind while he kept his eyes glued to the flight instruments. He finally glanced up for a brief instant, for as long as he could dare. "Lower left! Lower left! Four switches. Yellow lights above them. Yellow! Yellow! Turn them on. On!"

Crandall spotted them and passed her hand over all four switches at once, pushing them into the on position. "On! On!"

Berry looked down at the altimeter. Nine hundred feet. The rate of descent had slowed slightly, but they had lost some airspeed. They had less than half a minute before the Straton would hit the water. He called out to Sharon, "Back in the seat. Strap in." He stared at the center panel and watched to see if the Straton's engine instruments would come to life. He tried to think if there was anything else he had to do to fire up the engines, but couldn't think of anything. He focused intently on the four temperature gauges. Slowly, the needles began to rise. "Ignition! Ignition! We have power!" But he knew that the process of accelerating the jet engines and producing enough thrust for lift would take time, perhaps more time than they had left.

He glanced at the altimeter. Two hundred and fifty feet. The airliner's speed had bled off to 210 knots and the descent was slower, but he sensed he was very close to a stall. As soon as that thought entered his mind, the stall warning alarm began to sound—a synthetic voice repeating the word *AIRSPEED, AIRSPEED, AIRSPEED*. Berry knew that he should push forward on the wheel, lower the nose, and pick up airspeed to avert the stall, but he had no altitude left for that. Reluctantly, he pulled slightly back on the wheel and felt the nose rise. The Straton began to vibrate, the tremors shaking the airframe so violently that it became nearly impossible to read the instruments. The Straton was engaged in a test of strength between gravity and the thrust of its accelerating engines. As he glanced at his altimeter, he saw that gravity was winning. One hundred feet.

He looked down out of the side window. The hundred feet that was showing on the altimeter seemed less than that in reality. The swelling sea that sped by beneath him seemed to rise up to the wings of the airliner. He glanced out the front windshield. Huge, towering waves rose and broke only a short distance below him. If even one of those waves reached up and touched the Straton, the aircraft would lose enough speed to make a crash a certainty.

Berry scanned his instruments. Engine power was up, airspeed was good, but altitude was still dropping. Berry nudged the control column, trying to keep the nose up. He was walking a shaky tightrope, and one slip would put them into the violent sea at nearly 200 knots.

The synthetic voice announcing *AIRSPEED* continued, and so did the prestall vibrations. Berry worked the flight controls judiciously, trying to trade their few ounces of available energy for a few inches of extra altitude.

The altimeter read zero, though he guessed the airplane was still about twenty feet above the water. It was becoming obvious that the Straton was not going to make it, given the rate of increasing thrust against the rate of descent. Involuntarily, the muscles of his buttocks tightened and he rose imperceptibly from his seat. "Come on, you pig—climb! Climb, you bastard!" He turned to Crandall and shouted above the noise. "Locate the afterburners! Afterburners!"

She scanned the overhead panel again, near where the ignitor switches had been. She raised her arm and gave Berry a thumbs-up.

"Hit the switches!" He paused for a split second and said, "Then get into position to ditch."

Crandall hit the four switches.

Berry heard and felt a two-phased thud as the afterburners kicked in. He had no idea what would happen next.

Crandall called to Linda. "Put your head down! Like this." Crandall hunched over into a crash position, as well as she could with the copilot's wheel in front of her. Before she put her head down, she glanced up to see if Linda had done the same.

Berry felt the slight sensation of being pressed against his seat. The Straton was accelerating as fuel was injected directly into the jet exhausts and ignited to give extra thrust to the engines. The prestall airframe buffeting lessened, and he pulled farther back on the control wheel. The nose came up, and the ocean seemed to sink beneath his windshield. The stall alarm voice sounded one more time, then stopped. The altimeter showed 100 feet and climbing. "We're climbing! We're climbing! We're lifting!"

Sharon Crandall picked her head up. She felt the increased Gs against her body as the aircraft rose. "Oh, God. Dear God." Tears ran down her cheeks.

Berry held the control column with his left hand, reached his right hand out, and spread his fingers over the four engine throttles. For the first time since he had climbed into the flight chair, he was in control.

He called out to Sharon Crandall. "Afterburners— off."

She reached up and shut them down.

The Straton decelerated slightly and Berry worked the four throttles, feeling the aircraft accelerate again. He watched the engine temperature and pressure gauges rise and the altimeter needle move upward. Five hundred feet, six hundred. Berry sat back. The unknown terrors of flying the airliner, like most unknown terrors, had been exaggerated.

No one spoke. All the lights in the cockpit came back on, and most of the warning lights extinguished. Outside, the violent storm raged above them, but at their lower altitude it produced no more than rain and manageable winds. John Berry cleared his throat. "We're heading home. Sharon, Linda, are you both all right?"

The girl answered in a weak voice. "I'm not feeling good."

Crandall released her seat belt, stood, and stepped over the girl. She noticed that her own legs were wobbling. She took the girl's face in her hands. "Just a little airsick, honey. You'll be all right in a minute. Take a lot of deep breaths. There."

Berry recognized the automatic words of the veteran flight attendant, but the tone was sincere.

Crandall leaned over and gave Berry a light kiss on the cheek, then slid back into the copilot's chair without a word.

Berry concentrated on the instruments. He let the Straton come up to 900 feet, then leveled out before they rose into the bottom of the thunderstorm.

He listened for sounds from the lounge, but heard nothing that penetrated the noise of the rain, the hum of electronics, or the droning of the jet engines.

He shut off the windshield wipers, experimented with the flight control for a few minutes, then reached out and reengaged the autopilot. The amber light went off, and he released the wheel and the throttles and took his feet off the pedals. He flexed his hands and stretched his arms, then turned to Sharon. "That was about as close as it comes. You were very cool."

"Was I? I don't remember. I think I remember screaming." She looked closely at him. "John . . . what happened? You didn't do something . . . no . . . I read the message."

"Neither you nor I did anything wrong . . . except to listen to them."

"What . . . ?"

The alerting bell rang.

They looked at each other, then stared down at the data-link screen.

> TO FLIGHT 52: DO YOU READ?
> ACKNOWLEDGE.
> SAN FRANCISCO HQ.

Berry motioned toward the console. "Those bastards. Those sons-of-bitches."

Crandall looked at him, then back at the message. She had not had time to think clearly about what had happened, and had not yet come to terms with what she'd thought about, but her half-formed conclusions suddenly crystallized. "John . . . how *could* they . . . ? I mean, how could . . . why . . . ?"

"God, I can't believe what an idiot I've been. Hawaii. That should have been my tip-off. Shift the center of gravity. Fuel gauges. Those goddamned lying sons-of-bitches."

Crandall was still trying to understand all that had happened. "That was partly my fault. I talked you into—"

"No. I trusted them too. But I shouldn't have. I should have known. I *did* know, goddamn it."

"But *why?* Why, in the name of God, would they do that?"

"They don't want"—Berry jerked his thumb over his shoulder—"*them* back."

Crandall nodded. She'd thought of that for some time, but never pursued the thought to its natural conclusion. "What are we going to do? What are we going to answer them?"

"*Answer?* I'm not going to answer anything."

"No, John. Answer them. Tell them we know what they tried to do."

Berry considered, then shook his head. "Someone who is trying to kill us has control of the situation down there. Someone in that tight little room off the Dispatch Office. Talking to the man—or men—in that room is like shouting to the man who just pushed you into the water that you're drowning. I'm not going to tip them off that we're still alive. That's our secret, and we'll make the most of it."

Crandall nodded reluctantly. "Yes, I suppose. God, I wish we could tell someone. If we don't get back . . . no one will ever know."

Berry thought about the data-link messages. He tried to reconstruct them in his mind. "Even if we do get back, we'll have a hell of a time trying to make anyone believe us. It would be our word against theirs, and we are the ones who suffered decompression, and we are the ones who can't understand or follow the instructions of trained personnel."

Sharon Crandall was beginning to get a very clear picture. "Those bastards. Oh, those bastards. Damn them." She tried to imagine who in the Trans-United hierarchy would be capable of something like this. A few names came to mind, but she decided it could be anyone with enough to lose by having the Straton come back.

Berry was thinking of motives. "They probably don't want to have to admit that their airport security was bad. They'll discredit the bomb message we sent them—if they even bothered to pass it on, and try to pin it on someone or something else. The Straton Corporation. Structural failure. What a bunch of conniving, immoral bastards."

"God, I can't wait to get back and . . . But are they going to *believe* us?"

"We have to remember what we read, and believe that what we remember is correct."

Linda Farley spoke. "We can show them the words printed on the paper."

Crandall couldn't follow what the girl was saying. "Did you understand what we were talking about?"

"Yes."

Berry kept his eyes on the control panel and spoke to her. "Those men in San Francisco lied to us, Linda. They tried to . . . they told us things that would make us crash. Do you understand that?"

"Yes."

"What words?" asked Crandall.

"In the back. Near where I was sleeping before. It's sitting in a little door on the wall, and it printed while you were typing and—"

"John! There's a printer at the rear of the cockpit! I forgot about it." She tore off her seat belt and jumped down from the flight chair. She moved quickly to the aft bulkhead and peered into a space in the corner near the fuselage wall. "Here it is." She reached in and tore the narrow sheet from the printer, then grabbed a stack of folded messages from a collecting basket. She held them up and stretched them out. "John! It's all here. Everything."

Berry found that he was smiling. Nothing, he admitted, is as sweet as revenge. "Let me see them."

She brought over the stack of perforated paper, no more than five inches wide, and let the loose end fall. It reached down to the center console between the seats. Each small perforated section held a computer-typed message.

Berry scanned the messages hanging in her hand. "That looks like all of them." He turned back and stared out the windshield. He could see Sharon's reflection in the dark, wet glass, standing beside him, the paper trailing down from her hand as she read from it.

He watched her for a few moments, her movements, her facial expressions.

Sharon refolded the messages. "We have to get back and expose these people."

Berry nodded. If they died in the crash and the cockpit were destroyed, or if they put down at sea, the printouts would probably not survive. He turned to Crandall. "Give me those. Get life vests for all of us."

Crandall opened the pouch on the bulkhead and handed out the orange life vests. She watched as Berry and Linda put on their life vests, then put one on herself. She took a first-aid kit from the emergency locker on the bulkhead and treated a small cut on Linda Farley's forehead. She moved beside Berry. "Hold still. You have a lot of scrapes and cuts."

Berry watched her as she dabbed antiseptic cream on his arms and face. "Where did you get that kit?"

"In the emergency locker."

"What else is in there?"

"Not much. Most of the emergency equipment is in the cabins and lounges." At the mention of the lounge, Crandall looked toward the cockpit door. She had, until just then, forgotten about what was on the other side.

Berry handed her the printouts. "Put these into Linda's vinyl pouch on her life vest. Try to wrap them so they're waterproof."

Sharon Crandall understood that he was trying to prepare for the worst. She walked to the locker behind the observer's chair, took out two items, and brought them up front to Berry. "This is a waterproof flashlight. These are asbestos fire gloves."

Berry smiled. "Very good."

Crandall unscrewed the end of the flashlight, removed the batteries, and stuffed the printouts into the empty battery case. She screwed the end back on and slipped the asbestos gloves over both ends of the flashlight. She wrapped the entire package securely with a length of bandage from the first-aid kit and placed it in the pouch fixed to Linda's life jacket, then snapped it shut. "Linda, you know this is important. If anything happens to us, show this to . . ."

"A policeman," said the girl.

Crandall smiled. "Yes. A policeman. Tell him it's very important."

She nodded.

Sharon Crandall sat back in the copilot's seat.

Berry reached out and took her hand. He said to her, "No one can say you didn't earn your flight pay this trip."

She squeezed his hand and smiled. "When you first came aboard, I said to myself, 'That guy would make a good pilot. . . .' "

"You noticed me when I came aboard?"

"Well . . . you were wearing blue socks with brown shoes." They both laughed, then Sharon sat back and listened to the engines, and felt their power vibrate through the airframe. She turned back to him. "John, can you land it?"

Berry looked out the windshield. The rain was tapering off and the sky was becoming lighter. Below, the ocean seemed less turbulent. He glanced at the weather radar. It seemed less cluttered with images, and as far as he could determine, the weather to their front was clearing. "Depends on the weather in San Francisco." He knew it depended a great deal on his ability. He glanced at the fuel gauges. "Depends on the gas, too.

The afterburners drank it up. We're eating it up now at this altitude. But we can't use any fuel to climb back up there, and the weather at those altitudes might turn bad again."

"Do you think we have enough fuel to make it?"

"I don't know. Too many variables. But I'm willing to bet you a dinner that we at least see the coast before we run out." Berry smiled to hide his real feeling. He knew what a sucker's bet it was.

"I'll bet you we make it to the airport. I want to go to the Four Seasons in New York."

Berry nodded. "All right." Then his smile faded. "Listen, if we have to ditch at sea, I'll know in enough time and we can prepare ourselves. That close to the coast, we should be picked up." But he wondered if they would go down near a shipping lane. He thought about the possibility of sharks but didn't know how prevalent they were on the West Coast. He wanted to ask, but decided to wait until they were close. The more he thought about ditching in the sea, the more it seemed to be a beginning, not an end, to their problems. But something else was bothering him. Even a safe landing at San Francisco might not be the end of it. "Sharon, we've got to come up with a plan. Something for after we land in San Francisco."

"What?" She was puzzled. To her, getting the damaged Straton safely to the airport was all they had to do. "What are you talking about?"

"These people," he said, pointing to the data-link, "tried to kill us. They won't stop just because we've landed."

"That's crazy."

The two of them sat silently for a few seconds.

Sharon wondered if Berry could be right. Perhaps she was making too little of it. She said, "If we land at San Francisco in one piece . . . well, we'll have to be aware that not everyone on the ground is happy to see us."

Berry nodded, and dropped the subject.

Berry looked around the cockpit. He was trying to anticipate every one of their needs, no matter which way things went. "Is there a life raft in the cockpit?"

"No. The rafts are all back there." She paused. "But the inflatable escape chute from the emergency door doubles as a life raft. It's not as big as the others, but it would be okay for three people."

"Right." He thought for a moment. "I think I can put it down into a smooth sea. Let's go over the ditching procedures. Linda, listen to what Sharon—"

The alerting bell rang again.

    TO FLIGHT 52: DO YOU READ?
    ACKNOWLEDGE.
    SAN FRANCISCO HQ.

Berry shook his head. "Those bastards. I'd love to tell them we're sailing in and see what they have to say about that."

Crandall stared at the message. "This is so . . . obscene. What kind of person does it take to do something like this? To try to murder people . . . innocent people who haven't done anything . . . ?"

Berry remembered his earlier thoughts about climbing above the weather. If he had the fuel, the oxygen, and the confidence to fly, he would have done it. That climb would probably have killed dozens more passengers. Berry wondered if he was really any better than the people in San Francisco HQ, whoever the hell they were. "Sometimes it's a matter of expedience. It's not personal, usually. Maybe we shouldn't take it personally."

"I take it personally."

There were sounds coming from the lounge again, whining and moaning, some cries of agony from the injured, and the sound of scraping against the door. Berry heard someone striking the piano keys. For a moment he thought someone was trying to play.

Berry knew that everyone there would drown if he ditched at sea, and he admitted that he would do very little—nothing, really—to save any of them.

He took Sharon Crandall's arm and turned her wrist toward him. "It's two-twenty-four. We have a few hours before we reach the coast." He tried to think in terms of what they would need for an airport landing. He looked down and made sure the autopilot was still engaged, then unbuckled his seat belt and slid out of the flight chair.

"Where are you going?"

Berry laughed involuntarily. "Not far, you can be sure."

She smiled at her foolish question.

Berry knelt down behind the captain's chair and slid his hand beneath it.

"What are you looking for?" Sharon asked.

"Charts. I need them for radio navigation signals."

"The radios don't work."

"The navigation radios might. They're separate from the transmitters and receivers." Berry continued to fish around beneath the captain's seat, but he came up empty-handed. "Damn it. They were probably blown out. We could really use them. Damn." The possibility of finding San Francisco Airport without a good navigational signal was very remote, even if they had fuel enough to wander up and down the coastline, which they didn't.

"How important are they?"

"We'll get by without them." Berry slid back into the captain's seat. "We can search through all the frequencies on the radio dial when we get closer. We'll find the right one." But Berry knew there were too many channels and they had too little time.

Crandall unbuckled her seat belt. "I'll look over here."

"Okay."

She leaned forward and ran her hand beneath the copilot's seat. "Nothing. Wait . . ." She leaned as far to the right as the side console would allow. "I think I've got something. Yes." Sharon pulled out a stack of crumpled papers. "Here."

Berry took them quickly. "Charts," he said. "They must be the copilot's." He thought for an instant about McVary back in the lounge. These were his charts and this was his cockpit. Now it was Berry's, for whatever that was worth. Berry carefully opened the charts one at a time.

"Are they the right ones?" Sharon asked anxiously.

Berry smiled. "Yes." He pointed to one. "Here's San Francisco. This is the frequency I wanted."

"Will the radios work?" Sharon had her doubts.

"Not yet." Berry folded the charts so that the San Francisco area was faceup. "When we get within range, we'll see if we can pick up a signal."

"And if we can't?"

"Then wherever we see land is where we go. Could you recognize features on the coast?"

"I think so. I've seen it enough times."

"Would you know if we were north or south of San Francisco? Or if we were near any other city? *Any* airport?"

She didn't speak for a few seconds, then said, "When we get there, I'll have a better idea."

"All right. Think about it."

"I will." She stretched her bare legs out and leaned back in the seat. "Let's talk. Let's not think about what has to come later."

"Might as well. I've run out of things to do already."

Sharon closed her eyes. "Tell me about . . . your home."

Berry would have preferred to talk about something else. He settled back and tried to think of what to say. As he did, the autopilot disengage light flickered again, and the autopilot switch popped to OFF. Berry grabbed the flight controls. "Oh, for God's sake."

"Autopilot?"

"Yes." Now he knew that he couldn't trust it anymore. The autopilot had undoubtedly been damaged during their wild descent. He had no choice but to hand-fly the Straton for the rest of the flight. As Berry concentrated on retrimming the manual flight controls, he could hear from behind him the persistent scraping against the door and the dissonant pounding on the piano. It was beginning to get on his nerves. Then he heard the data-link alerting bell.

"John. They're sending another message."

Berry looked at the screen. It was a repeat of the message they had sent a few minutes before. The bastards were still sending out bait, on the chance that Berry had somehow managed to keep the Straton from falling into the Pacific. "Screw them," he said. He was, without a doubt, taking it personally.

# 15

Jack Miller walked alone through the long empty corridor outside the dispatch office. Edward Johnson had taken his detailed report and told him to go home, again denying him entry to the communications room. Jack Miller knew that his days at Trans-United were nearly over.

He heard footsteps coming quickly up the stairs at the end of the corridor. He stopped.

The figure of Chief Pilot Kevin Fitzgerald—tall, muscular, tanned, wearing faded jeans and T-shirt—appeared suddenly from the stairwell. He came quickly toward Miller, who stepped aside and exchanged nods with the man. Miller cleared his throat. "Captain Fitzgerald . . ."

The chief pilot moved quickly past him and turned his head back as he kept walking toward the door at the end of the corridor. "What is it, Jack?"

"Everyone is in the administration building. Executive conference room, sir."

# MAYDAY

"Damn!" He turned and headed back. "Nothing happening here?"

"No, sir. Communications with 52 has been lost."

Fitzgerald kept walking, retracing his steps to the stairs. "Screwed up, Jack. It's all been screwed up. No one knows what the hell is going on."

"Yes, sir," he called to the retreating figure.

Fitzgerald disappeared down the stairs.

Jack Miller stood alone in the corridor for a few seconds. He considered for a moment, hesitated, then broke into a run down the corridor and took the steps down, three and four at a time.

In the parking lot, he saw Fitzgerald get into a foreign sports car. He ran to it.

Fitzgerald started the engine and looked at him. "What is it, Jack?"

Miller found he couldn't speak.

"I'm in a hurry. Is it important?" Fitzgerald looked up at him. He put a softer tone in his voice. "What's up?" He turned off his engine.

Miller stepped up closer to the window. "Captain, I have to speak to you."

Fitzgerald had handled men long enough, and he knew Jack Miller well enough to know that he was about to hear something important and disturbing. "Get in the car. We can talk while I drive."

"No, sir. I think you'd better stay here."

Fitzgerald swung the door open and climbed out of the car. "Shoot."

"Well . . ."

"Forget all the modifiers, Jack. Give it to me straight and quickly."

"I think . . . I'm sure something here smells."

# MAYDAY

Fitzgerald nodded. "Go on."
Jack Miller began his story.

---

With the door closed, the Trans-United communications room had become hotter. Fumes from the color-reproduction machine lay heavily in the stagnant air. Edward Johnson sat with his sleeves rolled up and his tie loose.

Wayne Metz kept mopping the perspiration from his face with a damp handkerchief. He nodded in satisfaction. "I think that's it, Ed."

Johnson nodded slowly. He felt badly—there was no doubt about it—but he also felt that the weight of the world—the weight of the Straton—was lifted from his shoulders. He was annoyed that Metz was having trouble concealing his glee. The man didn't understand flying, didn't understand airlines or the people who worked for them. He only understood liabilities and how to eliminate them. Johnson reached out and pressed the data-link's repeat button and held it down.

The message printed.

TO FLIGHT 52: DO YOU READ?
ACKNOWLEDGE. SAN FRANCISCO HQ.

The message printed again and again as he held his finger on the repeat button. A long stream of printouts began to collect in the link's receiving basket. Johnson looked at his watch. "That should be enough to show one every three minutes for the last hour." He released the repeat button, then typed a final message.

# MAYDAY

They both waited in silence.

Metz looked at the clock. Two-thirty. He cleared his throat. "That's it."

"I suppose." Johnson thought for a moment. There was no possibility that a weekend pilot could have survived after a flame out of all four engines. At 11,000 feet, he would have had less than five minutes until impact. That was enough time to reignite the engines if he knew how, but Berry had neither the skill nor the knowledge to keep the Straton under control. *Five minutes.* He was momentarily overwhelmed by the thought of the huge Straton falling 11,000 feet into the Pacific. His mind conjured up a vivid picture of the scene in the cockpit as Berry and the others fell toward the sea. By then, they probably knew for certain that someone had murdered them—if they had time to think about it. "My God, Wayne. It's really over." His knees were shaking, and he hoped Metz did not notice.

Metz glanced around the room. "Did we forget anything?"

Johnson looked at him. "If we did, you wouldn't know what the hell it was anyway."

"Okay," said Metz, "none of this is pleasant. Don't take it out on me. I'm only trying to see if we left a loose end hanging around. Loose ends can become nooses. We've come too far to—"

"Do you have the printouts?"

"Yes." He pointed to the sports jacket hanging over a chair.

"Put the jacket on." Johnson took his own jacket and threw it over his shoulder. He walked toward the door. For an instant he wished he were back on the loading ramp, throwing around luggage in the bright sunlight with the other men, talking about women and sports, untouched by the years of compromise, untroubled by the corporate casualties he had engineered, and un-haunted by the specter of the Straton that he knew he would see every day of his life.

Johnson was aware of someone staring at him through the glass door. He looked up and saw Kevin Fitzgerald's form filling the doorway. The doorknob rotated.

Instantly, Metz could see the antagonism between these two men, and he could see also the change in Johnson's demeanor. He suddenly felt frightened again.

Johnson turned to Metz as he hurried to the door. "It's Fitzgerald. Follow my lead. Don't volunteer *any-thing.*" Johnson quickly unlocked the door. "How are you, Kevin?"

Fitzgerald stared at the door latch for a long second, then looked up. "What's the latest?" He walked into the communications room, and looked around.

"You've been briefed at the conference room?"

"No, I was beeped at the beach. I called in and got the message. No one mentioned the conference room, and I came here, naturally."

"Right." Had he forgotten to station someone in the parking lot? No, he had told Miller to do it. *That bas-tard. Damn.* Johnson knew he was lucky that Fitzger-ald hadn't arrived earlier. "This whole thing has been fucked up from the beginning. ATC mostly, although our people have stepped on their dicks a couple of times, too."

"There'll be time enough for public executions later. Who's this?"

Johnson turned his head. "This is Wayne Metz. From Beneficial Insurance—our liability carrier."

Metz extended his hand. "I'm very sorry about this, Captain Fitzgerald."

Fitzgerald took his hand perfunctorily. "Yeah. Us, too." He turned to Johnson. "Still no word from them?"

"No. It's been over an hour now." Johnson motioned toward the data-link. "I've been repeating my last message every three minutes. No response."

Fitzgerald strode up to the machine and ripped the paper from it. He strung out the messages between his outstretched arms, looked at them, then dropped them across the data-link. He turned to Johnson and seemed to stare at him a second longer than would have been considered polite. "I understand that this pilot—Berry—had the aircraft under control."

Johnson wondered where he got that information if he hadn't been to the executive conference room. "It seemed that way. At first, anyway."

Fitzgerald continued. "Damage to the aircraft was extensive, but not critical."

"Apparently it *was* critical." *Miller.* He had been speaking to Miller.

"He sent no last message indicating he was in trouble? No Mayday?"

Johnson's heart began to pound. Why was he asking questions like this? "There are the original printouts of the first messages on the counter. I had them copied and sent to ATC and to the conference room. They may answer some of your questions."

Fitzgerald spread the messages out on the long counter beneath the Pacific chart. He had already looked up the pilots' names on the crew scheduling sheet in the main dispatch office. Fitzgerald quickly scanned the printouts. *Stuart . . . McVary . . . Fessler . . . Brain damage. . . . Good God.* Miller's words did not have the impact of these actual printed messages from the damaged Straton. Fitzgerald glanced between the messages and the markings on the Pacific chart. "Why didn't someone get a pilot in here right away to give him instructions?"

"Things happened too fast. Look, Captain, if you have any questions, let's take them over to the executive conference room. This is hardly the place or time for this conversation."

Fitzgerald ignored him and looked back at Wayne Metz. "What's your function here?"

Metz felt immediately intimidated by this man. "Well . . . Captain, from a liability standpoint, I wanted to be absolutely certain that we had done everything humanly possible to minimize your exposure and ours." Fitzgerald kept staring at him, and he knew he was supposed to keep talking. "And you can imagine, Captain, how even a minor oversight could be blown out of proportion by the attorneys for the injured parties. Actually, your company rule book recommends that the insurance carrier be present during—"

"I know what the company rule book says." Fitzgerald turned to Johnson. "Where's our legal man? Where's our hull insurer? Where's Abbot, the Straton Aircraft representative?"

"At the conference, I suppose. Look, Kevin, I don't know why you have a bug up your ass, but if there are any questions, we'd better go and settle them at the conference." Johnson didn't want Kevin Fitzgerald in this room, though he knew it should no longer matter. "Come on, Captain. I have to lock up this room." He regretted the remark as soon as he made it.

"Lock it? Why?"

Johnson didn't speak for a few seconds, then said, "We're supposed to leave it intact for the government investigators."

Fitzgerald shook his head slowly. "Read your manual, Ed. That rule only applies to the scene of the accident. I don't think," Fitzgerald said, gesturing slowly around the room, "that this qualifies as the location where the accident occurred."

*Yes, it does.* Johnson was becoming edgy, and he tried to hide it with a show of impatience. "Then stay here. I have to go to the conference." He moved toward the door.

Metz followed.

Fitzgerald stayed where he was. "Hold on."

Johnson turned.

"I know you don't know anything about flying, but if you were a pilot, lost over the ocean, and your only means of communication was malfunctioning, you wouldn't want everyone at the other end walking out of the communications room. Would you?" He stepped up to the data-link and typed.

TO FLIGHT 52: IF YOU CAN RECEIVE US,
DON'T THINK WE HAVE ABANDONED YOU.
THIS LINK WILL BE MANNED

CONTINUOUSLY UNTIL YOU ARE FOUND.
SAN FRANCISCO HQ.

Fitzgerald looked up at Johnson. "Call Miller in here."

Johnson thought he had sent Miller home, but as he looked up, he saw him sitting at his desk. *Bastard.* "Miller! Get in here."

Jack Miller walked quickly into the communications room. He looked squarely at Johnson.

Johnson saw the defiant expression on his face and knew that Jack Miller was under the protection of Kevin Fitzgerald. *Son-of-a-bitch.* When this was behind them, he'd see to it that Miller never dispatched anything bigger than a lunch wagon. "The Captain would like to speak to you."

Fitzgerald indicated the data-link chair. "Jack, sit here and monitor. Send about once every two or three minutes, and then wait. Wait for an answer, Jack."

"Yes, sir." Miller sat at the data-link.

Johnson watched Miller hit the repeat button to send Fitzgerald's message again. The Straton was down, and no one could change that—not Kevin Fitzgerald, not Jack Miller, not all the company executives, not the company president or the chairman of the board. And he'd done this for them as much as for himself—but they'd never understand that, and never know it.

Kevin Fitzgerald picked up the company phone and dialed the executive conference room. "Let me speak to the president."

Johnson knew his uneasiness was starting to show. He took a cigar out of his pocket and clamped it in his jaws.

Metz wanted to leave but thought it wouldn't be a good idea. His hand reached into his jacket and touched the wad of data-link printouts. He noticed Johnson glaring at him.

Fitzgerald spoke into the phone. "Yes, sir. Fitzgerald. Just got the word. Damned bad business. I'm at the dispatch office with Ed Johnson and Mr. Metz from Beneficial. Yes. We're leaving a dispatcher here to keep sending and to monitor. We'll be along in ten minutes. Fine." He hung up and turned to Johnson. "Press conference for six o'clock. You're the star. Can you handle it?"

"Of course."

"There are relatives of the passengers assembling in the VIP lounge. I have to speak to them. I wish I was as confident as you." He looked at Johnson closely. "I don't know exactly what happened here, but when those reporters start firing away at you, you damned well better have your act together."

"Who the hell do you think you're talking to?"

Both men glared at each other.

Metz edged out of the door and stood awkwardly in the middle of the dispatch office.

Miller pretended to be concentrating on the data-link machine. He knew that Fitzgerald was proceeding very rashly and very dangerously. He hoped to God that his suspicions—vague as they were—had at least enough substance to ensure that the chief pilot was not sticking his neck out too far.

Fitzgerald finally broke the silence. "Johnson, we're going to find out what happened to Flight 52, what happened here, and who was negligent. And I don't care how long it takes or who gets burned."

Johnson took his cigar out of his mouth. "You act as though you think I planted the fucking bomb. Don't try to use this accident to discredit me, Captain. I know how to survive, and I promise you I'll come out of this looking just fine. Just fine." He turned and walked out of the room, breathing the clean air of the dispatch office. His head was pounding and his stomach was in knots. He walked past Wayne Metz, past the dispatchers whose heads were down over their desks, and out into the corridor that he had walked through not so long ago.

Retired Rear Admiral Randolf Hennings leaned heavily on the rail that ran along the passageway of the 0-2 deck of the *Nimitz*'s superstructure. The passageway was deserted, and it would most likely remain that way for some time. He looked up at the two white stars painted above the stairwell designating the Admiral's Passageway. This passage was off-limits to anyone of lesser rank without a specific duty there. It was another of the Navy's long-standing traditions to have an uncluttered passageway for an admiral. Hennings had always realized how anachronistic things like that were. Pointless traditions. But he also knew how much he enjoyed them. Codes of honor. Allegiances and oaths of duty. They were all manufactured from the same need, and they all served the same end. But they were artifacts of a vanished world, and like him, they belonged in a museum . . . or a tomb.

Hennings let out a long breath. He rubbed his fingers along the rope-lined handrail. Just the feel of the twisted hemp brought back a flood of memories. The South Pacific—or the South Seas, as it was called in old days. Blue water, sunny skies, palm-lined beaches, and the young officers in their tropical tan uniforms. Standing on the decks or sitting in the wardroom, listening to senior officers telling firsthand stories of the war. The great sea battles and the amphibious assaults. But those memories were tainted now. Like a submarine breaking through the surface of the sea, one word kept rising through the depths of his mind and formed on his lips: "Murder."

Hennings descended slowly down the deserted gray passage, then opened a hatch and stepped out onto the sunlit flight deck.

A moderate breeze swept the wide expanses of the nearly deserted deck. Seventy-five yards forward of the conning tower sat the S-3 transport. The pilots were giving it a final line check. An orderly had already collected Hennings's luggage from his stateroom, and it was sitting near the baggage door. It seemed so long ago that the S-3 had brought him here. Hennings turned and walked away from the aircraft.

The Pacific sun lay directly astern of the ship, and the asphalt flight deck gave off waves of undulating heat. He spotted a seaman working near the aft starboard elevator, and he turned to avoid him. He crossed the deck diagonally and walked toward the fantail. He approached the edge of the deck and stood with his hands on the chain rail. Below, he could see the white foaming wake left behind by the giant nuclear-powered carrier. Straight down, mounted on the stern, a huge American flag hung from its mast. The flag snapped nicely in the wind, its bright colors standing out against the white wake.

Randolf Hennings thought about his wife, Mary. He had spent most of their thirty-nine years of marriage away from her. And with her death coming so soon after his retirement, he had never really had the time to do the things with her that he had put off for so long.

He thought about his friends. Most of them were dead, some in battle, some from natural causes. The remainder were living out their lonely retirements. As a Navy man, he had no roots, no hometown, no family that knew him.

More and more he had come to understand that he was not only lonely, he was an anachronism as well. He had always believed that today's scientific advancements and solutions were going to require some unexpected and unacceptable payments tomorrow. Now he realized that tomorrow was here. And today's situation ethics as practiced by James Sloan, often led to more unhappiness and more dire consequences than yesterday's rigid moral code. It was this runaway technology, with no clear sense of ethics and no accountability, that killed the Straton and everyone aboard her. That killed Peter Matos. Hennings had tried to fit into the new scheme but had succeeded only in being an accessory to a monstrous crime.

He had heard the S-3's engines starting on the forward service elevator 200 yards behind him. They would be looking for him soon. Captain Diehl and a few officers and men would assemble quickly to pipe him off, then get back to more important duties.

Randolf Hennings stared into the churning wake. He thought of those officers he knew who were buried at sea, and whose lives had ended in the sea. They had lived shorter lives than his, but had died before anything could erase their heroic deeds.

Someday, he believed, on the Judgment Day, the sea and the earth would give up its dead, and give up its secrets as well. Then men would point to their murderers, their torturers, to those who falsely accused them, to those whose negligence and stupidity had caused their deaths. Then God would judge each man in turn and mete out a fitting punishment.

He heard the ship's address system call his name in the distance.

Randolf Hennings slid beneath the chain rail and strode purposefully to the edge of the ship's fantail. Without breaking stride he stepped from the carrier's deck, fell past the safety net, past the unfurled American flag, and dropped unnoticed into the white wake of the USS *Chester W. Nimitz.*

# 16

John Berry's shoulders ached from the strain of hand-flying the Straton, and his body was beginning to react to the beating it had taken during the violent descent and his battle with McVary. Bruises covered his face and arms, and there was a stiffness in his joints. His head was beginning to throb, and his eyes were blurry. He looked down at the fuel gauges. Less than one-eighth remained in the tanks. "What time is it?"

Sharon looked at her watch, set to San Francisco time. "It's five minutes to six."

The autopilot disengage light glowed a steady amber, as it had done for the last three hours. Berry felt an irrational anger at the malfunctioning machine. "Sharon, take the wheel."

She reached out and took the wheel in her hands.

Berry stretched his arms and legs, and rubbed his burning eyes. The life vest was becoming uncomfortable, but at 900 feet—less than one minute to the water—he thought everyone should leave the vests on.

"The first one to see land gets a bottle of champagne, just like on a ship."

"And I get dinner in New York if we make it to the airport."

"Right. And Linda . . ." He turned his head. "What do you want when we land?" Berry was sorry he'd brought it up.

Linda Farley looked up from her chair and shrugged. "I want something to drink. And I want to see if my mother . . . is . . . is okay."

Berry turned back to the front. He looked out the windshield at the ocean. The sea was becoming calmer, but there were still occasional high, rolling waves, any one of which could swamp the Straton if they ditched. The sky was dotted with white cumulus clouds—signs of fair weather—but that could change at any time. His prediction of sighting land no later than six o'clock raised their hopes too high. Sharon and Linda seemed to hang on his words. He'd have to be more guarded in what he said from here on.

He looked down at the radio console. Using the charts he'd found under the copilot's seat, he had set the captain's navigation radio to the Salinas Station frequency, south of San Francisco. Sharon had set the copilot's navigation radio to San Francisco Airport. The radios—which were more like electronic compasses than voice radios—had a limited range, but Berry thought that they should be close enough to receive a signal from either of those airports—unless he was so far off course that he would never be within range of them. "Do you see any movement in the needle there?"

Sharon Crandall looked down at the bearing indicator on the copilot's navigation radio. "Nothing."

*Perhaps,* thought Berry, *the antenna cables to those radios were severed along with the voice radios.* Voice communication was not that critical for a landing, but unless he could get a good radio navigation signal, and lock onto it, he would not be able to get a bearing for the final steer toward the airport.

Crandall glanced down at the West Coast radio chart in her lap. "Are you sure we've got the navigation radios set up right?"

"Let me see the chart again." Berry reached out for it, glanced at the chart and then the navigation radio, but he knew there was no mistake in the settings. Maybe he was still too far from the coast, or he was too far north or south, or worse, the radios simply weren't working. He didn't know, and he might never know. He handed the charts back. "We must still be out of range. Keep watching the needle on your side. If it moves, even a bit, let me know."

"Will do." Her eyes involuntarily passed across the data-link screen. The message sat there, then disappeared as someone at the other end pressed the repeat button. The alerting bell rang again, and the same message began to print across the screen as it had done every three or four minutes for the last three hours.

> TO FLIGHT 52: IF YOU CAN RECEIVE US,
> DON'T THINK WE HAVE ABANDONED YOU.
> THIS LINK WILL BE MANNED
> CONTINUOUSLY UNTIL YOU ARE FOUND.
> SAN FRANCISCO HQ.

"Maybe we should answer."

Berry didn't bother to look at the message again. Every time the alerting bell rang, he turned to the screen. He was beginning to feel as conditioned as Pavlov's dog. His will *was* weakening, and he wanted to answer. But then he might still be persuaded to do whatever they said.

"John, it's inconceivable that they would keep repeating this message if they—"

"They just want to be absolutely certain we're down."

He thought about that rapid succession of fifteen to twenty messages that had come in hours before. They had made the alerting bell ring continuously for more than a minute. "More probably they have to show that they're still trying to do something for us. They'll send messages until some government official or some airline executive determines that if we were still flying, we'd be out of fuel. It's probably standard operating procedure. I don't know exactly what's going on back there, but don't forget the Hawaii vector, and don't forget those informative instructions on how to shut off the damn fuel."

Crandall nodded. The words looked so sincere, sitting there on the screen. "John, maybe—"

"Change the subject." Berry had spent a good portion of the last few hours trying to imagine the scene at the other end of the data-link. *Bastards.*

"John? Do you think we should practice any more?" Sharon pointed to the flap handle.

"No. You've got that routine down okay." The two of them had been going over the landing sequence so that Sharon could operate the flaps and landing gear at Berry's command. That would free him to concentrate on the runway—or the surface of the ocean, if it came to that. "You don't want to be overtrained, do you?" Berry asked, smiling.

She forced a smile in return.

The cockpit grew silent and allowed the sounds of the lounge to penetrate. Berry could hear crying and some soft moaning, but for the most part it was quiet. They were sleeping, he thought. Then the piano began to play again, loudly this time, and Berry recognized the piece. It was unmistakably a passage from Tchaikovsky's Concerto No. 1, though in a terrible deranged arrangement. "Hold the wheel."

Berry ripped off his seat belt and moved quickly to the door.

"John, what are you doing?"

Berry pushed the door open against the stretched nylon and held it while he craned his head around the edge. He looked back into the lounge. The twisted forms of the dead and dying lay everywhere, like broken dolls strewn about the room of a disorderly child. Many of the passengers were still moving, however, roaming aimlessly over the body-strewn carpet. Daniel McVary was standing, facing the cockpit door, his face battered and one eye swollen shut. He walked slowly, with a limp, toward Berry.

At the piano sat Isaac Shelbourne, his long white hair wildly disheveled, and his hands moving dexterously over the keyboard as Berry had seen them move so many times on television. "Stop! Shelbourne, shut up! For Christ's sake, stop it!"

"John!"

Linda called out. "Mr. Berry . . . please close the door."

Berry drew his head back and let the door be pulled

closed by the tension of the nylon. He turned and walked slowly back to the flight chair and climbed in. He sat staring down at his lap for several seconds, then lifted his hands and took the wheel. "All right, I've got it."

Sharon Crandall looked at him and reached out to touch his shoulder. "Are you all right?"

"Yes. I'm fine."

There was an awkward silence in the cockpit.

Linda heard a noise behind her and turned in her seat. She screamed.

Berry and Crandall looked back quickly.

Several groping hands crept through the door opening. A few hands wrapped around the edge and pulled.

Crandall unbuckled her belt. "Damn it, you stirred them up again." She rose out of her seat.

"Stay here. I'll go."

"No. I can handle it. Fly the plane." She stepped to the bulkhead and took the fire extinguisher from its wall rack, then moved to the door and examined the length of panty hose. "You stretched it."

Berry didn't answer.

Crandall looked at the knot wrapped around the broken latch. The knot was secure, but the fiberglass door around the latch was cracked, and she couldn't remember if it had been that way before. The rivets on the latch assembly seemed loose also. She looked up and saw faces and bodies at the opening, which was about six inches wide. She raised the fire extinguisher and pointed it directly at Dan McVary's face. She pressed the trigger, and a rushing cloud of vapor blasted into the door opening. Excited squeals came from the other side of the door. Most of the hands disappeared. She raised the extinguisher and brought it down on one of the remaining hands, then struck out at the finger still gripping the door. She waited for a moment, then turned and replaced the extinguisher in its rack and sat down. "The door area around the latch is cracking."

Berry nodded.

"The copilot . . . Dan McVary . . . seems to be instigating. . . ."

"I know." Berry wondered how a single obsession could take hold in that damaged a brain. How was he communicating his leadership to the others?

"The extinguisher feels like it's nearly empty."

"Don't worry about it."

"Why not?"

"Look, I'm sorry. I got a little carried away. Okay?"

She nodded, and tears started to form in her eyes. "I'm sorry, too. It wasn't your fault. You've done so well, John. I don't know if any of our regular pilots could have done the same."

"No, they couldn't have. Because they would have realized it was hopeless from the start." He reached out and ran his hand over the side of her face. "I have a good crew." He turned and looked down at Linda Far-ley. "You've been a good member of the crew." He smiled at her.

Linda gave him an embarrassed smile.

Sharon Crandall put her hand on his arm. "Want me to take the wheel?"

"No. I've got it."

"Do you want to try to engage the autopilot again?"

"No. It's just as easy to fly it myself. I need the prac-tice."

"Okay."

# MAYDAY

Berry would have liked to have the autopilot, not only to relieve him at the wheel but because the autopilot might have made it possible for him to try for an automatic landing if they found the airport—although he didn't really know how to set that up, either. Without the autopilot, he would have to hand-fly the damaged Straton right into the touchdown. He scanned the horizon and watched his radio bearing indicator.

"John! It moved!"

Berry leaned far out of his seat and stared down at the indicator on the copilot's navigation radio.

They both looked at it for a long time, but the needle lay lifeless in the center of its scale. Berry saw too that the distance-to-go readout was blank.

"I thought I saw it move." She tried to sound emphatic. "I was sure I did."

"Nothing." He straightened up in his chair. "Keep an eye on it."

"Right."

Berry settled back again. Everything on the instrument panel remained unchanged. Dead voice radios. Dead navigation radios. Amber autopilot-disengage light on. Heading of 131 degrees. Airspeed of 340 knots. Altitude of 900 feet. The only change was the fuel gauge, which had sunk below the one-eighth mark. Even if they spotted land now, it was going to be very close.

Berry looked up at the horizon. Nothing. The long, uneventful three-and-a-half-hour portion of the flight had raised their hopes, but now with land supposed to be in sight, the tension was beginning to show. He tried to calm the mounting uneasiness within him.

Sharon pointed to the horizon. "What's that?"

Berry sat up and peered out the window. For the last half hour, every patch of low sea fog had become California, every hazy discoloration on the horizon had been San Francisco. Their imaginations and their hopes kept creating solid land out of each vapor, only to see it melt away as they approached. He stared at the low hazy line on the horizon and saw it move, then drift away as an ocean breeze caught it. "Nothing. More fog."

"It might be the fog of San Francisco."

"It might— What?"

"The San Francisco fog." She looked at her watch. "It's just past six. That's nearly always the time that the fog rolls in during the summer."

Berry looked at her. "Why the hell didn't you remind me? Damn! What am I supposed to do if the airport is covered with fog?"

"Well . . . you can make an instrument landing, can't you?"

Berry resisted the temptation to remind her of his meager qualifications. "No. A full instrument landing is out of the question." He had no business in the Straton's captain's seat. There were more instruments in the Straton's cockpit than there were combined in the last ten planes he had flown. "Damn, I should have headed north or south to another airport."

Crandall reminded him, "Since we don't know where we are, we may already be north or south of San Francisco." She tapped her finger against the fuel gauge. "We'll be lucky if we even see the coast. I wouldn't worry about the San Francisco fog yet."

Berry looked down at the gauge. *One-sixteenth.* "Yes. You're right."

"Maybe we can put it down near the beach," she said as she stole a glance at him. "Can we do that?"

"I suppose. If we get that far, and if I see that the coastline is covered with fog, I'll ditch it." Berry knew that a ditching into heavy fog would be suicide. "I'd like to try for the airport, but we would have to consider the people on the ground. . . ."

"Then don't try it. Whatever you want to do is all right. Just take it easy. You'll do the best you can when the time comes."

"Right." His nerves were becoming raw, and he hoped he had something left in him when the time came to put the plane down. From the first time he stepped into the cockpit and saw the disabled crew, he knew that, barring any midair catastrophe, he would have to put the Straton down eventually. That time—as the fuel gauges told him—was nearly here.

"It's not always foggy."

"What? Oh, right."

"And when it is, the fog usually comes in slowly. We may be able to beat it. And sometimes it doesn't get as far as the airport."

"Good." He noticed that no one offered to bet a dinner on it.

The Straton continued on its southeasterly flight path, the sinking sun casting the airliner's shadow onto the smooth ocean in front of its port wing. Berry scanned the horizon for land, and watched for other aircraft or ships that might recognize that the airliner was in trouble. But they were alone.

"John! It moved again!"

He looked quickly down at the copilot's panel. "It's not moving."

She stared at the navigation radio bearing indicator, but the needle was dead. "It did. There's no question this time. I saw it. Damn it, I saw it."

"Okay, okay." Berry watched the needle carefully. He'd heard stories of desperate pilots who had wanted to see runway lights or encouraging indications from their instruments so badly that they hallucinated into existence whatever they needed.

"I saw it move."

"Okay. Let's watch it."

They stared at it for a full minute. Berry picked up the radio chart and rechecked the frequency. The navigation radio in front of Crandall was unquestionably tuned to the San Francisco station. Berry turned and looked back at its indicator. "Still dead," he said in a whisper, as if his voice would scare away the signal.

She said nothing.

As they both watched, the needle finally gave a small, barely perceptible bounce.

Sharon Crandall jumped in her seat. "Did you see it?"

Berry's face broke into a wide smile. "I saw it. You bet I saw it."

The needle began to bounce more vigorously as the navigation radio received the signal more strongly. The electronic pathway to San Francisco suddenly opened to them.

As the small needle quivered with the electronic impulse of San Francisco Airport's directional beam, John Berry knew how all the lost and lonely aviators, seamen, and explorers felt when they laid eyes on the object of their search. "We're heading home. Not much farther to go now."

"John, we're going to make it. I know it."

"Our odds have certainly improved. Turn that dial. That one—until the needle centers."

She did as he said.

"Okay?"

"Yes. Now read me the number that shows on the display."

"One-three-nine."

"Okay." Berry faced the wheel and began steering the Straton through a shallow right turn until the compass heading of 131 degrees swung to the new heading of 139 degrees, then leveled out.

Sharon looked back at Linda Farley, who had maintained her usual silence. "We have San Francisco on the radio."

"I don't hear anything."

She smiled. "No. It's a . . . navigation radio. Like a compass. We know where the airport is now."

"Do they know where we are?"

Berry spoke. "Not yet. But they'll see us on radar soon."

Linda Farley leaned forward in her seat and asked, "Are you going to land the airplane, Mr. Berry?"

Berry nodded. "Yes, I am." He paused. "But we might still have to land in the water. You remember what Sharon told you about landing in the water?"

"Yes."

"Good." Berry set his navigation radio from Salinas to San Francisco. "I'll read it from here on. Look for land." He adjusted the dials and watched as the distance-to-go meter began cycling into place. He looked at the readout and smiled. "San Francisco Airport dead ahead—ninety-three miles."

"Ninety-three miles," she repeated. "How much longer?"

"About fifteen minutes. What time is it?"

"Eight minutes past six."

Berry nodded. "Well, we'll be on the ground no later than six-thirty."

"Oh, dear God, I can't believe it." Her voice became choked. "Oh, John—oh, God, I can't believe it." She put her face down into her hands and her body began to shake. "We're almost home."

"Yes," Berry answered absently. He had let his eyes drift toward the fuel gauges. The needles were almost on the empty marks. He had gotten good at translating the graduations on the fuel gauges into flight time. *By six-thirty,* he said to himself, *we'll be out of fuel.*

# 17

Hot lights always annoyed Edward Johnson, and today they seemed more annoying than usual. The long, walnut-paneled press conference room on the second level of the main terminal building was filled to overflow capacity with newspeople, camera crews, company officials. Everyone loved a disaster, reflected Johnson, except the people who were physically or financially involved. "Goddamn vultures," he said.

"Lower your voice," said Wayne Metz. Metz stood next to Johnson, trying to look inconspicuous, as though he had no direct connection with Johnson. "There are microphones in front of you."

Johnson was feeling reckless. "Goddamn vultures." There was such a din in the room, he didn't think anyone could hear him if he shouted out a full confession. He mopped his brow and noticed with annoyance that half the lights had not yet been turned on. "It'll be over soon." He glanced up at the clock. 6:08. "These goddamned things never start on time."

# MAYDAY

Hank Abbot, the Straton Aircraft Corporation representative, pushed his way through the crowd. "Hello, Ed. Bad break."

Johnson glanced at him. "Yeah."

Abbot turned to Metz. "Wayne Metz, right? Beneficial?"

"Right."

"Bad break for you, too."

Johnson broke in. "Have you notified your insurance carrier yet?"

Abbot looked at him for several seconds until he understood. "Hold on, Ed. One of those data-link messages mentioned a bomb."

"Did you see the damage, Hank?"

"No, of course not, but . . . ."

"Neither did an engineer. Do you think some half-hysterical, possibly brain-damaged passenger could tell the difference between a bomb blast and a structural failure?"

"Wait a damned minute—"

"If a wall or window blew out because the hull couldn't handle the air pressure, that would be your problem, wouldn't it?"

"Look, Ed, we've done business with Trans-United since before the war. On those rare occasions when an accident was caused by structural failure or faulty design, we've owned up and made good, but . . . ."

"Sorry, Hank. No aircraft, no survivors, no one knows anything. I don't think we should be speaking to each other at this time without counsel present."

"You bastard." Abbot stood in front of Johnson for several seconds, then turned abruptly and pushed his way to the back of the room.

Metz turned to Johnson. "God, you almost convinced *me* that it was his fault."

"It was." He looked closely at Metz. "It *was.*"

Metz nodded. "How will the government investigations be?"

"Not too bad." Johnson didn't think there was any way an investigating agency could unwrap the package in which he had sealed the Straton's fate. As he had basically reminded Abbot, there was a saying they used in these things: *No aircraft, no survivors, no one to hang—or everyone.* "I spoke to the president," Johnson said. He nodded toward a pleasant-looking man near the back wall. "He says your boss is pissed off at you."

Metz nodded. "Yes. I just spoke to him. He was all right this afternoon, but he turned nasty when he got an idea of what the bill might be from Trans-United."

"Does he have a check in the mail?"

"If he only knew how bad it *could* have been. Damn it, if he only *knew* what I did . . ." He looked around him. "I have to go to New York tonight. See him first thing in the morning. Christ. I hope we can stick the Straton people with this."

"We have a good shot at it. And, Wayne," he lowered his voice, "don't even hint to Mr. Wilford Parke that his fair-haired boy helped deep-six the Straton for the good of the company—because if you do . . ."

Metz nodded. It had occurred to him, as he spoke to Parke, that he had committed mass murder for nothing. His days at Beneficial were definitely numbered. Johnson, on the other hand, seemed to be coming through this intact. "Life can really suck—you know?"

"Tell me about it." Johnson wanted nothing more

out of life at that moment than a drink and a good night's sleep. He wanted to get into his car, drive out to the beach, check into a motel, and get far away from this airport.

A voice yelled out, "Two minutes!" Evidently, they were going with live TV coverage rather than videotapes.

For Metz, the television and press coverage was a foreign and overwhelming event and a further addition to his problem. He hoped Johnson could handle it. He had a sudden desire to disappear into the shadowy corners of the room. "Should I move farther away?"

"How about Brazil?"

"I mean—"

"Stay here. Just step back out of camera shot, but don't get too far."

Metz had a sudden inspiration. "I wouldn't mind answering questions. I could say something."

"Don't try to save your job on my time. I might have enough trouble saving my own. Step back."

Metz stepped back. He could see that Johnson was still volatile, but he knew that as soon as he settled down, he would begin to think in terms of helping Metz save his job. He had no choice, really. The two of them were in it together.

"One minute!"

Johnson took a cigar out of his pocket and lit it. He looked around the room. Kevin Fitzgerald stood with Trans-United's public-relations man and a few other executives. The president stood with the chairman of the board and presumably God stood beside them both, though Johnson's irreverent eyes could not see Him. Everyone had agreed that this conference was too important to be left to the public-relations people, and too sad an occasion to have the president's face and name associated with it. *Bastards.* He straightened his tie and wiped his brow.

"Thirty seconds!"

Johnson looked at the clock. Twelve after six.

A TV technician shouted from across the room. "We're ready, Mr. Johnson."

Johnson nodded. He turned and faced the cameras squarely as the last of the bright lights were turned on.

Metz stepped even farther back from Johnson. Out of nervous habit, he felt inside his sports jacket for the data-link messages, as a man feels for his wallet, and his heart jumped when his fingers found nothing. Then he remembered, with some embarrassment, that he and Johnson had stopped on the access road between the Trans-United hangar and the administration building to burn them. They were no more than a pile of ashes now. But, still, his fingers went deeper into his inside pocket. He had the sudden, irrational fear that he had somehow left one of them in his pocket, and that the TV camera would suddenly swing around and zero in on it like an X-ray zeroing in on a suspicious spot. His fingers felt the line at the bottom of his pocket. He patted his other pockets quickly. He saw Johnson giving him an annoyed look. *Calm down. Almost over.*

A young woman with a clipboard called out, "Mr. Johnson, watch for the red light."

Johnson glowered at the production assistant. "I know that."

"Right. Begin with your prepared statement, then we'll go into the Q and A from the newspeople."

"Fine." It seemed to Johnson that the newsmen—or

newspeople, as they called themselves—were literally licking their lips over the assignment to cover the first air crash of a supersonic transport. *If the bastards only knew the story they almost had.*

The camera's red light came on.

"You're on."

Johnson cleared his throat and put on an expression that was appropriate to the gravity of the first sentence he could speak. "Ladies and gentlemen, I regret to announce that Trans-United Flight 52 has apparently crashed at sea. The flight, a Straton 797 supersonic airliner, left San Francisco International Airport this morning at eight-thirty A.M., on a nonstop flight to Tokyo. Onboard the aircraft were 302 passengers and a crew of fourteen. Approximately midway across the Pacific, there was an in-flight emergency, the exact nature of which is unknown but apparently involved the hull—the fuselage . . ." *Fuck Abbot.* ". . . and cabin pressure was lost. The aircraft turned around and headed back to San Francisco." Johnson paused and took a breath. "What you may have heard concerning a passenger piloting the aircraft is true."

There was an excited murmur in the room, and Johnson could see pencils moving and cameras clicking away at him. He continued, "Because of a malfunction in their voice radios, we established contact with them via data-link—a computer screen for typed messages. The last message was received from Flight 52 at approximately one P.M., San Francisco time. Since then—"

A wall telephone rang loudly in the back of the quiet room.

Johnson glanced up at it with unconcealed annoyance, and saw Kevin Fitzgerald pick it up. He glanced at the production assistant who was motioning him to continue. "Since then, an extensive search-and-rescue operation has been mounted by military and civilian authorities. . . ." Johnson saw that Fitzgerald was speaking excitedly into the telephone, and something inside him signaled a warning. "Flight 52 had . . . still has not been found as of this moment . . . and if they were still flying . . . their fuel would probably have been consumed by now . . ." Fitzgerald had motioned for the president and the chairman of the board. *What the fuck is going on back there?* "And is still . . . that is . . . we have many of the relatives and friends of the passengers here at the terminal . . . in our lounge . . ." Fitzgerald was speaking into the phone and relaying a message to the people around him. There was a stir in the back of the room. "And the chief pilot, Captain Kevin Fitzgerald . . . has been with the passengers . . . the passengers' relatives . . . constantly . . . until now. The search will continue until—"

"Wait!" Fitzgerald held the phone in his hand and was signaling to Johnson.

Johnson dropped his cigar on the floor and stared at Fitzgerald.

Everyone turned toward the back of the room.

"It's the control tower," said Fitzgerald. "The radar room."

The production assistant barked an order and the camera turned toward Fitzgerald. Technicians ran across the room with hand microphones and the electrical crew swung several of the white lights around. The shadow of Kevin Fitzgerald holding the telephone in his outstretched hand rose up on the stark wall behind him. "The control tower says," shouted Fitzgerald over the rising noise, "that they have a large unidentified aircraft on their radarscope. The aircraft is headed directly toward San Francisco Airport. It is now sixty-two miles west of here, flying at a low altitude, and at an airspeed of three hundred and forty knots. They believe the aircraft may be . . ." He glanced up at Johnson, then finished the sentence with the words that were already on everyone's lips: ". . . the Straton."

The room exploded with sound. Some reporters rushed up to Fitzgerald, and others grabbed the phones on the long conference table. The Straton executives had already positioned themselves at the door in the rear of the room. They disappeared into the corridor and headed for a small VIP conference room across the hall.

Wayne Metz pushed through the crowd and grabbed Johnson by the shoulder. "*How?* How can this be possible? Johnson?"

Edward Johnson looked at Metz as if he hadn't understood the question.

"Johnson, damn it! Can it be true?"

Johnson was in a daze. A few reporters, unable to get to Fitzgerald, crowded around Johnson. Questions bombarded him from all sides. He pushed through the reporters and broke out into the corridor, half walking, half running toward the staircase.

Wayne Metz came up behind him, breathless. "Johnson! Is it true? Is it *true*?"

Johnson turned and spoke distractedly as he bounded down the stairs. "How the hell do I know?"

Metz followed. "Where are you going?"

"To the damn ramp, Metz. At the speed that aircraft is traveling, it'll be here in less than ten minutes."

Metz followed him to the lower level, down a long corridor that led to a satellite terminal, then to a door that led to the aircraft parking ramp. Johnson put his identification card into an electronic scanner, and the door opened. The two of them walked outside, onto the airport ramp. "Can it be the Straton? Tell me. Please."

Edward Johnson ignored Wayne Metz and looked up into the setting sun, shielding his eyes with his hands as he moved. He tried to think clearly, but his mind was unable to absorb all the ramifications of what had happened. Stunned with a terror he had never before known, he ran across the parking ramp. He felt that the Straton was sweeping down on him as he ran, like a winged nightmare from hell, a dead thing that came back from a watery grave. He thought he saw a small dot coming out of the sun, but realized it was too soon yet to see it. *Please God. Not the goddamn Straton.*

# 18

Sharon Crandall looked at the distance-to-go meter. "Twenty-three miles."

Berry held the wheel tightly in his hands. He stared at the fuel gauges. They were within a needle's width of empty; two low-fuel warning lights glowed a brilliant red, probably for the first time since the aircraft was built.

"John, do we have enough fuel to reach the airport?"

The time for thin assurances was ended. They could flame out before he drew his next breath. "I can't tell. Fuel gauges aren't accurate when they're that low." He saw the electronic needle nudge against the empty mark. Technically, they were already out, but feasibly the engines could run for as long as ten more minutes. There was no way to tell until that first sickening sensation of power loss, which he remembered from when he had put faith in the data-link instructions and almost landed in the sea. He felt the muscles in his stomach and buttocks tightening.

"Twenty-two miles. Still on course." She paused. "We're going to make it, you know."

Berry glanced at her and smiled. "What time is it? Exactly."

"Six-twenty-one."

Berry looked down at the unbroken top of the low white fog that stretched out in all directions. Some of the vapor rose up and obscured his windshield. "Damn it, if we're twenty-two miles from the airport, we can't be more than ten miles from the Golden Gate Bridge. We would be able to see the bridge or the city by now if it weren't for this fog."

"We'll see it soon."

"We're going to have to see something soon. We're less than five minutes' flight time to the airport—and we'll be coming up to congested airspace. Linda, keep watching for other airplanes."

"Okay."

He turned to Sharon. "I hope to God they've spotted us on radar and kept everyone away from us."

"I'm sure they have." A calm had come over her, brought on in part by the presence of the fluffy white blanket of vapor beneath them, in part by fatigue, and the feeling that it would be all over, one way or the other, in less than five minutes.

Linda Farley called out. "Look! What's that?"

Berry and Crandall turned back to her, then followed her outstretched arm.

Berry peered hard out of the Straton's left-side window. Off the wingtip, he saw a ghostly gray mass rising through the layer of fog. A mountain. Its peak was at least 1,500 feet higher than the Straton. "I see it. Sharon, look."

"Yes, I see it."

"Do you recognize it?"

"I don't know. Wait . . . I can't tell." She leaned closer toward Berry. "Yes, It's Mount Tamalpais. In Marin County."

"Okay. Give me the charts." He looked at the navigation chart and studied it. "That's north of the Golden Gate Bridge?"

"Yes. The bridge should be ahead. A little to the left."

"Okay." He looked over his shoulder and forced a smile. "Linda, you win the champagne . . . the prize. We'll get you something nice when we land."

She nodded.

He turned to the front and began a shallow turn to the left. "I'm going to try to steer directly over the bridge. We have to stay over the bay." He knew he was too low to try to cut across either San Francisco or mountainous Marin County. At 900 feet he was below the summit of at least three of San Francisco's famous peaks, and below the tops of a few of its newer skyscrapers. The Golden Gate Inlet to the bay was just that—a gate into the harbor, the same for an aircraft at 900 feet as for a sailing ship. "Sharon, Linda, look for the bridge—we may be able to see its towers."

"I'm looking," said Crandall.

Berry continued the left turn toward a course of due east, trying to find the inlet to the bay, trying to feel his way across the top of the fog. It occurred to him that one of the arguments that must have been used against bringing the Straton home was that he would be endangering the city, but Berry had no intention of endangering anyone on the ground. He'd keep the flight over the water no matter what the cost to him or the others. "Sharon, if we don't see the inlet very soon, I'm going to put it down in the ocean. We can't risk hitting a hill or a building."

"Can't you climb higher?"

"That takes too much fuel and too many miles. We don't have either." He looked down at the fog. He could see a few breaks in it now, and caught a glimpse of the water. He could see that the fog went all the way to the water's surface. A blind landing in the sea would mean almost certain disaster. He consoled himself with the knowledge that this close to the coast, they might recover the bodies. He thought he felt a sinking sensation in the seat of his pants, as if the airliner were suddenly decelerating. "Did you feel that?"

"What?"

He sat motionless for several seconds. "Nothing." *Damn it. There it is again.* Was he imagining it? From this altitude, his glide time after a flame out would be less than thirty seconds, and there would be no restarting of the engines this time. And a thirty-second powerless glide on this heading might put him into the bridge, or into the city, but not into the bay beyond the city. "I'm going to put it in the water. We can't keep heading this way."

"Wait, John. Please. Just a bit longer."

"Damn it, Sharon. I might be heading into a mountain or into a building. We have no right to fly over the city. I'll put it in the ocean while I know we're still over it. They've seen us on radar. They know where we are."

She looked at him and said very definitely, "No. Keep going. I know the inlet is straight ahead."

He looked at her. There was something in her voice and her manner that made him think she had some information from a source not displayed on the instrument panel. "Sharon . . ." He saw a picture of the Straton plunging down through the fog, the fog parting, the city of San Francisco rising up through his windshield, and the nose of the huge airliner pointed into the streets below. He shook his head quickly to clear the image from his mind. He said softly, "I've *got* to put it down right now."

*"No."* She turned away from him and stared out the windshield as though the argument was over.

He realized that he'd known her for less than seven hours, yet he felt he knew her as well, certainly, as he knew Jennifer. Sharon Crandall had given him her complete and unquestioned trust, but now she was withdrawing it in favor of her own instincts, and he saw that she meant it. It was his turn to show the same perfect trust, though as a technical person he mistrusted instincts and always went with the odds and the gauges. "Okay. A little longer," he said.

The Straton flew on. Hovered above the blinding fog, a sense of unreality filled the cockpit. For Berry, Flight 52 had ceased to be a real flight long ago, and the fog only added the final dimension to that feeling.

Sharon Crandall stared placidly out at the rolling fog, an odd smile on her face. She raised her arm and pointed out the front windshield.

Berry looked out to where she was pointing. A glint of red caught his eye, and he sat forward. It disappeared, then reappeared again. Directly in front of the Straton, about seven miles in the distance, the twin towers of the Golden Gate Bridge rose majestically through the solid blanket of white.

Sharon Crandall's eyes nearly filled with tears. "Oh, God, yes! Yes!"

Berry felt a constriction in his throat as he stared out at the faraway reddish towers.

As she always did when she made the announcements from a returning overseas flight, she said, "Welcome home."

Berry nodded. "Yes, welcome home." He watched the bridge towers grow quickly in his windshield as the Straton approached at six miles a minute.

"Look," said Crandall. "Look beyond the bridge."

Berry looked out toward the bay. As if the Golden Gate were a wall, the bank of fog ended abruptly at the bridge. The entire bay, as far as he could see to Berkeley and Oakland on the opposite shore, was clear.

"I told you we could beat the fog, John." Crandall laughed. "Look to the right."

Berry glanced out the right windshield. Indistinct angular forms rose out of the fog—the shape of a city. Golden sunlight glinted from the tops of the Bank of America Building and Transamerica Pyramid, like El Dorado, thought Berry, but this was no spectral city, and a sense of reality began to return to him. The buildings grew rapidly as the Straton hurled toward them at 340 knots. Berry steered the Straton to the left, away from the city, and lined its nose up between the bridge towers, like a helmsman navigating the approaches to the bay.

The airliner passed through the inlet and sailed over the Golden Gate Bridge, the twin towers barely a hundred feet below the aircraft. Berry spotted Alcatraz Island coming up below him. He banked the Straton to the right and followed the curve of the bay, south toward the airport, which he knew was less than three minutes' flight time away. Even if they flamed out now, he thought, he'd be able to avoid the populated areas. "Okay," he said matter-of-factly, "we're approaching the airport. Sharon, get ready to begin the landing procedure we practiced."

"I'm ready."

Berry felt that there was, between them, that bond that instantly develops between pilot and copilot, helmsman and navigator, observer and gunner; the knowledge that two must work as a perfect team, become nearly one, if they are to beat the long odds against survival.

The skies were clear, and out of the right-side window, the city of San Francisco lay among the hills of the peninsula. Flight 52 was a sudden intruder on the city's hectic rush hour. Along Fisherman's Wharf, cars stopped and pedestrians turned to gawk and point at the huge aircraft lumbering over the bay. On Nob Hill and Telegraph Hill, people watched the aircraft sail past at eye level. Vehicles pulled off the road, and children shouted. Many of the onlookers spotted the holes in the sides of the Straton, the jagged wounds highlighted by the low angle of the sun. Even those who had not seen the damage could see that the low-flying Trans-United airliner was in trouble.

Berry saw the silvery San Francisco–Oakland Bay Bridge lying straight ahead across the Straton's flight path. He knew that this bridge was the last obstacle to a successful ditching in the bay. He held his breath until he was certain that the Straton's glide path in a sudden flame out would carry it over the bridge.

As he passed over the bridge, he allowed himself to look out at San Francisco International Airport. It sat on a small piece of lowland jutting into the bay, less than fifteen miles ahead. "There it is." He knew he should be applying the flaps if he was going to try for the airport. But the flaps would cause extra drag and burn off too much fuel. He thought he wanted to get as close to the airport as possible before he made the decision on where to come down, or had it made for him by a flame out. He let the Straton streak along at 340 knots.

Crandall looked at the rapidly approaching airport. Instinctively, she knew they were coming in too fast. "John, too fast. Too fast."

Berry tried to calm himself. There were so many things to do and so little flight time left in which to do them. Everything had to be a trade-off from here on; every maneuver would be a compromise between the right thing and the expedient thing, always trying to avoid the dead-wrong thing. "All right. All right. I'm going for distance. We can hit the brakes later." He looked at his fuel gauge. The electronic needles were lying dead against the empty mark.

Berry recalled his first solo landing in a Cessna 140, an older tail-wheeled aircraft he had some trouble checking out in. When the instructor finally got out, Berry kept finding excuses to continue with other kinds of practice rather than land, until his fuel was too low to put the landing off any longer. *No excuses this time. Bring it right in.* Sweat started to form on his brow and neck, and his hands were starting to become unsteady on the control wheel.

Berry yanked back on the four throttles, putting the engines at idle power. He watched as the ship's airspeed began to bleed off to a lower, more reasonable indication for landing. Intent on the cockpit instruments, Berry failed to see what was passing a few miles to his left. On the east side of the bay was the Naval Air Station at Alameda, and farther south was Oakland's giant airport. Either one of those airports was a minute or two closer, but John Berry was focused, physically and mentally, on San Francisco International. That was where he had started, and that was where he intended to end. He hoped that the emergency equipment would be waiting there. "All right," he said softly, "all right. No ditching. We're going into San Francisco International." Berry saw that the airspeed was now low enough. "Flaps down."

Sharon sat motionless for a second, mesmerized by the sight of the rapidly approaching airport jutting into the bay in front of her. In her mind she had already arrived home safely. The realization that they were still hundreds of feet off the ground and miles from the runway jarred her.

"Flaps down! Flaps!"

She reached out mechanically with her left hand, as she had done dozens of times in practice during the last three hours, and grabbed the flap handle.

"Pull it to the first notch. Quickly."

She pulled the handle, and the flaps dropped.

Berry felt the aircraft slow even more and saw the speed bleed off on his airspeed indicator: 225 knots. Altitude 700 feet. To his right he saw Candlestick Park pass beneath his wingtip. "About five miles. We're coming home. Coming home. Put out more flap. Go ahead. Now."

Crandall pulled back at the flap lever and moved it to the next setting.

The Straton began to decelerate more quickly, and the nose jumped up. The aircraft began to pitch up toward the sky.

"John!"

Linda screamed.

"Calm down! It's all right. It's all right. I've got it under control That was normal. Just relax. We're doing okay. Okay. Coming home. A couple more minutes."

The giant airliner was more of a handful than Berry imagined. It was heavy, ponderous, a hell of a lot different from the Skymaster . . . yet the principles of flight were the same. *It is the Skymaster,* he said with conviction. *Nothing is different.*

Suddenly, the wheel began to vibrate violently in his hands and the stall warning synthetic voice filled the cockpit. AIRSPEED . . . AIRSPEED. "Oh, Christ." He had allowed the Straton to slow too much. The airframe began to shake badly. "Power, Sharon, power." He held on to the wheel with both hands, knowing that if he let go with even one, the aircraft might get away from him.

Crandall reached out and grabbed the four throttles. She pushed them a few inches forward. "Power."

"Not too much. Easy, easy. We don't have much fuel." Berry lowered the nose of the Straton to pick up airspeed. He prayed that he hadn't asked for too much from the fuel-starved engines. The control wheel in his hands stopped vibrating and the flight smoothed out.

But Berry could see that he had very little altitude left; he certainly couldn't afford another approaching stall. Yet he had to ration every ounce of fuel, to balance engine power against altitude, altitude against speed, speed against lift and drag. The airport was coming up fast. He reached out and pulled the throttle back to a lower setting. "Okay, coming home, coming home, Sharon, full flaps."

Crandall pulled the flap lever to its last notch. "Full flaps."

Suddenly, another cockpit horn sounded, followed by another synthetic electronic voice. LANDING GEAR.

Berry looked down at the instrument panel. "Damn. . . ." He realized now that he had put out full flaps without lowering the landing gear, and that had automatically triggered the warning. A gentle reminder to pilots like himself who had too many problems to think about trivialities like landing gear. "Sharon—the landing gear. Put it down. Down!"

Crandall knew she also should have remembered—it had been part of the drill they had practiced. She reached out and lowered the big handle directly in front of her. "Gear down."

The airport was almost beneath the nose of the Straton, and Berry knew it was too late to try to put it down on the shorter runway in front of him. He swung the Straton to the left, toward the widest part of the bay, away from the airport.

"John. The airport."

"No good, I need room to maneuver." The landing-gear voice continued, and he wondered if the gear was functioning. He focused on the three unlit landing-gear lights directly in front of him. "Forget it. No gear.

We're going to put it down in the bay." Suddenly, the horn stopped and three bright green lights glowed in front of him. "Gear down! Gear down. Okay. Hold on. We're turning in." Berry banked the aircraft back to the right, but as soon as the airport came into sight again, he saw that his turn had been too wide. *Christ, Berry, do something right. Get a grip on yourself.*

"John, we're too far left of the airport."

"I know. Take it easy. I can slide it back." He applied the proper amounts of rudder and aileron, and the Straton began sliding back toward the airport. "We're okay. Coming in, everything is all right." Berry felt that he could negotiate the approach with some degree of skill and confidence. But it was the last five or ten seconds to touchdown that killed—that transition between approach and landing, those moments when the lift of the aircraft had to end and the forces of gravity had to fully take over again.

He looked down at the airport, a right-angle cross of double runways jutting into the bay. He could see the main terminal and the long passageways radiating from it to connect the satellite terminals. He saw movement and activity on the ground, and knew they were waiting for him. There were two parallel runways in front of him now. He expected to see the runways foamed, but remembered that it was no longer considered useful in a crash situation. The white approach lights that ran out into the bay were blinking to show him they wanted him to use the left runway. "Okay, I read you. I read you."

The touchdown zone lights embedded into the runway were on and the green runway lights were visible even in the daylight. There was no question about where they wanted him to land. The only question was what kind of landing it would be. All he could promise them was that he wouldn't kill anyone on the ground.

The Straton kept sliding right as it descended on its long, shallow glide slope toward the runway in front of it. Berry stopped the slide and lined up the nose with the centerline. "Okay. Soon." He had no idea why the engines were still running. He glanced at the altimeter. Three hundred feet above sea level, and the airport was at about thirty feet above sea level. Two hundred seventy feet to touchdown. He looked out the windshield. The runway was about two miles ahead. They were low by normal standards, but nothing about this flight had been normal. The airspeed was slow, but not slow enough for a stall. He grasped the wheel with one hand and pulled off more power from the throttles with the other. "Okay, we're going in. Going in. Sharon. Linda. Just hold on. Hold on. I'll touch it down as easy as possible. Sharon, read off the speeds to me the way I told you."

Crandall looked down at the airspeed indicator: "One hundred sixty knots."

"Right." Berry felt he could do it, as long as the fuel lasted another fifty or sixty seconds. As long as he didn't fall apart within the next minute. He drew a long, deep breath. In front of him, a series of sequence strobe flashers in the bay drew his eyes toward the runway centerline. *Very elaborate system. Very nice airport.* "Speed."

"One hundred fifty knots."

Berry held the wheel steady and felt the huge aircraft sinking slowly from its own weight, down toward the earth.

He heard a sound behind him, the sound of ripping—ripping fiberglass. John Berry kept his eyes on the runway, but he knew what that sound meant.

Sharon Crandall turned and saw the panty hose lying on the floor with the latch still attached to them. She looked up. "No! No!"

# 19

The president of Trans-United Airlines, the chairman of the board, and government officials looked out from the control tower. The entire emergency and rescue operation was being coordinated below.

Jack Miller stood off to the side, not exactly sure how he had gotten into the control tower, but knowing that there was no longer time to get to the runway. He watched and listened as the operation unfolded around him.

The curious and the morbid were arriving by the thousands, choking the airport access roads and covering the grass boundaries of Route 80. Police in the area of the airport, trained for just such a situation, began clearing a lane for outside emergency vehicles to reach the airport.

Outside the main terminal, and inside along the security corridors, people had begun assembling, even before the news of the radar sighting. Those on the outside stared up at the sky, waiting, on the remote chance that the Straton would return. Those on the inside watched the flight information board or just listened to the public address system for updates. They waited and watched, like wives of sailors once waited and watched, on the quays and from the upper windows of their houses, for sight of the ship that was lost.

Since the radar sighting had been announced, the airport was increasingly jammed with friends and relatives of the passengers on Flight 52. With them stood other passengers and airport employees who had temporarily abandoned their jobs. For everyone outside, all eyes were turned eastward as they followed the huge silver Straton as it swung slowly around to the south. It flew low over the bay, flaps down and landing gear extended, like a gull about to light on a rock.

From the moment the Straton had been spotted on radar, all other air traffic had been diverted to Oakland and other airports, and rapid intervention vehicles—RIVs—had been cutting across the deserted runways, trying to position themselves for any eventuality. Equipment was being massed by RIVs and helicopters at the point where the two pairs of runways crossed. A platform truck from which the officer-in-charge who would supervise the operation was brought out to the crossway, complete with field desks and cell phones. Medical supplies, wheelchairs, hundreds of stretchers, water, and burn units were flowing toward the center of the airfield. Aluminum trestles were set up to convert stretchers into examining tables. A unit stood by to identify and mark the dead. Another unit of paramedics, nurses, and doctors was breaking open crates of medical supplies. The entire acre at the juncture of the runways resembled a hastily assembled military bivouac. But as quickly as the emergency services were assembling, they were still not ready to handle a disaster of the potential scope presented by the onrushing Straton.

Edward Johnson and Wayne Metz stood on a small taxiway a few hundred feet from the runway. Around them, on the road and on the grass, stood scores of police, reporters, airport officials, and Trans-United people. About a dozen news cameras stood in the grass, all pointed toward the end of the runway. RIVs sped past, taking up positions on both sides of the runway.

Wayne Metz looked out across the bay and watched silently as the Straton made its turn. His mouth kept forming words, but no sound came out. Never before had he wanted so badly to see one of his insured risks destroyed. He stared as the Straton came out of its turn far east of the runway. "I can't believe this is happening. I can't believe that's the Straton."

Edward Johnson watched, fascinated, as the aircraft made its final approach. "It's the Straton, all right. I don't know how he did it. I don't know how he could have recovered from a flame out . . . but he did, didn't he?" He had stopped being frightened and had gotten control of himself again. A cold, calculating impassiveness took hold in him, and he watched with grudging admiration as Berry slid the aircraft back toward the runway. "I'll be damned. Jesus Christ, this guy has his act together. I might sign the son-of-a-bitch for a pilot job with Trans-United. He does a better job than half our overpaid crybabies."

Metz looked at Johnson as though the man had gone completely out of his mind. But as he stared at Johnson, he knew why Johnson had come so far. Edward Johnson believed that he had not been a participant in what had happened in the communications room. He was now Edward Johnson, vice-president of Trans-United Airlines, and very concerned about the fate of his flight.

Trans-United's chief pilot, Captain Kevin Fitzgerald, moved closer to the runway than anyone else dared. He stood by himself at the edge of the grass, staring down the long expanse of concrete. He raised his eyes and looked out into the bay, then looked at the head-on silhouette of the Straton. His airplane was coming home. He whispered, "Come on. Come on, you bastard. Hold it." His voice became louder, "Hold it! You got it! You crazy bastard, it's yours, it's yours! You're in control. In control."

The police and emergency services crews who had gathered on the grass became excited as the Straton came in over the bay and began dropping toward the runway. Many of those people realized the dangerous position they had put themselves in and began running back toward the hastily assembled disaster-control area, a little farther from the Straton's target area.

Johnson, Metz, and Fitzgerald, along with most of the firemen, a few reporters, and all the cameramen, stayed dangerously close to the runway.

Johnson turned to Metz. "It's going to be hard to convince anyone that the pilot of that aircraft is in any way brain damaged."

Metz shook his head. "Damn it, you can say he was temporarily confused."

"Right. But if those data-link printouts exist, we

have to get to them before the FAA people start crawling around that cockpit."

"I hope to hell he crashes. I hope the airplane explodes."

Johnson nodded. He'd never been so ambivalent about anything in his life. "God, Wayne, I hope he makes it and I hope we make it."

The two men looked at each other for a long moment.

About ten yards away from Metz and Johnson, Fitzgerald stood at the edge of the runway, shouting. "Push down. Push down! That's it. That's it. Gently. Gently."

Some of the firemen, policemen, and reporters began to cheer. The Trans-United people were screaming, "Down! Down! Down!"

All around the airport and, as the word spread, inside the terminal building, people were weeping and hugging each other.

Johnson stood frozen by the scene in front of him, not knowing if his behavior appeared appropriate, and not caring.

Wayne Metz unconsciously grabbed Edward Johnson's arm. Talking about crashing an airliner was one thing; seeing it coming out of the sky in front of him was something else. He opened his mouth and drew a short breath. "Good God, I've never seen . . . anything . . . Oh, my God, look at it." Metz felt like running, and in fact had slipped his hand in his pocket and found his car keys. He turned, dazed, toward Johnson. "We're finished."

Johnson shook his head. "Not yet."

The Straton glided in closer to the approach lights, hardly more than a mile away now, barely 200 feet above the airport, dropping a few feet every second, its long landing wheels reaching out tentatively.

The crowd was becoming almost delirious with emotion as the drama of the moment swept away the last inhibitions. Men and women, reporters and emergency personnel shouted, jumped, wept, and embraced.

In the cockpit of the Straton airliner stood First Officer Daniel McVary and more than a dozen passengers— mostly men, some women, and a few children. They were babbling and wailing, their residual instincts telling them that they were in danger. Their faces and arms were covered with freshly coagulated blood from the battering they had taken during the descent into the storm.

Sharon Crandall stared at them. "John . . ."

Linda Farley fought to keep from screaming. Her body began shaking.

"John!"

Berry's whole existence had been reduced to the controls in front of him and the runway looming up outside his windshield. "Ignore them! Stay in your seat! Linda, put your head between your legs and don't move." It was hardly more than one mile to the threshold of the runway. Thirty more seconds. The Straton's speed was too high and its altitude too low. Berry could feel someone's hand brush against the back of his neck. He tried to ignore what was behind him. He concentrated on the airport and his approach path.

Berry could see the crash trucks racing in from all directions, converging on the entire length of the runway. He glanced quickly at the airspeed indicator. Still too fast. They would overshoot the runway and land in the bay or veer off and crash into the buildings outside the airport boundary. He made another adjustment with the throttles and the flight controls.

As the airliner streaked toward the threshold of the runway, Berry became more aware of the press of bodies jammed into the cockpit of the Straton. He suddenly realized that someone was standing barely inches from him. Berry glanced to his right.

Daniel McVary stood at the rear edge of the center console. His body leaned forward, hovering threateningly over the flight controls. The other passengers stepped to the front of the cockpit, cautiously, tentatively, like unwelcome visitors.

Sharon Crandall drew away from McVary. Her voice came out in a barely audible whisper. "John . . ."

"Stay strapped in. Don't move. Don't provoke them."

McVary reached out and put his hand on the co-pilot's control wheel.

Berry felt the pressure on his wheel, then felt a cold, clammy hand on his face. He heard Linda trying to fight down a mounting hysteria. "Christ, Jesus!" The threshold of the runway was half a mile away. The excessive speed was dropping off and the nonexistent fuel was still flowing to the engines. *Please, God.* He eased farther back on the throttles and felt McVary's hand on his. "For God's sake, get the hell out of here!" He swiped at McVary's hand.

With the other hand still wrapped around the co-pilot's control wheel, Daniel McVary pulled hard. This was *his* control wheel, that much he remembered, although he had no idea what it was for.

Berry could feel the man's pull. He pushed forward against the captain's control wheel with as much force as he could, to counterbalance what McVary was doing with the copilot's wheel. Berry's arms ached. "Get away, you stupid son-of-a-bitch. For Christ's sake . . ."

Crandall struck out at McVary with her fists. "Stop! Stop! Go away! John. Please!"

"Steady . . . steady . . ." They had only a quarter of a mile to go, but Berry knew that he was losing in this battle of brute strength. Whatever the copilot had lost in mental ability hadn't affected his muscle power. "Sharon! Get him off! Now! Fast!"

Sharon tried to pry the man's fingers from the control wheel, but McVary held to it with an incredible strength. She bent over and bit savagely into the back of his right hand, but McVary was almost totally beyond pain.

Daniel McVary pulled against the copilot's control wheel even harder, and it caused the Straton to suddenly pitch up and its right wing to dip low as the tail began to yaw from side to side. The stall-warning synthetic voice began to fill the cockpit again with its frightening chant. *AIRSPEED. AIRSPEED.* Several of the passengers howled. Linda screamed.

Many of the people standing in the cockpit were thrown off balance by the sudden erratic motions of the Straton. They lurched back toward the bulkhead; some of them fell against the circuit-breaker panel.

McVary held firmly onto the wheel and kept his balance.

"You bastard! Let go, you son-of-a-bitch." Berry

knew he had only a few seconds left to get the Straton back under control. If he didn't, they would die—right here, right now. The runway was only a short distance ahead. "Sharon! Help me! Help!"

Sharon Crandall felt the flesh in McVary's hand break under her teeth, and blood run over her chin and down her neck. Still, the hand would not move. She picked her head up and shot her hand out, jabbing a finger in McVary's eye.

The copilot screamed, and released the wheel.

Berry pushed his control wheel abruptly forward, rotated it to the left, and pressed hard against the rudder panels. The Straton seemed to hang in its awkward position for a long second. The stall-warning synthetic voice was still sounding, the repetition of its one-word vocabulary now continuous. *AIRSPEED, AIRSPEED, AIR-SPEED.* Berry could see the ground streaking by outside his windshield at an incredible angle, then suddenly the horizon straightened and the runway centerline swung back to the middle of the windshield.

But the Straton had lost too much airspeed. Even without the continuous blaring of the stall-warning voice, Berry could feel the sickening sensation that told him the airliner was nearly done flying. In another moment the Straton would fall uncontrollably, like an elevator cut loose from its cable, its 400 tons crashing to the runway below.

"John!" Sharon screamed. The ground rushed up toward them. She covered her eyes.

Waiting as long as he dared, Berry made one last and desperate pull on the flight controls with all the strength he had left.

# MAYDAY

Captain Kevin Fitzgerald's experienced eye told him instantly that the pilot had suddenly lost control. He found himself running toward the plummeting airliner, shouting as he ran. "He's losing it! It's pitching on him! Oh, goddamn it, he's losing it. Christ Almighty!" The pilot had managed to get the giant airliner within a half mile of the runway, and now, inexplicably, he was letting the ship get away from him. He shouted like a coach trying to play the game from the sidelines. "Goddamn it! Goddamn you! Hold it, you bastard, hold it! Kick the rudder. The rudder! Kick the goddamn rudder, you son-of-a-bitch!" He suddenly stopped running.

Just before the Straton's wheels hit the runway, Fitzgerald could see that the pilot had made one final, desperate control input. That, coupled with the aircraft's low airspeed, was all that averted instant and total catastrophe. But the aircraft's unspent downward energy was still far too great for its designed limits of strength. As Fitzgerald watched, the Straton sank down onto its undercarriage, then the huge sets of landing gear snapped off as if they were made of glass. Broken wheels and struts catapulted in all directions. The airliner fell onto its belly and skidded down the runway at over a hundred knots, a shower of sparks rising beneath and behind it. The aircraft yawed left and right, dangerously close to a complete spin. Fitzgerald could see the speed brakes extend above the wings. The rudder was still working back and forth; Fitzgerald knew the pilot had not given up.

The crowd on the grass began running as the uncontrolled airliner, as tall as a three-story building and as long and wide as a football field, began skidding toward them. Some of the crowd jumped on retreating vehicles; others hit the ground.

Fitzgerald knew that no place was safer than any other if the Straton went off the runway, and he stood his ground and watched. Around him, four news cameramen stood in the grass, recording the progress of the giant airliner plowing across the runway less than 3000 feet away. The sound of scraping and tearing metal rose above the screaming of the engines as the tortured Straton 797 came closer.

Wayne Metz said to Ed Johnson, in an awed, faraway voice, "Did he make it?"

"Sort of."

"Will it explode?"

"Maybe."

They both watched as the huge aircraft continued its crabbing skid down the runway, leaving a trail of sparks, coupled with an unbelievable sound of scraping, tearing, tortured metal.

Metz asked, "What should we do if it doesn't explode?"

"We should go out to the aircraft and be among the first to meet the pilot."

Metz glanced at Johnson, then back at the Straton. He said softly, "Explode and die."

Berry felt the Straton settle hard on its landing gear, and heard the incredible sound of the gear ripping off. The airliner's 820,000 pounds dropped jarringly onto the runway and the aircraft began to slide. Berry's only emotion as the landing gear collapsed was anger. Anger at himself for getting it so far and losing it at the last moment.

But it wasn't all lost yet. He was alive, and he intended to stay that way. He glanced toward Sharon. As his hands reached for the fuel shut-off switches, she was looking at him, and apparently had been since the impact, watching his face, trying to see by his expression if they were going to live or die. He nodded to her, as if to say, *It's okay.* But it wasn't.

Berry raised the spoilers on top of the wings to act as speed brakes in a last desperate attempt to slow the careening airliner. His feet worked the rudder pedals, but he could see it was having little effect on keeping the aircraft pointed straight down the runway, now that the fuselage was in contact with the pavement.

For a split second, right before touchdown, he had seen himself taxiing the crippled airliner up to the parking ramp, but now he knew he would be lucky if he could avert an explosion. For the first time since he had begun flying, he wanted to run out of fuel. But even if the tanks were dry, there was probably enough volatile fumes in them to blow the airplane to pieces.

He saw the crowd scattering to his left, and noticed the crash trucks moving away as well. He motioned for Sharon to get into a crash position, but she shook her head. He looked quickly over his shoulder and saw that Linda had her head between her legs. The passengers were stumbling and falling; the deceleration had thrown many of them back into the lounge.

The sickening sound of tearing, scraping metal filled the cockpit with a noise so great that he literally could no longer think clearly. He turned back to the front and waited out the final seconds. There was nothing left for him to do concerning the Straton, and that, at least, was a welcome relief.

---

The Straton skidded toward Fitzgerald. As it came within a hundred feet of him, it suddenly spun out of control, its seven-story-high tail coming around in a slow clockwise direction. Fitzgerald dropped to the ground. The massive Straton filled his whole field of vision and he could actually smell its engines and feel its heat as its wing passed above him. He looked up and saw the left wing dip down and plow into the grass. The outboard engine fell from its mounts and rolled end over end in the grass, leaving a trail of blazing earth behind it.

People began to yell, "Fire!"

Fitzgerald looked up at the aircraft spinning and sliding away from him. He could see that the wing section around the lost engine was a maze of severed wires, tubes, and cables. Long plumes of orange flame and black smoke trailed off the damaged wing. Within seconds the entire left wing was ablaze, flames shooting up to the full height of the fuselage.

Fitzgerald stood quickly and began running after the moving airliner. Incredibly, on his right, he saw Edward Johnson and Metz running too. Johnson he could understand. There was nothing cowardly about the man, no matter what one thought of him. But Metz . . . *What the hell was going on here?*

The Straton had slowed considerably as soon as its wing and engine ripped into the ground, and the spinning action further slowed its forward momentum. The aircraft came to rest a hundred yards from Fitzgerald.

Rescue units began rushing toward the Straton, and fire vehicles converged on it with nozzles spewing foam over its length, trying to smother the fire before the fumes and fuel in the tanks exploded.

———————

From the captain's seat, Berry could see the wall of flame that engulfed the left wing.

Before the airliner came to a complete stop, Berry ripped off his seat belt, stood, and reached across to Sharon Crandall. He grabbed her arm and shook her. "Sharon! Sharon!" She was dazed, and he could tell from the gray pallor of her face that she was in shock. He opened her belt and pulled her out of the chair.

She clung to him for a second, then picked her head up. "I'm all right. We have to get out of here."

Berry looked around. The cockpit was jammed with twisted, moving bodies. The first whiffs of acrid smoke had already floated up the circular stairs into the lounge, and drifted into the cockpit. Passengers from the lounge were beginning to respond to the smoke, and began heading toward the cockpit.

Berry shouted above the noises of the injured and the sounds of the emergency units outside. "Open the emergency door. I'll get Linda."

She nodded quickly and pushed her way through the stumbling forms around her.

Berry pulled away a lifeless body draped over the observer's seat and unbuckled Linda's belt. The girl was barely conscious, and he lifted her over his shoulder.

He pushed his way to the door, which was still closed. "Sharon! Open the door. Open the door."

She knelt beside the small emergency door, tears running down her face. "It's stuck! Stuck!"

He thrust the girl into Sharon's arms and pulled at the emergency handle. It held fast, and he pulled again, but it wouldn't open. *Damn it. The airframe is probably bent.* He looked around wildly. Through the cockpit door poured a stream of passengers, crawling, clawing, staggering, and with them came clouds of black stinging smoke, darkening the cockpit. The passengers pressed against him; they were thrashing, howling, terrified. Foam splattered against the windshields, and the cockpit became almost black. He looked up and saw that Sharon and Linda had disappeared. He reached for them, but other bodies were forcing him back against the sidewall. Berry dropped to one knee and rammed forward until he found the emergency door again. He grabbed blindly for the handle, and finally located it. The smoke was overcoming him, and he couldn't find the strength to pull. "Sharon! Linda! Where are you?"

"John, here." Her voice sounded weak. "We're over here. In the front."

"Hold on. Hold on." Berry looked up, but he couldn't see more than a few feet through the smoke and the frightened, milling passengers. He turned back to the emergency door. He grabbed the door handle and pulled on it with every bit of strength he could summon. He kept pulling until he thought he would black out.

The door suddenly flew open, followed by a loud explosion as the nitrogen bottle fired into the inflatable emergency chute. Berry drew in a long breath. He grabbed at the figure standing in front of him, but his eyes were burning and he couldn't see through the clouds of black smoke that billowed out the door.

The passengers began tumbling past him, their residual intelligence directing them toward the sunlight and air. Berry shouted as the stream of passengers fell over him. "Sharon! Linda!"

"John. Here. We're here. Against the copilot's chair. Please, we can't move."

Berry crawled toward the voice, trying to stay below the smoke. Through his watering eyes he saw a bare leg and grabbed at it. But the people around him were moving like a tidal wave now, like the escaping air that had started this nightmare so many hours before. They pressed against his kneeling figure, and before he realized what had happened he was on the bright yellow escape chute. He grabbed wildly at the sides of the chute, but he could not stop himself from sliding down, headfirst, toward the runway below. Before he hit, he heard himself screaming, "Sharon!"

# 20

John Berry's head throbbed and waves of nausea passed over him. In the distance he could hear sirens, brakes screeching, the shouts of rescue workers, bullhorns, radios squawking, and the cries of injured people around him.

He got himself into a sitting position and tried to look around, but his right eye was blurry and he rubbed it; his hand came away with blood. "Damn . . ."

He glanced at the Straton towering over him. The huge jetliner sat on its belly, but the aircraft was tilted to the right and its nose was pointing back toward the direction from which he'd landed. *Incredible*, he thought, looking at the size of this thing that he'd brought in. The cockpit had been so small. . . . He suddenly felt a sense of overwhelming awe and pride. "My God . . ."

Berry thought he'd been unconscious for only a short time since hitting the concrete, because the scene around the Straton was still chaotic with trucks and ambulances rushing toward the aircraft. He looked up at the left wing. Small wisps of smoke were still rising from the areas around the fuel lines, but the flames were out. Several fire trucks were positioned on both sides of the airliner, spraying foam across the wreckage from a safe distance.

Berry took a deep breath. It was strange, he thought, that his body still felt as if it were in the Straton; he still felt the vibrations of the airframe, the pulse and sound of the engines—like a sailor who steps off a ship and walks with a swaying gait. He ran the palms of his hands across the warm concrete, as if to assure himself he had returned to earth.

He took another deep breath to try to clear his head, but there was an acrid smell in the air and his stomach heaved again.

Berry stood unsteadily and looked around the runway. About twenty people were sprawled on the concrete, some unconscious, some moaning, a few crawling. Berry looked for Sharon and Linda—looked for the orange life vests among the injured passengers. But neither Sharon nor Linda was on the ground.

He looked up and saw that the yellow escape chute was still attached to the cockpit emergency door. Berry shouted up at the open door, "Sharon! Linda!"

A figure appeared at the door, and Berry saw that it was the copilot, Dan McVary.

McVary stood at the threshold for a second, then took a step forward, as if he were walking down a flight of stairs. He fell backward and careened quickly down the chute, howling as he accelerated. His feet hit the runway and the sudden deceleration pitched him forward, and he tumbled right into the arms of John Berry.

Both men stared at each other for a few long seconds, and as Berry looked into the eyes of this man who had caused him so much trouble, he realized that anger and hate were totally inappropriate emotions. He said to McVary, "I brought your plane home, buddy. You're home."

McVary kept staring at Berry, showing neither comprehension nor aggression. Then he seemed to slacken in Berry's arms, and a tear rolled down his cheek.

A medic pushing a gurney was racing toward the people at the foot of the chute, and Berry called out to him, "Hey! Take this guy. He's the copilot. He needs help."

The medic detoured to Berry, and together they forced McVary onto the gurney. Berry said, "You'd better strap him in."

The medic nodded, and as he fastened the straps, he asked Berry, "Hey, what's with these people?"

Berry replied, "Brain. . . . Lack of oxygen. They're all . . . They're not well. Unpredictable."

The medic nodded. "You okay?"

"Yeah."

"You're not supposed to be moving around. Just lie down here and wait for a stretcher."

"Okay."

The medic pushed the gurney down the runway toward a dozen parked ambulances and a few dozen trucks that had been pressed into service to transport dead and injured.

Berry tried to make sense of what was going on around him. It appeared that most of the rescue workers and vehicles were staying a respectable hundred yards or so from the Straton until the firefighters gave assurances that the airliner wasn't going to blow. There were no ladders or hydraulic platforms at any of the doors or at the holes in the sides of the aircraft. All Berry could see were hoses shooting chemicals at the huge aircraft, nose to tail, top to bottom, wingtip to wingtip. The giant airliner was dripping, glistening, as pools of chemicals collected around the craft. Berry noticed that a fire truck was shooting white foam at the tail, obliterating the Trans-United logo. This, he knew, had less to do with fire fighting than with public relations.

He noticed, too, that a number of medics had braved the risk of explosion and were removing the passengers who had slid down the only deployed chute, which was the one from the cockpit.

Berry looked up at the cockpit emergency door and shouted again, "Sharon! Linda!"

He grabbed the arm of a passing fireman and shouted, "My wife and daughter are in the cockpit! I have to get up there!"

The fireman looked up at the towering dome of the Straton 797, the place where the first-class lounge and cockpit were. The man shook his head. "We don't have anything on the scene that can reach that high."

"Then get a goddamned truck and ladder here! Now!"

"Steady, fella. We're going in through the passenger doors in a minute. We'll get into the dome and get your family." He added, "I have to ask you to clear this area. Back where the ambulances are. Go on."

Berry turned and hurried toward the tail of the aircraft.

He felt dizzy, and guessed he had a slight concussion. He surveyed the area around him, and in the far distance he saw the main terminal and more vehicles headed his way. He spotted a number of vans with antennas and dishes on their roofs, and he knew they were television vans. A line of police cars with rotating lights kept them at bay and kept the growing crowd from getting closer.

It occurred to John Berry that somewhere around here was the person or the people who had access to the data-link and who had tried to put him and everyone aboard the Straton into the ocean. *Undoubtedly*, he thought, *someone from the airline. Someone high up who could commandeer the company data-link and clear everyone else out of the area.* But that was not his main concern at the moment. His main concern was the two people he'd left behind.

---

Trans-United's chief pilot, Captain Kevin Fitzgerald, moved around the ambulances, between the wheeled gurneys, and among the aluminum trestles on which lay stretchers. He spoke quickly to medics and doctors and looked at each of the twenty or so passengers who had slid down the chute and were being taken here, far from the aircraft that could potentially explode.

Based on what Jack Miller had told him, and on the passenger manifest, Fitzgerald was looking for passengers John Berry, Harold Stein, and Linda Farley, and flight attendants Sharon Crandall and Barbara Yoshiro. But so far, no one answered to those names. In fact, he realized, no one was answering to any name. Within a few minutes, the enormity of what had happened struck him.

Fitzgerald came to a gurney about to be loaded on an ambulance. On it lay a man wearing a bloodstained white shirt with epaulettes, and a black and white name tag that said "McVary."

Fitzgerald motioned the attendants to hold up a moment, and he leaned over McVary, seeing that he was conscious and strapped down. Fitzgerald recalled meeting Dan McVary once briefly at a training seminar. Fitzgerald said, "Dan. Dan. Can you hear me?"

McVary looked at the chief pilot, a man who yesterday was his boss, a man with whom he'd always wanted to have a few words. But today, First Officer Daniel McVary wouldn't have even recognized himself in the mirror and certainly did not recognize Chief Pilot Kevin Fitzgerald. "Aarghh!"

"Dan? It's Kevin Fitzgerald. Dan? Dan, can you . . . ?" *No*, Fitzgerald realized, *no, you can't, and no, you never will.* "Damn it! Oh, my God, my God, my God . . ." Suddenly, he realized what Edward Johnson and Wayne Metz were about.

---

A fire truck came by, and Berry jumped on the running board beside the driver. He said, "Drive under the wing."

The driver did a double take, but rather than argue a small point with someone who looked like he meant it, the driver turned slightly and drove toward the tilted wing.

Berry climbed up a small ladder fixed to the side of the cab and balanced himself on the roof. As the fire truck passed beneath the wing, Berry jumped forward and landed on all fours on top of the wing.

He scrambled up the slick, foam-covered wing toward the fuselage where the wing-top emergency door was located. He slid precariously sideways, then found some traction and finally reached the door, grabbing for the recessed emergency latch.

He caught his breath and pulled at the latch, but the small door wouldn't open. "Damn it!" He propped his knees under the door and kept pulling, but the door held.

Down below, firemen were yelling to him to come down. Berry stood and edged toward the front of the wing, pressing his body against the fuselage for friction even as his shoes slipped on the foam. He inched his body closer to the hole in the fuselage, which was just above and forward of the wing.

A fire truck pulled up to the Straton only a few feet below him. The firemen were still shouting at him, and he saw now a hydraulic platform rising up toward him with two rescue workers on it.

Berry realized he couldn't quite reach the hole in the fuselage, and he conveyed this to the firemen below by turning toward the rising platform and nodding his willingness to come down. The platform came up to a level position with the wing, and one of the rescue workers held on to a safety rail while reaching out to Berry with his other hand. Berry grabbed the rescue worker's hand and jumped onto the platform.

Before the platform began to descend and before either of the rescue workers could react, Berry broke the man's grip and dove off the platform into the hole in the side of the fuselage.

He found himself on the floor amid the pulverized and twisted wreckage. A few bodies lay in the swath of destruction, and Berry could hear a few people moaning. He pitied these men, women, and children who had lived through the terror of the explosion and decompression, then the oxygen deprivation, followed by the crash landing and smoke inhalation. It occurred to him—no, it had always been there in his mind—that he should have just pushed the nose of the airliner into the Pacific Ocean.

But he hadn't done that, so he had left himself with some unfinished business.

The two rescue workers on the platform were shouting to him to come out. "Hey, buddy! Come on out of there! It could still blow. Come on!"

Berry glanced back at them standing in the sunlight and yelled, "I'm going up to the cockpit to get my wife and daughter!"

The Straton listed to the right and was pitched slightly upward. Berry made his way up the left-hand aisle toward the spiral staircase.

The windows were covered with foam, and the farther he got from the two holes in the fuselage, the darker it got and the heavier the smoke became. He heard people moving around him, and he felt someone push past him in the dark. It was strangely silent, except for an eerie sort of growl coming from somewhere close by. Berry thought it could be a dog.

He had given up on Barbara Yoshiro and Harold Stein a long time ago, but he had to give it a try. He shouted, "Barbara! Barbara Yoshiro! Harold Stein! Can you hear me?"

There was no reply at first, then someone, a male, close by in the dark, said, "Here."

"Where? Mr. Stein?"

"Weah. Mista. Heah."

"Damn it! Damn it! Shut up!" Berry felt himself losing control, and tried to steady his nerves. He was fairly certain that Yoshiro and Stein were either dead or unconscious, and beyond his help.

He continued on in the dark, crouching lower because of the smoke. Finally, he found the spiral staircase and grasped the handrails, discovering that the whole unit was loose. He took a few tentative steps up the stairs, then stopped and glanced back toward the shaft of sunlight passing through the holes in the midsection. He tried to see if any of the rescue workers had followed him, but all he could see was one of the brain-damaged wraiths stumbling around, his hands over his eyes, as if the light were blinding him.

Berry took another step up, and the spiral staircase swung slightly. "Damn. . . ." He shouted up the stairs, "Sharon! Linda!"

A voice shouted back, "Shaarn. Linaah!"

Berry took a deep breath and then another step, then another, carefully making his way up the swaying staircase, shouting as he went, "Sharon! Linda!"

And each time he was answered with "Shaarn! Linaaah!"

He could hear people now at the bottom of the stairs, and also people in the lounge at the top of the stairs. Smoke from the cabin was rising up the staircase and, he guessed, out the open emergency door in the cockpit, so it was as if he were standing in a chimney. He found a handkerchief in his pocket and put it over his face, but he felt nauseous and dizzy again, and thought he might black out.

This was more than heroics, he thought. For one

thing, he knew he couldn't live with himself if he survived by getting down the chute and they died in the cockpit, so close to safety. Also, there was the matter of the data-link printouts, which would prove that he wasn't crazy when he told the authorities that someone had given him instructions that would put the Straton into the ocean. And then there were his feelings about Sharon Crandall. . . .

He took another step up the staircase. A shadow loomed at the top, and a hand from below grabbed his leg. A voice shouted, "Shaarnn!" Someone laughed. A dog growled.

He was back in hell.

---

Edward Johnson and Wayne Metz stepped out of the rapid intervention vehicle a hundred yards from the massive Straton, which was surrounded by yellow fire trucks that looked small by comparison, and Johnson was reminded of carrion-eating beetles around a dead bird.

Johnson surveyed the evacuation site—the aluminum trestles and stretchers, the gurneys, empty wheelchairs, ambulances pulling away. He found a woman with a clipboard who looked official, and he identified himself as the senior vice president of Trans-United, which he was, and which he wanted to continue being, which was why he was here; he had to control the situation to the extent possible, and with any luck, the man named Berry would be dead, and so would the flight attendant, and the data-link printouts would be sitting in the collecting tray in the cockpit. If none of that was true, Johnson knew he'd have to make some tough decisions and do some unpleasant things.

The woman with the clipboard identified herself as Dr. Emmett of the airport Emergency Medical Service.

Johnson asked her, "Doctor, how many people have you pulled out?"

Dr. Emmett replied, "We haven't *pulled* any out. Some came down that chute. Twenty-two, to be exact."

Johnson glanced at the yellow chute in the far distance.

Dr. Emmett continued, "The rescue workers will enter the aircraft shortly. Then we'll have our hands full." She thought a moment, then said, "Unless, of course, they're all dead from smoke inhalation . . . which is possible since we've seen no one inside trying to get out, and no one has deployed any other emergency chute."

Johnson nodded and asked her, "What's the condition of the people you've got here?"

Dr. Emmett hesitated, then said, "Well, they all seem to have suffered some physical trauma . . . bleeding, contusions, and such, but no burns. All seem to have experienced smoke inhalation—"

"Their mental state, doctor," Johnson interrupted. "Are they mentally well?"

Dr. Emmett considered a moment, then replied, "No. I thought at first it was just shock and smoke inhalation—"

Johnson interrupted again and said, "They experienced a period of oxygen deprivation when"—he pointed to the hole in the distant fuselage—"when that happened."

She nodded. "I see."

"Have you noticed any people who look mentally . . . normal?"

"I don't think . . . Some of them are unconscious and I can't—"

Johnson said, "We know there were at least three people who were not affected by the loss of oxygen—a man, a female flight attendant, and a young girl. There may also be another female flight attendant— Oriental—and another male passenger who is not . . . brain damaged." He looked at Dr. Emmett and asked her, "Have you seen anyone like that?"

She shook her head. "No. No women in flight-attendant uniforms for sure, and no young girls. About ten men, but. . ." She glanced at her clipboard and said, "We've taken identification from those who had ID on them—"

"The men were named Berry and Stein."

Dr. Emmett scanned her list, then shook her head. "No . . . but there *was* one man in a pilot's uniform . . . name tag said McVary. . . . He was not well."

Johnson nodded to himself as his eyes scanned the people in the stretchers around him.

Dr. Emmett said, "Another gentleman was asking about those people."

Johnson turned back to her and described Kevin Fitz-gerald, right down to his tan.

Dr. Emmett nodded.

Johnson asked, "Where is that gentleman now?"

She shrugged and motioned around at the controlled chaos spread up and down the runway. "I'm sure I have other things to worry about."

"Right—"

It was Dr. Emmett's turn to interrupt, and she said,

"We're taking everyone who got out of that plane and who might get out of that plane to Hangar 14, where a field hospital is being set up." She added, "The field morgue is in Hangar 13. Please excuse me." She turned and walked quickly away.

Johnson took Metz's arm and steered him toward the aircraft.

Metz asked, "Where are we going?"

"To the Straton, Wayne."

"What if it explodes?"

"Then we don't have to face charges of attempted murder. We'll be dead."

Metz broke free of Johnson and said, "Hold on. If it explodes, the evidence goes with it. I'm waiting here."

"Wayne, don't be reactive. Be proactive."

"Don't give me that management-seminar shit. I came this far with you, but no further. If you want to get closer to that . . . that fucking aluminum death tube filled with gasoline—"

"Kerosene."

"—and brain-damaged people, go right ahead." He added, "I'll stay here near the ambulances and see if our friends get this far."

Johnson looked at Metz and asked him, "And if you happen to see them, what will you do?"

Metz didn't reply.

"Will you kill them?"

He shook his head.

Johnson reminded Metz, "Wayne, if that guy Berry lives, you and I will spend at least ten, probably twenty years in a state or federal prison. I have better ways to spend my golden years than walking around an exercise yard in blue denims."

Metz seemed to stare off into space for a long time, then said, "I didn't do anything wrong. I don't know what you're talking about."

Johnson laughed unpleasantly. "I figured you'd say that." He turned to Metz, then said, "Okay, partner, you can stay here and watch the store. But if I don't get to Berry and Crandall, and if I don't get my hands on those data-link printouts, then you can be certain that you'll be in the cell next to mine." Johnson turned and walked toward the Straton.

Wayne Metz watched him go, then turned suddenly and ran toward an ambulance. He shouted to the attendants, who were about to close the doors, "Wait! I need a ride!" He brushed past them and jumped into the back of the ambulance.

The attendants shrugged and closed the doors.

Wayne Metz found himself crammed among three stretchers on which were three people. The first thing he realized was that there was a smell of vomit, feces, and urine coming from them. "Oh . . . ah . . . ah . . ." He covered his face with his handkerchief.

The ambulance suddenly took off at high speed, and Wayne Metz stumbled into a stretcher that held a middle-aged man whose face was smeared and crusty with things Wayne Metz didn't want to think about. Metz's stomach heaved, and he made a retching sound. One of the patients let out a howl and another began to grunt.

Metz backed up to the doors and called out to the two men in front, "Stop! Let me out!"

The driver called back to him, "Next stop, Hangar 14. Pipe down."

Metz would have opened the doors and jumped, but the ambulance was going very fast.

As the vehicle streaked toward Hangar 14, the three patients on board began screaming and babbling, then one of them howled again.

Metz felt a chill run down his spine, and the hair on the back of his neck stood up. "Oh . . . God . . . get me out of here. . . ."

"You jumped on board," said the attendant in the passenger seat. "Now, keep quiet."

"Oh. . . ." Metz forced himself to look at the faces of the three people strapped into the stretchers. "Oh, my God. . . ." The term "continuing liability" suddenly struck home.

He realized he was out of a job, but that didn't seem so important anymore compared to spending a decade or two in the penitentiary.

Metz turned and looked out the rear window of the ambulance and focused on the retreating Straton. He said a quiet prayer. "God, let the Straton explode, killing everyone on board, especially Berry and Crandall, and anyone else who has the mental capacity to testify against me, and please, God, let the data-link printouts burn, and let Ed Johnson go up in smoke, too. Thank you, God."

But as he watched the Straton, nothing happened. It smoked, but didn't blow. "Please, God."

The patients were babbling, the ambulance reeked, and Wayne Metz's heart was racing. He had never in his life been so miserable. He began sobbing and choking.

The attendant had climbed out of his seat and come up behind Metz. "Here. Take these. Tranquilizers. Take the edge off. Make you feel good. Here."

Metz swallowed the two pills whole. "Oh . . . get me out of here. . . ."

"Sit down."

Wayne pounded on the doors of the ambulance. "Stop!"

One of the patients shouted, "Stob!"

The attendant said to Metz, "Sit down, pal, before you fall down."

Suddenly, Metz felt light-headed and his knees felt rubbery. "Oh . . . what . . . what was . . . ?"

The attendant said, "Did I say tranquilizers? I meant sedative. I always get them confused."

"But . . . I . . ."

"You cause trouble, you get a Mickey Finn. Lie down." The attendant helped him to the floor.

"But . . . I'm not . . . a . . . I wasn't . . . I'm not . . . a passenger."

"I don't care *who* you are. You're in my ambulance, and you're causing trouble. Now you're out like a light."

Metz felt his bladder release, and everything went dark.

----

Ed Johnson surveyed the scene at the port side of the Straton. The fire chief had declared the aircraft safe from combustion, and rescue workers wearing fire suits and oxygen masks were being lifted on hydraulic platforms into the body of the dead beast.

Johnson saw the main guy with the gold trim and went up to him. "Chief, I'm Ed Johnson, VP of Trans-United. This is my plane."

"Oh, hey, sorry."

"Yeah." He asked, "Anyone alive in there?"

The chief nodded. "Yeah. The rescue workers are reporting on their radios that they have dozens—maybe hundreds in there." He added, "We're strapping them into scoop stretchers—immobilizing them—you know? Then we'll begin to start taking them out."

Johnson nodded. His mind was working on his own problem.

The chief thought a moment, then said, "These people . . . They don't seem right, according to what I'm hearing on the radio. . . . I mean, nobody tried to get out. . . ."

"They're brain damaged."

"Jeez."

"Right. Hey, can you get me in there?"

"Well . . ."

"It's my aircraft, Chief. I have to be on it."

"It could still catch fire," said the chief, though the possibility had greatly diminished. He added, "Toxic smoke and fumes."

"I don't care. I have to be in there with my passengers and crew." Ed Johnson gave the chief a man-to-man stare, not entirely phony, but partly recalled from the old days before all the politics and compromises. He added, "This is my aircraft, Chief."

The fire chief called out to one of his men and said, "Get this man a bunker coat, gloves, and an air pack, and get him up into the craft."

"Thanks," said Johnson.

As he waited, he stared up at the hole in the side of the craft and said, "What the hell . . . ?"

The chief followed his gaze and said, "Yeah. It's,

like, blown *in.* One of the guys said he thought it could be a meteor strike. You know? Or a piece of satellite. But the two holes are in the *sides*—horizontal. The other one is blown *out*—and a lot bigger—like something went in this side and out the other. Maybe a missile. What do you think?"

"Jesus Christ . . ." It suddenly hit him. *A missile.* A runaway missile. A fucking runaway military missile. Or a drone. Something that operated at 60,000 feet and didn't explode when it hit the Straton. Some military fuckup of the first order, like all those stories about TWA Flight 800. But this one had actually happened. A missile. That *had* to be it. And he'd been worried about structural failure or a bomb smuggled aboard through lax Trans-United security. And all the time it wasn't their fault. "Jesus H. Christ. What a fuckup."

"What's that?"

Johnson glanced at the fire chief. "Wish me luck."

"Right."

Two firemen helped Ed Johnson into a bunker coat, showed him the fireproof gloves and flashlight hanging from Velcro straps on the coat, and fitted him with a Scott Air-Pak. Johnson let the mask hang on his chest. He said, "Let me have one of those axes."

One of the firemen shrugged and handed Johnson a steel-cut ax. The fireman said, "Be careful with that. It's sharp as a razor."

*Good.* "Thanks."

A hydraulic lift raised Ed Johnson up to the rear catering-service door, that had been opened by the rescue workers.

Johnson stepped from the sunlight into the cavernous

Straton 797, lit now by battery-powered lights. He waited for his eyes to adjust to the dimness.

After half a minute he could see, but he could not comprehend. "Oh, my God . . ."

Slowly, he made his way up the left aisle, past rescue workers, past dead and injured passengers strapped in their seats or lying on the floor.

He came to the holes in the fuselage and examined the swath of wreckage from left to right. He had no doubt that something had passed through the Straton, something that could be called an Act of God, or an Act of Nature, or an Act of Man—but not an act of Trans-United negligence. The irony of the situation struck him, and he would have laughed at himself or cursed his take-charge personality, but he could philosophize later, when he was on vacation or in jail. Right now, he needed to get into the cockpit and to the data-link printout tray.

He moved forward in his cumbersome bunker coat. The farther he got from the holes, the worse the smoke was. He strapped on his oxygen mask and drove on.

It was darker toward the front of the aircraft, so he took his flashlight and turned the beam toward where the spiral staircase should be.

The beam of light picked out the galley and toilet cubicles and also illuminated figures moving around toward the front of the aircraft—but he couldn't see the staircase.

He moved up the aisle, past the rescue workers who were clearing the aisles of the dead and putting them in seats. Johnson noticed that the rescue people were also strapping the injured onto stretchers and back-boards, as much to protect them from internal injuries as to keep them from wandering around like the living dead. "Jesus Christ, what a mess, what a mess . . ." *Total decompression at 60,000 feet. Let the Straton Aircraft Corporation bright boys explain that to the news media.*

Ed Johnson got to the place where the spiral staircase should have been, but it wasn't there. It was, in fact, lying on its side in the aisle ahead, looking like some giant corkscrew. "Damn. . . ." But then it occurred to him that this was better.

Johnson stopped a passing rescue worker and spoke loudly through his oxygen mask, identifying himself as a National Transportation Safety Board investigator and asked, "Are any of your people in the dome?" He pointed the flashlight up at the circular opening in the ceiling.

The rescue worker looked up at the opening. He said, "No, sir . . . I don't think so." He called out to the people around him, "Hey, do we have anyone up in the dome yet?"

A woman called back, "No. There was that chute deployed there. Everyone up there either got out or is probably dead." She added, "If we have unconscious people up there, they'll have to wait. We have our hands full here."

The rescue worker near Johnson said, "We've got about two or three *hundred* dead and injured here, but I'll get some people up to the dome—"

"No. You've really got your hands full here. Just give me a boost up there, and I'll look around."

"Okay." The man called out for help, and two men appeared who made a cradle by joining hands with the third. "Step up."

Ed Johnson shouldered the fire ax and stepped onto the three men's hands and arms, steadying himself on one of their shoulders with his free hand.

One of the men said, "Check first for bleeding, then breathing, then—"

"I'm trained in CPR. Lift!"

The men lifted in unison, and Johnson felt himself lifted—propelled, actually—up and into the opening. He grabbed at the upright newel post that still stood on the floor, and swung himself up into the first-class lounge.

He remained on the floor and looked and listened, the sounds of his own breathing into the oxygen mask filling his ears. The lounge was completely dark, its windows thick with foam. He heard someone moaning nearby and smelled the same evil odors he'd smelled below. *God.* . . . He breathed deeply and stayed motionless awhile and listened.

He oriented himself without turning on the flashlight and began crawling toward the cockpit, dragging the ax with him.

The carpet—which Johnson knew was royal blue and cost too much—was wet with different liquids, all of which felt disgusting. He stopped, wiped his hands on his coat, and pulled on the fireproof gloves. He renewed his resolve and crawled on.

Johnson knew the layout of the lounge, and with only one detour to get around a body, he came to the cockpit door, which he discovered was open.

Johnson shouldered the steel-cut ax and made his way in a crouch through the opening and into the cockpit.

He stopped, kneeling on one knee, and looked

around. The windshields were covered with foam, but light came through the small emergency door. The smoke here was very light, and what little remained was being suctioned out the open escape hatch. Johnson rose up a bit and peered out the door, spotting the sloping yellow chute. He turned back to the cockpit, but his eyes took a minute to readjust to the darkness. When they did, he spotted a man lying on the floor at the base of the copilot's seat. The man was dead or unconscious. Johnson glanced all around the cockpit, but there was no one else there, dead or alive.

Still in a slight crouch to stay beneath the curls of smoke on the ceiling, he made his way toward the observer's station, then snapped on the flashlight and scanned the beam until he saw what he was looking for—the data-link printer. The beam rested on the tray and illuminated a page of white paper. *Thank God.*

Johnson stood, pulled off his gloves and his oxygen mask, and went to the printer, where he retrieved six sheets of paper from the collecting tray. *Mission accomplished.* He scanned the papers with his flashlight, then turned them over. "What the hell?"

A voice from behind him answered, "Blank printer paper from the machine."

Johnson swung around and pointed his flashlight toward the voice. The dead man was sitting up now, his back to the copilot's seat. Johnson's heart literally skipped a beat, then he got himself under control.

Neither man spoke for a few seconds, then Johnson said, "Berry?"

"That's right. And who are you?"

"None of your fucking business."

"I'd like to know the name of the man who tried to kill me."

Johnson held the ax out in front of the flashlight so Berry could see it. Johnson said, "And may still kill you."

Berry's eyes focused on the big ax. He hadn't considered facing a weapon.

Johnson said, "You're a brave man, Mr. Berry."

"You're a heartless son-of-a-bitch."

"Not really. You of all people understand why I had to do what I did. And after what I saw down there, I wouldn't change a thing I did."

Berry said, "You shouldn't try to play God."

"Why not? Someone has to do it."

"Who *are* you?"

"It really is best if you don't know."

"If you intend to kill me with that ax, what difference does it make if I know who you are?"

Johnson said, "The reason you're still alive and may stay alive is that you don't know who I am."

"The only reason you're still alive is that ax."

Johnson ignored him and said, "If you can produce those data-link printouts, we can make a deal for your life."

Berry stood, and Johnson yelled, "Don't move!"

Berry stared at the man in the dim light for a few seconds, then said, "The printouts were hidden on the person of the girl who survived."

"Where is she?"

"I put her and your flight attendant Sharon Crandall down that chute into the arms of medics. They were both breathing but unconscious. If either of them dies, I'll see that you're executed or I'll kill you myself."

Johnson stood motionless for a second, then said, "Brave talk for a weaponless man facing an ax."

"Look, pal, I don't know who you are, but the game is up. Drop the ax."

"I'm not so sure the game is up. I have the option of bashing in your skull—it'll look like contact trauma— then I'll slide down that chute and go to Hangar 14, where the survivors are, and find Linda Farley and Sharon Crandall."

Berry tensed, and his eyes darted toward the emergency opening.

Johnson moved a few feet and blocked Berry's path. Johnson said, "If you have those data-link sheets with you, I give you my word I won't harm you. Or them."

"Of course you will."

"I don't want to kill you. I'd rather we just called one another liars during an investigation. Even if I wind up in court, I'd trust a California jury to find me not guilty. Hell, they find *everyone* not guilty. Then I'll write a book and make a lot of money. I'll even make you a hero in my book." Johnson laughed and continued, "Come on, Berry. Give me the sheets. Save your life. You've come too far to die now."

Berry took a deep breath and replied, "I told you, the evidence is gone. Down the chute with the girl." He shrugged. "You're finished."

"No. *You're* finished." Johnson hesitated, then raised the ax.

From the lounge came the opening notes of "Jingle Bells" on the piano. A few seconds later, a voice called out, "I never got much beyond this. In fact, it's the only piano piece I know."

Johnson swung around and peered into the dark lounge. "Oh . . . my God. . . ."

The piano music stopped and a man approached through the murkiness. The man's big form filled the cockpit door. Kevin Fitzgerald said, "Hello, Ed."

Ed Johnson stood frozen.

Fitzgerald said, "Can you massacre both of us with that ax? I doubt it. I doubt you even want to. So drop it."

"You . . . what?" He looked over his shoulder at Berry, then back at Fitzgerald. Suddenly he realized he'd put his foot in a trap and his neck in a noose.

Fitzgerald addressed John Berry and said, "Thank you, Mr. Berry, for agreeing to act as bait."

Johnson's eyes widened, and he said, "You mean . . . you've met . . . ?"

"Just before you arrived," Fitzgerald replied. Fitzgerald said to Berry, "The gentleman with the ax is Mr. Edward Johnson, senior vice president of Trans-United Airlines. A good company man who has the best interests of the airline at heart. Not to mention the best interests of Ed Johnson." Fitzgerald said to Johnson, "I sort of figured it was you."

Johnson snarled, "Bullshit!"

"No, really, Ed. You have the right combination of balls, brains, selfishness, and total lack of conscience."

"Oh, fuck you, Kevin. I don't need a fucking lecture from you. I tried to save this airline. You and your fucking pampered pilots wouldn't do that."

Fitzgerald lost his patience and snapped, "My pilots save this airline every damn day they're up there, you desk-bound son-of-a—"

"Enough!" yelled Berry. He had a feeling this was

an old argument. "Enough." He said to Johnson, "Drop the damned ax, or so help me God, I'm coming right at you, and I'm going for your eyes. Drop it!"

Johnson stood motionless for a second, then swung the ax in a wide arc and with incredible strength sent it sailing into the front windshield, which shattered in a thousand pieces. He said to Fitzgerald, "Fuck you. Try to prove it." Johnson strode over to the emergency door and stood crouched at the yellow chute for a moment, then looked back over his shoulder and said to Berry, "If you had any real balls and any conscience whatsoever, you would have put this fucking planeload of living dead into the water instead of trying to save your own ass. You can both go to hell." And with that, he propelled himself, legs first, down the long yellow chute.

Fitzgerald said to Berry, "Don't pay any attention to him."

Berry didn't reply.

Fitzgerald continued, "As I said to you before, and I'll say again, you did the right thing, and you did it well. Regardless of Mr. Johnson's opinion, Trans-United is grateful."

"Good. Do you think I'm too old to get a job flying commercial airliners?"

Fitzgerald smiled and replied, "You're obviously capable."

Berry smiled for the first time in a long time. He looked around, then said, "I've seen enough of this cockpit."

Fitzgerald nodded.

Both men slid down the yellow chute into the sunlight and landed on their feet.

# 21

John Berry passed through the ornate iron gate into the tea garden. He walked slowly down bamboo-railed paths, over grassy slopes, and beside red-leafed Japanese maples.

He crossed small stone bridges that passed over little streams and lichen-covered rocks, and came to a chain of five pools filled with water lilies and goldfish. Over a still pond in the distance curved a wishing bridge, its reflection in the water completing a perfect circle. Waiting on the bridge was a woman and a girl.

He moved toward them, passing fantastically misshapen bonsai trees and delicate trees of plum and cherry. The day was still and the smell of camellias and magnolias hung in the air. The setting sun cast elongated shadows of stone lanterns over the paths and dappled the grass between the trees.

John Berry quickened his pace, and found that his heart was beating rapidly. Then he stopped abruptly at the foot of the bridge, as though the vision in front of him would vanish if he came closer. He looked up and smiled hesitantly.

Sharon Crandall, dressed in a light blue sundress and straw hat with a wide brim, smiled back. "We've been waiting for you."

Linda Farley waved a greeting. "We thought you got lost."

Berry stepped onto the bridge and approached them. He stood awkwardly for a moment, then impulsively bent down and kissed Linda Farley on the cheek. "How are you feeling?"

She nodded. "Good."

"Good." He straightened up and handed her a large box of chocolates. "Here. The prize for spotting land first."

Linda took the chocolates and smiled. "Thank you."

"You're welcome." He turned to Sharon. "I wanted to bring you something, but I didn't know—"

"Dinner in New York."

"Yes. We made it to the airport, didn't we?" He paused. "You're looking well."

She put her hand on his cheek and frowned at his cuts and bruises. "You look as though you lost a fight."

"You should have seen the other guy." He looked out at a red-tiled pagoda surrounded by carefully pruned vegetation. "This is quite a place."

"Yes. I thought you'd like it. It's a beautiful example of how man and nature can live in harmony."

"You come here often?"

"Whenever I have a lot of thinking to do." She looked down at her reflection in the pond. "I used to come here with Barbara Yoshiro sometimes."

"I . . ." He didn't know what to say. "I think she

would have been happy to know you came here and thought of her."

"Let's take a walk."

They crossed the bridge. On the far side they passed through a thicket of leafy bamboo and took a path to the west. They walked in silence for a long time, came to a grassy slope, and climbed it. A breeze came up, and Berry stood on the summit of the hill. Small puffs of white clouds rolled across the sky. Gulls circled in the distance and the vapor trail of a high-flying jet left a white line on the deep blue sky. "No fog today," he said.

"No." Sharon Crandall walked a few yards down to the western slope, took off her hat, and lay in the sunny grass. "No. No fog today. We could have used this weather yesterday at this time. But then, that wouldn't have been consistent with yesterday's luck."

"No." Berry sat down beside her.

They both watched in silence as Linda walked slowly down the grassy slope and toward a brook at the base of the hill.

"Don't go too far," Crandall shouted after her. She turned to Berry. "She has her good and bad moments. She just finished crying before you got here. She hasn't come to terms with it yet."

"Her mother?"

"She wasn't one of the survivors."

Berry nodded. It was, in his mind, better that way. Easier, in the long run, for Linda.

Sharon Crandall looked down at the young girl and watched her for a few seconds, then turned back to Berry. "I spoke to Linda's grandmother."

"What did she say?"

"She's the only relative, except for some cousins in Kansas or someplace. Linda's father died years before. The grandmother lives in a small apartment on the south side of the city. She's going to take custody of Linda now, but she is very concerned about being able to raise a young girl by herself. When I told her I'd like to help out, she was very happy."

"I'd like to help out too, if I could."

"Sure."

Neither of them spoke for some time, then Berry said, "Golden Gate Park reminds me of Central Park."

Crandall smiled. "Does it?"

She closed her eyes and stretched out in the grass and kicked off her shoes. "I don't really want to hear the latest, but you might as well tell me."

Berry looked down at her face. The sun lay on her features the way it did in the cockpit of the Straton and highlighted the nice cheekbones and soft lips. "The latest. The latest is that we have to speak with the FBI again tomorrow morning."

"I figured that. What else?"

"Well, Commander Sloan was flown in to Alameda Naval Air Station this morning from the carrier *Nimitz* and is under custody there. Incidentally, even though it was a top-secret test, all the radio transmissions to and from the fighter were automatically recorded in the *Nimitz* central radio room. It's some kind of electronic recording loop that they keep for safety investigations, and it erases itself every twenty-four hours. Apparently, Sloan didn't know that, because only safety officers have access to that stuff. You'd think people would be more careful about recordings these days. Anyway, the Navy got to the recordings before they automatically erased, so the charge against Sloan is evidently going to be murder."

"How about the other two Navy men?"

"The pilot is still missing at sea. Admiral Hennings hasn't been found onboard yet. Apparently he jumped. But they want that downplayed. The Navy's not saying much about what exactly was on the recordings, but they did tell me that it proved conclusively that Sloan was the instigator. My impression was that Sloan conned and bullied the Admiral and the pilot into the cover-up. And the original mistake was Sloan's, too. After the Straton's late departure from San Francisco, Sloan never received updates from Air Traffic Control because of a technical problem. He just assumed that the area was clear of traffic, even though he was supposed to check."

"He sure doesn't sound technically competent. What about Edward Johnson and Wayne Metz. They almost pulled it off, didn't they?"

"Johnson's made a full confession. He says he was pulled both ways the entire time—save the airplane or save the airline."

"Sure," Crandall said sarcastically. "He says he did it all for the airline? Nothing in it for him?"

"That's his story."

Trans-United was certainly going to be under the microscope for a while, Berry thought. But his gut feeling was that the airline would survive it. Even the press seemed to be playing up the actions of individuals rather than organizations. Maybe that's the way this thing would ultimately wash out. But Berry did understand, at least a little, why Johnson had not wanted

Flight 52 to come back. He thought about Daniel Mc-Vary.

"Has there been any improvement in Dan McVary or the others?" Crandall asked, as if she had sensed his thoughts.

"No. The same. There's no hope for any of them. The doctors told me that the brain damage is unquestionably permanent."

"That's what I had guessed," she answered softly, shaking her head.

Berry nodded. "Me too." He remembered a similar conversation with Harold Stein. Stein had been right, at least about his family. It was hopeless. Berry could feel his emotions begin to slide again. He was becoming increasingly maudlin. He pulled out a handful of grass and scattered it down the hill. He forced his mind to change gears. "Metz hasn't said much yet, except to hint that it was all Johnson's idea. He says he didn't know what was happening with the data-link."

"I doubt that."

"Hell, I *know* he understood where we were going. The federal prosecutor knows it too."

They both looked down the hill and watched Linda for a while as she walked along a brook. Berry coughed lightly to clear his throat. "I called home this morning."

"How is everyone?"

"They're fine." He stood up, then helped Sharon to her feet.

"I'll bet they can't wait for you to get back," Sharon said.

Berry considered. "Yes . . . that's the way they sounded."

Sharon Crandall didn't speak for a few seconds, then said, "Why . . . why didn't they fly out here?"

"Well, the kids have finals now, and Jennifer doesn't like flying anyway. She never came with me when I flew. All our vacations were by car or, sometimes, by ship. I don't think Flight 52 helped her overcome her fear of flying."

"I shouldn't think it would." She watched a flight of gulls sail overhead. "When are you going back?"

"I'm not sure. I have to stay here for the next few days, just like you. We have a lot of questions to answer for a lot of people. I've taken a month's leave of absence from work." He hesitated, then went on. "They were good about giving me the time, but there's something . . . demeaning in having to ask for time off after nearly twenty years, you know? I mean, they could have offered before I asked. And Jennifer could have arranged for the kids to take their finals some other time, had three martinis, and flown out here. My mother, who is seventy-two and not well, wanted to come out." He lapsed into silence for a while, then said, "My wife started off predictably enough . . . great concern . . . terrible anguish. But ten minutes into the conversation I could already pick up the old line." He pulled out another handful of grass and threw it into the breeze. "Things would be okay for a few months. . . . We'd make the round of cocktail parties and country clubs, and I'd have to perform for everyone for a while. Then it would wear off. . . ."

Sharon Crandall reached out and took his hand. "What do you *want* to do?"

He felt the pressure of her hand and returned it. "I'm not sure. But I'm going to stay here for a few weeks until I know. Sometimes I think I'd like to fly for a living. That's what I wanted when I was young."

"I don't think anyone would doubt your ability to fly."

"No." He laughed. "It's my ability to land that's in some doubt."

She sat up. "Do you have to go back to the hospital?"

"No. I'm discharged. I've got a hotel room at the Mark."

She turned and looked at him. "Stay with me. I have a place in North Beach."

He stared out at the sky for a long time. An aircraft came toward them, heading over the city toward the airport, and from a distance it looked like a Straton 797. They both saw it, but neither commented on it. John Berry thought about what lay ahead. Investigations, grand juries, courtrooms, news coverage. Like it or not, he and Sharon were going to be news for some time. "It wouldn't look right. We have no private lives. At least for a while. It took me a half hour to shake the reporters on my way here."

She released his hand and stood. "I have to get Linda back." She slipped on her shoes and picked up her hat.

Berry stood beside her and took her arm. "You know I want to. . . . It's easier for you to . . ."

"Why? Because I have less to lose? You've got *nothing* to lose." She turned to him. "What were your first thoughts when you got out of the cockpit and realized you were alive? How you couldn't wait to go home and get back to work?"

"No . . . I thought about you. . . ."

She stared at him for several seconds, then turned

and called to Linda. "We have to go, honey." She looked back at Berry. "I'll see you tomorrow, I guess. I'm sorry if I put you in a difficult position, but . . . I care about you. And I can see that you're unhappy." She watched Linda running up the hill. "I keep thinking about all the friends I lost on that flight. I think about Captain Stuart. He was a good man. A no-nonsense guy. You remind me of him. He once told me that he had family problems, too, and he couldn't resolve them. Now he doesn't have to. But you do."

Berry thought for an instant about those he had brought back, the survivors who would never be able to go through more than the barest motions of life. Were they any better off than those who had died? He couldn't decide. Was survival enough, or should there be more?

Linda scampered up the hill and ran toward them. "Are we going?"

Sharon smiled at her. "Yes." She took Linda's arm and began walking down the slope.

Just before she reached the bottom, Berry called after her. "Sharon."

She stopped and turned. "Yes, John?" Linda was clutching her hand, and the two of them looked up toward Berry.

John Berry took a few tentative steps toward her. As he moved down the hill, he could see in the distance the tall towers of the Golden Gate Bridge. They stood majestically, bathed in the late afternoon sun, their rigid beams framing the scene in front of Berry. More than any other single moment, the first sighting of the Golden Gate Bridge towers had marked the beginning of their salvation, the beginning of their new lives.

# MAYDAY

He stopped halfway down the hill and asked, "Can we have dinner together tonight?"

"I can't. One of my old boyfriends asked me to dinner."

"I'll pick you up at eight."

"He's picking me up at eight-thirty."

"You won't be there."

Sharon laughed. "Do you know where I live?"

"I'll find you."